PREPARED TO DIE

THE DCI PETER MOONE THRILLERS BOOK 3

MARK YARWOOD

This novel is entirely a work of fiction. The names, characters and incidents portrayed in it are the work of the author's imagination. Any resemblance to actual persons, living or dead, events or localities is entirely coincidental.

BiscuitBooksPublishers © Mark Yarwood 2023

The author asserts the moral right to be identified as the author of this work Published by Amazon Kindle All rights reserved. No part of this publication may be reproduced, stored, or transmitted in any form or by means, electronic, mechanical, photocopying, recording or otherwise, without the prior permission of the publishers.

For Rosie

ACKNOWLEDGEMENTS

Once again I need to thank a few individuals who made possible the writing of this third DCI Peter Moone book. First of all, I shall thank Inspector Paul Laity, whose advice on police matters has been, as always, invaluable.

Secondly, I want to thank John Hudspith, my editor who always puts up with my 'fluff'.

As always I shall mention my mum, dad and brother for all their love and support. But I mostly want to thank my wife and daughter and, of course, little Mittens, my writing partner.

PROLOGUE

He saw beauty in everything. Even the dead things. Especially the dead things, with their hollowed-out pallor, and the odour that stayed long after they had gone like some lingering perfume. Yes, it was a kind of perfume, a scent that teased and played with his desires.

He took his eyes away from the thing that stared back at him, its face half hidden by matted dirty hair, the bars of the cage hiding the rest of it. It wasn't beautiful yet. It was still so full of life, an exquisite kind of life that crackled with electricity powered by pure fear.

He looked down at the pen in his hand that hummed, sending a sweet vibration up his arm as he pressed the needle to its flesh. A blank canvas, only tiny, light-coloured hairs and freckles decorating its pale skin, the beautiful imperfections that would become magnificent in that final stage of existence.

How many dead things had he seen, had he touched? So many, but it only occurred to him in these last few months to put a mark on them, to show off what they become when released.

He smiled as he finished off the second wing of the butterfly. He sat back, admiring the colours, the blaze of red and orange. It was perfect, and she was almost perfect. In a moment he would put on the gloves, grip her neck in his hands and take her beyond beauty, beyond any understanding of that word. And he would breathe out a kind of fire, and feel it charge along his back and into his heart.

CHAPTER 1

He could hear the rain hitting the canopy of trees overhead, the patter of it filling his ears as he tried not to stumble over the stumps and bushes. DCI Moone stopped as he got closer to all the fuss, the uniforms scattered through the trees, searching for more evidence. The sun was barely up, the soft, hazy pink glow of it showing behind the harsh and skeletal outline of the autumn trees. As he climbed down a steep bank, his feet sliding a little, his eyes jumped to the SOCO tent which had been erected between two thick and ancient trees. Voices called out somewhere and crows seemed to answer with a sound like violent complaining, perhaps upset at being woken so early.

    He took out his phone, checking for any message from Butler.

    Mandy. She had a name, she just preferred not to be called it, as if some kind of familiarity would grow between them, and heaven forbid that should happen. Every time he felt as if they were on solid ground, she would withdraw, stop calling him Pete and bring down the shutters. It had been like that lately, but he assumed it was the fact that her father was unwell, something to do with his chest. The details were scarce as always with Butler.

Moone pulled himself out of his dark mood as he spotted the familiar stocky figure of Sergeant Kevin Pinder trudging towards him, a smile appearing on his face.

'Your face says it all, boss,' Pinder said, then turned and looked towards the tent.

'How're you, Kev?' Moone took his chilled hands from his pockets and blew on them.

'Better now that this whole Covid business seems to be buggering off. Where's your other half?'

'Ha ha.' Moone passed him, heading towards the tent, listening to the squawking above, hearing his name in their voices, a warning not to go any closer. 'Is it a young woman?'

'Yeah. In her mid-twenties, they reckon.'

Moone sighed and shook his head and stepped closer, watching the SOCOs coming out. Mid-twenties, no age at all; his stomach twisted and knotted itself at the thought, the image of him having to deliver the bad news. 'Any ID?'

'Nothing. Not even any clothes.' Pinder

caught up with him as he headed to the tent, more purpose in his stride now. He could feel the uniforms' eyes turning to him and he didn't want to show hesitation.

'They found her naked?' Moone asked.

'Yeah, the doctor said she's been dead at least two days, give or take. Want to hear a joke?'

Moone stopped, Pinder's words sinking in, mixing in with the grey and thick mud that seemed to be coating his insides as well as his shoes. 'Is this really the time, Kev?'

Pinder shrugged. 'Just thought it'd break the tension. Gallows humour and all that. Maybe I'll save it for later. It's a good one.'

Moone nodded, knowing that Pinder's heart was in the right place, he just didn't know when to pick his moments. But he never felt like he had the right to criticise him, not since he had saved his life. The memory came in like an icy cold wave, bringing with it a high-pitched whine as his heart began to thud in his chest and ears. He moved to a tree, gripped the bark, hanging his head. DS Carthew's image passed by his eyes, an expression of evil and emptiness on her face. He hadn't seen her that day, the day he knew, but couldn't prove, she had pushed him off the viaduct, but the image of her had grown in his mind, birthed by a fearful imagination. Moone took out his vape, his hand trembling. He looked at it, feeling pathetic, longing for a real fag. He took a puff and put it away in a hurry.

'You OK?' Pinder asked from behind him.

'I'm fine.'

'What about Alice? How's she doing?'

Moone let out a sigh as he faced Pinder, his mind racing back to the day on the viaduct, his stomach folding in on itself, his heartbeat starting to speed up. 'She's OK. She says she's OK, at least.'

'Are you sure you're all right?' Pinder raised his eyebrows, but Moone turned back and kept walking.

'Anything else I should know?' Moone reached the tent, pulled on a glove and opened one of the flaps.

'Best you take a look.'

Spotlights had been set up by the SOCOs in each corner, bleaching out any shadow and burning his eyes as he got into the small space. His vision jumped to the shape on the ground, an ivory-coloured collection of limbs given more luminescence by the lights and outlined by the deep dark earth beneath them. The scent of the ground, the earthy fungus and moss stench, rose up and mixed with that other macabre odour and joined together to choke him as he stepped closer. He almost didn't take it in at first, so taken was he with the glaring whiteness of her arms and legs, but then his eyes travelled to her back. He crouched down, staring at her sharp and almost milk-white shoulder. A couple of inches below her shoulder blade was a tattoo, a perfect and beautifully drawn image of a butterfly, around four inches wide. He pulled out his phone and took a snap of it.

'That looks fresh, doesn't it?' Moone turned to find Pinder by the open door of the tent. 'Hasn't had a chance to heal, the doctor said.'

'Is Parry still here?'

'No, it wasn't him. It was someone else. A woman. Forget her name. Parry couldn't make it, even though he was supposed to be on call. Not like him, she said.'

'Oh, right. That is unusual for him.' Moone looked at the body again, took a mental photo to go with the actual one and headed out in the chilled morning air. 'So, she's dumped here. Did I see marks round her neck?'

'Yeah, strangulation it looks like, the doctor said. What do you make of the tattoo?'

'It's perfectly drawn. Must have been done by a real artist.'

'There's loads in Plymouth.'

'Wonder if it's a particular kind of butterfly...'

'Painted lady,' Pinder said, taking out his radio. He caught Moone's stare. 'Don't look at me like that. I know a bit about nature. I'm not just a copper.'

Moone gave an empty laugh. 'A painted lady.' He felt a shudder travel down his back as he took out his vape and had another desperate puff, knowing that this might be the beginning of something. Then he wondered what Butler was up to. He would need her for this one.

She reached for the mug of tea on the hospital table, felt it was tepid and let go again as her eyes jumped back to her dad who was lying under the starched white sheets and grey blanket. Outside the windows of the hospital ward, the late autumn sun was rising, taking away the dark night sky and replacing it with a blue-grey that did little to cheer her mood. That colour was how she felt inside, she decided as she heard her father mumble something.

They had strict visiting hours these days, especially since Covid had done its worst, but she had flashed her badge and had not taken no for an answer. The nurses were kind enough to turn a blind eye, and even brought her the tea that had now grown cold. She picked up the mug and drank it anyway, as a kind of punishment.

Moone came to mind, the image of his untidy self, his messy hair, that tired and nervous look in his watery blue eyes. He would be at the job by now, going over the scene, trying to take it all in without showing his absolute panic. She huffed out a laugh at the thought.

'What's funny?' her dad's voice said, then his deep, painful cough followed and stabbed at her ears and heart.

'Nothing. Nothing's funny.'

He turned his head, trying to shuffle himself up the bed a little, obviously hoping to get a better view of her. 'Something's always funny. Even in here. Take the old fella across from me. He used to be a farmer. Broken hip. Thing is, they have to keep moving the poor sod, cause he keeps wetting the bed.'

'Hasn't he got a pot or something?' Butler looked over at the withered old man lying under the sheets, his grey skin covered in a peppery stubble.

'Course. But he can never sit up properly to pee into it. I keep telling him, you can't pee uphill, Norman.'

Butler allowed herself a laugh, then stopped when she saw he had turned his eyes towards the windows, his smile having sunk away. 'What have they said?'

'You know what they said. Dockyard for most of my younger working life. Back then we didn't know about asbestos. Used to kick it round back then, use it as a football. Course all the dust ends up in the air. Stupid...'

'You didn't know. Nobody knew.'

'Someone always knows.' He looked at her,

a faint smile returning. 'Least there's some good come of it. You're here.'

'Yeah, well, I don't mean to make a habit of it.' She couldn't look back into his eyes, so she looked down at the carrier bag at her feet and lifted it a little. 'Popped to the Co-op on the way. Got you a sandwich, a Snickers...'

'They were better when they were Marathons.'

'I think the name was the only thing they changed.'

'How's it going with your partner, that Moone fella?'

She looked at her father, saw his watery eyes taking her in, trying to burn through her flesh. 'It's alright. He's a bit of a faffer, but he seems to know what he's doing.'

'High praise from you.'

'Yeah, well, I'm saddled with him. And he needs me to guide him. He doesn't get us Janners.'

The old man laughed. 'I think you're actually pretty fond of him.'

She jerked her head up, staring at him. 'What's that supposed to mean?'

'Nothing. I know you, Mandy. I know you don't suffer fools gladly.'

She huffed, staring towards the windows again, a conversation playing over in her head against her will. She tried to turn it off, to eradicate the words of DS Faith Carthew, the smug way she suggested that her and Moone were more than just partners. She laughed, shaking her head, then felt it, a tightening in her stomach and a strange nervousness following it.

'What's funny now?' her dad asked.

'Nothing. Just laughing at him being on the job without me, probably causing all kinds of havoc.' She got up, straightened her trousers and did her best to smile at him.

'Looks like you're off, then?'

She folded her arms across her chest, looking away from him, staring round at the withered bodies under the light grey blankets that looked as if they used to be blue. She watched the nurses doing their thing, taking the observations of the patients and admired them for it. Dealing with the dead was sometimes better than the living. 'I better get back to work. A DB's turned up.'

'Where?'

'Ham woods.'

The old man tutted. 'Gets worse. I'm sure you and your fella will solve it.'

She stared at him. 'He's not my fella.'

He laughed, shaking his head. 'Go on, get going. Send my regards to Moone. Tell him to come and see me. Or I'll see him down the pub when I get discharged.'

She nodded as he started coughing again and then turned away, walking out of the bay and down the corridor. She passed the nurses' desk and then went back out towards the doors to the ward. Porters were bringing in a bed, so she pushed herself back out of the way, her eyes travelling over a skeletal old lady who was mumbling in her sleep. She rushed out, her chest feeling tight, her breath pounding into her mouth. She felt the tears running down her cheeks, then wiped them away, trying not to think of what the doctor had told her about her dad's condition.

She straightened herself, coughing away the ridiculous emotions that welled in her chest and throat, then stormed on, heading for the lifts. Why the hell was she feeling sad about him when she hadn't forgiven him for the past? She huffed and called the lift, determined not to go soft on him, even if he might die. She couldn't hang around being morbid, there was work to be done.

Moone pushed his hands into his pockets, stamped his feet a few times against the ground that had hardened somewhat from the morning frost. Things were slowly thawing out, helped by the clear sky, the rise of the tepid sun. He watched the bodies still coming and going, the uniforms heading along the paths that spread out deep into the woods, following the stream. He walked a little way, watching the uniforms on their search, then turned when he heard a car coming from the direction of Weston Mill. He saw Butler's car pull in, then waited, trying not to shiver as he stood in the shade of the tall trees.

'What's the story?' Butler asked, her hands buried in her coat, a plume of steam popping from her mouth as she hurried past him.

'Woman in her twenties,' Moone said, catching up with her. 'Strangled. Naked. Fresh butterfly tattooed on her back.'

Butler nodded, then headed down the steep slope, holding on to a tree as she headed toward the path that would lead to the SOCO's tent. 'No ID, then?'

'No. How's your dad?'

She stopped at the bottom of the path and faced him. 'He's fine. Just a bit...under the weather. Bad chest.'

'I see. I'm sure he'll be fine.'

'I know, Moone. I'm not daft.' She turned and hurried towards the tent and stopped again, seeming to stare towards it then getting out of the way when the white bodies of SOCOs emerged from the glowing interior like aliens from a UFO.

Moone approached her, took out his phone and brought up the photo he'd taken of the tattoo. 'Unless the search team turn anything up, this is all we've got to go on.'

After a couple of beats, Butler looked at the screen. 'That's excellent work. There's a lot of skilled tattooists down here. Not many quite that good. I'll start on a list.'

'You all right?'

She looked at him. 'Yeah, why wouldn't I be? You know me, hide of a rhino.'

He smiled but sensed the wave of thick unease coming off her and knew with regret that she wouldn't talk about it. There had been something else, just before she mentioned her dad was unwell, something troubling her, another thing she wouldn't talk about or even admit to. *Was it something he had done?*

Butler had taken her notebook out and stepped away before he could say any more, so he watched her, feeling the cold grip him again, half listening to the squawk of complaints from the crows high above as he pushed his hands into his pockets. He turned towards the tent, staring in as the cameras flashed, trying to clear his head of background noise, to focus. He could see her lying against the ground, her slender, pale and lifeless body. Who does this? Who was the predator who had taken her out into the woods and strangled her? Was she strangled in the woods at all? He straightened himself then poked his head into the tent. 'Is there dirt under her nails?'

One of the plastic covered bodies turned their face towards him, then lowered their mask. A pink, quite pretty face looked back at him. 'A little dirt on her fingers, where she's been laid on the ground, but nothing deep under her nails.' The woman got up, staring at him, then back at the body. 'You're thinking she was strangled somewhere else and placed here. Right?'

He nodded, not wanting to say too much.

She seemed to eye him carefully, then bent down again, staring at the body. 'I'm only guessing, but it looks as if she was strangled by someone's hands. Judging by the bruising, I think her killer was facing her.'

'Meaning he wanted to see the life drain out of her? I'm sorry, who are you?'

She smiled, then stepped out of the tent and took down her hood, revealing light, mousey brown hair pulled back in a ponytail. 'Dr Dawn Jenkins. I was on call to... well, you know.'

'I do. Sorry, I missed you before. Nice to meet you.' He momentarily put out his hand, then lowered it again. 'I'm DCI Peter Moone.'

'Oh, right, yes, I had to take a phone call. I came back to get a better look at the victim. You're from London, by the sounds.'

'Yep. Born and bred.'

'I'm from Wales, originally. Moved about a bit. My father was in the navy, that's how I ended up here.'

'It's a lovely part of the world.'

'It is.' She laughed, then pulled a face as she looked back towards the tent. 'Sorry, shouldn't be laughing.'

'No, I guess not. I wonder who she was.'

'I'd say she was an artist.'

Moone laughed. 'An artist? Who, the tattooist?'

'No, the dead woman. Didn't you notice the calluses on her index fingers? I'd say she draws a lot.'

'Are you Sherlock Holmes?'

She laughed. 'Just observant. Anyway, she is definitely dead. Unfortunately. So, I'd best be going.'

He smiled, nodded to her, then watched her walk past Butler and towards the main road.

'Where's Parry?' Butler asked as she pushed herself away from the tree she'd been leaning against.

'Off sick? Holiday? I don't know. Maybe he's got the corona?'

Butler huffed and showed him the list she'd made. 'Twelve tattooists in Plymouth that I'd say are capable of that quality of work, but...'

'But?'

'A butterfly?'

Moone shrugged, looking down the list. 'If a customer asks for a butterfly, then they do a butterfly, don't they?'

'Yeah, but there's places you go asking for a butterfly...'

'Is there? Search me.'

She looked him up and down, scrutinising him. 'So, you haven't got any hidden artwork on you, then?'

He laughed. 'Do I look like the tattoo type?'

'I don't know. There don't seem to be many people without tats these days. Especially down here. There's going to be a lot of care homes filled with tattooed old people. Come on.'

Moone followed a little behind, thinking about it all, the case and everything, but especially about Butler and what had been bothering her a few weeks back.

'You heard about Carthew?' Butler asked, still walking up the path towards her car.

'No?' Moone caught up, his blood running cold at the mere mention of her name. His mind flashed back a few months when he'd issued his warning to her and she had fired back hers. 'I haven't seen her around.'

'She's in Bristol. Fast tracked up there, by all accounts.'

'Phew. For a minute I thought you were going to say she's been made Chief Super or something.' He laughed but felt his stomach's lack of sense of humour.

Butler stopped and faced him, her arms folded across her chest, eyebrows raised in a disappointed way. 'You know what that means, don't you?'

'No, why don't you tell me?'

'When they fast track these buggers, sometimes they send them up the line, you know, up to the smoke or Bristol.' She stared at him, eyebrows raised.

'So she's in Bristol. Good riddance.'

Butler huffed, shaking her head. 'You really are cakey sometimes. It means, they send them off to get more experience, or reprogram them, or whatever the bloody hell they do, but when they come back, they come back with a stick up their arse and more letters in front of their name.'

Moone felt the shudder down his spine as his stomach pulled the knot tighter. 'Jesus. So she'll be coming back here as what?'

As they arrived back at their cars, Butler said, 'Well, Stack's still on gardening leave. There's talk he might not even come back, so she could come back as our boss.'

'Shit.'

Butler climbed in her car, then wound down her window. 'Don't worry, if she does, then she'll have me to contend with. It'll be her who gets pushed off a bridge next time.'

'Viaduct.'

'Whatever it was, she'll be going off it.'

CHAPTER 2

He slapped his hand down on the sheet of paper, feeling its roughness against the cool of his palm. He lowered his head, muttering, swearing under his breath. When he looked up and peered at the design he had spent the last hour on, he sighed and shook his head. It was amateurish, so he screwed up the paper and hurled it at the wall. Feeling a pulse of fury welling in his chest and thundering up through his arms, he jerked out of his seat and let out a shout that echoed round the low beamed ceiling. He spun his head round to the cage as the thing jerked backwards into the shadows. He breathed hard, watching for a moment, balling his fists. He stepped closer, making a hushing sound, smiling, the best feature he had. His smile lit up his eyes, he'd been told and so he used it when he needed to. But the smile quivered as the anger remained as a thick red fog that clogged up his chest. He put his hands round the bars and peered in, watching her as she sunk back, whimpering.

'I don't want to hurt you,' he said in a soothing tone, turning up the smile again, but the thing just whimpered, sniffing, and he could almost smell the streams of phlegm that would be congealing on her upper lip and seeping into her mouth. He shuddered, then fetched a pack of tissues and held them through the bars. 'Here. Wipe your nose.'

He could make out her wet eyes through the mat of dirty hair. She would need a shower before he started work. He grimaced when he realised the design wasn't ready, wasn't perfect enough. He managed a smile again, gently shaking the packet. 'Here. I'm not going to bite.'

She stared at him, judging him, a scared little animal so full of loathing. Then she edged out, taking small, scared steps, shivering. Her hand snapped out and grasped the packet, leaving his hand empty.

'See, I told you I wouldn't hurt you, didn't I?' He pushed his face between the bars, letting the smile fade as he looked her over, turning his head a little, a critic of fine art stood in a gallery in London. The Tate, perhaps. 'Turn round,' he said, his voice quiet.

She looked up, the tissue still at her nose. Her eyes narrowed, the spite rising above the fear.

'Go on, turn round. Be a good girl. Turn around for me and I'll make sure you get a shower.'

She frowned, her body trembling as she moved, her awkward blackened feet crossing over each other, turning her bony back towards him. He sighed as he saw her muscles move beneath the tight flesh of her back. He didn't allow his eyes to drift down, just held off, keeping his desire at bay for a while. He let out another sigh and saw her tremble even more.

'You're a canvas,' he whispered. 'The most beautiful canvas. But you're dirty. I'll turn on the water and you can wash yourself. Don't worry, I won't watch.'

He retreated backwards, his eyes still dancing over her skin, and then turned his face away at the last moment and found the stopcock. He turned it on and listened as the water started to cough and splutter its way out. His eyes rose to the paper on his drawing board, the thud of inspiration beginning to burn through his veins. 'Yes, yes, my beautiful painted lady,' he whispered and sat down, letting his hand take the pencil to the paper and scrawl away.

Moone parked up behind Butler just up the road from the newly developed Barcode shopping and cinema complex. He climbed out, looking around at the people passing by, noting the lack of masks. Things were pretty much returning to normal; he shrugged and took a puff from his vape. He wasn't sure if the return to normality was a good thing or not as the normality he was used to seemed to be anything but.

'Still puffing on that thing, then?' Butler said, folding her arms across her chest. 'They still don't know the long-term effects of vaping.'

Moone looked down at his vape, then up at her with his eyebrows raised. 'You told me to get one! You said you couldn't stand the thought of me puffing away on those cancer sticks. *Your words.*'

'I know.' She smirked, then pointed across the road. 'See that shop?'

Moone sighed, put away his vape and stared across the road at a narrow shop painted dark red with a window covered in various artistic paintings. 'The Redhouse?'

'It's a tattooist. One of the best in Plymouth. Come on, and try and be a bit, you know...'

'What?' Moone quickly followed her across the street, feeling a little rain being blown into his face.

'Cool.' Butler pushed open the glass door and headed into the shop.

'I'm a copper, I'm not,' Moone began to say, then his eyes jumped to the interior of the shop, which was narrow, but stretched far back. Expensive looking wood floors lay under several comfortable black chairs where customers were reclining as the staff buzzed away, scribbling at their skin. 'So this is where it all happens?'

Butler looked at him, let out a huff and then walked towards one of the tattooists, a young woman who had her arms and neck covered in thorny flowers. Her pink hair was kind of bobbed one side, shaved short the other side. Moone mentally shrugged, feeling ancient, as Butler said, 'Who's the boss round here?'

The young woman hardly lifted her eyes from her work as she said, 'No boss. Only Kris, he owns the place. He's round here somewhere. Do you want a tattoo?'

'Me?' Butler laughed. 'No, but my friend here would like a big rose rising up between his arse cheeks.'

'I really wouldn't,' Moone said when the woman looked up at him. Then her eyes jumped behind him. 'That's Kris.'

They both turned to see a tall, solid and muscular man in his forties, with a shaved head which was almost completely covered in a barbed wire design that had spiders entangled within it.

Moone took a breath and headed over to the man who was laughing with a client who was lying back in one of the many chairs. He took out his ID, which Kris barely glanced at as he picked up and then swigged from a bottle of water.

'You want me to tattoo FILTH across your forehead, bey?' Kris laughed, shaking his head. 'All above board here, officers.'

'You recognise this tattoo?' Moone held up his phone, the dead woman's tattoo lit up on his screen.

Kris took a brief look, then smirked. 'A little pretty fuckin' butterfly? Give me some fuckin' credibility, bey.'

'Take a closer look,' Butler said, scowling at him.

Kris looked into her eyes, then looked down at the screen. His eyes narrowed, then his chunky tattoo-covered fingers enlarged the image. 'I was wrong. That's a fine piece of art. Not mine, but it's intricate. Look at the detail.'

'So, do you know who might've inked that?' Butler asked.

Kris shook his head. 'Na, but I'd like to meet them. I'd like to offer them a job.' He smiled.

'This is part of a murder inquiry.' Moone folded his arms, watched the surprise and shame spread a little across the man's tattooed face as he turned to look at the image again.

'You know what,' the tattooist said, pointing at the screen. 'That looks like writing. Tiny writing or something. Rio, what you reckon?'

A red-headed girl with a bob cut, who was just sitting down with a customer, looked over at him. 'What's writing?'

'Take a look at this,' Kris said, and the girl came over and stared at the image.

'Do you mind?' the girl said to Butler, and then took the phone off her and enlarged the image. 'Yeah, think you're right. It looks like, maybe, I don't know, Arabic? Something like that. Usually people ask for Chinese letters or sometimes Latin. But looks more like Arabic.'

Butler took back her phone and peered at it. 'I think they're right. Maybe we can get it translated. So, neither of you have seen this type of work before?'

'Na,' Kris said. 'People don't come here for butterflies. We leave that to the low-end shops. But that butterfly, well, it's the best I've seen.'

Moone signalled to Butler that it was time to leave, so they thanked the tattooist and stepped outside.

'What do you reckon?' Moone asked.

'There's still a lot of tattooists to check out,' Butler said, looking at her phone again. 'Probably a lot with the skills but who aren't practicing. We better print up this photo and circulate it. In the meantime, let's find out what those words mean, if anything at all.'

The lecture theatre was only half filled. Most of the police officers were sat close together, only about half of them wearing masks. DS Faith Carthew looked them all over, then focused on the lecturer who was still getting himself ready for the talk he was about to give. The slightly overweight DSU tucked in his shirt as he looked up at the rows of police officers that were sat quite far from him, then smiled. His name was Charlie Armstrong. DSU Armstrong, and rumour had it he was heading down to Plymouth to take over from DSU Stack. She stared at him as she sat down, a few seats away from the other police officers. She noticed their strange looks but smirked to herself and got out her pad and pen. When she looked round again, she saw the Indian girl, Cara, looking her way. Then she quickly looked down. Carthew smiled to herself.

'Is my deodorant not working?' DSU Armstrong asked, stepping towards the front row. 'Why is everyone sat so far back? You'll give a man a complex.'

The other police officers laughed, then got up and moved closer, but Carthew stayed where she was. DSU Armstrong's gaze jumped to her, so she looked at him, not moving. He smiled, nodded, then turned to start his lecture. She was staying in the Premier Inn just up the road, the same place he was staying. In fact, she had made sure she was only a few doors away from him. She had carried out her research on him meticulously, especially his rumoured adulterous nature. When he kept looking her way throughout the lecture and stumbling over his words and forgetting his place, she knew it wasn't just rumours. She smiled at him, concentrating on the night ahead.

The rain was lashing down by the time they got back to the station and headed into the incident room. Moone had braved the elements on the way back and bought an Americano, which he nestled between his cold hands, trying to warm them up as he thought about the dead girl. He stared at one of the printouts of the butterfly image, an enlargement that allowed him a better, if not more pixelated view of the writing. He took his pen and drew over the image, playing connect the dots.

'I've got a spot the difference, if you want to have a go,' Butler said, appearing by his desk.

'Very bloody funny.' He looked up, then tapped the butterfly. 'Do we think our killer tattooed that on her?'

Butler leaned over his desk. 'A painted lady? Could be a coincidence. She recently gets a tattoo, then some nutter attacks her.'

'Could be. I suppose it probably is. Did you look at missing twenty-year-olds?'

'Yeah, there's a few. Both in Devon and Cornwall. A few similar to her. I've sent uniforms to deal with it.'

Moone nodded. 'What about a translator?'

'Found a lecturer at Exeter uni who's an expert in Arabic and the Middle East. Think he's actually from there, somewhere. But chances are they're actually just squiggles, or they'll translate as "I love butterflies".'

Moone smiled, but his stomach curled in on itself, tying itself in that same tight knot it always did. Then his mind drifted to his other problem, the one that had seemed far off behind him, but now edged much closer. 'Bristol, you said?'

Butler looked up, then sighed. 'I shouldn't have said anything, now you'll worry about that all day. She's off in Bristol, not here. I'm sorry I said anything.'

'Are you talking about Carthew?'

Moone turned to see Harding stood behind him, holding a stack of the murder books he'd asked him to put together, including an enlargement of the butterfly on the victim's shoulder. 'That's right.'

'She's been fast tracked, I hear,' Harding said. 'Do you think she'll be sent back here as our boss?'

Butler put her face in her hands. 'Why did I open my big mouth? Let's cross that bridge when it comes, shall we?'

'Is Stack even coming back?' Harding asked. 'I heard he isn't.'

Moone turned to Butler. 'Is he?'

Butler sighed. 'I had a word with him. I tried my best, but I don't think he can face it. Poor sod, after what he went through, who can blame him?'

Moone nodded, trying to push away the image of Carthew the last time he'd seen her, her eyes so full of intent. She wouldn't just go away, he knew that. She would be somewhere, planning her next move. He shook his head, telling himself not to fixate on her. He stood up, rubbed his hands together. 'Right, let's stop all this moping and get on with the job in hand. Are uniforms visiting the tattooists?'

'Yes, sir,' Butler said and saluted, then gave him the middle finger. 'You know they are. They're expecting us at Derriford in a couple of hours for the post-mortem. We know she was strangled though...'

'And he was facing her,' Moone said, staring off into the distance. 'Staring into her eyes as he did it. He must've enjoyed it.'

'It's getting worse here,' Harding said, shaking his head. 'More and more nutters doing random shit.'

'I blame Moone.' Butler sat back, arms folded.

'Why me?'

She huffed. 'I think you brought the weirdness with you.'

'Isn't that a Crowded House song?' Harding laughed as he started handing out the murder books.

'Probably, Mr Eighties.' Butler shook her head and started going through the murder book.

Sergeant Kevin Pinder came through the door, the usual cheeky grin on his face, hands in pockets. 'Do you lot do any work? I should become a detective. Looks like an easy life.'

Butler turned to him. 'You couldn't detect your way out of a carrier bag.'

'Well, you manage to keep your job.' Pinder grinned at her. 'Heard the one about…'

'Why're you hear, Pinder?' Butler asked.

'That translator guy's here. Happened to be in Plymouth, about to give a lecture or something. Do you want him in an interview room?'

Moone got up. 'Yeah, room one. Make him a tea or coffee or something.'

Professor Joseph Kahlil was sitting at the metal desk, a cup of coffee by his hands that were clasped together. He looked to be in his early forties to Moone, with dark curly hair that was greying at the temples. He was thick set, dark skinned, and wore black rimmed glasses. He stood and put out a hand towards Moone as he entered.

'Joseph Kahlil,' he said, with a brief and wide smile. 'Someone said you needed a translation?'

Moone shook his hand, wondering how to continue as Butler came in behind, not wanting to upset the man with the details.

'We've got a murder,' Butler huffed, pulled out a chair and sat down.

Kahlil opened his eyes wide, looking between them, frozen as he stood there. Moone pointed to the chair behind him. 'Sit down, professor. I'm DCI Peter Moone, this is acting DI Mandy Butler. Thank you for coming in.'

'You're welcome.' The professor sat down. 'Is this terror related?'

'We don't think so,' Butler said, sitting back and folding her arms. 'Moone, show him the photos.'

Moone stared at her for a moment, shaking his head, noting she was back to being her sulky self, then took out the two photographs. He pushed them towards Kahlil, who stared down at them, taking off his glasses and replacing them with another pair.

'As you can see, the tattoo was found on the back of a murder victim.' Moone watched the professor drag the photos closer to him, leaning in closer to get a better look.

Kahlil's brow furrowed. 'I'm sorry, I cannot see the writing you want me to…'

Butler tapped the close-up image of the butterfly. 'It's kind of woven into the design.'

Kahlil nodded, staring down, adjusting the image. 'Yes, of course. Now I see what you mean...'

'Where are you from?' Butler asked, sitting back.

'Butler...' Moone shook his head.

'Just a question, Moone. Keep your pants on.'

'It is OK,' Kahlil said, looking at her. 'I'm from Ghuma in Lebanon.'

'Where's that to?' Butler asked.

'She means where's Lebanon,' Moone added. 'It's in the Middle East.'

'I haven't been back there for several years,' Kahlil said, looking down at the photo again. 'But you are right, there is writing here. This seems to be an early form of Arabic, but it is still used today.'

'Can you tell us what it says?' Butler asked, raising her eyebrows.

The professor raised a thick finger, lifted his briefcase onto the desk and started rifling through it. He produced a worn, leather bound notebook and a pen and started making notes.

'Is that a *yes* or *no*?' Butler said.

Kahlil looked up. 'I apologise, but I'll need a moment to work out the words.'

Moone stood up and pointed a thumb at the door. 'Come on, let's give the man some peace.'

Butler shrugged, then dragged herself to her feet and followed Moone into the corridor. He stood, leaning his back against the wall, staring at the interview room door, his mind buzzing away, once again on a desperate hunt to make sense of it all.

'You're overthinking things again.' Butler huffed, then folded her arms, staring at him.

'Probably. But who tattoos a butterfly on the shoulder of a girl before throttling her?'

'A nutter. A nutter out there doing his weird little thing. We'll catch him, like we've done before. But as for the overthinking, I was talking about Carthew...'

'Faith? You're the one who said about her being fast tracked and everything...'

Butler nodded. 'I know, I know. Chances are she'll disappear, given any luck. Go off and badger some other poor sods.'

'Do we really want someone else lumbered with her? We know what she's capable of.'

Butler held his gaze. 'She's definitely the one who pushed you off the bridge?'

'She is. I'm sure of it. And don't forget she set fire to my caravan.'

'How could I forget? You mention it twenty times a day.'

'Maybe we should talk to Laptew?'

'Good luck with that. He's on holiday.'

'Where?'

'Deepest Cornwall, I think. Him and his missus like to get lost there, walking or hiking. Sounds like hard work to me.' Butler looked down for a moment, then up, her face having changed, her cheeks a little scarlet. Her mouth opened a couple of times, he noticed before she said, 'Moone. Pete…'

Then the door of the interview room opened and an excited looking Kahlil came out, looking between them both. He held up his notebook and said, 'I think I have it.'

Moone stepped over. 'What does it say?'

Kahlil looked down at the words he'd scribbled down. 'The butterflies know and accept the beauty of change.'

Moone looked at Butler, but she shrugged.

'I think that's what it says,' Kahlil said. 'I'm pretty sure.'

Moone looked at the words. 'Then this is probably our killer's message to us. Or to someone.'

CHAPTER 3

The hotel restaurant was on the ground floor, a sizeable rectangular room, black steel beams and glass creating the exterior walls, giving the effect of being in a massive greenhouse, decked out with tables covered in white tablecloths, and a long chrome bar on one side. DSU Charlie Armstrong picked up his pint of bitter and sipped it as he stared round the room. It was dark beyond the large windows, the lights of the city and shapes of people moving past. He hadn't been in Bristol long, and soon he would be moving on again, heading farther south. It was fine by him, as it got him away from the wife and the stagnant cesspit their marriage had become. He had had this feeling lately, a strange sense that she might be seeing someone else; he just couldn't seem to make himself care about it. He sighed, took another drink and looked at the people at the bar, a real mix of Bristol's young and old citizens. A few of his students were there too, propping up the bar, necking shots, no doubt ready for the night ahead.

He couldn't help notice the strawberry blonde wasn't among them. Faith Carthew. DS Carthew. He'd looked her up, curious about the way she separated herself from the chaff. He admired her for it, but what really had got a grip on him was the way she'd stared so intently at him all the way through his lecture. There had been the occasional smile too, he noticed, when he caught her eye.

A dark-haired young woman came to his table, a tablet device in her hands, a polite smile on her face. The waitress took his order, then went away, taking his menu with her.

He sighed again, his eyes jumping to the wine menu, thinking he might have a glass of red with his steak and chips. He shook his head, knowing full well what Kate would think, how boring and predictable he had become. Fuck her, he thought, then flinched a little when he saw someone was stood at his table.

He put a hand to his chest, half laughing as DS Carthew looked down at him with a subtle smile.

'You scared the life out of me,' he said, burning with embarrassment.

'I'm sorry.' She smiled, looking into his eyes. 'I hope you haven't got a heart condition.'

'No, nothing wrong with my ticker, don't you worry.'

She nodded, then looked around the restaurant, her eyes fixing on her fellow students. 'Looks like they're in for a rowdy night.'

'Yeah. Not your thing?'

'No. Give me a glass of wine, a good book, or Gogglebox on the TV and I'm happy.' She looked down at the chair opposite him.

'Did you want to join me?' His heart began to pound in his chest.

She shook her head. 'No, you're OK. I don't want to disturb you...'

'You wouldn't be. Honestly. Go on, sit down, if you want.'

She looked around again, seeming to hesitate, then shrugged and pulled out the chair. 'No point eating alone, I guess.'

'No. Do you want a drink?' He managed to signal one of the waitresses, who slowly came over.

'Wine,' Carthew said. 'White. Sauvignon blanc. Please.'

The waitress went away, leaving them in silence, a silence that he started to feel in his chest, his mind whirring to find anything to say. Be charming, he told himself, you used to be charming. He looked over at the bar again, trying to dredge up some kind of witty conversation, but he caught sight of the dark-haired female officer from his lecture. She seemed to be staring at Carthew.

'Don't look now, but I think someone's staring at you,' he said.

Carthew turned round and looked towards the bar. The dark-haired officer turned away.

'She keeps doing that,' Carthew said and laughed. 'Must have a crush on me. You're married, then?'

She was looking at his left hand. His heart thudded as he looked down at the thick band of silver. 'Eh, yeah, twelve years. Twelve very long years.'

'Kids?' Carthew picked up and opened the menu, her eyes starting to scan it.

'No. We never. We didn't...'

She looked up. 'Sorry, I shouldn't be prying.'

'You were in Plymouth?'

She nodded, looking down at the menu again. 'Yep. Now I'm here.'

'That's where I'm heading... Plymouth, I mean.'

She looked up, seeming surprised. 'Really? You're not taking over from...'

'DSU Stack? I am, for my sins.'

She seemed to look to his right for a moment, entering a dream state.

'You OK?'

She flickered out of her dream, smiled at him. 'Fine.'

Her wine was put down next to her by the

waitress, who moved away again after asking if Faith wanted to order anything. She shook her head as she picked up her glass and stared right into Armstrong's eyes. They were alone again, and he delved into his brain, trying to ignore his pulse that thudded in his neck.

'I looked you up,' he said, then instantly regretted it as her eyes narrowed.

'Really? What did you find?'

'You've been on quite a trajectory.' He smiled, sipping his drink.

She nodded. 'I suppose. I know where I want to go, and I don't let a lot stand in my way.'

'I see. That's to be admired.'

She smiled. 'I suppose it is. Some wouldn't agree. Some would call me a bitch.'

'Not me. All the more power to you. Women have been side-lined for far too long.' He worried he sounded far too woke, but shrugged it off.

She leaned forward, as if she was about to impart a dark secret. 'Tell me, what are you doing in a couple of hours?'

'Er... nothing. Probably watching the TV in my room, doing some paperwork. Why?' His heart thumped again.

'I was thinking maybe I could pop by your room. We could have a nightcap. Or would that be terrible?'

He didn't react for a moment, held in his shock. He quickly sipped his drink, his mind racing. He had a flash of his wife. Fuck her. Why not have some fun? How could she possibly find out? 'Maybe... maybe I can get a bottle of Champagne?'

'And celebrate your promotion?' She smiled. 'Sounds like a plan. I'm hoping to climb the ladder myself soon.'

'Good luck. Though I'm sure you won't need it.'

She smiled, lifting her drink as if to toast. 'You're right. I won't need luck. I have a plan.'

He smiled, leaning forward, knowing that it was going to be a good night. 'Tell me more.'

'I will. Soon. I'll come to your room in two hours. Then we'll have a night we'll never forget.'

It was dark by the time Moone had parked up at Derriford. He sat in his car for a moment, staring down towards the bus stops, watching the smokers coming out of the hospital, some dressed in pyjamas. He took out his vape, took a puff, then grimaced. He shook his head, then threw it on the empty passenger seat. Butler had gone home early, making the excuse that she had things to do at home, stuff to sort out, but he felt the barriers going up again; he couldn't help feel that there was something she was keeping from him, some secret she was keeping close to her chest. He shrugged, then climbed out, tempted to go over and ask one of the smokers for a fag. No, he wouldn't give in. Then, as he crossed the road, he made himself a deal. If he solved the case, if he found whoever tattooed the dead young woman, then he'd have one cigarette. Just the one as a kind of reward.

He took the lift to the bottom floor, then headed to the big plain white door. He pressed the buzzer and was let in by a young man in scrubs. He went right, and passed the large metal cabinets where they kept the dead, then headed into the autopsy room.

Dr Lee Parry was absent and only a dark-haired woman, perhaps in her early forties, was stood at the head of one of the long metal tables. A body lay in front of her, covered by a green sheet.

The woman looked up from the notes she was making and smiled and Moone realised they had met earlier. 'Hello again. Sorry, what was the name?'

'DCI Peter Moone,' he said, flashing his ID. 'No Dr Parry again?'

The woman turned her wrist, looking at her watch. 'No, he's running a bit late. Not like him either, apparently. Do you remember my name?'

'Dr Dawn Jenkins. From Wales.'

'Very good. How come we haven't met before this morning?'

Moone stepped further into the room, his

eyes resting on the shape under the sheet. 'I don't know. Not a very big place.'

'No, not very.' Dr Jenkins filled in some more paperwork, then followed his eyes to the table. 'Your unidentified victim. Awful business…'

'It always is.'

She nodded. 'Mid to late twenties. Such a waste. I hope you find out who did this. I wish you luck.'

'I'll need more than luck.' He raised his eyebrows. 'Anything you can tell me?'

'We're waiting on toxicology. Fingerprints have been taken, swabbed for DNA. Hers or her killers. She was strangled. Thumb and finger marks on the front and sides of her neck. Petechial haemorrhaging, all the signs of strangulation. He was looking in her eyes. By the way, my guess is that the tattoo was made a few days prior to her death, judging by how much it had healed.'

Moone was about to say something when the door at the far end of the autopsy room opened and Dr Lee Parry hurried in, pulling on a pair of gloves.

'Sorry I'm late,' Parry said to his colleague, then his eyes jumped to Moone. 'DCI Moone, how are you?'

'I'm all good, thanks,' Moone said. 'Not like you to be late.'

Parry gave a short laugh as he shook his

head. 'No, it's not. Traffic was bad. Gets really snarled up round here.'

Moone nodded, then watched as Parry approached the table, his eyes travelling over the shape beneath the sheet.

'You've completed the post mortem?' Parry asked, putting his gloved hands together, still looking at the table.

'Yes, and it was definitely strangulation,' Dr Jenkins said, getting shoulder to shoulder with Parry.

'There's a tattoo on her back,' Moone said, pointing at the table. 'Near her shoulder.'

'There is?' Parry asked as he lifted back the sheet, revealing the washed, almost grey skin of the woman, the dark bruising on her neck now looking angry.

'Yep.' Moone folded his arms. 'A butterfly.'

Parry started turning the woman's body as Dr Jenkins joined him. Then he bent down, staring at the tattoo.

'Painted Lady,' Parry said, then straightened himself. 'Interesting.'

'What do you make of it?' Moone asked.

'Beautifully designed.' Parry still stared down at the body.

'Why would somebody do this?' Jenkins asked, shaking her head.

'We've got a theory that he's releasing them,' Moone said, then shrugged, a mild burn of embarrassment travelling up to his face as

Dr Jenkins turned to him. 'It's just a theory.'

'So, he captures them,' Jenkins said, stepping closer to Moone. 'Then he marks them, then releases them. But why?'

Moone shrugged. 'I wish I knew. We managed to translate some writing we found hidden in the tattoo. It basically said that butterflies understand the beauty of change. Which seems to suggest he's changing them somehow or something. But why do any of these crazy people do this stuff?'

'Who knows?' Jenkins said, before her eyes lit up. 'Oh, there was something else. I noticed a cannula had been put in your victim's arm recently. And it was done quite well.'

'Probably used it to keep her drugged,' Moone said. 'Then our killer might have medical knowledge. Interesting.'

'Where's your charming companion?' Parry asked, a smile stretching his face.

'She had errands to attend to, apparently,' Moone said. 'She's become a bit of a mystery lately.'

'Really?' Parry looked at Jenkins. 'Do you mind giving us a moment, Doctor?'

'No, it's fine,' Jenkins said, but her smile looked rather fake to Moone as she turned and headed out of the room.

Parry folded his arms, his eyes narrowing. 'A mystery? You should be able to solve it.'

Moone laughed. 'The living are more

difficult to interpret.'

'True. They're very complex. But it's probably something simple. Maybe to do with her father.' Parry turned away, concentrating on the body again, and the autopsy report that Jenkins had left for him.

'Her father?'

'Yes, didn't you know? He's in this hospital.'

'What's wrong with him?'

'Not sure, but he worked in the dockyard for years, and judging by the ward he's in, I'd say asbestosis.'

Moone looked down, shaking his head, his stomach twisting into a tight knot. 'Why didn't she say anything?'

'You know DS Butler,' he said, looking down at the report again. 'She doesn't exactly wear her heart on her sleeve, does she?'

'No, she doesn't. What ward is he on?'

'You're thinking of visiting him?' Parry raised his eyebrows. 'Do you think that's wise? This is Butler we're talking about.'

'Yes, I know. She plays her cards close to her chest, and she wouldn't be happy about me poking my nose in.' Moone watched Parry nod as he started perusing the autopsy report again, as more curiosity found its way to his lips. 'Talking of poking my nose in…'

Parry looked at him expectantly. 'Yes?'

'Why were you late? You're never late. And

there's not much traffic at this time of day.'

Parry straightened himself, a smile stretching his face wide as it always did. 'Well, you are a good detective, after all. No, it wasn't traffic. I lied. It's...well, it's a family thing. Bit of a crisis.'

Moone held up his hand. 'Say no more. I hope everything's OK.'

'It's nothing really. You know family.'

'I do, only too well. If you need to talk about it, any time.'

Parry smiled. 'Thanks, that's kind of you.'

'Anyway, what ward is her dad in?'

Moone buzzed the door to the ward, looking through the window, watching the masked nurses going about their business, all looking pretty frazzled. He adjusted his own mask, then shivered a little at the thought of having to do their job, but thought about his own, and the fact that he had a young woman as yet to identify. Parents. His stomach sank as a voice crackled from the intercom and asked him what he wanted. He told the female voice that he was the police, and the door buzzed open. As he got close to the nurses' station, he had to press himself against a wall as a bed came past, pushed by some porters, a tiny old lady at the centre of it. She smiled at Moone, waving her withered arm at him. He waved back, then carried on down to the ward, the cacophony of noise, patients coughing or shouting, hitting his ears.

He showed his ID to an Indian-Looking nurse on the desk. 'DCI Peter Moone. Is Alf Butler here?'

The nurse looked up, staring at his ID, then up at his face. 'Is he in trouble?'

'No, nothing serious. But I would like a word with him, if I'm allowed.'

The nurse shrugged, then looked on the computer screen. 'Bay G. Bed two.'

Moone smiled, then headed along the corridor, dodging doctors and cleaning staff. He went into the bay and saw the old man sat up, a paper in his hands. He seemed thinner, certainly frailer than the last time he had seen him. Moone stepped closer, his eyes jumping over to the other patients lying in their beds, reading or playing on their phones.

'Moone, isn't it?'

He turned and saw Alf Butler had put down his paper and was staring at him, a wide smile on his face. 'That's right. Peter.'

'No, I'm Alf. You're Peter.' The old man laughed and then pointed to the chair close to his bed. 'Sit down, lad.'

Moone sat down, delving into his mind, trying to find some conversation and slowly regretting his decision to visit Butler's father. He kept seeing the doubt in Parry's eyes.

'You here to arrest someone?' Alf asked,

sweeping his eyes over the room. 'One of these old codgers committed armed robbery or something? No, you usually deal in murder, don't you? One of them done a Shipman?'

Moone laughed. 'Nothing like that. I came to see you.'

'Oh, I see,' he said and coughed. 'She told you, did she?'

'No, she didn't mention you were in here.'

The old man shook his head, gave a deep laugh. 'No, course not. She doesn't like to share, our Mandy. So, she doesn't know you're here. Interesting.'

'No, she doesn't. She'll probably kill me.'

'Probably. Don't worry, I'll have a word.'

'Thanks. How are you?'

Alf gestured to the ward, then shrugged. 'See, this is what you get for working for years with asbestos. To tell the truth, there's not much they can do. Just a waiting game.'

'I see.' Moone looked down, feeling weak, his stomach knotting, flashes of the dead girl appearing in his mind.

'But it's Mandy you're concerned about.'

Moone looked up and saw the old man had a knowing look in his eyes.

'Sort of. She just seems to have grown distant of late… But maybe it's because you're not well.'

'Doubt it's that. But you're right. She's got something on her mind. Who knows what's going on in that head of hers.'

'I hoped you would.'

'Sorry, Pete.'

'It's all right.'

'She was here this morning. Before work. Brought me a couple of treats, which is unlike her. I don't know. Something's definitely bothering her. Maybe it's that woman police officer you've had trouble with.'

'She's mentioned her?'

'Yeah, a little.'

'Well, hopefully we've seen the last of her. Think she's in Bristol. Anyway, I better go.'

'Thanks for coming to see me, Pete. Hopefully we can go for a drink soon, when I'm out of here?'

'That'd be great.'

The old man smiled, then Moone watched it crumble as Alf said, 'We'd better make it soon, I don't suppose I've got long left.'

Moone opened his mouth, but nothing came out for a moment, as he saw old man was perhaps expecting some words of comfort. 'We'll go for that pint. And many more, I'm sure. Take care, Alf.'

Moone left the bay, hurried down the corridor, then stopped outside the ward, his stomach all churned up at giving Alf false hope. If Parry was right, and he usually was, then it wouldn't be long before the asbestos did its worst. He started walking again, his mind turning to Faith, who was out there somewhere. He hoped she was behaving herself.

Charlie Armstrong had just finished shaving and was tending to a slight cut on his neck when there was a knock on the door. He froze for a moment, then turned and stared out of the bathroom. He listened, his heart starting to thud.

She was here. She was actually here. He looked at himself, feeling sweat trickling down his back. Was this really about to happen?

There was another knock, so he pulled himself together, ran a hand through his hair and adjusted his shirt as he walked towards the door of his room.

As soon as he opened it, the scent of her perfume engulfed him, making his heart swell in his chest. He also felt a deep cavernous desire unfolding within himself, while an echo of guilt called out somewhere at the back of his mind. He quietened it all down, somehow reconciling the fact that he might be about to cheat, with the knowledge that his marriage was pretty much dead in the water.

'Can I come in?' she asked, raising a perfectly formed eyebrow, a subtle smile on her now red-painted lips.

'Yeah, yeah, of course,' he said, stepping aside. As he was about to close the door, his eyes jumped to a woman stood in the corridor, dressed to go out, a handbag clutched in her hand. Her eyes were on him, but she quickly looked away. Eyewitness, he thought. But she didn't know Kate, had no way of knowing that he was married. He shut the door, then swore when he looked down at his left hand and the silver ring on the appropriate finger. He gripped it, then eased it off before slipping it into his pocket.

'Everything OK?'

He turned and saw her stood by the bed, a bottle of white wine in her hand. She had changed into a deep red dress that was quite short and low cut.

This was happening. His mind began to fill with self-doubt, wondering if he was up to the task. She had to be ten years younger than him, if not more. Dirty old man, some would say, but he pushed it all away, put on a smile, and walked towards her.

'All good,' he said, then looked at the small desk where the TV and beverage making area was, pleased that he'd ordered the more expensive bottle of Champagne, which was nestled in an ice bucket, two flutes by the side.

'Champagne?' he asked.

'Not yet. This first.' She handed him the wine. 'Champagne gets me a bit, you know...I like to be eased in.'

Charlie felt his face burn a little, and his

lower regions tingle for the first time in a long time.

'Of course,' he said, opening the wine. 'Wouldn't want you getting too…you know. Well, maybe I would.'

She giggled. And his hand trembled a little as he poured the wine.

He handed her a glass.

'Bottoms up,' she said and clinked his glass.

He smiled at her words, imagining her with no clothes on, her bottom up, waiting for him to…

'Drink up,' she said.

His cheeks were burning. His heart pounding. He downed the wine in one go, his mind racing, trying to fathom what his next move would be. *At what point should he make a move, and did she even want him to?*

'I should warn you,' Faith said, sitting on the bed and crossing her legs. 'Wine makes me a little flirty, but Champagne gets me all turned on.'

His eyes were drawn to her hitched-up dress, the triangle of white panties. He was getting hard. She was smiling, a devilish look in her eye. *This was happening.* There were no crossed wires, she was definitely here for one thing only. He knew these days you had to be careful, had to be aware of the line; he had taken too many statements from young and older women who had been in the company of men who didn't know where the line was, or either didn't give a shit if there even was a line.

No, there was no misinterpreting this. She knew where this was heading. So did he, and he felt the more powerful stir of desire.

She put her wine glass on the floor, straightened back up and patted the bed. 'Why don't you sit down?'

He nodded, his heart pounding more than ever as he sat down, his eyes finding her shapely legs, then the low cut of her dress, the flesh of her breasts. He wondered if he should try and kiss her yet. He needed more Dutch courage. He never used to be nervous with women, but that had all been a long time ago, long before he met… he buried his past, promising himself that he should live only for the moment.

She leaned right over, giving him a good look at her breasts as she picked up her glass from the floor. 'You look all hot and bothered. Drink this, then we'll hit the Champagne.'

He took the glass, tried not to tremble as her hand touched to his leg. She was stroking him. *Actually stroking him.*

'Drink up,' she said, 'I'm really feeling a bit turned on already. Shall we have some Champagne?'

He chuckled. 'I'm feeling a bit turned on myself.' He drank the wine down in one.

She took the glass from him. He watched her as she walked away. Bottoms up.

He was going to fuck her. Or maybe she'd fuck him. He didn't care either way.

Her shapely legs went out of focus. And then back again. He'd only had a couple of beers with his meal, but he already felt a little dizzy. Maybe he should lay off the Champagne.

No, this wasn't drunkenness, he decided, his eyes going out of focus and whole room seeming to lurch. He felt strange, a little sick. He looked at her, noticing how her look of mischievousness had gone and now she stared at him, watched him carefully.

'I don't feel so good,' he said.

'That'll be the Rohypnol,' she said.

'What? You're joking?' He tried to get up, but he had no strength in his legs. 'What've you done?'

'Drugged you.' She stepped right up to him, smiled, folded her arms. 'Was that not clear? Did you really think I'd want to sleep with you? A middle-aged, cheating husband? Give me some credit.'

'You fucking…'

Her hand pushed against his chest, knocking him backwards, turning his vision towards the white ceiling, the light fitting going in and out of focus. He could hear her moving, then a door opening. Was she leaving? He struggled to move, screaming in his head to move. He tried to speak, to call out, but only mumbled incoherent sounds.

Then her face appeared over him, free of any discernible expression, an animal, a snake examining its prey. He tried to shake his head, plead with his eyes as she produced a needle and syringe.

'This isn't personal,' she said, looking briefly at the syringe. 'I don't want you dying and thinking that I had it in for you. It's not that. It's just, well, you're in my way. I need to get to where I'm going, you see? This won't hurt.'

He was screaming, the sound echoing deep inside him, spreading out to every part of him. He didn't feel the needle go in, only watched her as she stood up and stared down at him. There came a bubble of sickness, then a deep grey mist from the corners of his eyes. His heart pounded in his chest, then slowed, as he sunk backwards, deep into the bed.

CHAPTER 4

'When does the new guy take over?' Harding asked, his eyes appearing over the monitor and fixing on Moone.

'I don't know,' Moone said, sipped his morning Americano, then went back to his reading, absorbing all the information in the murder book, which wasn't much, truth be told. Most of the book consisted of the stack of crime scene photos piled high, the grey images of the girl, her naked body so powerful and stark against the undergrowth. Someone's daughter, sister, or even a young wife. The sickness tried to overtake him, but he swallowed it back down. Then his head swam, a vision flashing in front of his eyes. He was holding onto the stone of the viaduct, the brickwork crumbling under his nails, the drop below him out of focus. His heart began to hammer in his chest, an icy sweat running down his sides.

'Next couple of weeks,' Butler said, as she

was sitting at her desk, a phone in her hand. 'DSU Charlie Armstrong.'

Moone tried to calm down, reminding himself that the moment had passed, he was no longer hanging off the old viaduct. Sergeant Pinder had saved him, just in the nick of time. 'You know him?' Moone asked, merely to distract himself.

'Worked with him once,' she said. 'Bit of a ladies' man. It's weird, cause I can't see him being in charge of... well, anyone.'

'People change,' Moone said, going back to staring at the crime scene photos. They still didn't know who the girl was. He hated that they didn't know who she was, and now she was alone in the morgue, filed away, no one coming for her. But then when she was identified, they would have to tell someone. His stomach wrapped around itself, constricting.

'No, they don't,' Butler said.

He looked up to see her staring at him. 'Don't what?'

'Change,' Butler said. 'People, they don't change.'

'OK, maybe they don't...'

'But he's one of the good ones, luckily,' Butler said, just as Sergeant Pinder came waltzing into the incident room, a smile on his face.

'Morning, you beautiful people,' Pinder said, folding his arms, looking round at them all. 'How's life?'

Butler turned to him, glowering a little. 'How can you be so bloody cheery at this time?'

'It's nearly half past eight,' he said, then looked at Moone, shaking his head. 'I guess I'm just a morning person.'

'That makes one of us,' Moone said, reaching for his coffee. 'Haven't seen you around for a bit, Kev. Apart from the other morning, that is. You first responders keeping busy?'

Pinder laughed, then raised his shoulder. 'Haven't you noticed? I'm an Inspector now. I'm working my last week with the first response team. It's all changing the way things are done in the force. From next week I'm going to be head of a team with neighbourhood policing. We'll be based in Devonport, so won't see you lot much any more.'

Butler put on a sad face. 'Say it's not true, Kevin. I'll miss you so, especially your dad jokes.'

Pinder nodded, narrowing his eyes at her. 'Funny. Listen, I came by because I've got some intelligence for you.'

'You've got intelligence?' Butler said, laughing at herself.

'Well, sort of good news. Depends if you're a half empty...'

'Don't faff, just spit it out.' Butler huffed.

'We think we might have an ID on your

victim,' Pinder said. 'The butterfly girl.'

Moone stood up, staring at Pinder, his stomach going into spin cycle again. It didn't help that he kept seeing Pinder reaching for him, about to pull him up from the viaduct over and over, usually throughout a sleepless night. Sometimes it was in a nightmare, playing over again, but this time Pinder didn't seem to care, and didn't grab for him. Moone couldn't hold on any more, the clumps of brickwork coming away in his hands. Then he was falling...

'Moone, you all right?' Butler asked, staring at him. 'You went into some weird trance.'

'Sorry. Yep, I'm fine. Who is she?' Moone stepped closer to Pinder, his stomach still spinning.

Pinder looked at the notebook in his hand. 'The name's Bobbi-Jane. Apparently, she was staying temporarily in Milehouse Road. There's a halfway house...'

Butler gave an audible huff, so they all stared at her, but it was Moone who asked, 'Something wrong?'

Butler sat back, arms folded, an unimpressed look on her face. 'Milehouse Road. Don't tell me she was living at Ryland House.'

Pinder looked down at his notebook. 'OK, I won't tell you.'

'What's wrong with Ryland House?'

Moone asked, looking from Butler to Pinder.

But it was Butler that came over and said, 'It's a kind of halfway house, the sort of place they house all the waifs and strays, junkies, young people who've just got out of prison, care of the community, all those sorts. There's a few places like it dotted around Plymouth. Most people don't know about it.'

It was Moone's turn to sigh. 'But if she is one of these waifs and strays, as you put it, doesn't mean we don't try and find who killed her...'

Butler raised her eyebrows, letting out another deeper huff. 'Did I say I wasn't going to find her killer? No, bloody well right, I didn't. I just don't like going there, that's all. And once you've been there, you'll see why.'

Moone looked at Pinder and caught the look of sympathy he was throwing him. 'So, Kev, how do we know this might be our potential victim?'

'A young-sounding man called it in,' Pinder said. 'Didn't give a name, but said this girl had been staying there with him, then vanished. Said she had a tattoo of a butterfly on her back. By the way, Butler's right. They're an interesting bunch at Ryland House. The lad who called in, he's probably on drugs or mentally ill. Maybe your dead girl might be the same.'

Butler grabbed her coat as she said, 'Then

we've got another killer who preys on the weak. Can't wait to bang this one up.'

It was Butler who drove them past Pennycomequick at speed, Moone having only a brief chuckle at the name as he always did. Then they headed past the Britannia pub, where Moone had enjoyed a few Sunday afternoons with Alice. Plymouth was certainly starting to feel like home, and he hardly ever missed the grind and noise of London any more. The only trouble he had was when he walked anywhere, finding the locals dawdling along, while his gears were still set on fast mode. He turned to look at Butler, thinking about her dad, wondering if it was the right time to mention that he knew he was sick. But did she want him to know, that's what he was wondering, or did she want to keep it to herself?

'Had your penny's worth?' she said, still watching the road.

He looked away. 'Don't know what you mean.'

'I know I'm beautiful, Moone, but try not to drool.'

'I'll try. It is difficult.'

'How's things on that front?' She looked at him briefly.

'The drooling? I manage to keep it to a minimum...'

'Ha ha. I meant the old love life, you wally.'

'Oh, right.' Moone let out a sigh at the mere flicker of memory of recent love life events. 'Well, there's been little of that malarkey since you know who.'

'Yeah, well, the least said about all that, the better.'

'Yep, you're probably right. What about you?'

Butler glanced at him. 'What about me what?'

'The old love life?' he said, and instantly regretted continuing the subject when he saw her face redden.

'As if I'm going to discuss that with you.' She huffed, shook her head, then pointed at the windscreen. 'Here we go. Hellhouse. Sorry, I meant Ryland House.'

'They've got to live somewhere, haven't they?'

Butler shot him one of her looks, one of the severe ones that always put him in mind of the Paddington Bear stories that he read as a kid. But of course he wouldn't dare tell her that as he liked his testicles where they were.

Butler parked then swung round to him. 'That's the problem with you, Moone, you take liberalism to extremes. If I cut you open, the word liberal would probably be written all the way through you. And, plus, you make assumptions, like the one you've made about me hating the residents in there. Yes, it's always noisy in there, always chaotic, but that's not it. It's just, well, there's someone I don't want to see.'

She climbed out in a flash, hardly giving Moone a chance to ask who the person was. He jumped out, hurrying to catch her up as she headed to a large, quite ornate building that was set a little way back from the main road.

'Excuse me,' a voice called from across the road, so Moone and Butler turned to see a woman, maybe in her sixties, stood staring at them.

'Yes, madam?' Moone said, calling across the road as the traffic groaned past.

'You two from the council?' she asked in a London accent, seeming a little annoyed.

'No, we're not,' Butler said and huffed. 'We're police and we're very busy.'

Moone smiled at her. 'Can we help you?'

The woman looked both ways, then scurried across the road and stood, arms folded, staring up at Moone. 'You sound like you're from London.'

'That's right, madam. Enfield.'

'You're joking. That's where I'm from. What a place Enfield is now, a right mess, and stabbings every five minutes. Don't get me started... anyway, you seen the state of the road round here. Litter everywhere...'

'Well, I'm afraid that's not our

jurisdiction.' Moone pointed a thumb behind him. 'We've got police business to deal with.'

'In there?' The woman rolled her eyes. 'Good luck. Madhouse in there. They were kicking up a right stink the other night. Hope you're here to sort them out.'

'Well, sort of,' Moone said, then smiled, and turned back towards the building.

'One of your lot?' Butler said, then headed into the grounds of the house.

'From Enfield, yes. Said there was something going on here the other night.'

Butler pressed the buzzer by the big glass doors, the only modern looking detail of the old building. 'There's always something going on here, and it's usually quite loud.'

'Isn't that a Madness song?'

'You're daft, Moone.'

'I know.' Moone flinched when a large shadow banged against the frosted glass of the door. 'What the hell!'

Then there were raised voices inside as two figures seemed to dance and struggle behind the door.

'Here we go,' Butler said, huffing again like there was no tomorrow.

The door opened eventually, revealing a stocky, strawberry blond man with ruddy cheeks. His eyes jumped from Moone to Butler, widening as they did, while a big smile appeared on his face.

'As I live and breathe,' the man said, pulling the door fully open. 'DC Mandy bloody Butler. How you doing, bird?'

Butler pushed past him, a barely polite smile on her face as she entered the large, dusty hallway. 'I'm good, as always, Leroy, but it's acting DI Butler now. This is DCI Peter Moone.'

Leroy stuck his thick hand into Moone's and shook it hard with a tight grip. 'Nice to meet you, Pete. Don't mind me calling you Pete?'

'No, it's fine.' Moone nodded, then looked round the hall, hearing the shouts and music echoing loudly round the building. He followed Butler towards the back of the house and a small kitchen.

'Leroy used to be on the job,' Butler said, then filled the kettle.

'Really?' Moone turned to face the stocky ex-copper, but he was speaking to a giant young man who was holding a football and wearing shorts far too small for him. He turned back to Butler, who was setting out three mugs. 'Is this who you wanted to avoid?'

'Yeah, but don't you say a word.' She glared at him.

'I won't. Why though?'

'Never you mind, here he comes.'

'So, how come I've got the pleasure of your company, Mandy?'

Butler finished making the coffees, then

handed them out as she said, 'Like I said, it's acting DI Butler to you. We're here on official business.'

Leroy exchanged raised eyebrows with Moone, then said, 'She doesn't get any less uptight, does she? I tell you, I've got plenty of stories about Mandy Butler. Oh, the cock-ups she made when she was first on the job.'

Moone looked at a red-faced Butler. 'Oh, really?'

'That's enough of that,' Butler snapped. 'If you both want to keep your privates where they are.'

Leroy exchanged a cheeky smile with Moone before he said, 'Go on then, what's this about, Mand?'

'Bobbi-Jane,' Butler said, folding her arms.

'I'm sorry?' Leroy looked between them. 'Am I supposed to know that name?'

'She's been staying here, apparently,' Moone said. 'Someone from here called us to report her missing. They didn't say who they were, but sounded like a young man, apparently.'

Leroy sighed, then tutted. 'You can't rely on what these lot say. Probably just pulling your chain.'

Butler stepped towards him, folding her arms. 'But what if they're not? What if she was staying here?'

Leroy huffed, shook his head, then sipped

his coffee. 'You got a photo of this girl?'

Butler took out her phone and brought up the image of the girl that had been taken on the morgue table. She was about to show him, then said, 'Hope you're not squeamish, Leroy.'

He gave her a strange look, shook his head then stared at the photograph. Then his eyes closed and he rubbed a hand down his face as he let out a deep breath.

'You do recognise her?' Moone asked.

Leroy nodded, looking at Moone. 'Yeah, there's a lad on the top floor. Drug problems. Daryl. Daryl Pawsey. He had some girl here the other night. They're not supposed to, but I turned a blind eye. I didn't like to think of her out on the streets by herself. Just don't tell anyone. Anyway, I think that might've been her.'

'We'd better talk to Daryl then,' Butler said, finishing her coffee, then putting the cup in the sink. 'Show us the way.'

Leroy sighed again, then led them off towards the stairs that travelled up through the centre of the building. Moone let Butler go before him, then slowly climbed the stairs, listening to the racket that echoed around him, shouts and singing, and televisions blasting out nonsense. Occasionally he passed an open room and saw a skinny man or woman, usually pretty young. Some of them just stared back at him, a kind of vacant look in their eyes.

Sometimes they would start shouting stuff, half chasing him as he went up the stairs. Leroy would bark orders to some of the more energetic boarders, telling them to stay in their rooms.

They came to a room halfway along the hallway, where Leroy went in, followed by Butler. Moone stood in the doorway, looking into the small, plain, musty smelling room. A small TV was on, some music channel pumping out dance music. Only the top of a man's shaved head was visible over the duvet that was pulled over the rest of him.

Leroy folded his arms and stood over the bed, then nudged it with his knee. 'Daryl. You awake, son? Police are here to ask you some questions.'

'I'm sleepin',' a muffled voice said. 'Tell 'em to fuck off.'

'Why don't you tell us yourself?' Butler said, standing at the end of the bed.

Slowly the covers came down, revealing a pale, bony face, a sharp nose and two quite bulbous eyes. 'I ain't done nothin', you can't prove I 'ave.'

'They're here to ask about that girl,' Leroy said, pulling the covers down further.

Daryl pointed a finger up at Leroy. 'Stay back, you. I don't want your Covid. Or you two for that fuckin' matter. Anyway, I don't know no fuckin' girl.'

Butler took out her phone and showed him the photo of the dead girl.

'She asleep?' he asked, staring at the photo.

'Kind of,' Moone said, then cleared his throat.

'Kind of?' Daryl sat up, then brought out a pack of cigarettes. 'What's that supposed to mean?'

'Means she's dead,' Butler said. 'So, was she here or not?'

The lad looked down at his pack of fags as he shook his head, a strange look coming over his face. 'Na, don't know no girl.'

'Don't give us that rubbish.' Butler huffed.

Daryl didn't look up as he took out a cigarette and rolled it between his fingers. 'How come she ended up, you know, dead?'

'That's what we want to know,' Moone said.

'You can't smoke in here, Daryl,' Leroy said.

'I need a fuckin' smoke, don't I?' Daryl glared up at him.

Moone had an idea, so stepped closer. 'Is there somewhere outside you can smoke that?'

'Courtyard,' Leroy said. 'But you haven't answered their questions, Daryl.'

'It's all right,' Moone said, holding up a hand. 'I'll go with him.'

Moone ignored the look Butler shot him

as he followed the young lad down the stairs, watching him take out his fag as he prepared to smoke it. Moone was getting the itch, the almost overwhelming desire to leech a fag off the lad. Butler wouldn't see him. But she would know, would be able to smell it on him. He shook his head, closing his mind off to the noise of the building that clattered and screeched its way to his ears as they headed out a back door and into a large, concreted yard. There was a couple of benches and a metal garden table that the seagulls had covered with their disdain. The young lad sat down and lit up, then offered his cigarettes to Moone who remained stood up.

'No, thanks,' he said, 'I've given up.'

'What the fuck do you want to do that for?' The lad spat onto the concrete then gave a deep cough. 'You're just depriving yourself of life's little pleasures.'

'Very true.' Moone sat down, staring towards the wall at the end of courtyard and the ivy that had enveloped it. 'Tell me about Bobbi.'

Daryl shrugged. 'Not much to tell.'

'Must have been something. That's what she called herself, was it? Bobbi-Jane?'

'Yeah, think so. Yeah, Bobbi-Jane. Pretty sure.'

'Did she tell you anything about herself? Where she was from?'

'Fuck all.' He hunched over, staring at the ground. 'I was a bit... you know, bit out of it.'

'Where did you meet her?'

'The park. I like to go there sometimes. I watch Ali, that's the big lad with the footie. He fuckin' loves footie, but he can't even kick the fuckin' ball straight. Anyway, I was smokin', watchin' Ali trying to score. Then I look round and she's there, just bleedin' stood there smiling at me. Jesus, I thought, she's either mental or off her head on drugs.'

'Was she?'

'Off her head? I don't think so. But something was up, 'cause she wanted to talk to me, and no one wants to talk to me...'

'I am.' Moone smiled, feeling a small spike of sympathy stab his chest.

'Only 'cause you have to. It's your job. She didn't have to. She just came over. It was like we were old mates or somethin'.' The lad seemed to follow Moone's eyes that had fixed themselves on the cigarette. 'You sure you don't want one?'

'No, like I said, I'm trying to give up. Got one of these.' Moone took out his e-cigarette, but Daryl laughed and shook his head.

'That's like giving up sex to DIY yourself every night. Fuckin' madness lies that way, mate.'

'I think you might be right. Listen, so was it you who called us about Bobbi?'

Daryl looked down. 'Might've been. Thing

is, she promised to come back to see me. Swore on her mum's life that she'd meet me in the park, but she never turned up.'

'Things get in the way.'

'I know. I'm not stupid. But it's the way she promised. Like her life depended on it. And she seemed scared about something, or someone.'

'Well, I'm afraid she won't be coming back, Daryl. I'm sorry.'

Daryl stared at him strangely. 'How do you know that? She might.'

Moone's stomach twisted in on itself. 'My partner showed you the photo… she's dead.'

'I told you. I don't know who that was, but it's not Bobbi. Looked a lot like her but wasn't her.'

Moone stood up. 'You're sure?'

Daryl dropped his cigarette and stamped it out before he stood up. 'Course I am.'

Moone took out his phone, thinking about the tattoo that had been recently performed on their victim. 'When you called in, you mentioned a butterfly tattoo. The girl we found, she had a recent tattoo on her back. Recognise it?'

Daryl took the phone from him and stared at the photo for a while. Then he shook his head and handed the phone back. 'Na, that's not her tattoo. Her one was much better. A real craftsman did hers, mate. Told you it wasn't her.'

Moone put away his phone. 'Did she have any other tattoos?'

'Yeah, she had this flowery thing right over her arse. Sexy, it was.'

Moone turned away from him, the hair flickering to attention over his back as he realised Bobbi wasn't their dead girl, which meant they were still yet to identify her. Then he pondered on Bobbi and how much Daryl said she looked like their victim. He didn't want to think it yet, but the thought barged its way to front of his mind anyway, making him ask himself whether they had a serial offender on their hands. No, don't jump the gun, he told himself. It was unlikely.

CHAPTER 5

DI Vincent Crowne took another sip of his coffee, then rubbed his eyes, trying to wake himself up. It seemed as if he'd only just finished his sixteen-hour shift, been asleep for half an hour before he'd been woken up by the alarm on his mobile. He was stood in the foyer of the hotel, resting his back on the reception desk, watching the boys and girls in their white plastic outfits carry the tools of their trade back and forth. He rubbed his tired eyes again, then drank some more coffee.

'Is that not doing the job, Vin?'

DI Crowne straightened himself when he saw DSU Tucker coming his way, decked out in her usual dark blue trouser suit, her dark hair piled up on her head.

'You know how it is, boss,' he said, nodding to his coffee. 'Never enough in this job.'

'No. Never is. Didn't get much sleep?'

'Nope. Never enough of that, either. Don't often see you here at these parties.'

Tucker looked at him as if he'd asked her the colour of her pants. 'Parties? Jesus, Crowne, you never change. Anyway, it's one of our own. DSU Charlie Armstrong.'

Crowne's eyes lifted towards the ceiling, a strange coldness washing over him. He'd worked with Armstrong before, a couple of years ago, part of an investigation into an honour killing. It had been a complicated case with long hours, but he recalled Armstrong always lightened the mood. 'Shit. They said murder. He's been offed?'

'For want of a better phrase, yes. Bludgeoned and stabbed, they tell me. They also found a bottle of quite expensive Champagne in his room and two glasses. Looks like he was going to entertain someone, but the bottle hadn't been opened. Wasn't he married?'

Crowne felt uncomfortable. 'Yes, I think he was. But maybe his date never turned up.'

'But somebody turned up and killed him.'

'Bloody hell. I wonder if it's a revenge thing.'

'Well, that's what you're paid to find out.' Tucker turned and pointed to the restaurant across the foyer, where a female uniform was on guard. 'Armstrong was lecturing to a small group, so I've had them put in the restaurant. Talk to them, find out what they know. Oh, and they don't know that he's dead. You can break the news.'

Crowne nodded, then put his empty coffee cup on the reception desk. 'All on the job? Can't see it being one of them, can you?'

'Nothing shocks me. Just get on and talk to them. I'm off to a budget meeting.'

He watched his boss leave, then stuffed his hands into his pockets and headed through the frosted glass doors of the restaurant, giving a nod to the uniform on guard. The lecture group were mostly on separate tables, with only two young officers sat together. He went over, smiling at them all in turn, nodding his head.

'What's happened?' a young lad said, a bottle of water in his hand.

Crowne cleared his throat. 'I'm afraid I've got some bad news. Your lecturer, DSU Armstrong, is dead.'

'Oh God,' one of the girls said. She had caramel-coloured skin, long dark hair. 'Heart attack or something?'

Crowne shook his head. 'No. Someone murdered him. But I can't say much else.'

'Hang on,' the young lad said, looking round at his fellow students. 'You think one of us did it?'

Crowne shrugged. 'I don't know who did it. I do know that he had ordered some Champagne and two glasses. Were any of you expected in his room tonight?'

They all shook their heads and looked blankly at him.

'Well, I know that you lot were among the last people to see him alive.'

'That's not true,' another of the young ladies said. This time it was a blonde with bobbed hair and a sharp face. 'Sorry, I'm Danielle Halligan. I'm a detective constable, in North London.'

'So, Danielle, one of you weren't the last to see him alive?' Crowne asked and pulled up a chair and sat down. 'Tell me more.'

Danielle looked at the dark-haired woman. 'It's not, is it, Cara? You said you saw him with the other woman, the DS from the course, didn't you?'

'That's right,' Cara said, then turned round to Crowne. 'He was with her in here. I saw them sat together, like they were having a meal together. Looked proper cosy.'

Crowne took out his notebook. 'What's your name? Cara, was it?'

'Yes. DC Cara Banerjee.'

'What's this detective sergeant's name?' Crowne asked.

The group all looked at each other for answers, but they all came back blank, so Crowne sighed and put his notebook away again. 'I guess someone will have a list.'

The doors to the restaurant opened, and Crowne turned to see a male uniform coming in, escorting a slender, attractive and strawberry-blonde young woman.

'Boss, this young lady wants to talk to you,' the uniform said.

'That's her,' whispered Cara.

Crowne stood up. 'And you are?'

'DS Faith Carthew,' she said, putting out her hand, and looking over the others. 'Has something happened?'

'There's been an incident,' Crowne said. 'DSU Armstrong is dead.'

'Heart attack?' Carthew asked.

'No, murdered. Where have you been?'

'In my room.'

'Alone?'

'Yes, why?'

He folded his arms, looking round the room. 'Had any of you met Armstrong before?'

The group looked at each other, then collectively shook their heads, so he faced Carthew. 'Have you ever met him before?'

'No. Never.'

'But you had a meal with him?'

'No.'

'You didn't have a meal with him? But you were seen…'

'Sitting with him? Yes, I sat at his table. I was picking his brains. Then I went to my room. That's it.'

Crowne nodded, taking his notebook out again. He wrote some stuff down, thinking for a moment, occasionally looking at Carthew, trying to get a feel of her. Then he turned to the others. 'Where were you all tonight?'

It was Cara who said, 'Us girls went to a couple of bars, but we got back around midnight, didn't we?'

The rest of them nodded, so Crowne looked at the young man. He'd been taking a swig of his water, the look of realisation appearing on his face. 'Me?'

'Yes. What's your name?'

'DC Jason Wise. I went for a late run, then went to back to my room. I had no reason to kill him. I'd never met him before. This is probably someone he put away or something.'

Crowne faced Carthew again and almost flinched when he noticed she was staring right at him, a very enigmatic smile on her lips. 'And you're sure you've never met him before?'

'No, I've never met him before. Why would I want to kill him? Go check my clothes, if you want, get them forensically examined.'

Crowne gave an empty laugh, then looked round at the male officer who didn't seem flustered by any of it at all. No, he didn't think the lad had anything to do with it. But he was definitely getting a strange vibe from the female officer, Carthew. 'Where are you stationed?' he asked her.

'Down here for a bit,' Carthew said, eyeing him all the time, almost as if she was trying to stare him out. He found it a little unnerving. He nodded, smiled and looked them all over, thinking, knowing in his gut that he needed to get her to the station to ask her more questions. There was something off about her whole manner, but he didn't want to put her on edge.

'Right then,' he said, rubbing his hands together. 'I think we need to get you lot down to the station, get your statements taken and then it's safe to say you can be on your way again.'

'You don't think it was one of us, then?' Cara asked, looking around, a little bit of a relieved laugh in her voice.

'One of you lot?' He laughed. 'No, I don't think so. Maybe it was a revenge thing. We'll have to dig a lot deeper, check his movements. Anyway, let's get you lot out of here.'

Moone stifled a yawn, then sipped his coffee, watching the sun settle over the horizon across from the station, glowing a deep hazy orange. He rubbed his eyes, feeling his back ache. He'd only been living in his new mobile home for a couple of weeks, but for some reason he didn't feel comfortable. Butler had laughed at him for forking out for another one, and couldn't understand why he hadn't bought a flat or a house. He didn't know himself, he would have to say if he was honest. The first one he'd bought had been on a whim, a kind of quick decision because he didn't see himself settling in Plymouth for good. But he recalled his first morning, getting up at the crack of dawn, driving to the city to buy a coffee and feeling this strange sensation that he was where he belonged. So why was he living in a mobile home? It was easy. He just didn't like to admit it. Carthew, Faith, had burnt his last one to the ground. Getting another was a kind of middle finger up at her. He wondered where she was, hoped she might be happier there, and not pushing anyone off viaducts. He shook his head, knowing that he was being naive. She wouldn't just stop her ruthless and meteoric rise to the top, wouldn't just become a nice and shy police officer, the way he thought she'd been. She was his responsibility, and he needed to find out what she was up to.

'You're up early, boss,' Harding said, hanging up his coat and heading to his desk. 'Couldn't sleep?'

'Must've wet the bed,' Butler said, following Harding into the room.

'Very funny,' Moone said, smiling at Molly as she went to her desk. 'I was just thinking about this whole case...'

'Here we go.' Butler sighed, then sat at her computer.

'What?'

Butler shrugged. 'Nothing. Just when you start thinking, then we get in trouble. We've got one dead girl. Still unidentified. Probably a runaway from God knows where...'

'But she had that tattoo, with that writing,

the Arabic...'

Butler sat back, huffing. 'Yes, a tattoo with writing. A foreign language, just like every other bugger gets. Most people don't even know what their tattoos say. They think it says something wise or profound, but what it actually says is, I'm an enormous twat.'

'I've got writing tattooed on my back,' Harding said, sounding a bit pissed off.

'That's because you're an enormous twat,' Butler said. 'Anyway, she probably got picked up by the wrong guy. Maybe she was short of money, so decided to try her hand at, you know what, but her luck wasn't good and she met some nutter...'

'Maybe.' Moone sipped his coffee, then opened up the file in front of him that had been sent over from the pathology department. He started reading it, the technical words that meant hands had been used to strangle her. Average sized hands, most likely belonging to a man. Then his eyes jumped to her stomach contents. He expected to see a burger or chips, something grabbed from a fast-food place. No. He read it again.

'Hang on,' he said and looked up at Butler.

'What?'

'Her stomach contents. Her last meal consisted of salmon and steak and prawns. Sounds a bit classy.'

Butler stood up, then came over, looking

suspiciously at him. 'Where? Let's have a look.'

Moone pushed the file towards her. 'So where did she eat salmon, steak and prawns in Plymouth? Doesn't sound like something you're average Plymothian eats, does it? At least not at home.'

Butler straightened up. 'Maybe she picked up some posh bloke. He takes her to a restaurant or back to his place, then...I don't know. Anyway, maybe we can check the menus of local restaurants. Look at the posher ones first.'

Moone nodded, then turned to Harding, holding out the report. 'Steak, salmon and prawns. Check out the local restaurants, Harding, see who serves these.'

Harding took the report then started typing at his desk, leaving Moone to face Butler again. 'So, what're you thinking?'

Butler shrugged. 'I don't know. Like I said, young, pretty, runaway girl gets picked up by some rich weirdo. There's plenty living round here. Most of them come from elsewhere, buy some flashy place down here. Loads of them came flooding down here when Covid hit. Bloody idiots.'

Moone nodded, thinking it all over. 'What about the other missing girl? The girl who Daryl met in the park?'

'Oh, come on. You can't take anything that kid says as gospel. He might've imagined the whole thing.'

Moone sighed and sat back, put his hands behind his head. He couldn't deny she was right. They had two possible missing women, one of them dead, and now waiting to be identified in the morgue. He looked over at Molly. 'Anything from missing persons, Molly?'

'Plenty of young women,' Molly said, blushing a little. 'But nobody matching our dead girl, I'm afraid. I'll keep looking.'

'Jesus,' Harding said, so Moone swung round to face him, and said, 'What?'

Harding looked horrified as he stared up at Moone. 'I can't believe this. This is criminal.'

'What? What's happened?' Moone rushed to Harding's desk.

'Nearly fifty quid for a platter of steak, salmon and prawns,' Harding said. 'Are they famous prawns? Celebrity cows? It's ridiculous.'

Butler huffed. 'Where do you take your missus for a meal? KFC?'

Moone let out a sigh. 'Bloody hell, come on you two. So, who has those items on their menu?'

Harding looked up. 'There's a few restaurants dotted around Devon and Cornwall with similar platters on their menus. But the closest one is a posh restaurant not far from here.'

'Where's it to?' Butler asked as she came

over.

'It's Mario Jean Black's restaurant.'

'The one on top of the Holiday Inn?' Moone asked.

'Yeah, that's the one,' Butler said. 'I knew it. Some rich weirdo has taken her there, filled her up with grub and then done away with her.'

Moone sat back, then pointed at Harding. 'Phone the restaurant, check they're still serving that meal. Sometimes they change their menus.'

'Will do,' Harding said and picked up his phone.

Moone's mobile phone started ringing. He didn't recognise the number, so headed out into the corridor to answer.

'DCI Peter Moone,' he said, backing up against the wall.

'At last,' the gruff voice said on the other end. 'Been trying to get hold of your boss, but had no luck.'

'He's in the wilds of Cornwall,' Moone said. 'Who's this?'

'Sorry. I'm DI Vincent Crowne. Bristol division.'

'Right, OK. What can I do for you?'

There was a sigh on the other end. 'Well, I wanted to ask if you know a DS Faith Carthew?'

Moone's stomach wrapped itself tightly around his spine and squeezed. 'I do. What's happened?'

'Well, it's just that we've got a situation here. I'm dealing with a murder...'

'Murder? Carthew's been murdered?' He felt bad as a kind of relief followed his shock.

'No, she's fine. Well, I think she is. No, it's DSU Charlie Armstrong. He's been found battered and stabbed in his hotel room. He was giving a lecture to some police officers. Thing is, I checked the CCTV and I've got Carthew heading to his room about three hours before he was found dead. Got her leaving too a few minutes later, but she's not covered in blood. I know, it's stupid thinking that she may have done something like this...'

'Where's she now?' Moone felt like throwing up, his heart pounding.

'In the station, making a statement. Then I'll have to let her go...'

'Don't.'

'What? Why? What do you know?'

Moone silenced himself, thinking, wondering what to say or what to do for the best. 'I'm going to come to you.'

'There's no need, I just need...'

'Trust me. I better come to you.'

'Really? If you've got information that's relevant, you can...'

'I promise you, it's best I talk to you in person. It's delicate. I'll get there as soon as I can. Keep her there.'

'OK, I'll try...'

Moone hung up, then stared ahead, his heart still thudding, his stomach still on spin cycle. Then he walked back into the incident room, still trapped in a terrible nightmare.

'They've got steak and salmon on the menu,' Harding announced to the room, seeming victorious.

'That's no good, you wally,' Butler said. 'It has to be prawns too.'

'Well, they used to have steak, salmon and prawns cooked in some special sauce, but I was told they don't serve it any more.'

Butler huffed. 'Well, looks like we should visit them and find out when they took it off the menu. What do you reckon, Moone?'

Moone looked at her, realising he didn't hear what she'd asked. 'Sorry?'

'Black's place used to have steak, salmon and prawns on the menu. You all right? You look like you've lost a tenner and found a turd.'

'It's Carthew,' he said, and watched Butler's face go through a flurry of emotions, ending on annoyance.

'What's she done now?' Butler asked.

'Not sure. There's been a murder in Bristol. A DSU Armstrong. Why do I know that name?'

Butler clamped her hands over her face, then took them away, her face now red, the fury clear in her eyes. 'That *fucking bitch*. DSU Armstrong? He was meant to take over here. Jesus, she's only gone and offed him, so she can get the job here. She's a complete psycho...'

'We don't know...' Moone held up a hand.

'We don't bloody know? Come on, you daft sod...'

Moone looked round the room and saw his team staring at them both. 'Let's do this in the corridor.'

'Jesus, Pete,' she said, as they got out into the corridor. 'What the hell're we going to do?'

Moone leaned against the wall, blowing the air from his cheeks. 'I don't know. I really don't. Could she really have knocked him off?'

'She's bleeding well capable. It's like Richard the Third, knocking everyone off or sticking them in jail to get to be next in line.'

Moone gave a laugh.

'What?' Butler stared at him.

'You, talking about Shakespeare.'

Butler huffed. 'I got dragged to see it a couple of years ago at the Theatre Royal. Anyway, the thing I don't get is, if she was going to murder the new boss, to get a chance of being our boss, then wouldn't she be more cunning about it? I mean, I don't like her, but she's smarter than that.'

Moone nodded, thinking it all over, remembering the viaduct, his body flooding with adrenaline at the mere thought of it. 'You're right. If she is guilty of this, then she's obviously got a plan up her sleeve.'

'So, what's she up to? She must have an

alibi. I can hear her now. She'll say something like, do you think that if I was going to murder someone, I would do it in such an obvious fashion? Then there'll be some kind of alibi. There'll be something.'

'I'll ask her.' Moone sighed.

'What do you mean, you? We'll both go.'

'You need to take charge here while I'm gone. We still haven't identified the girl. You need to find out who she is, before he does it again.'

Butler stared at him, then shook her head. 'You're so convinced he'll do it again. I bet we never hear from him, or whoever they are.'

'I hope you're right. I really do. Right, I'm off to Bristol.'

Butler stood back, watching him for a moment. 'Moone,' she suddenly said, so he stopped as he was about to go down the stairs.

He looked at her. 'What is it?'

'There's another possibility.' Her face had lost all emotion, and there seemed to be a darkness deep in her eyes.

'What possibility?'

'Carthew. She could be doing this for attention.'

'What? Attention from who?'

'You. She murders a man and you come running.'

CHAPTER 6

He stood in the darkness for a moment, leaning against the door frame, listening to the beats of breath coming from deep down in the basement. Panicked breaths poisoning the dank air. He soaked it up for a while before he headed down the stone steps. He stood at the other end, staring across the basement. Her eyes were tiny spots of fear in the blackness of the cell. There were only iron bars lining the end of room, separating her from him. She would be released soon, but before that he would have to catch another, ready to be prepared. She would be an ugly creature that he would make so beautiful. He had to. He had no choice in the matter.

The crying started as he came closer, her eyes probably only able to pick out his silhouette as the pleading started. He put his finger to his lips, hushed her. The crying and whimpering lessened, leaving them staring at each other in the darkness, her eyes so wide.

'Please,' she whispered. 'Please don't hurt me.'

'I'm not going to,' he said, and he truly believed his words. But she needed to be released, set free, the butterfly caught on a breeze, then trapped in a net.

'My name...' she said, her words catching in her throat.

'Don't,' he said, his voice rising, his fists clenching.

'...Is Chloe,' she said, tears coming. 'My name's Chloe.'

He lowered his head, shook it, cursing her in his mind, screaming and shouting for her to take it back. *'Why did you say that?'*

She sniffed, breathing hard, staring at him. 'I have a family. A mum and dad. They'll be worrying...'

'Shut up,' he said. 'I didn't want to know your name.' He stepped closer, let her see how angry she had made him.

'What's your name?' She smiled, but it crumbled away, more tears coming.

He knew there would be moments like this, points of weakness where he would be tempted to set them free. Yes, they were to be eventually released. But that was something entirely different. He breathed it down, counted a few seconds, trying to erase her name from his mind. 'You think I'm weak, is that it?'

She shook her head, so he stepped closer. 'Yes, you do. You think that if you tell me your name, tell me about your mum and dad, how much they'll miss you, then I'll have pity on you. Mercy.'

'Please.'

'It's not up to me. Don't you understand that?'

But she started crying again, retreating into the darkness, leaving him alone in the half light, trembling all over with guilt, shame, and fury.

Moone showed his ID to the security guard on the gate of Bishopsworth police station in Bristol, then watched the barrier lifting. He parked up and took a puff of his vape, examining the two-storey, modern built building in front of him, all cream-coloured brick, disabled ramps and sliding doors. It looked more like a doctor's surgery than a nick. He took another puff of his vape, then stared at the little device, a strange bitter taste filling his mouth.

'You taste like shit,' he said, and threw it on the passenger seat. He reached for the glovebox and dug around until he found what he was looking for. He opened the box of twenty he had bought in a moment of weakness a month or so ago. He opened the box, sniffing the scent of tobacco that rose to his nostrils, then found his lighter. He lit one, and took a deep puff, filling his lungs. Then he climbed out, locked the car and stared at the police station, trying to imagine her sat there, waiting for him. She knew he was coming.

He took a few more hungry puffs, trying to steady his nerves, forming a kind of speech in his mind, then stubbed out the cigarette. He took out a pack of mints and put one in his mouth as he headed to the entrance of the building.

There was a tired-looking, middle-aged man stood by the doors, wearing a creased grey suit. He stared at Moone, then came towards him, extending his hand.

'DCI Moone?' the man asked.

'That's right,' Moone said, shaking his hand. 'Crowne?'

'DI Vincent Crowne. I suppose I should call you sir, or boss.'

Moone laughed. 'Moone will do. Where is she?'

Crowne looked round at the building. 'In an interview room. Nice and cosy with a cup of tea and some biscuits.'

Moone nodded, his stomach knotted itself. 'Good. Can I see her?'

Crowne took out a lanyard with a visitor badge attached. 'You'll need this. I'll sit in with you.'

'Is it possible for me to have a private word

with her first?'

Crowne's forehead creased. 'Why? You worked with her, yeah? Do you think she's capable of this?'

Moone sighed, thinking it all over, wondering if he could trust the detective in front of him. The way he saw it, he didn't have much choice. 'Can I be honest?'

'Please. I'd appreciate it.' Crowne gave an empty laugh.

'Yes, I think she might be capable of it.'

'Jesus. Why?'

'It's a long story. This officer who's been murdered…'

'Armstrong.'

'Yes, Armstrong. He was going to be our boss. She wants to be our boss.' Moone stared at him, watched the detective's face going through a range of emotions until the inevitable laugh of disbelief came.

'Is this a wind up? She offs her own boss to take his place? What is she? Detective sergeant? She's got quite a few ranks to get through…'

'She was being fast tracked…'

'Even so. Why now? Why not later?'

Moone shrugged. He didn't pretend to know the rhyme or reasoning behind Carthew's motives, but he knew what she was capable of. 'She pushed me off a viaduct.'

'What?' Crowne's eyes widened. 'She did what?'

'It's a long story. I know her true nature, you see. I'm a risk to her future career.'

'Well, if that's the case, why isn't she locked up?'

'I haven't got any proof.'

Crowne laughed again. 'I see. Jesus, mate. What now, then?'

'What have you got?'

'CCTV footage of Carthew heading to Armstrong's room that night, about three hours before he was murdered. But I've also got her leaving a few minutes later with no trace of blood on her, just calmly walking away. I confronted her with the CCTV footage, and she admitted she popped into his room for a few minutes and left. I've also got an eyewitness confirming the same thing.'

'None of her returning?'

'No. Armstrong also had a fresh needle mark in his neck. Maybe his killer incapacitated him, then came back later to finish him off.'

'Anyone else turning up to his room later?'

Crowne nodded. 'Yes, there was someone, but they're wearing a hood. Looks like a woman to me, you can see some long blonde hair poking out of the hood, but that's about it. Dressed in jeans, boots, that sort of thing.'

'She changed her clothes, wears a hoodie. Gives her deniability. Where does she say she was?'

'In her room.'

'Alone?'

'Alone.' Crowne turned and looked at the building. 'Why don't you have your chat now?'

Moone opened the door to the interview room and looked in, his eyes jumping to Faith Carthew. She was sitting opposite a female uniform who was taking her statement. Carthew's eyes rose and took him in with a subtle look of victory.

'I believe you can leave us now,' Carthew said, causing the uniform to look round at Moone. Moone showed his ID, then nodded for her to leave.

When she had left, Moone sat down opposite Carthew and folded his arms across his chest, giving his best disappointed parent look.

'You took your time,' she said, smiling a little. 'Traffic bad? Always is between here and Plymouth. And if you're heading to London...'

'You knew I'd come running.'

She smiled a little brighter, then leaned towards him. 'I did. I knew you wouldn't be able to resist.' She looked towards the door. 'You didn't bring that cow, Butler, with you?'

'No, Butler's back at the station. It's just you and me. No one's listening.'

'They're always listening. You know, I'm really starting to think that DI Crowne believes I murdered DSU Armstrong. Can you believe it? No, don't answer that. I know you believe I murdered him, or you wouldn't have come.'

Moone leaned back. 'I know what you're capable of.'

'Excellent police work?'

He huffed, then felt uncomfortable as he heard Butler's huff in his own. 'You pushed me off a bridge…'

'Viaduct.'

'You admit it, then?'

'As if. Word gets around. I heard it was a viaduct. How's your living arrangements?' She raised her eyebrows.

He managed to keep another huff from escaping his lips. 'Fine, as if that's any of your business.'

'Please don't tell me you're living in another caravan. You are, aren't you?'

'Do you know what I'm trying to figure out?' He leaned forward, rested his elbows on the desk.

'Why am I living in another shitty caravan?' She smiled.

'Very funny. Why? I mean, I know you need to get him out of the way, so you can step up, but you're not there yet. You're not a DSU, not even close.'

'You know why you're living in a caravan, don't you?' She copied his posture.

He sat back. 'Go ahead and tell me.'

'Mobile home. It's not a real home. That's

the way you think of it. It's not bricks and mortar. Not stuck in the ground, cemented in. You don't think you're here permanently. You think one day you'll be back in London.'

'Can't think of a place I'd less like to be.' He folded his arms again, trying not to show that she was right on the money.

'You left to follow your family, but you lie awake thinking about all the dark terrible things happening back there. You wonder if you could help.'

He stared at her. 'You're not going to get away with this one, you know that, don't you?'

'There's nothing to get away with. I didn't kill him. I was in my room. It's all circumstantial.'

'That's all they'll need. You know that. You've got motive. Means. You wore a hoodie…'

'No, I didn't.' She stared at him, leaned closer. 'I didn't kill him.'

'Do you want my help?'

'Yes, tell them you were in my room with me, fucking my brains out. That should help.'

He laughed, then shook his head. 'Was this some attempt at getting attention?'

'From you? That's funny. In fact that's hilarious. I'm over you. But I know I'm still in your head. You even had a crafty cigarette before you came in here. Tried to cover it up with those stupid mints you carry around, but I can still smell it. You needed it to steady your nerves before facing me. I either plain scare you or turn you on so much that you can't trust yourself.'

'You scare me. I don't mind admitting it.'

She nodded, then looked round the room. 'Remember when you used to shag my brains out? We were perfect together, weren't we?'

She laughed. 'If Crowne is listening, which I think he is, then he should be in here any second.'

'Listen, Faith, this can't go on,' he said, leaning towards her, making eye contact. 'You've got to stop. I can help you...'

The door to the interview room opened and DI Crowne poked his head in.

'DCI Moone, a word, please,' Crowne said, a tremor of anger in his voice.

Moone followed Crowne out into the corridor, then faced him, watching the DI pacing the floor, shaking his head. Then he swung round to him, pointing a finger at Moone. 'Is that true what she just bloody well said?'

'Which part?' Moone looked down.

'You know which part.' Crowne blew the air from his cheeks. 'Listen, I know you're my superior, but Jesus... What the fuck is going on here?'

Moone looked up. 'Yep. It's true. But it was over a long time ago.'

'Fuck me. Did she bloody well do this? Did

she murder Armstrong?'

'I think so.'

'For a bloody promotion?'

'To prove a point. I don't know really, I can't figure out what makes her tick. But she's capable. She's highly intelligent.'

'Then she's a psychopath.'

'I don't think they use that term now. Personality disorder or...'

'I don't care. How the fuck do I prove it? If she's so bloody clever, how do I prove it?'

Moone turned away, staring towards the door. 'Honestly, I don't know. I'm not clever enough.'

Crowne stood next to him. 'But two heads are better than one. Give me something.'

'Who's your other suspect?'

'A young probationary officer. Went out jogging, he says, then went back to his room. Alone. Just like her.'

Moone nodded. 'Yep. Just like her. She won't leave herself without an alibi.'

'What? You think she's got one stored up?' Crowne pulled Moone round to face him.

'Well, the way that it stands is she's the last person to see him alive. She's got motive and means. There's no physical evidence, is there?'

'No, but if we do find her prints or DNA, she's already admitted going to his room.'

Moone nodded. 'She's leaving herself very

open for attack. No. She'll have something. Come on.'

Moone headed back into the room, followed by Crowne. The two detectives sat down, opposite the smiling DS Carthew.

'Is it threesome time?' she asked, looking between them.

'I don't think this is a time for jokes, do you, Officer?' Crowne huffed and folded his arms.

'Who said I was joking?' Carthew smiled and leaned back.

'See, the problem is,' Crowne said, smiling, 'well, you say you were in your room alone.'

'I wasn't expecting to need an alibi,' Carthew said, raising her eyebrows. Then she leaned forward again. 'Are you interested in hearing my theory?'

Moone watched as Crowne exchanged a surprised look with him, then turned back to face Carthew. 'Yes, I'm very interested.'

Butler looked over at Pinder as they drove towards the city, heading for the Hoe and the large concrete monstrosity sat back a little way from it that called itself a hotel. He was masked up, his eyes fixed with concentration. Part of her wanted to ask his advice, to get a man's perspective on her problems, but she suspected that he couldn't be trusted to keep his trap shut and would probably turn it all into one big joke.

He looked at her, caught her staring.

'I know I'm beautiful, Butler,' he said, smirking. 'But you don't have to stare.'

She huffed. 'I can only see your beady eyes, mate. Don't get any ideas. You know you look stupid wearing a mask in your car.'

He pulled it down. 'Didn't want to give you my germs. So, are you missing Moone?'

'Why would I be? I just left him five minutes ago.' She looked towards the flats and cheap council houses that were looming towards them. 'Anyway, he's a pain in my arse.'

Pinder parked up in the spaces on the other side of the strip of grass that separated one side of the road from the other where the hotel had been built. There was a light rain hitting the car, covering everything in a blurry mist.

Pinder turned off the engine. 'I don't believe that. I know you, how much people irritate you, and the amount of time you spend with him…'

'I have to, it's the job.' She climbed out, the irritation starting to crawl over her neck and shoulders, hoping that he would leave it alone.

'I definitely touched a nerve there,' he said, grinning as they approached the brass framed glass doors of the hotel. Butler pushed through the doors, avoiding a crowd of guests, who looked ready for a wedding. Pinder followed her past the long and quite glitzy reception desk, then left to the bank of lifts. They went up in the lift in silence for a moment, but Butler noticed Pinder looking at her every now and again, the cogs turning behind his daft eyes.

'What is it, Kev?' she asked with a huff.

'Well, I hear Moone's gone to Bristol,' he said, leaning against the glass wall of the lift.

'That's right.'

'To see Carthew, I hear. Has she really done someone in?'

'Maybe. Shouldn't come as a surprise to you though, seeing as you had to rescue Moone from that bridge.'

'Viaduct, actually. But, yeah, I know. But to kill someone like that. Stabbed and beaten, wasn't it?'

'That's what I heard.' But the more she thought about the situation, the more her mind rebelled at the notion of trying to put the pieces together. 'But it's weird though, isn't it?'

'Isn't murder always weird?'

'You know what I mean. She's smarter than that. She would have come up with a better way to knock him off.'

The lift doors opened, so Pinder walked out, with Butler following, heading along to the restaurant, a huge rectangular room surrounded by tall glass that allowed a stunning view of the city and the wild sea beyond.

'You think she's up to something?' Pinder

asked.

'Definitely. My guess is, she's worked it out. She'll have an alibi. Watertight like a duck's arse, and we won't stand a chance of breaking it.'

'Can I help you?' an attractive, tanned, young woman said as she appeared from out of the kitchen door. 'I'm afraid we're closed at the moment.'

Butler took out her ID and flashed it. 'That's OK, love, we're here to ask a few questions.'

The young woman looked concerned but tried to put on a smile. 'Right, OK. Ask away.'

Butler took out her phone and brought up the post mortem image of their victim. 'Have you seen this young woman in your restaurant?'

The woman looked at the photo but shook her head. 'I don't think so. If you've got a name...'

'No, we don't have a name.' Butler folded her arms. 'Let's talk about your menu.'

The woman frowned and looked at Pinder, as if to find some kind of clarification. 'The menu? Is there a problem with it?'

'Maybe I should talk to the boss. Is Mr Black here?'

She gave a quick laugh. 'No, Mr Black doesn't actually work here. It's his name above the door, but we don't see him very often, maybe once a month, if that.'

'Then who's the cook?' Pinder asked.

'James Hammett is the head chef,' she said. 'Do you want to talk to him out here?'

'No, we'd like to shout at him in the kitchen,' Butler said, then sighed.

The young woman narrowed her eyes, then stormed off into the kitchen. When the doors opened again, a tall and broad man in his mid-thirties, with shaved ginger hair came out. His face was ruddy, his brow covered in sweat.

'You wanted me?' he said in a Cornish accent.

Butler nodded. 'You used to have steak, salmon and prawns on the menu. Yeah?'

Hammett stared at her, his eyes narrowing. 'Yeah, but not for months. It used to be cooked in this special sauce that Mr Black invented, based on a Japanese recipe. Why? Has someone complained or something?'

'Someone's dead.' Butler watched the young man's face change colour, getting paler. 'Not from eating the food though. Someone killed her. But she did eat steak, salmon and prawns, not long before she died. Take a look at her photo.'

The chef's face regained some composure as he straightened up, a tinge of annoyance appearing beyond his eyes as he looked up from the photo Butler showed him.

'I've never seen her before,' the chef said.

'Like I said, she had steak, salmon and prawns before she died.'

'She could've eaten that anywhere.'

'Really? It's quite an unusual mix of foods.'

He pointed at her. 'I could name you several places in Cornwall that have similar items on their menus.'

'We're checking them out,' Pinder said, taking out the list of her stomach contents. 'Look at this. She had steak, salmon and prawns and some other ingredients in her stomach. Recognise them?'

The chef snatched the list. 'I should think so, I'm a bloody chef, aren't I?'

He shook his head, his face reddening, as he stared at the list. 'As I thought, this is the ingredients that we used to serve. Not any more. I didn't cook this.'

But Butler noticed a strange look cross the chef's face as he folded the list back up.

'What?' she asked.

'Nothing.' He handed her the list.

'Yeah, you noticed something. What was it?'

He shrugged. 'Well, it's just those herbs and spices. They seem like the selection that we used to prepare our salmon and steak rub with a few months back.'

'Whose recipe was that?' Butler asked, feeling she was getting closer and closer to the rich wanker who had picked up a girl, had his fun with her and thrown her away again.

'Well, it was based on Mr Black's recipe,' the chef said. 'But a guy I was working with always improved it a little. Added a few spices and stuff. But the boss hated that, so he gave him the elbow.'

Butler huffed. 'So, sounds like we need to talk to your boss and this other guy. What's his name and where is he?'

'His name's Paul Fabre. Last I heard, he was portering at Derriford. Bit of a step down, but there you go.'

'A job's a job,' Butler said, 'and the NHS need all the help they can get. What's he like this, Paul Fabre?'

'Nice enough, bloke. Well, bit finicky in his ways, if you know what I mean. He got on some people's nerves, but he's all right.'

Butler nodded, then thought of something. 'Does he go in for tattoos?'

The chef looked at her strangely. 'Tattoos? No. What's this all about? That girl's dead, you said and now you're asking about tattoos? If you're talking about tattoos and expensive food, then it sounds like you should be talking to Mr Black.'

'Why's that?' Butler asked.

'Well, his past girlfriends have usually ended up as his walking canvases. He designs tattoos for them and covers their skin in them.'

'He actually tattoos them himself?' Pinder

asked.

'Oh yeah, he's obsessed with tattoos. Don't tell him I said all this, but he is a bit weird about it all.'

Butler nodded. 'Don't worry, we won't let on you told us.'

CHAPTER 7

Carthew nodded, then smiled as she sat back in her chair in the interview room. 'Who do you normally look at first when it comes to a murder like this?'

'A murder like this?' Moone asked, his stomach doing its usual nosedive, then tying itself into a knot.

'Yes, a man found dead alone in a room,' she said. 'A married man. Under suspicious circumstances. Well, you have to look at his family first, don't you? Isn't that what we do first?'

'We'll talk to his family.' Crowne sat back, staring at her.

'He didn't have any,' she said. 'I mean, he has a brother in Australia, but they haven't talked for years. Mother and father dead. No kids, just a wife.'

Crowne gave an empty laugh. 'You seem to know a lot about him.'

'We chatted quite a bit in the restaurant,

then in his room. Anyway, my point is, he's married. Not happily. He suspected his wife was playing away.'

'He told you that?' Moone asked.

She nodded. 'Sometimes married men are after someone to listen to them. Aren't they, DCI Moone?'

'I wouldn't know. I'm divorced.'

She smiled. 'Anyway, my money's on the wife. She either did it herself or paid someone.'

'That's your theory?' Crowne said, pushing himself to his feet.

'Yes. I'm sure you'll find I'm right.' She smiled. 'Now, am I free to go?'

Crowne looked at Moone, so he shrugged.

'Yes, you're free to go,' Crowne said.

'She did it, didn't she?' Crowne said as he drove himself and Moone to a housing estate on the way to Portishead.

Moone struggled for something to say as his eyes took in the motorway. He still had trouble putting it all together, trying to understand how she could be so blatant. Unless Butler was right, and what she was doing was crying out for attention. No, that was too crazy, even for her.

'Moone?' Crowne said. 'Did she do it, or what?'

Moone looked at him. 'More than likely. I just don't know how she thinks she's going to get away with it.'

'Maybe she doesn't plan on it. Could be a self-destructive thing... some killers...'

'Not her. Not Carthew. She's clever, driven. She knows what she's doing, and that's what scares me. One day I came home to find my caravan on fire... I watched it burn. Then she stepped out of the dark, watched it burn beside me, then walked off...'

'Jesus. Doesn't seem much point asking where Mrs Armstrong was last night then. Except for the reasons of procedure, I mean.' Crowne tapped the indicator and slowed the car down, getting ready to turn left into a road filled with terrace houses.

'I don't know, but I'm guessing she sent us here for a reason.'

When the car was parked, close to a response car, Moone climbed out and headed to the neat house with a tidy driveway and large double front doors. His stomach tightened at the prospect of facing another grieving widow, and watched with regret as Crowne rang the bell. A young woman with light brown hair pulled back in a tight ponytail answered and let them in.

'Mrs Armstrong's in the kitchen,' the female detective said and nodded a greeting to Moone. 'She seems OK to me.'

Crowne stopped and faced her. 'What do you mean by that, Castle?'

She shrugged. 'Nothing. Just doesn't seem a lot of love lost between them by the sounds, that's all.'

Crowne nodded, then looked towards the kitchen. 'Well, you keep doing your job, liaising with her, OK?'

'Sir.'

Moone followed Crowne into the kitchen, where Mrs Armstrong was putting away dishes in the cupboards. She looked round slowly, then stared at them all.

'I've never had this many people in my kitchen,' she said, with a smile that quickly faded. 'Are you here to ask more questions?'

'I'm afraid so,' Crowne said, then pointed at the kitchen table. 'Why don't you sit down?'

Mrs Armstrong stared at the table, let out a sigh, shrugged, then sat down. Crown sat opposite, while Moone rested himself against the work surface.

'I'm DI Vincent Crowne,' he said, showing her his ID. 'This is DCI Peter Moone. We're very sorry for your loss.'

She looked at Moone briefly, then down at the table. 'Thanks. Any idea who did it?'

'It's early days, I'm afraid.' Crowne sat back. 'I'm here to ask all the same old questions. Ones you've already been asked.'

She nodded. 'Do I know anyone who might want to hurt him?'

'Yes.'

'No. I don't know anyone who would want to kill Charlie. I've racked my brains, and all I can think is it was some criminal he's put away. Are you looking into that?'

'We'll be looking into every possibility, believe me, Mrs Armstrong.' Then Crowne looked at Moone briefly, exchanging stares that he interpreted as "here come the awkward questions". Crowne cleared his throat. 'I know this a deeply distressing time for you, Mrs Armstrong...'

'Please don't keep calling me that,' she said, shook her head and gave an empty laugh. 'Mrs Armstrong was my mother-in-law's name. Makes me feel old.'

'OK, sorry. What can I call you?'

'Kate.'

'OK, Kate. Thing is, in terms of procedure...'

'You want to know where I was?'

He looked up at her. Her eyes were fixed on him, her neck a little flushed. 'I'm sorry, but yes.'

She nodded. 'It's always the family, isn't it? That's whose personal life you dig around into first, isn't it? That's what Charlie always said. He'd watch the appeals on TV, the family asking for information on their lost... or dead kids, wives, whatever, and he'd say he thought the family had done it.'

Crowne gave an empty laugh. 'Sometimes

it seems that way. Stranger crime is still pretty rare, but…'

'It probably wasn't a stranger,' she said. 'Was probably some junkie or murderer he put away.'

'Thing is,' Moone said, stepping away from the work surface, 'Your husband hadn't been on any cases like that for quite a while. That's why I guess he'd fought to get in charge of one…'

Mrs Armstrong looked at him strangely. 'Fought to get on one? You mean he volunteered? He told me…' She gave an empty, tired laugh. 'He told me that he had to. That they didn't have enough detectives…'

Moone didn't know what to say so settled for, 'I'm sorry.'

'Yeah, well,' she said and shrugged. 'I guess he just wanted to get away from me…'

'I'm sure that's not it,' Moone said, his stomach knotting.

Crowne sighed, took out his phone, and brought up a photo of Carthew and held it up. 'Have you ever met this woman?'

Moone watched Mrs Armstrong as she stared at the photo. He saw it, just for a brief second, a flicker of recognition before she shrugged and shook her head and said 'No, I've never seen her before. Who is she?'

Crowne put down his phone. 'Just someone of interest, someone we need to talk to.'

She nodded, looked down then up again, staring towards Crowne. 'Was he... was Charlie in a, well, was he in a bad way?'

'I've seen much worse,' Crowne said. 'Let me just say that we will catch the person who did this.'

'Thank you,' Kate Armstrong said as she watched Crowne stand up. They both bid her farewell, then went out into the hallway and left the house.

Crowne lit up a cigarette when he got to the end of the front garden. He blew out some smoke, stared at Moone, then nodded towards the house. 'Did you see that?'

'Her reaction to Carthew's photo?' Moone said. 'Yep, I saw. She knows her, or at least recognised her from somewhere.'

'Yeah, they've met all right. So let me ask you this, Moone. What the hell is going on here?'

Moone let out a sigh. 'I wish I knew. Like I said before, Carthew's clever. Extremely clever. We'll have to wait and see where she's taking us.'

'But we're not going to like where she's taking us, are we?'

'No, you're not.'

Crowne narrowed his eyes. 'I'm not? Does that mean you're leaving me to deal with her?'

'I'm sorry, but I've got a murder

investigation back at home. But I'll be around, just down the motorway if you need me.'

Inspector Kevin Pinder led the way into the busy Derriford Hospital, following the steady stream of patients and staff heading through the sliding doors. Butler turned and saw the cafe, her stomach rumbling, while her mind travelled up the floors to where her father would be. Shit, she thought, knowing he was only going to get worse. That's what the doctor had told her. His need for oxygen had got more regular, his lungs starting to pack up. She shook it all away as she stormed on, following Pinder towards the bank of lifts. But he stopped, scratching his head, looking around the place.

'Are you lost?' Butler asked him.

'No. Just need to find where the porters hang out.' Then he pointed at a middle-aged man in a grey polo shirt, pushing an empty wheelchair.

'Where would I find the porters?' Pinder asked.

'Where would you find the porters?' The man straightened himself up, smiling a little. 'Most of them are hiding away somewhere, trying to look like they're working. You need someone taking somewhere?'

Butler showed her ID. The porter raised his eyebrows, then pointed towards the next corridor on their left. 'Follow me, then.'

They followed the porter down the corridor that was lined with treatment rooms and machines for scanning. At the end they found a small room tucked back where a middle-aged woman was talking on a phone behind a glass screen. Butler lifted her ID and pressed it against the glass, waiting for the woman to end her call.

'What's happened?' the woman asked as she put down the phone. 'Is this about that bloke who broke into the women's changing area?'

'No,' Butler said. 'I'm looking for one of your porters. Paul Fabre. He around today?'

The woman stared up at Butler for a moment, open mouthed, then turned her eyes to the screen in front of her. 'He should be here somewhere. Try the staffroom round the corner, through the doors on your right.'

Butler turned and headed towards the doors that buzzed and opened as they approached. Pinder followed her as she went into a cramped staffroom that was filled with chairs, most of them taken up with men and women in grey or white polo shirts.

Butler lifted her ID and showed the room. 'Police. Is Paul Fabre here?'

Most of the eyes of the room sprang to the far corner, where a skinny man sat holding a mug, as if he was about to take a drink from it. He looked up at Butler, then the rest of the room as he said, 'I'm Paul Fabre. What have I done?'

'Can you come and have a word with us?' Butler asked, pointing a thumb at the door.

Fabre slowly stood up, allowing Butler to see that he was a tall man, with very little meat on his bones at all. In fact, to Butler he looked more like a patient than a porter. She followed him out into the corridor.

'What's this about?' he asked, a touch of annoyance in his voice. 'Has someone complained about me?'

'Why would anyone complain about you?' Butler asked, sidestepping to let a couple of nurses pass by.

He shrugged. 'Some call me a jobsworth. Look at this for instance.'

Butler watched as a hospital bed came down the corridor, pushed by a couple of porters. An old lady was on the bed, her eyes closed.

Fabre tutted and grabbed hold of a plug that was trailing behind the bed, 'Look, guys, you can't have this hanging off the bed. It's an accident waiting to happen.'

'Sorry,' one of the porters said, taking the plug before the bed disappeared round the corner.

'See what I mean?' Fabre asked, shaking his head. 'They're new, and they get training, but nobody tells them how to do the job the right way. People think it's just moving people from here to there, but there's more to it than that...'

'I'm sure,' Butler said. 'Where were you between eight last night and one this morning?'

'Working here. I did the night shift. Extra money. You can check.'

'We will. You used to be a chef, didn't you?'

Fabre stared at her. 'Who have you been talking to?'

'You worked for Mario Black?' Pinder asked.

Fabre nodded. 'Yeah, for my sins. He trained me. You know he's a psycho, right? You should see the way he screams at his trainees. You put a foot wrong...'

'There's a dish you pretty much created.' Butler held up the recipe.

Fabre leaned in, staring at the sheet of paper. 'I didn't create it. That's Black's recipe.'

'We were told you changed the dish,' Butler said.

'Yes, I added some ingredients, gave it a little more substance, and flavour, and didn't he scream at me for it. What's this to do with? Is he saying I've done something? This can't be just about food, surely? Unless... did someone have an allergic reaction?'

Butler folded up the sheet. 'No, nothing

like that. Tell us about Black, your former boss.'

Fabre folded his bony arms, while his eyes narrowed. 'Black? The man's made a fortune from TV shows and opening up expensive restaurants where he trains young chefs to work in then pays them shit money.'

'We hear he's fond of tattoos, that right?'

'Yeah, that's right. Not so keen on receiving them, but he loves to give them. Why? What is this all about?'

Butler straightened up, then moved out of the way for a porter pushing an empty wheelchair. 'We can't discuss the case. Could you look at this though...'

Butler brought up the photo of the butterfly tattoo on the dead girl, then held it up for him to see. Fabre leaned in, staring at it for a moment.

'Yeah,' he said, eventually. 'That looks like Black's style. You know who you want to go and see?'

'No, we don't,' Pinder said. 'Why don't you tell us?'

Fabre shot him a tired look, then turned to Butler. 'There was this waitress he had a thing for. It all happened when he first came down here to open up his restaurant. He was here for a couple of months. He hooked up with her for a while. She already had a couple of tattoos, but it didn't stop him using her as a walking canvas.'

'What's her name?' Butler asked, taking out her notebook.

'Let me think,' Fabre said, looking towards the ceiling and narrowing his eyes. 'Anna? No. Not Anna. It was like that, though. Or Allie? No, Alina. That was it. Alina. Think she was from Poland, maybe.'

'Surname?'

Fabre shot her a look. 'I can't do your job and mine. It's bad enough here, having to go around correcting all the mistakes I find in this place. It's a health hazard around here, you know that? They thought Covid was bad, but it's human error that'll kill you.'

Butler huffed. 'I'm sure you're right. Why did you quit working in a kitchen?'

'I was tired of being screamed at and being paid shit money. Also, I didn't like making food for the rich. I decided I wanted to help people instead. Here I am.'

Butler nodded and smiled politely. 'Let us know if you think of anything else to help us.'

'Oh yeah, I'm sure I'll have plenty of time.' Fabre shook his head, then headed up the corridor tutting to himself.

'What a character,' Pinder said, as they headed back towards the main entrance.

'Yeah, what a jobsworth. A total wanker, actually, but that's interesting what he said about Black and the waitress.'

Pinder nodded. 'Yep, the fact that he likes

young women, tattoos, and cooks the kind of food we found in our dead girl's stomach. Got to be him, right?'

'Could be.' Butler stopped at the entrance, something nagging at the back of her mind, a little irritating voice telling her, in a London accent, that it couldn't be that simple or straightforward. She looked at Pinder. 'We're never this lucky, are we?'

'Not usually. But you never know.'

'Check the porter's alibi, make sure he was working last night, then contact Black's restaurant, find out the whereabouts of this waitress so we can see what she knows. Let's see if she's got any butterfly tattoos.'

The other door had to be closed. There was no light coming into the long, inky black room like there was when he came down the stone steps to visit her in the cold and damp basement. Chloe shook her head, her heart beginning to thud in her chest, the sickness being woken from its slumber in the pit of her stomach. She gripped the bars of the cell, felt the wire mesh dig into her skin, pushing her face closer to it. Her stomach felt hollow and ached. She was hungry but she didn't like to admit it somehow, as if she did, it would mean that life down there had become ordinary, that she had accepted that she would never leave that room. Hunger was for home, for when she smelt dinner cooking. She clenched her eyes shut, holding back the tears.

The dead girl. She shook the image away.

His hands round her throat.

She lowered her head, let out a sob.

Her head shot up, her eyes jumping to the darkness of the ceiling. There were the usual sounds, the TV coming on loud, distant footsteps, his footsteps. Her heart pounded again, waiting, knowing that he might be coming down. She wondered what mood he would be in. She could never tell. Sometimes he came down and talked to her like she was actually human, other times he would only stare at her through the darkness, stood by the door. There was only ever a little spray of light from the stairway, and not nearly enough to get a good look at him. Only on one occasion had he stood closer to the light source so she could see that he wore a mask. That's when she became most terrified, imagining that he wore it to distance himself from what he might do at any moment. Other times she could tell that there was nothing covering his face, only the thick blackness of the room. His breaths would poison the air, his voice free from anything muffling his lips.

She flinched and stepped back. The door had opened at the top of the flight of stone steps, and now she listened, holding her breath as he came slowly down them. The light flickered on, then there was the squeak of wheels. She stared at the doorway, watching for his silhouette to appear, wondering whether he would be masked or not.

The squeak of the wheels got closer, then the dark outline of him merged into the deep grey darkness of the room. He was pushing the cart towards her, his outline growing.

He stopped, his muffled breaths reaching her ears. She whimpered, wrapping her arms around herself as she backed up against the wall.

'It's time,' he said, his voice sounding a little deeper. She shook her head, noting the pleasure in his words. He was excited. 'It's time to make you more beautiful.'

CHAPTER 8

Moone headed into Charles Cross police station, sipping his takeaway Americano that had an extra shot of espresso, just for good measure. He had hardly slept since his return from Bristol, his mind having spent the night helter-skeltering, flashing him images of a smug-looking Faith Carthew. But that's what she wanted, a fact that part of his mind had tried to remind him of several times during the dark hours that slowly bled into light. Sleep now, you've got four hours to get some rest. Three and a half if you sleep now.

Three. Two.

He told himself to stop thinking about it all and headed up the stairs and into the incident room to find Butler talking on the phone heatedly with someone.

'Well, you better get on to him or his solicitors or someone,' she growled into the receiver, then slammed it down.

Moone edged carefully into the room and placed his coffee down on his desk. Her gaze immediately jumped to him, the venom still clear in her eyes.

'Oh, there he is,' she said, the growl fading a little. 'You've finally come home after swanning around Bristol...'

Moone stared at her for a moment, then turned to make eye contact with Harding and Molly. 'Did me and Butler get married? Did I miss that party?'

'Very bloody funny,' she said, and came over to his desk. 'You remember we went to Mario Jean Black's restaurant?'

'I remember. What did you find out?'

'That he's our number one suspect.' Butler folded her arms and raised her eyebrows.

'You're kidding me? How?'

'That food in her stomach. It's his recipe or something similar to a dish he created.'

'That can't be all.' Moone sipped his coffee.

'No, of course not. We talked to a former employee of his, a porter at Derriford, and he told us Black loves tattoos...'

'So do half of Plymouth.'

Butler shot him a look. 'Shut up for a minute. He loves designing and *giving* tattoos.'

'What about the porter? Has he got an alibi?'

'He was working the time the victim would have died. We checked.'

'I see. We need to look at Black's work then, see if it matches...'

'I've been trying to while you've been visiting that crafty bitch. How is the cow anyway?'

Moone sighed, then sipped his coffee, images of Carthew swamping his mind again. He'd known that there would be no avoiding talking to Butler about her, but somehow he'd still hoped he could leave it all behind in Bristol, leave it to Crowne to tidy it all away. 'Crafty as ever, I'm afraid.'

'Don't tell me, they can't pin it on her?'

Moone nodded. 'They've only got circumstantial evidence at the moment. She was at the hotel, went to his room, but left again. There's CCTV footage of what looks like a woman arriving at his floor before he was murdered, but it could be anyone. She's got deniability. Thing is, she's got no solid alibi either.'

'She was alone in her room?' Butler gave an empty laugh, shook her head.

'How did you know?'

'I know, cause I know her. She's stringing them along, dancing in the limelight. She wants to be suspected, wants to show how clever she is.'

'But she's risking her career. If she gets done for this, or they think she might've had a hand in it, then that's her career over. She wouldn't risk that, would she?'

'You talked to her?'

'Yeah, but she didn't say much.'

'Did she give you another suspect?'

Moone felt a cold hand brush up his back. 'Yes. The wife. Said her and Armstrong weren't on the best of terms, all that stuff.'

'They weren't. Last thing I heard from him, was that he suspected she had been cheating.'

Moone stood up. 'With who?'

Butler shrugged. 'He had no idea. Just had a suspicion. You're not giving any credence to what she says, are you? Come on, don't be a wally all your life, Moone.'

'I know, but what if the wife is involved? What if Carthew helped her do away with him? It's a win for both of them, isn't it? The wife probably gets money as well her freedom back, and Carthew gets a job here lording it over us.'

Butler sighed. 'I'm not doing this. I'm not giving her one more thought. Come on, let's come up with a way to find this girl that Black liked to draw all over. One sick bastard at a time, thank you.'

Moone followed her to her desk, watching her search through her notebook, then pick up the phone on her desk.

'Who're you calling?' Moone asked, doing his best to shut down any thoughts of Carthew and failing miserably.

'I'm calling the chef we talked to yesterday, to see if he knows where this girl might be.'

It was nearly an hour later when Butler drove them along Hoe Road, then onto JennyCliff Lane. As the sea came into view, along with the grass covered cliffs high above it, Moone's gut tightened up as he recalled the councillor he had chased through the mist that horrific day. Butler pulled into the car park that looked down across the cliffs, and the cafe that sat across the road.

'You all right?' Butler asked, as she turned off the engine.

'Yep, fine.' Moone climbed out, blotting out that day, even though he pictured the misty outline of the councillor racing off before him, heading for the cliffs.

'I know what you're thinking about,' Butler said, and pushed him towards the cafe, jerking him from his nightmare. 'Don't dwell on it. What's done is done.'

'Easy to say.' Moone headed across the road, then along the front of the cafe, feeling the wind tugging at his clothes. The sun was out, and a few customers braved the colder weather as they sat nursing tea or coffee at the bench tables out the front of the cafe.

There were more customers inside, the sound of cutlery scraping, and cups chinking echoing round the ceiling. It reminded him of his old school's canteen. He walked up to the counter, smiling, feeling Butler coming up behind him.

'What'll it be, love?' the young woman asked him, getting a notebook ready to write down his order.

Moone showed his ID. 'I'm DCI Moone, this is DI Butler. Do you have a woman called Alina working here?'

The young woman frowned, then looked back at the kitchen area behind her where a middle-aged woman and a dark-haired young lady were preparing food. Moone's eyes jumped to the dark-haired woman. He noticed her slender, pale arms were daubed with intricate tattoos.

'Alina?' the woman called, her eyes returning to Moone. 'There's some people who want a word with you.'

Alina looked round, her eyes growing fearful as they jumped to Moone. He had seen the look before, on many occasions, the look of dread when they turned up in their suits. She put down the knife in her hand and came over, a stony look coming over her face.

'What is it?' Alina asked, and Moone noted a Polish accent.

'Can we have a word outside with you?' Moone nodded to the open door.

'Am I in trouble?' she asked.

'No, we just need a word,' Butler said. 'Come on, let's take a walk outside.'

They all ended up with coffees and sat at the very end table outside, closest to the car park. The girl still looked half scared, her tattooed arms now covered by a navy-blue cardigan as she nursed a mug of latte.

'Where are you from?' Butler asked, sipping her Latte. 'Originally.'

'Poland.' She smiled, then stirred her coffee with a wooden stirrer. 'Been here for five years. I came to learn English.'

'Your accent's perfect,' Moone said. 'You looked scared when we turned up. Did you think we were from immigration?'

She shrugged. 'I just saw your suits. After the whole Brexit thing, people can be a bit funny. You understand?'

'I do. I like your tattoos,' Moone said, causing the girl to look down at her wrist, where part of a tattoo was poking out of her clothing.

'Thanks,' she said. 'Can't really afford to have them finished now.'

'I heard you had them done for free,' Moone said, sipping his Americano. 'Some of them at least.'

She nodded. 'Have you been talking to the people at Black's restaurant?'

Moone smiled. 'That's right. They told us that you and Black struck up a kind of relationship. Is that true?'

She shrugged again. 'I think you could call it that. But I didn't feel he was there really. I mean emotionally. Which was fine really.'

'So you let him draw all over you?' Butler asked with a huff.

'I like tattoos and he offered.' Alina sipped her coffee.

'What was he like with you?' Moone asked. 'Did he treat you well, I mean?'

'He was fine. He has a temper, but that's something you see in the kitchen, not at home.'

'He never laid a finger on you, then?' Butler asked.

'No, never. What's happened? Why're you asking me this?'

Moone sighed. 'I'm afraid we can't discuss that. But we need to ask you a favour.'

Alina looked worried again as she stared up at Moone. 'What do you want me to do?'

'Your tattoos.' Moone gestured to her arm. 'We'll need photographs of them. If you come to the station, we'll get a police photographer to take some snaps of them.'

She looked down at her arms, then wrapped them around herself. 'Why? Why do you want photos of them?'

'It's part of a murder inquiry,' Butler said. 'You either help us, or we drag you in. Up to you.'

Moone flashed her a look. 'I'm sure it won't come to that, Alina. You'd be helping us out if you would let us take some photos. It could save someone's life.'

'Alina, it's getting busy in here,' the other server called from the doorway, then vanished inside.

'I better go,' Alina said. 'OK, I'll come to the station.'

'We'll send someone to collect you, after your shift.' Moone stood up. 'Thanks. We really appreciate it.'

Alina got up, still looking a little confused, then smiled and disappeared inside. Moone got up and stretched, his eyes finding the hazy horizon where the blurry silhouette of boats and ships hovered. He tried to keep his mind off the events of that horrific day but they kept playing over and over, then seemed to mix together with the day he hung off the viaduct. His stomach lurched, his heart pounding.

'I think we're onto something,' Butler said as they walked up the steep path towards the road.

'Do you?'

'Yeah, of course.' She sighed and shook her head and walked across the road to the car park. 'Black's got a temper. He likes to humiliate the people he works for. Bet he gets a real kick out of humiliating the young women who work for him...'

Moone stopped by the car, watching Butler unlock it, thinking back to what the girl had said. 'She didn't have a bad word to say about him.'

Butler stared at him. 'Do you really think she's just going to come out with all the stuff he's probably made her do? There's definitely something more to this. He convinces her to let him use her as a sketchbook? When she comes in, I think we need to talk to her. Maybe I should do it, lend an ear and see what she divulges.'

Moone laughed as he climbed in. 'You've really made up your mind, haven't you? Black is guilty. He's some rich psychopath who likes to tattoo women and then strangle them? Really?'

She faced him. 'You're not buying it? Why not?'

Moone faced the view, then shrugged. 'I don't know. Just doesn't sit right with me.'

Butler huffed, then started the engine. 'I know what's wrong with you.'

'And what's that?'

'Her.' Butler reversed the car, then turned and crept the vehicle towards the road, the dust rising around them, the gravel crunching under the tires.

'Her? Carthew? I'm trying not to think about all that.'

'But she's in there, rattling round, rearranging the furniture.'

'That's because she killed our potential new boss. I mean, what is she up to?'

'God only knows. But I know that we need

to keep our distance, just let the Bristol lot do their thing. Let them worry about her.'

Moone hung his head, looking down into his hands, thinking it all over and getting that dull sense something was very wrong with it all. 'I don't know if I can do that.'

'Jesus, Pete. I've got enough to worry about without having that cow running around in my head.'

He looked at her, his mind racing along to the hospital. 'Your dad, you mean?'

She swung her eyes to him, all narrowed and accusing. 'What do you know about it?'

'Nothing. Just that he isn't well. I hear he's in the hospital.'

She huffed. 'Yes, he's in Derriford. His body is shot. Working at the dockyard has finished him off. Asbestosis.'

'You're talking like he's already–'

'It won't be long.'

Moone paused for a moment, his mind whirring, questions building in his skull, questions that he knew he shouldn't ask. The pressure kept building. 'What is it with you two?'

He felt the engine groan, her foot squeezing the accelerator. 'Nothing. Snout out trout.'

'That's a new expression. Proper Plymouth one?'

'No.'

'It's obvious you two don't get on, I just wonder–'

She flashed her angry eyes at him. 'Don't wonder. Just keep your mind on the job at hand.'

Then Moone's phone was ringing, and he thought of saying that old cliché, saved by the bell. He couldn't fathom whether she had been saved or if he had. He took out his mobile and saw Parry was ringing.

'Hello, doctor,' he said.

'DCI Moone,' Parry said, the same old smile in his voice. 'I was giving the DB another going over and noticed something. Can't believe I didn't notice it before.'

'Maybe you're getting old. I can't remember what I had for breakfast. We'll be right there.'

Moone had suggested to Butler that she take the chance to visit her dad while they were at the hospital, and mentioned the fact that he was quite capable of talking to Dr Parry by himself, but she brushed him off with a well-placed huff. So they headed down into the bowels of the hospital and then into the autopsy room that shone and gleamed as always. The stench of cleaning fluids, that did little to hide the scent of death, burnt at his nostrils as always. Moone stood with a mask on, near the table where Parry and his helpers had already brought out the dead girl. Butler stood behind him, and he could feel the anger radiating from her. He was trying to keep his mind on the job, but there seemed to be so many personal issues piling up that also needed seeing to. Number one being Butler and her father, who still seemed at odds over some issue in the past. It bothered him that her old man might die without a reconciliation with his daughter, and Moone made a little pact with himself to try and bring them back together before it was too late. He also desperately wanted to find out what had come between them.

'Thanks for coming back so promptly,' Dr Parry said, pulling on some gloves, giving them a fleeting grin that quickly dissolved. Moone couldn't help but think that there was something not quite right with Parry, his usual big smile having deserted him. Then he recalled how he had been late previously and lied about it.

'No problem,' Moone said. 'What did you find out?'

Parry nodded, then his eyes jumped to Butler. 'Afternoon, DI Butler. Haven't seen you in a while.'

'I've been busy.' Butler pointed to the body under the blanket. 'What's new?'

Parry nodded, then walked to where the dead girl's left hand would be and pulled back the cover. Her hand, thin, delicate, and pale, was wrapped in a plastic evidence bag, secured by a plastic tie at her wrist. 'It's her hands. Well, her nails actually.'

Moone stepped closer, staring at the dead girl's black nails. 'What about them? You found DNA?'

'No, but I have noticed that someone painted over her pink nail varnish with this black varnish.'

'How do you know she didn't do it?' Moone asked.

Parry shrugged. 'Doesn't seem like a goth to me. But the thing is, when I took off the black, very carefully, you can see the pink has been there quite some time, and her nails have grown quite a bit since she had them done.'

Moone nodded, staring at her hand again. 'Meaning that the killer might have had her for quite a while. That's interesting.'

Butler barged past Moone with a tut, then bent down to examine the dead girl's hands. 'Underneath the black nail polish, I see it. Looks like an expensive job. Let's take some photos and get some uniforms to show them round town. Then we might at least get an ID on her.'

She looked at Moone, so he gestured to her hand and said, 'Would you like to do the honours?'

With her usual huff, Butler took out her phone and took a few snaps. Then she stood back, seemingly deep in thought, before she said, 'I'll meet you by the car in about half an hour.'

Moone nodded, watched her leave, then turned back to Dr Parry, his eyes still on the door.

'Think she's going to visit her dad,' Moone said, then had a thought. 'Don't suppose you know what the situation is between Butler and her dad?'

Parry looked up, blinking for a moment, then shook his head. 'Sorry. My job is to get answers from the dead, not the living. And, anyway, getting information from Butler is like trying to get blood from a particularly pissed-off stone.'

Moone nodded in agreement, then decided to take his mind off her and examined Parry, watching him going about his work as he started to clean up. He realised he equally knew very little about him and Butler, even though they had worked together for almost a couple of years.

'What happened with your situation the other day?' Moone asked, causing Parry to stop collecting some instruments together and look up blankly.

'Sorry?'

'Your family thing? You were late.'

Parry nodded, then smiled. 'Oh, yes, that. It's families... and they are people and I'm not very good with people. Well, the people who are breathing, that is.'

Moone suddenly wished he hadn't brought it up, feeling as if he should have some kind of advice. 'Well, they're your family and you've just got to get on with it.'

'You have to get on with it?' Parry shook his head and laughed. 'Is that the best you can do, DCI Moone?'

'I'm afraid so. You can call me Pete when no one's around, you know.'

Parry made a face, then picked up a mat full of instruments and rolled it up. 'That feels like it would be weird. I think I prefer DCI Moone.'

Moone laughed and nodded. 'Yep. OK.'

Parry was about to turn away, then stopped. 'I heard you came here the other day to question someone. One of the porters, wasn't it?'

'That's right. Well, Butler did. Why? Do you know him?'

'Only to say hello to. He's brought down a few of the cadavers during a night shift. But I know he used to work for Mario Black. That's your prime suspect, isn't it?'

'He seems to have become a person of interest. Do you know Black?'

'Well, no, but I have dealt with one of his former customers.'

'Really?'

Parry looked towards the dead body on the table. 'A young woman. Was barely twenty-five, I think. Shame.'

'How did she die?' Moone's stomach tried to constrict itself.

'Anaphylactic shock,' Parry said. 'She consumed a little peanut oil. Thing was, they couldn't find any traces of peanuts or peanut oil in the dishes he served, so he got off. At the time I thought it was all a bit neat.'

'What do you think now?'

Parry shrugged. 'Well, I didn't really think much of it at the time, but now you're looking into him... well, the strange thing was, that the girl had previously worked in one of his London restaurants for a short time. Coincidental, wouldn't you say?'

Moone felt a shudder pass up his back. 'Very, very coincidental, I would say.'

CHAPTER 9

Crowne ambled into the incident room at Bristol Major Crime unit, then sat down, taking the lid off his fourth coffee of the day. He let out a breath, took a sip, his eyes finding the murder book on his desk. He opened it, finding the crime scene photos of Armstrong, beaten and stabbed to death, lying on the hotel room floor. Carthew had been let go, they had nothing to hold her with. Moone was right, she was clever, and she knew the job well, knew perfectly what to say and when to hold her tongue.

'Hey, boss,' a female voice said and he looked up to see the half smile that DS Maxine Rivers was giving him, stood with her arms folded.

'Hey, Max,' he said, then took another sip of his coffee.

'Thought I'd let you know DSU Tucker's been looking for you,' she said, her eyes following his movements as he sipped his drink. 'She's on the warpath.'

'She always is. She wants this closed

yesterday.'

'Everyone does. Whoever did this, killed one of our own.'

He nodded, then looked more carefully at Rivers. 'Don't let it cloud your judgement though. We need to think clearly.'

'I know. I am. By the way, the toxicology report came back. Armstrong tested positive for a small amount of Rohypnol.'

'Of course he did.' Crowne sighed. 'With all the alcohol in his system, he would have been at his killer's mercy.'

'None was found in his room though. Which meant his killer probably brought it with them and left with it.'

Crowne nodded. 'Which means it looks likely that his mysterious date drugged him. Carthew could have slipped him something.'

'But there's no physical evidence to support that she did. Anyone could have.'

'What about the needle mark?'

River looked at the notes on her desk. 'Nothing. Whatever she used hasn't been detected. Some drugs disappear from the system in a few hours.'

Crowne sighed. 'Yes, they do. Anyway, how are you? You've got a new girlfriend, I hear?'

'Nothing serious. Early days. How's your wife?'

'Good. Always unhappy I'm always

working. But there you go.'

She nodded. 'Listen, you'd better brief everyone. They're all pissed off that one of our own has been killed.'

Crowne looked at her for a moment, saw the determination in her eyes, then he switched his view to the other members of the team who also seemed to be staring at him. He sighed, then stood up, holding up a hand. 'Listen, people, I know this is about one of our own, but we can't let ourselves get worked up. We need to get this right…'

'Do you really think it was this DS Carthew that murdered Armstrong?' one of the team asked.

Crowne raised his shoulders. 'I don't know. DCI Moone seems to think she's capable of it. But I really don't know what to believe any more. I mean, we've so far got nothing, nothing concrete tying her or anyone to this…'

'Aha,' Rivers said, holding up a finger. 'That's where you're wrong, boss.'

As Rivers headed over to her small desk in the corner, Crowne followed, his heart beating into life. He wasn't sure if it was the excitement of a possible lead or too much caffeine. 'Please, Rivers, tell me we've got a suspect.'

'Well, maybe.' She brought up some CCTV footage. 'You know that detective constable who was on Armstrong's course?'

'The jogger?'

'That's right. DC Jason Wise. Well, he said he went for a late-night run, then went back to his room, alone.'

'That's right.' Crowne stared at the paused screen. 'Didn't he?'

Rivers tapped the screen. 'Well, he definitely went for a run, but he didn't go back to his room straight away. Look…'

Crowne moved closer to the screen, staring at the grainy images of the city centre. Rivers sped up the footage until a blurry figure came into shot. She slowed it down, allowing Crowne a good view of what looked like the young Detective Constable Wise. Then the detective was slowing down, decked out in what seemed to be a tight-fitting running outfit. He then stopped and looked about him, before he took out his phone.

'He's texting someone,' Crowne said, then looked up at Rivers.

'Keep watching,' Rivers said, then sped up the footage.

Crowne watched the figure hurriedly put away his phone then retreat backwards, his head turning quickly side to side until a dark car pulled up. Rivers slowed down the footage, allowing Crowne to see the young jogging detective climb in. The car quickly drove off.

Crowne looked at Rivers with his eyebrows raised. 'Please tell me you got the registration number of that car.'

'Sorry. Can't see it from that angle, and there isn't a good camera along that road. Can't even get a good look at the driver, either. I'm still searching though.'

Crowne rubbed his eyes. 'So, the bastard lied to us. Let's go and drag him back in.'

As he turned to leave the incident room, Crowne's eyes landed on DSU Tucker who was heading towards him with a determined look on her face. He stopped, folded his arms, waiting for her rebuke.

She slowed a little, folding her arms and looking round at his team, nodding to them before she laid her steely eyes on Crowne. 'DI Crowne, I'm glad I caught you. A word out there.'

He sighed, then followed Tucker into the corridor, where she faced him with only a hint of anger in her grey eyes.

'You've let Carthew go, I take it?' she asked, raising her eyebrows.

'As I was told to do.'

She nodded. 'Good. I mean, the suggestion that one of our own... it's not the sort of publicity we need at the moment.'

Crowne rubbed his stubble, his stomach churning a little. 'Thing is, ma'am, I'm not convinced she's not involved.'

'You're not convinced? She's never met the man before...'

'He was about to start the job she

wanted…'

'So she offs him for the job? Who told you this rubbish?'

Crowne looked down. 'DCI Moone knows her, he's worked with her before.'

'DCI Moone? Jesus. Are you sure he's not got some involvement with her? Some jealously or…'

Crowne looked up, doing his best to hide everything he had learnt about Moone and Carthew. 'We have got another lead, ma'am, but I'm not sure you're going to like that either.'

She closed her eyes for a moment, shook her head slightly and looked at him. 'Go on.'

'DC Jason Wise. He told us he was out jogging until late, then went back to the hotel, alone. Well, we've got him on CCTV getting into an as yet unidentified car and then being driven off. He never mentioned that.'

Tucker huffed. 'OK, find out what he was up to. I'm sure there's a reasonable explanation. Then, I want you to do some real police work and find out who the lowlife scumbag is who really did this. It's probably a revenge thing, it usually is. Got that?'

He nodded, then watched her turn on the spot and head off. He poked out his tongue, then turned back to the incident room.

'Hey, boss,' Harding said, and stood up behind his monitor.

Moone had only just stepped into the incident room, a hastily made coffee in his hand that tasted bitter. Butler wasn't around, and he wondered where she had gone now. He had picked her up after he'd left the crime scene, and they had travelled back from the hospital in silence. But he had felt the tension thick in the air, could see the way she gripped the wheel, the angry way she drove and swore at the other drivers who came anywhere close to cutting them up. He couldn't figure out a way to get her to talk to him, to divulge what was going on with her dad and what had happened in the past to make them so estranged. They were meant to be partners, and he knew that was only meant to mean working together, trying to help each other get the job done, but he also knew it was more than that. You were meant to be there for each other, he just didn't know how to be there for Butler.

'What is it?' Moone asked, sipping his coffee and grimacing.

'Alan Fenwick is opening a new restaurant in Padstow today,' Harding said, raising his eyebrows like Moone should be impressed.

'OK. You offering to buy me dinner there?'

Harding laughed. 'No, boss, I couldn't afford it on my pay grade. But Fenwick and Mario Black are mates, they did that travel show programme together. Just seen on X, formerly known as Twitter, that Black's probably going to show his face.'

Moone put down his coffee, then looked at Harding's monitor where an X feed was up. He read Fenwick's post. 'Jesus. Then we'd better go along and see if we can ask him some questions.'

'His managerial team won't like it.'

'Well, stuff them. We're not going to arrest him, just have a little chat.'

'What would Laptew think?'

Moone shrugged. 'Thing is, he's on holiday in deepest, darkest Cornwall. We can't exactly ask him. And it looks like I'm pretty much in charge. It can't hurt to have a private word.'

Harding shrugged, then sat at his desk. 'All right, you're the boss. I'll print out the directions.'

Moone nodded, then almost walked away, but a thought occurred to him. 'Harding, you've worked with Butler a long time, haven't you?'

'Been nearly seven years working with Mand. Don't tell her I called her that. She'll cut my balls off.'

'I won't. Do you know anything about her and her dad?'

'I know he's in hospital, not well. Really bad she told me.'

'What? She told you about it?'

'Yeah. We chatted one morning, a few days back. I noticed she looked particularly pissed-off...'

'Jesus. So, it's just me she's not talking to?'

Harding shrugged. 'I wouldn't take it personally, boss. You know what she's like. Forget I said anything.'

Moone nodded, put on a bit of a smile as he walked away from a worried looking Harding, but he couldn't forget it. He thought he'd made headway with Butler, had become not just a partner but a friend too, but it seemed he had been mistaken all this time. After all they had been through, and she still kept him at arm's length.

Butler came into the incident room, hung her coat up, then sat down at her desk and started typing at her keyboard, her usual look of mild annoyance on her face. He took a breath and went over and stood by her desk, waiting for her to look at him.

She didn't lift her eyes from her screen as she said, 'Had your penny's worth?'

'How about I take you for a nice meal?'

She looked at him, her face seeming to flush a little, her eyes narrowing. 'What're you after?'

'I hear Padstow is nice.'

'It is. One of my favourite places. How did you know?'

'Just so happens that Mario Black might be putting in an appearance at a restaurant opening this evening.'

Butler huffed. 'Should've known it had to do with work. Right then, we better get a move on and get down there.' She got up and started collecting her stuff together.

'You should make an evening of it,' Harding said, popping his head over his monitor with a smirk. 'Might be late by the time you're finished.'

Moone listened to what he said, thinking it over, liking the idea of a change of scenery for the evening. He was getting pretty tired of staring at his flimsy four walls every night, and his stomach had already started rumbling at the thought of a slap-up culinary meal. 'What do you think, Butler?'

Mandy stopped and stared at Harding then Moone, a strange look on her face. 'What're you talking about? Staying at a hotel or something? You and me?'

Moone shrugged. 'Why not? We deserve a treat.'

'And the taxpayer's going to fork out for this treat, are they?'

'No, I will.'

Her face reddened, he noticed, as she said, 'Too late to book anywhere.'

'There's a bed and breakfast just a short walk from the harbour,' Harding said, still smirking. 'Shall I book it?'

Butler stared at Harding, her eyes narrowing. Then she sighed and said, 'I'll have to pick up some… bits. Change of clothes.'

'OK, that's settled then.' Moone rubbed his hands together, a plan forming in his mind, imagining Butler with a few drinks inside her, loosening up a bit, maybe spilling the beans about her old man. He smiled to himself as he was about to follow Butler out of the incident room.

'What're you grinning about?' Butler snapped, making him flinch.

'Nothing. I'm looking forward to a nice meal. And great company, of course.'

She made an unimpressed sound then turned and stormed out.

She was swamped by nausea as her eyes fluttered open, a blurry image of darkness dancing opposite her. It was only the shadows, the shape of herself and the objects in the room being thrown up the wall by the lamp that swung over her head. There was a gag over her mouth, strapped tightly round her head, the corners of it cutting into her lips. She was sitting in the centre of the cold basement, strapped into the chair.

The chair.

She tried to let out a scream as she writhed, fighting with the straps that bound her arms and legs to the seat. She panted, her chest pounding, the tears in her eyes.

She was cold. Her teeth chattered.

She looked down at her bare skin, her naked flesh that was puckered with the cold and the fear that had dug its way into her. She trembled, the way the other girl had trembled as she had woken to find herself in the same chair, strapped to it in the exact same way. She sobbed, shaking all over, her hands tearing at the leather straps again.

It was no good.

Then her head swung round, the sound of the door opening far above her. Then the steps, his steps. Coming down the flight of stone stairs, slowly. She tried to keep it in, the bubble of panic and fear that raced up through her, finding her mouth that began to let out a gurgle of crying. She swallowed it all down quickly, her heart still pounding as her eyes watched the doorway.

The light came on, flickering for a moment, then nothing, no movement.

Panting hard, she watched the doorway, her eyes widening as his dark shadow came slithering out as it always did. Then the step, the sound of his boot, the shape of him, filling her with a deep, dark sickness. She shook her head as she saw the case in his hand, letting out a muffled scream.

He stared at her, shaking his head, lifting his hand and pointing upwards. Then he shushed her, putting his finger to his lips before he brought the case closer to her. He opened it and took out the tattoo machine, the dark gun shape of it glistening in the lamplight.

He set it up, his eyes staring at her, visible above the mask that covered his mouth and nose. Then he pressed the trigger, the loud buzzing sound of the machine making her jump. He seemed to see her flinch, and his eyes smiled, a show of some kind of kindness. He seemed that way, sometimes, she thought, her mind racing, trying to put it all together, the reason why he did what he did. First the tattoo, then he… he… she couldn't think about it, couldn't allow the terrible images of what he had done to the other girl to enter her mind.

His eyes looked kind, that's what she grasped hold of and held on tightly to. She sniffed away her tears, cleared her throat and tried to speak, but her voice was muffled by the gag.

'It won't hurt,' he said, his voice again sounding kind. 'Not very much. Then it will heal. It'll scab over and then it'll heal.'

She shook her head.

He looked down at the tattoo gun, then up at her. 'I know, it's not this you're afraid of. It's what comes after. Isn't it?'

She nodded, tears filling her eyes, her mouth sending out muffled pleading.

He gave an empty laugh, then looked down at the machine in his hand. And when he looked up, there was genuine sorrow in his eyes, and she felt a glimmer of hope. She had got him in a good mood, had found the light inside him.

'I'm sorry,' he said, moving closer, the sadness clear in his eyes. 'I'm so sorry, but I have to do this. It won't hurt. I'll make sure it won't hurt at all.'

CHAPTER 10

DC Jason Wise looked uncertain, maybe even a little shifty as he was escorted through the custody suite, then up to the interview rooms. His cheeks were a little ruddy, Crowne thought as he watched him from a distance, nursing a takeaway coffee. DS Rivers was sitting in the interview room, waiting for the DC with a warm smile and a cup of tea or coffee if he wanted one. Crowne wanted him at ease, didn't want his suspicions to be aroused too soon.

He watched the detective head into the interview room, then gave it a couple of minutes before he knocked on the door and went in. Wise's eyes jumped up to Crowne, then he gave a respectful nod.

'Is this all official?' Wise asked, his eyes jumping between them.

Crowne sat down, exchanged pretend shocked looks with Rivers, then shrugged. 'Official? Why would it be official? Why, what have you done?'

Wise gave an empty laugh. 'Nothing, of course, I just wondered why I was being brought in like this.'

'Well, it's an ongoing murder investigation, and you were at the scene...'

'But like I said, I went out for a run and then went back to my room.' Wise sat back, while Crowne watched his face, and his hands for any signs of nervousness. He had a good poker face, but his reddening cheeks gave his lie away.

'Do you know DS Carthew very well?' Rivers asked, looking down at her notes.

'Never met her before this business,' Wise said.

'You're sure about that?' Crowne leaned forward.

'Of course,' Wise said. 'Do you think I'm lying?'

'Why would you lie?' Crowne stared at him.

'I wouldn't. I'm not.'

'What about Mrs Armstrong? Kate?' Rivers asked. 'The victim's widow?'

Wise looked at her, his cheeks burning. 'I don't think I've met her...'

'You don't think you have?' Crowne asked, then looked at his colleague. 'DS Rivers, the photo please.'

Rivers slipped the photo out of the file she had brought in with her. Crowne took it and turned it over, then slid it towards the Detective Constable. 'Here she is. She's an attractive woman, wouldn't you say?'

Wise looked down, but only briefly. 'Some might say. Listen, I get the feeling this is leading somewhere. Do I need my union rep?'

Crowne gave a short laugh. 'You're very defensive, DC Wise. Now, let's go back to the night of the murder...'

'I went for a run...'

'So you say.'

'You don't believe me?'

Crowne stared at him as he folded his arms. 'I know you went for a run, because we've got CCTV footage of you on said run.'

'Good,' Wise said, but Crowne noticed he didn't look good at all, and in fact the colour, even the redness of his cheeks had drained away.

'Well, it would be, but there is a little discrepancy in your original statement.' Crowne let the words hang there for a moment, watching the worry twitch its way across the young copper's face. 'You know what I'm referring to, don't you?'

Wise shook his head. 'No.'

'Well, I'll refresh your memory.' Crowne looked towards Rivers, ready to ask for the next still taken from the CCTV footage of Wise, but she was already slipping it towards him. He took it and showed Wise. 'There's you, stopped halfway through your run. Stood outside this old shop, seeming to wait for someone.'

Wise tried to hide the shock from his expression, but it was there, a flutter of surprise and horror crossing his face, enlarging his eyes for a split second. 'So, I stopped. What of it?'

'You waited. Nearly ten minutes. Then a car pulled up. You got in. Remember that?'

Wise went back to staring at the photograph, his desperate thoughts, his confusion clear behind his eyes. Then he looked up, nodding, putting an ill-fitting and awkward looking smile on his face.

'Oh, right,' he said, nodding. 'I forgot. I got a taxi...'

'Why? Why in the middle of a run?'

He shrugged. 'Suddenly felt tired. It'd been a tough week.'

'You weren't that far from the hotel. You couldn't just walk back?'

'Just a lazy moment, I guess.'

Crowne nodded. 'Thing is, you show up on CCTV again, jogging towards the hotel, no sign of this mysterious car.'

'I got them to drop me off a little way from the hotel. Didn't want to seem lazy, did I?'

'OK, so what taxi company picked you up?'

Wise shrugged. 'I don't remember really. It could've been any of them.'

'You don't remember?' Crowne raised his

eyebrows.

'No, sorry. I just jumped in. I haven't broken any rules, have I? OK, I didn't mention the taxi before now, but that's OK, isn't it? I was in my room when this all happened, when he got...'

'Murdered?' Crowne sighed. 'Thing is, that's what you said to us originally, but now we've got you gallivanting around in a taxi. We don't even know where you went in this taxi. Where did it take you?'

'I just got him to drive around. That's all. Didn't want to come back from my run too soon, did I?'

'We'll be able to pick up this mysterious taxi on CCTV, and we'll either confirm your story or...' Crowne let it hang there, watching Wise's response. He was still agitated, definitely nervous about something. It wasn't right, he wasn't right, or at least he was hiding something, but he just couldn't put his finger on it.

'Is that it?' Wise asked, flicking his eyes between them.

Crowne nodded, knowing sadly that he had nothing much more to question Wise on, only the troubling feeling in his gut, and that didn't count for much. Then his mind raced, desperate for any connection he could drum up.

'Have you ever worked with DSU

Armstrong, the victim?' Crowne asked as Wise stood up.

There was that flicker, the nervous tremble in his eyes and mouth before he said, 'Don't think so. If I'm honest, I can hardly remember what he looks like.'

Before Wise could head to the door, Crowne brought out the photograph of Armstrong that came from his police file. 'Here, take a long look. Jog your memory. Not that you should need it. He gave you a lecture not that long ago.'

Wise stared at Crowne, then down at the photograph. He shrugged. 'I might've come across him sometime before now. There're so many officers I've met so far…'

'OK, go on your way.' Crowne watched the young detective leave before he turned to Rivers, who he noticed was still staring at the door. 'What do you think?'

She looked at Crowne. 'He's hiding something. This whole cock and bull story about the taxi. Didn't look like a taxi to me. I think he arranged to get picked up by someone. We just don't know where he went. It's like the car just disappeared.'

'Well, keep searching. It must be somewhere.' Crowne turned back to the doorway, mulling it all over. 'Cars don't just disappear.'

The day was slowly melting into dusk by the time they took the turning into Padstow and found a space in the long car park that ran parallel with the harbour. As Butler parked up, Moone sat for a moment, staring out at the sea and the boats that gently bobbed there, their silhouettes rocking against the deepening orange glow of the sun. The bodies of tourists kept cutting across his view and his thoughts as the engine grumbled and fell silent.

'That Polish waitress came in,' Butler said.

Moone nodded. 'Good. They took photos of her tattoos?'

'Yeah. They're very good, but not sure they're a match for the one on our DB. No butterflies.'

'Shame.'

'Well, here we are,' Butler said, staring out at the view.

'Do you think we should've got in contact with his people before turning up here?' Moone asked, wondering what Laptew would be saying about the whole business, knowing he would probably be obsessed with the PR angle of it all.

Butler looked him up and down. 'What's happened to you? Worrying about appearances now, are we? Come off it, you know as well as I do that if we started pussy footing around, then we could wait ages before we get to talk to him. People like Black, with all their money and their rich friends, are protected. They have lawyers, teams of them. We need to catch him off guard. Come on.'

He watched Butler climb out and stared at her as she started storming off towards the town. He hurried out of the car, then jogged to catch up with her, his eyes being dragged away to the heart-stopping views. This was a place where he could see himself growing old, maybe getting himself a shaggy dog, perhaps even an old boat. He laughed at the ridiculous image of himself wearing a captain's hat and smoking a pipe, then followed Butler into the harbour that was crawling with tourists, the stomach-growling smell of fish and chips being deep fried finding his nostrils.

'It's up there, then round the corner,' Butler said, pointing and half looking down at her phone.

They found the restaurant in one of the winding streets, which was rammed with surf shops and touristy places. It was set back a little, with a garden out the front. The building had obviously been an old Victorian villa at some point, owned by someone wealthy. Now it had been converted, modernised, a glass frontage added, the restaurant's name written across the front in large rustic style letters. The garden area was busy with diners waiting to go in, drinks in their hands. The interior was bustling already, Moone could see as they approached, but Butler was already storming in, taking out her warrant card.

Before Butler was approached by an attractive woman with light brown hair, Moone grabbed her elbow and whispered, 'We're not supposed to be official about this, are we?'

Butler pulled her arm away from him, a glare of annoyance coming his way. Then she huffed and put away her warrant card as the woman smiled at them expectantly, a tablet device in her hands.

'Hi, welcome to Fenwick's,' she said. 'Have you booked?'

'No, but we'd,' was all Butler managed to say before the woman tilted her head to one side, a sorrowful look coming over her face as she said, 'I'm so sorry, but if you haven't booked, then I doubt we can fit you in. It's opening night...'

Moone smiled and held up his hand. 'It's fine. Is Fenwick here?'

'Of course. He's busy in the kitchen at the moment. I'm sorry, I've just got to see to these people...'

Moone looked round to see more customers piling in, so stepped aside, getting ready to follow Butler who was already heading outside. He turned back to the woman before she could approach the expectant diners, and said, 'Is there a good fish and chip place round here?'

The woman laughed, then nodded and pointed towards the door. 'Go back to the harbour, turn right, there's a place on the corner. Harbour Fish and Chips. Sorry again.'

He smiled, then had another thought. He took out his warrant card and flashed it before slipping it back into his coat. 'DCI Peter Moone. I'm sorry to keep you, but is Mario Black here?'

The woman was still staring at his pocket, a look of surprise on her face when she said, 'Not at the moment, but Mr Fenwick has a table reserved for him in case he makes it up from London.'

Moone took out his card. 'My mobile number's on there. You couldn't let me know if he turns up, could you?'

She looked down at the card, then up at him with a smile and a shrug. 'OK, I guess so. Sorry, I'd better see to these people.'

'Yes, sorry. I'll see you again.'

She smiled. 'I'll see you, drectly.'

He turned away, her words lingering in his ears, wondering what the last phrase meant as he walked back towards the harbour. Butler was stood looking round at the view, the town and harbour now being soaked in a deep orange glow as the sun submerged itself behind the warrens of tourist shops and galleries.

'What does drectly mean?' he asked

Butler.

'See you soon. As in I'll see you *directly*.'

Moone nodded. 'That's what I thought. She was very helpful.'

'Who was?' Butler looked over her shoulder. 'The beautiful brunette? Yeah, I bet she was. After her tip, no doubt.'

'Fancy fish and chips?'

Butler followed his eyes along to the large, glass fronted fish and chip restaurant that faced the harbour and gave a huff. 'Is that where you take your dates? For fish and chips? No wonder you're still single.'

Moone followed her as she stormed on, heading into the restaurant, thinking about her last words. It wasn't meant to be a cruel jibe, and he knew in his heart that Butler would never mean to upset him, but even so it seemed like a bit of a low blow. After all, he thought, as he followed her to a table near the windows, she knew his history, and especially his recent history with women. His mind travelled back to Carthew, wondering how DI Crowne was getting on with her. He'd heard nothing since he had left, so he tried to convince himself that no news was good news.

Butler had seated herself near the windows, allowing them both to look out at the harbour and the steady stream of tourists going past. She put down the menu as he seated himself and said, 'Cod and chips. But I don't want a pile of chips. Got to watch my waistline, haven't I?'

He smiled awkwardly, finding himself facing one of those questions that could easily be a trap. So he looked down at the menu instead, thinking it was best to stay quiet.

'No, Mandy, you look gorgeous and slim, Mandy,' Butler said sarcastically, shaking her head.

'You OK?' he asked, then sat back, facing her. 'Anything you want to chat about?'

She narrowed her eyes. 'If you try and bring up my father, I will have to lamp you one.'

He sighed, then looked down at the menu again, deciding he would have cod and chips too. Or maybe haddock. 'Wonder what the haddock's like.'

'Exactly the same as the cod, I should think. You ever seen a cod and a haddock next to each other?'

He looked up, unable to keep the smirk from his face. 'What, you mean like in a police line-up, or in a queue at the bank? No, can't say I have.'

She made a face. 'Funny. They look exactly the same, except for a black line round their side. One has it and the other doesn't. Something like that.'

He nodded. 'Interesting. I wonder when Black will get here.'

'If he gets here.'

Then Moone flinched as a shape darkened the window at the same time a tapping sound filled the air between him and Butler. The young woman from Fenwick's restaurant was stood outside, waving and smiling. She gestured for him to come outside, so he got up and hurried out.

The young woman was stood with her back resting on the harbour wall, her tablet device in her hands by the time he reached her.

'Sorry, I've forgotten your name,' she said, smiling awkwardly.

'DCI Peter Moone,' he said. 'I didn't catch yours.'

'Lisa, Lisa Brunning,' she said. 'You don't sound like you're from round here.'

'No, from London originally. Moved down here a couple of years ago.'

She smiled. 'My dad was from your neck of the woods. Notting Hill.'

'I know it well.'

'Sorry, you probably don't want me wittering on. I came to tell you that Black is on his way. He's being driven down as we speak. Should be here about nine tonight.'

'That's great. Thanks. I hope you're not going to get in trouble.'

She shrugged. Then Moone noticed the strap of her dress slipped off her shoulder, revealing the start of a tattoo, which looked to Moone as if it was the beginning of a butterfly's wing. He tried to take his eyes away from it, not wanting her to think he was some creepy weirdo, but he couldn't help notice it was a very intricate, delicate in places. It seemed to start at her left shoulder and carry on down her back.

She lifted the strap, letting out a laugh as she covered up the tattoo. 'I think this dress is too big for me, the straps won't stay up.'

He nodded, his eyes flickering back towards her shoulder, the hairs standing up along his neck. He was onto something, getting closer. He tried to let it go, to not mention the art on her back, but he found the words bubbling up in his throat. 'Nice tattoo, by the way.'

She looked towards her shoulder, then gave an empty laugh. 'Thanks. I'm not sure I like it any more. Had it done in a moment of madness.'

'Where did you have it done?' he asked, trying to sound at ease.

'Why, are you thinking of getting one? Are the police allowed to have tattoos?'

He laughed. 'Only if we don't have them on show. By the way, just so you know, I have a massive, multicoloured peacock on my back.'

She laughed. 'You're funny.'

'My daughter wants to get one. I wanted to find somewhere…'

'You have a daughter? That's nice.'

'And a boy and another little girl. Well,

she's nearly three now.'

'A nice little happy family.'

He shrugged, his stomach knotting. 'It would be, if we lived under the same roof.'

'Oh, I see.'

'Do you have any children?'

She opened her mouth, seemed to hesitate, then shook her head. 'No. No children.'

He nodded, his eyes jumping back to her shoulder, trying to find a way to bring the subject back to the butterfly tattoo. It couldn't be just a coincidence. 'How well do you know Mario Black?'

Her eyes flickered with surprise for a moment. 'Back into policeman mode already? Just when I thought you were about to ask me out.'

He felt his face redden, his heart cough into life and start hammering. Of course, he had noticed she was very attractive in a natural, not very much make up way, and the scent of her had made him far too aware of himself, but he hadn't even considered she might be interested in him. What should he do? His eyes jumped to the blurry form of Butler who was sitting on the other side of the restaurant's window, then focused in. She was staring back but looked away far too quickly.

'Perhaps we can go for a drink sometime?' he said, unsure of what else to say.

She smiled, a little redness rising to her cheeks. 'That would be very nice. I have your card. I could text you.'

'Good,' he said, his mind racing back to the tattoo, telling himself that spending more time with her might be beneficial, if she knew anything more about Black. But his eyes travelled down her, taking her in, the beauty of her engulfing him and making his desire yawn and stretch.

'I'd better go,' she said, straightening herself, then smiling at him. 'Until next time we meet.'

He smiled, then watched her walk back towards the restaurant. She stopped, turned and faced him.

'Sorry,' she said. 'You asked about the tattoo, and I never said. Your daughter's out of luck, I'm afraid. A friend did it for me.'

CHAPTER 11

'So she didn't tell you who her friend was that did the tattoo?' Butler asked with a huff as they got up from their table and hurried out into the harbour.

Moone struggled to keep up with Butler as she strode ahead, aiming for Fenwick's restaurant. It had only been a few moments ago that Moone had received a text from Lisa Brunning, informing him that Mario Black had just arrived in a chauffeur driven Mercedes. Moone especially took notice of the fact that the text had come with two kisses attached, but then started to wonder if this was how she normally corresponded with her contacts. But then again, he thought, he had only just met her.

'You going to answer me or what?' Butler snapped, swinging round and facing him as they reached the restaurant's entrance. 'What goes on in your head, Moone?'

'Nothing much. No, she didn't say who

gave her the tattoo, only that it was a friend. But that says a lot, doesn't it, that a *friend* did it?'

Butler made an unconvincing sound as she turned back to the restaurant and started walking again.

'Come on,' Moone said. 'It's a very intricate tattoo of a butterfly and her friend did it? That can't be just a coincidence.'

'Can't it? This is the South West, the world and his wife knows a tattooist here.'

'We need to get a photo of the tattoo.' Moone went to head into the restaurant, but Butler blocked his way.

'Hang on,' she said, her eyes narrowing. 'How exactly are you going to get a photo of her tattoo?'

He shrugged. 'I'll just ask her if Black did it for her, and if he did, I'll get a photo of it and compare it to the one on the dead girl. It's not rocket science.'

'You can't just ask her,' she said, sighing.

'Why not?'

'Because if Black did do the tattoo and she lets onto him that we've been asking all manner of questions, then he'll know we're on to him.'

Moone nodded, knowing full well she was right. 'Then I'll find another way.'

She stared at him, her face darkening a little as she turned round and started moving towards the restaurant again. He caught up with her, his stomach knotting itself automatically, knowing she wasn't best pleased about something.

'What's up now?' he asked, cutting her off.

She let out a quiet huff, then shook her head. 'I saw the way you were looking at her.'

'What way was I looking at her?'

'You know. Puppy dog eyes. Haven't you learnt your lesson from last time? Remember the psycho cow who aided and abetted a killer? And do you remember the nutter before that one? The one we're still dealing with?'

He couldn't find anything to say, so looked away, staring towards some tourists who seemed to be gawping at them.

'Are you planning on seeing her again?' Butler asked, her eyebrows raised.

He looked at her, thinking it all over carefully. Even though he didn't like lying to her, he knew it was the only way he was going to get past this awkward moment. Anyway, he thought, he didn't have any solid plans to see her again, apart from the fact that they would need a photograph of the tattoo. 'No, I'm not. But we still need to find out about the tattoo. Maybe there's another way we can find out…'

'You and I both know the only way that'll work is if you go and see her, take her for a drink and get the information out of her subtly.'

Butler seemed to calm down as she barged past him and walked towards the restaurant and then past it. Moone followed her, watching her as she stormed on towards some stone steps that led up to a car park that was situated a little way from the town. Lisa had told him in her text that it was a private car park, reserved for important guests and that Black would be arriving there at any moment. As he closed in on Butler on the last few steep steps, he heard a car engine getting louder, then saw a Mercedes pulling into the car park. It parked, then sat in silence.

Butler was already heading for the car, producing her warrant card as she reached the vehicle as Black was getting out. Moone recognised him from the press photos he'd seen in the papers and around his restaurant. He was tanned, with shoulder length dark hair. His eyes were deep set, with dark rings underneath them. Those eyes took in Butler's warrant card with a blank expression as he moved past her, towards the steep path they had just come down.

'Excuse me,' Black said. 'I'm expected at my friend's restaurant.'

Moone blocked his way and folded his arms. 'We're the police, Mr Black.'

Black looked him over with disdain. 'I could tell. Have I done something wrong?'

'We need to have a chat with you.'

Black turned round to face a woman who was striding towards him dressed in a short black dress, her dark brown hair piled up on her head, a large mobile phone in her hand.

'Amber,' he said. 'The police are here being a pain in my arse. Deal with them, would you?'

Black barged past Moone, leaving him looking into the bored eyes of Amber, who he took to be the arrogant chef's PA. But her attention was half on her phone.

'Are you looking to charge Mr Black with a crime?' she asked, tapping away at her phone.

'No, not at this juncture,' Moone said.

'So I don't have to get his team of incredibly expensive lawyers involved?' She looked up, neat eyebrows raised, a smirk on her lips.

'No, not right now.'

Amber smiled without emotion, then walked past Moone, hurrying after Black as she called out, 'Send whatever questions you've got to us. We might answer them.'

Butler walked up to him and folded her arms across her chest. 'Well, that went well. What now?'

Moone shrugged as he turned to watch Black and his people heading towards the steps that would take them down to the harbour, the anger slowly simmering up in him, flashes of a smug Carthew flickering before his eyes. Then he found himself hurrying after Black and his sycophantic crew, his heart pumping as he went down the steps. He managed to get ahead of them as they entered the restaurant and cut Black off. He raised his ID, his hand trembling, his heart pounding even more. 'Mr Black, I don't know who you think you are, but I'm from the police, and I'm investigating the death of a young woman. A murder, in fact. I think that's a little more important than you getting a free meal, don't you?'

'I'm busy.' Black put on a fake smile, then went to move on, but Moone found his own palm pushing the chef back a little.

'Excuse me?' Black glared at him, his eyebrows raised. 'You realise who I am? The people I know? The people who owe me favours?'

'I know who you are. You don't know who I am. But let me tell you about my very interesting career in London, the people I got out of some really serious jams. There's a lot of people, some of them journalists that owe me favours. I can get the word out that you weren't willing to help solve the murder of a poor young woman. Worse, I could get them to make out you've got something to hide. Oh, and don't I recall some talk about a young woman having anaphylactic shock in one of your restaurants? Wouldn't it be inconvenient if that story found its way back into the papers?'

Black stared at him, his dark eyes digging

into Moone, sizing him up. Moone stared back, but noticed the chef's PA sidling up as she said, 'Mr Black, I think you shouldn't...'

But Black held up a hand. 'Shut it. Come on, policeman, step into my office.'

Moone followed Black towards the kitchens, then through a double door, where the shouts and noises of the kitchen rose in volume to an almost deafening degree. The chef headed to a door marked private, then went in. He was standing by a large desk, his arms folded, staring at Moone as he came in.

'You've got some balls,' Black said. 'Is any of that true?'

'Some. Believe me, I can make your life difficult.'

'I'm sure. What's this about?'

'I told you. Murder. I hear you like to draw.'

'Draw?'

'On young women. Tattoos.'

Black laughed, shaking his head. 'I do. I do, it's true. It's amazing what those shallow little girls will let you mark their skin with. Let me guess, your dead young woman had a tattoo on her?'

'Yes, she did.'

'And you'd like a nice little example of my work to compare it to?' Black laughed, then looked at his hands, seeming to examine the cleanliness of his nails. 'No way, Detective. Now, you're thinking that sounds like some kind of admission of guilt, aren't you?'

Moone raised his eyebrows, but kept quiet, a little curious to see where Black was heading.

The chef folded his arms, leaning his back against the wall. 'It's not. It's really not. I didn't murder anyone. I'm not capable of murder. Some people might tell you what an arsehole I am, and they probably would tell you I'm pretty much evil, but that's just the people who couldn't stand the heat in my kitchen. Yes, OK, I'm an arsehole, but I'm not a murderer. I'm an artist.'

'Then let's have a look at your artwork.' Moone smiled politely.

Black stared at him. 'How come you ended up here? Who pointed you in my direction? Who told you about the tattoos? Please tell me, I'm curious.'

'I can't discuss that. Police business.'

Black nodded. 'Then what if I had information that might help you? Even another suspect?'

'That would be handy.' Moone took out his notebook and pen, but all the time his suspicions were growing as he looked into the dead dark eyes that stared back at him.

Black stepped closer. 'Have you heard of a little boy called James Dyer?'

Moone looked up. 'The kid who went missing in Spain about five years ago? What's he got to do with this?'

'Nothing really. He's the son of my friend, Tom, Tom Dyer. Another chef. Not quite as successful as me, but he's pretty good.'

'So?'

'They don't get much info from the Spanish police, or our police either for that matter.'

'You want me to make enquires?'

'Well, yes. You see, I paid a private investigator to look into it last year. He obviously didn't find the kid, but he came up with a name. A suspect.'

'Well, I suggest you go to the appropriate police with that…'

'Grader. Loy Grader.'

Moone's stomach turned over, then seemed to try and find a comfortable spot in his shoes. 'Like I said, go to the police dealing…'

'We've tried. They don't want to hear it. But if you talk to them…'

'They probably won't listen. Now, why don't you tell me what you know about the murder of the young woman…'

'Well, that's the thing, I may know someone with a penchant for tattooing young women. They're also a complete psycho.'

'Then just tell me.'

'After you go and talk to whoever you have to talk to about this sick Loy Grader person. He's a paedophile, right?'

'Amongst other things. But yes, he's a

monster.'

Black nodded. 'Then you go and find out if he was in Spain at that time, when James went missing and then you can find out from me who killed your victim.'

'The person you suspect murdered my victim?'

'That's right, Detective. I'll even throw in a free meal.'

Moone gave an empty laugh. He took out his card then put it on the desk. 'Here's my number, for when you grow a conscience and decide to tell me what you know.'

Black kept staring at him, his face blank. 'You'll be waiting a long time. And your killer will probably have killed again by then, won't he?'

'We've got one victim, we don't...'

'Come on. I watch telly, I read. If you've got a killer on your hands who likes to tattoo his victims, then he's not going to just stop, is he?'

Moone looked into the dark eyes staring back at him, wondering what lay beyond them, suspecting it was probably pretty bad stuff. 'No. Probably not.'

'Definitely not.' Black smiled and stepped closer. 'He obviously enjoys marking their bodies. Gets off on it. It excites him. He'll want more.'

'Will he?' Moone felt a strange sensation travelling up his back. His instinct was to turn and run.

'You know I'm right, don't you?'

Moone nodded. 'I think so. This is probably just the beginning.'

'Then run along and come back when you know what I need to know.' The chef waved to the door, then smiled briefly.

Moone sighed, then headed out of the office and back out into the restaurant that now roared with scraping cutlery and chatting people. He was glad to be out of the room with the creepy chef. Butler met him halfway across the restaurant and cut him off as she folded her arms.

'So?' she said, raising her eyebrows. 'We all set?'

Moone emptied the breath from his cheeks, then looked back at the office. 'Not really. He wants to make a deal.'

Butler huffed. 'A deal? A bloody deal?'

'He denies committing any murders, unsurprisingly, but he seems to have someone in mind for it.'

'Who?'

'Some tattoo obsessed psycho,' Moone said, then pointed to the exit. 'Let's go outside. I can't hear myself think in here.'

When they got outside, and leaned against the wall that surrounded the harbour, Butler said, 'So, what's this psycho's name?'

'He wouldn't say.' Moone looked at her,

then shook his head.

'What the fuck, Pete.'

'I know. He'll tell us if we look into something for him.'

'What? That arrogant bastard!' Butler went to storm toward the restaurant, but Moone grasped her arm as he said, 'Wait. Listen to the rest.'

She glared at him, her face red around the cheeks. 'Go on. Spit it out. Stop faffing.'

'Apparently, Mario Black's friend is one of James Dyer's parents.'

'James Dyer? The kid that vanished in Spain? What the hell is this about?'

'He says Dyer's parents can't get any joy from the Spanish police or the Met either. He wants us to find out what's going on.'

'He's taking the piss. He's made all this up just to buy him some time.'

'Maybe. But this is the weird, and rather unsettling part…'

'Go on.'

'Apparently, Black hired a private investigator and he came up with a suspect that he reckons was in Spain at the time.'

'Oh God. Who?'

'Loy Grader.'

Butler turned away, then gave a choked laugh. Then she looked at Moone again, her face losing any kind of mirth. 'No way. We're not getting involved with that… that piece of shit again. The thought of it makes my blood...'

'What if he knows something?'

'He doesn't. And if he does, he won't tell us. You know he won't. He'll just tease us for a while and get his kicks from the attention.'

'But what if he really does know something or can help somehow?'

'He's not Hannibal Lecter.'

'I know. Listen, I'll talk to the Met, see if I can find out something, I'll tell them about Grader, and see what they say first.'

Butler stared at him for a while, before she said, 'You promise you'll talk to the Met first?'

'Scout's honour.'

She glared at him, then gave a deep huff. Then her eyes turned back to the restaurant. 'You know it's probably Black who's behind our murder and the possible kidnapping of this other girl, don't you?'

'Probably. You should have heard him in there, talking about our killer as if he knows them.'

'He does. Him.'

'Then we keep an eye on him. I want his background too, anything he's ever done wrong. If it is him, we'll nail him.'

'And what about this tattooed woman he's got working for him?'

'Well, like you said, I should go and arrange to meet her for a drink.'

Butler sighed. 'So you can pump her for

information, or just pump her?'

'For information, obviously.' He laughed, but Butler turned away with an even more aggressive huff than he was used to. He tried to catch her up, to ask her what was wrong, but she kept on storming back towards their car.

Crowne found himself driving for a while, not wanting to go home quite yet. Everything was going round in his head, his interview with DC Wise playing on his mind especially, the fact bugging him that they still didn't have any evidence he was involved. All they had was him catching a lift in a mysterious car or taxi near to the hotel. No, not a taxi. They couldn't find any cab company that picked up anyone fitting Wise's description from where he had been waiting that night. And no cameras seemed to pick up the car anywhere else. But Wise was lying, that was for sure. Crowne looked around him, coming out of his zombie-like trance, and saw he was heading towards the estate where Mrs Armstrong lived. Maybe it was his subconscious, but he did have a couple of questions he wanted to ask her. He was about to park up, when he noticed a figure walking up her driveway and ringing her bell. The person, who to Crowne looked a lot like Jason Wise, was looking around, seeming a little cautious. Crowne pulled up along the street, then headed to the house, just in time to see Mrs Armstrong letting the young man in. He let out a laugh, shaking his head, the hairs standing up along the back of his neck. He stopped for a moment, hesitating, wondering what the best course of action was, then smiled to himself and produced his warrant card. He rang the bell, then slapped the letterbox a couple of times. He could hear it or rather he couldn't hear it; there was a sudden silence, and he imagined the panic, the beating breaths as they rushed about, deciding what to do for the best. He banged on the door, then bent down towards the letterbox and opened it.

'Mrs Armstrong, this is DI Crowne, please let me in,' he said in his best authoritative voice, then headed towards the narrow alleyway that led down the side of the house towards the back gardens. When he got close to the back of Mrs Armstrong's house, he heard a door opening and panicked voices, a man and a woman's. He stepped out as Mrs Armstrong and DC Jason Wise stood at the back door, two startled rabbits, half in an embrace, staring at him.

'I thought I might find you here,' Crowne said, lying, putting on a smug little smile.

'I just came round...' Wise started to say, but Crowne shook his head and raised a silencing hand.

'To pay your respects, DC Wise?' Crowne said. 'Then you thought you'd better sneak out the back way? Come off it. Let's go inside and talk.'

The caught lovers, panic still burning in their eyes, stared at each other for some kind of support. But it was Mrs Armstrong who breathed it all down, straightened herself up and said, 'I'll make some coffee.'

Crowne followed them in, watching as they went about their awkward business. Mrs Armstrong made the coffee, her chest still rising and falling, while Wise sat down with his eyes fixed on Crowne.

'I suppose we're in trouble?' Wise asked.

'That depends,' Crowne said. 'How long has this been going on?'

They looked at each other, then Mrs Armstrong said, 'Almost a year.'

'Eleven months, two weeks,' Wise said, then the room fell into strained silence.

Crowne cleared his throat. 'This is where you came that night? The night her husband, DSU Armstrong was murdered?'

Wise nodded. 'Yeah. This is where I was. I wasn't at the hotel murdering anyone.'

Crowne nodded. 'I guess you're each other's alibis then. Nice.'

'We had nothing to do with it,' Mrs Armstrong said.

'Can anyone else confirm that?' He looked between them and he thought he saw a flutter of something, an almost imperceptible twitch of their collective eyes. Then it occurred to him, a sudden thought or idea breaking out into the front of his mind.

'DS Faith Carthew,' he said and watched the flutter of quiet panic cross their faces once more.

CHAPTER 12

Moone had found himself being ignored by Butler as she drove them to the Bed and Breakfast that Harding had booked for them. It turned out he had booked them into a large, nicely decorated room with an adjoining bathroom. The only issue was that there was only one king size bed, which was obviously a nice little joke set up by Harding. After the middle-aged woman with bleach blonde hair had shown them around, Butler stood at the end of the large bed and said, 'Harding's dead when I see him.'

Moone pointed at the sofa that sat at the other end of the room, near the large screen TV. 'I'll take the sofa.'

'Yes, you will.'

Then Moone's phone was ringing and he was thankful for it, to have someone else to talk to for a least a few seconds. It was Inspector Kevin Pinder calling.

'Hello, Pinder,' Moone said, sounding far

too relieved, so lowered his voice and sat on the sofa.

'Sorry, I've got some bad news,' he said.
'What is it?'
'We've got another one.'

Moone ran his hand over his face. 'Another dead girl?'

'Yep. This time dumped in Plympton, on the edge of the woods near Saltram House.'

'Right, OK, secure the scene. We'll be there as soon as we can.' Moone ended the call to find Butler staring at him, a strange look on her face, which he assumed was either her usual annoyance or sadness that another victim had turned up.

'Another vic?' she asked.
'I'm afraid so.'
'You should be pleased with yourself. You said it was a serial offender.'
'Well, I'm not.'

They arrived at Saltram House, taking the back entrance, passing through the stone gateway and parking at the edge of the grounds as the darkness swallowed the day. There was already a cluster of police incident cars and vans parked halfway to the house, some of which had their blue lights flashing, lighting up the trees momentarily in an eerie way. The crime scene tape was tied round several trees, twisting in the light breeze, while the silhouettes of the uniforms and SOCOs flickered in the light, making them seem to dance.

It was Inspector Pinder who came out of the deep black shadows of the trees, his face illuminated with blue light every few seconds. He approached Moone and Butler with a heavy sigh as he turned and pointed a finger towards the tape and beyond it.

'Young woman,' he said with a shake of his head, his usual bravado seeming to have deserted him. 'Tattoo at the centre of her back.'

'Butterfly?' Moone asked, stepping towards the tape, his eyes jumping to the duckboards that lined the way towards a white SOCO tent that stood between two twisted and ancient trees.

Pinder nodded. 'Yeah, but if you ask me, it looks even more intricate than the last one. More colour too.'

'Listen to the art critic,' Butler said, huffed and pulled on some latex gloves, then slipped under the cordon, and hopped onto the duckboards. Moone followed, staring towards the tent that flickered blue, already yearning for a cigarette, his hands trembling a little, half with the chill of the wind, but mostly due to the dread of what was lying inside the tent. Butler opened the tent door, allowing Moone to slip into the glowing yellow interior, where the SOCOs where busy, mostly taking photos and examining the ground. The girl's body glowed white against the deep green undergrowth, the slender shape of her broken up by the occasional twig, as if the ground was giving her up. There was something strange, kind of out of place about the position of her body, Moone decided, but he didn't truly understand what that meant and decided to keep his observations to himself.

'He's right,' Butler said, taking out her phone and snapping the tattoo on her back, which glowed a deep orange, almost red against her pale skin.

Moone nodded. 'He's used more colour. He's getting better or taking his time.'

'Sick bastard. What's wrong with a canvas?'

Moone ignored her comments, half watching the SOCO with the camera that was knelt by the feet of the DB.

'Who found her?' Moone asked.

'Late night dog walker,' one of the SOCOs said, then added, 'It usually is with a body dump like this.'

Moone nodded and stood up, then took a photo himself, his stomach wrapping itself tight around his spine, and threatening to use it as a ladder to climb up to his throat. Then he noticed something when he looked towards her pale, thin hands. The nails had been painted black, just like the first victim. He looked away, his hands trembling even more, the desperate urge for a cigarette coming in a wave.

'Her nails,' he said. They've been painted.'

'Like our first DB,' Butler said and sighed. 'They've still had no luck tracing whoever did the original nails.'

'They should keep looking.' Moone left the tent and breathed in the night air outside, smelling the scent of flowers. He looked around the scene, watching the uniforms spreading out already, searching the undergrowth. 'Is Dr Parry here yet?'

'He's not coming,' Pinder said, leant up against a tree. 'There's someone else on the way.'

'I see. Not sure what's up with Parry at the moment. He's off his game.'

'People have lives.'

Moone nodded. 'I think he's got family problems.'

'Doesn't everyone?'

'Is he at work, though?'

'As far as I know. He just said someone else would examine the body in situ.' Pinder stepped closer, lowering his voice. 'What's happening about our other little problem?'

'Carthew, you mean?' Moone allowed her image to penetrate his brain, bringing the usual dark cloud that always swamped his head when he allowed her in. 'She's someone else's problem now.'

'You really think she murdered our potential boss?' Pinder raised his eyebrows.

'Remember you saved me from falling to my death?' Moone walked away, his heart thudding with the terrifying memory of hanging from Bickleigh viaduct.

'I know. I just can't get my head round it all.'

'Well, you better had,' Butler said with a huff as she walked up to Pinder. 'Do you know anything about James Dyer?'

Pinder rested his hands on his stab vest, narrowing his eyes. 'The kid who went missing in Spain? What's that got to do with Carthew?'

'Nothing,' she said. 'Moone here has made a deal with Mario Black to find out what he can about the case. It's a long story, but Black might know something about these murders.'

Moone swung round, facing them, his mind buzzing. 'How long has she been dead?'

Pinder looked at him. 'On-call doctor said roughly eight to ten hours. Why?'

Moone looked at his watch. 'We were with Black not that long ago. About an hour and a half ago. Then before that, as far as we know he was travelling down from London.'

'We need to find out if that's true,' Butler said. 'What's the betting he arrived here a long time before that?'

'Then we better find out from one of his

people where he was exactly before he arrived at the restaurant,' Moone said.

'You're going to go creeping after that woman, aren't you?' Butler asked, shaking her head.

Pinder looked between them. 'What woman? What have I missed now?'

'She doesn't even work for Black,' Moone said, then he thought it all through as he turned to Pinder. 'We met someone at the restaurant who might have a tattoo done by Black. And I suppose she might know someone who might know exactly where Black was.'

'I bloody well knew it,' Butler said as her phone started ringing. She sighed, then answered the call as she started walking back towards their car. 'DI Mandy Butler. Yes. When? OK, I'll come now.'

Moone was half listening to her call as he turned back to Pinder. 'Better check any cameras they've got round here. Must be some.'

'Already on it.' Pinder nodded, so Moone hurried to catch up with Butler. As he caught up with her and saw her end the call, he asked, 'Was that work?'

'No, it wasn't.' She stormed on.

'The hospital?'

She stopped dead a few yards from their car, then swept round and faced him. 'Keep your snout out. I'll drop you off at the station.'

Moone shrugged and climbed in,

watching her start the engine, then reverse and head back out of the grounds of the house and race back towards Plymouth. He struggled to know what to say, guessing that her dad might have taken a turn for the worse. He had always found it difficult to know what to say to anyone suffering grief, but with Butler it was a million times worse. He still didn't know what exactly the issue between her and her dad was. He couldn't fathom what could have pushed a wedge between them and with every passing moment he became more and more determined to find out what it was and try and bring them back together before it was too late.

'You can drop me at the hospital,' he said.

She looked at him briefly. 'Why there? Don't think you're going to nose in on my business, mister.'

'I'm not. I want to see Dr Parry. I want to check a few things with him.'

'Right,' she said, with her usual huff.

He stood in the quiet darkness of the room, staring towards the cell, the hose in his hand. He had his finger on the trigger, his hand trembling a little with the excitement of it all. There was also fear, the great gulf of fear of being caught and sent to prison, but that only heightened the excitement to an almost glorious degree. He was aroused, there was no hiding the fact, dressed in the latex suit he had constructed to protect himself from their DNA and hair and to prevent him leaving evidence on them. He looked down to see how proud and excited he truly was. He gently put down the hose gun on the tattoo chair and stepped towards the cell, a sound growing in his ears, the pulse of his heart deep within him. But that wasn't the only sound he could hear; there was a scream echoing out to him, playing over and over, sometimes muffled, other times bellowing out. He saw her, the latest one, strapped in the chair as the wings of the butterfly grew, stretched, fluttered and prepared to give flight.

It was a magnificent moment, and now he was filled with it, his heart thumping, his erection straining as he stood inside the cell that still held the stale scent of her. It was a scent that contained so much fear. If only he could bottle it, he thought as he lifted his arms up as if he himself was about to fly around the room.

Then he lowered one arm, reaching for his latex covered glory and began to relive all the pleasure.

'Did you hear what I said?' Crowne asked, staring from DC Wise to the back of Mrs Armstrong. He could see her whole body had tensed as she rested her hands on the kitchen work surface. After a second, she went back to making the coffees and turned around with a mug in her hand, her face clearly drawn.

'Thanks,' Crowne said as she put the mug in front of him and withdrew again, watching him, then looking towards Wise with a look close to pleading.

'Is anyone going to talk?' Crowne asked. Nothing. 'Fine. Then I'll talk. I do love the sound of my own voice. I think you know DS Faith Carthew. One of you or both. I think she murdered your husband, Mrs Armstrong.'

Mrs Armstrong's eyes shot back to Crowne, staring at him, her head starting to slightly shake. Her mouth opened, a sound beginning to emerge. She was going to say something.

'Don't,' DC Wise said, his voice snapping. 'Don't say anything.'

Mrs Armstrong lowered her head, her cheeks scarlet.

Crowne sighed, knowing he had been so close to the truth. She was the weak link, something that he made a mental note of. He took a breath, trying to put it all together, and only coming up with one plausible scenario. He stood up, putting his hands behind his back. 'Let me try and put it together, see if I'm still a good detective. DC Wise... Jason, you must've met Carthew on the job, or at another conference or something, and you get friendly, and you tell her about this policeman's wife that you've fallen for. Is that right so far?'

Wise looked up at him, his face blank, save for a distant glimmer of anger.

'Now, I suspect, and have it on good authority, that Carthew is a sociopath, so she probably told you that she could sort the problem out, yes? She probably promised she could eliminate the competition. That right?' He looked at them both, but Wise looked away and Mrs Armstrong kept her eyes to the floor.

'I'm wondering though,' Crowne continued, 'what did she want in return for committing murder for you? Money? I mean, what else is there? So, did you pay her?'

Wise was staring at Crowne again, then stepped forward. 'You haven't got proof of anything. Everything you've said is... bollocks. We don't know her. We had nothing to do with his murder. If you had any proof, you'd arrest us, take us in for questioning. But you haven't, have you?'

Crowne stared back at him, his own annoyance raising its head as he realised that Wise wasn't as stupid as he looked.

Crowne nodded. 'You're right, Jason. I don't. But soon I will. One of you will crack. It won't be Carthew. She doesn't have feelings like guilt. But one of you two, does. It's only a matter of time.'

Moone left Butler after she parked opposite the

noodle bar and coffee shop that sat beneath the newly built multi-storey car park. Then he walked across the hospital grounds, knowing she wouldn't be far behind, still gathering her thoughts and locking up. His mind still buzzed with the idea of discovering Butler's secret, which was quickly becoming an obsession. Something had definitely happened between them all those years ago, and Moone was determined to find out what and patch them up before the old man passed away.

First, he decided to pay a visit to the morgue to talk to Dr Parry about the latest victim. The body would be soon making its way to him, to be delivered to his cold metal table. As he took the empty lift to the basement, Moone pictured the young woman's body among the earth and grass. The more colourful butterfly appeared to him, seeming even more realistic than the first, and almost moving its wings in his mind's eye. He took out his phone and stared at the image as the lift reached the basement with a thud and a creak.

The metal doors opened, so he headed down to the section of wall, where he knew the plain white door was, with no markings telling anyone that the dead resided inside. An eerie feeling always arrived at the centre of his back at that moment and travelled up to the base of his skull. He was about to knock on the huge white door, when he heard the squeak of wheels and the tap of sensible shoes coming from down the gloomy corridor. A bony shape came out of the shadows pushing an empty trolley, which they parked close to the morgue doors.

Moone saw the gaunt frame and face of the man in a grey porter's uniform who took him in blankly for a moment. He recalled Butler's description of the skinny, sick-looking porter she had questioned as the man went to turn away.

'Paul Fabre?' Moone asked and saw the porter stop, then turn around slowly.

'That's right,' Fabre said, then stepped closer as he seemed to scrutinise Moone. 'Do I know you?'

'No, but one of my colleagues talked to you recently.' Moone showed his ID. 'DCI Peter Moone.'

'I remember. Something about tattoos.' Fabre looked at the ID with a shrug. 'Late-night visit to the morgue, is it? Try not to make a mess. The dead don't mind, but we porters do.'

'Why the empty bed?' Moone tapped the bed.

'It's not empty.'

Moone flinched, yanking his hand back. He stared closer to the sheets and realised that there was someone or something beneath them.

'You're not squeamish, are you?' Fabre

gave a laugh. 'You must deal with the dead all the time.'

'I do. I did tonight. I was just surprised. You deliver them here often?'

'Sometimes. When the need arises. Which is more often than you'd think. I don't like doing it, but some of the other porters really haven't got the stomach for it.'

'I bet. You know the pathologists?'

Fabre looked towards the door, then shrugged. 'A little. They keep themselves to themselves. They don't really like us being in there. Don't want any contamination. Thing is, we're probably cleaner and more careful than they are. And I've witnessed so many trip hazards in there that's it's not funny...'

'Do you know Dr Parry?'

Fabre narrowed his eyes at Moone. 'What's all this about? Why're you asking questions about the pathologists? Don't tell me they've been up to no good? You hear stories...'

Moone let out an exhausted breath as held up his hand. 'No, he's a friend...'

'Doesn't sound like you know anything much about your friend...'

Moone had had enough. 'Thanks for your time, Mr Fabre.'

The porter huffed, then went to turn away again. 'Did you get hold of Mario Black?'

'I can't really talk about that.'

The porter nodded. 'No, I suppose not.

But take it from me, he's got a real dark side. Anyway, night night. Tell them to come out and get Mrs Jones, will you?'

Moone was left alone, staring down at the slight shape under the sheets, almost convinced it was about to move or was in fact already moving a little. He backed away, his heart thumping, then turned and knocked on the door of the morgue.

After a moment, the door slid open and a grey-haired orderly looked out at him.

'There's someone out here for you,' Moone said, stepping back, so the man could see the bed.

'Cheers,' the man said, taking the brake off the bed and dragging it inside the grey entrance of the morgue. 'Another guest. I hope we've got room.'

'Is Dr Parry here?' Moone asked, showing his ID.

'No, he's not. Dr Jenkins is here.'

'OK, thanks,' Moone said, putting away his warrant card and heading towards the door of the pathologists' office. He buzzed, then waited.

Dr Jenkins opened up then smiled when she saw him, a mug of coffee in her hand.

'I just made myself a coffee, would you like one?' she asked, letting him into the small office.

'Thanks, but it's a little late for me.'

He went in and stood with his back against the bare brick wall, watching her clear away the coffee making equipment from the small kitchen area in the corner.

'Afraid you won't sleep?' she asked, facing him.

'I've just met one of your guests outside. I'm pretty sure I won't sleep now.'

'I don't believe that, what with all the death you've been exposed to.'

He nodded. 'So, Parry isn't here?'

She looked round. 'Unless he's hiding under the autopsy table, no he isn't. Why, do you need him?'

'Not really. You haven't had our latest victim turn up here yet?'

'No, but I've been informed she's on her way. Another tattoo on her back I noticed when I examined her at the scene.'

'Yep. Even more...'

'What?'

'I was going to say beautiful, but doesn't seem appropriate, does it?'

'Some people consider the dead more beautiful than the living. You think of the Egyptians, the way they treated their dead. All that beauty that went into preparing them for the afterlife.'

Moone nodded, thinking it all over. 'Do you think that's what our killer is doing? Preparing them for some kind of afterlife?'

She shrugged. 'No idea. Could be. That's for you to find out. I did notice that she had also had a cannula inserted recently, just like your first victim. So it could be someone medically trained.'

'We're looking into it.'

'Why did you want Parry, anyway?'

'No reason. Just concerned about him. It's not like him to keep going missing like this.'

'I think he's got a lot on his mind. Some kind of family trouble, I think he said.'

Moone looked up, imagining Butler at her dying father's bedside. 'He's not the only one.'

'Is something going on upstairs?'

'Just my partner visiting her poorly dad.'

'DI Butler?'

He nodded. 'That's right. She's another one acting strange these days.'

Jenkins sipped her coffee. 'I believe Dr Parry has a theory on that.'

'Really? What does Parry think?'

'He thinks she's got a crush on someone.' Jenkins raised her eyebrows.

'Really? Butler with a crush on someone? Who?'

'Who do you think?'

Moone shook his head, totally confused by Parry's theory, then noticing that Dr Jenkins was raising her hand, then directing her index finger towards him.

'You've got to be kidding?'

'I'm afraid I'm not. Looks like you might have a slight problem.'

CHAPTER 13

Moone had tried to spend the morning concentrating, trying to put some kind of order or meaning to the two murders so far. But just when he thought he was getting somewhere, his eyes would drift up to the open doorway of the incident room where he saw movement. Usually it was a passing uniform or a detective from another team, but never Butler. His mind kept jumping back to the narrow pathologist's office where Dr Jenkins' finger kept pointing directly at his chest. No, he shook it away as a ridiculous notion.

'You're early, boss,' Harding said, standing in the doorway, munching on a bacon roll.

Moone sat back, nodding. 'Trying to make sense of all this.'

Harding came over, still chewing, staring down at the latest crime scene photos. 'Jesus. I heard there'd been another. Enough to put you off your food.'

'Not you, though?' Moone said and watched Harding take his breakfast to his desk and keep on munching as he sat down.

'Nope. Not me.'

'Harding,' Moone started to say, then thought better of it. Saying anything about last night's conversation with Dr Jenkins was a sure-fire way to get it all round the office by the afternoon.

'Yeah?' Harding looked at him over his screen.

'You've got ketchup on your chin.' Moone turned back to the photos on his desk, staring at both sets of murder scenes, then at the butterflies. He leaned in, glancing from one image to the next. They were both obviously created by the hand of an expert tattooist, but one was even more... he hesitated at that word again: *beautiful.* It made him sick to think of the killer drawing his design on their victims, knowing full well that moments after he was going to take their lives. So far, they hadn't found a tattoo artist that was as good as the one who had created the butterflies, at least not one working in a shop.

Moone's mind returned to his other problem, the matter of what Black had propositioned him with last night. It was all crazy, a potential killer demanding they bring him information about another unsolved mystery. Moone tapped his pen on his desk, thinking it through, knowing they had little else to go on. He turned round and faced Harding again.

'Harding?' Moone said.

Harding appeared like a ketchup-stained meerkat, almost making Moone burst out laughing. 'What do you know about the James Dyer disappearance?'

Harding stood up, wiping his face with a serviette. 'As much as anyone else. It's crazy, that kid just vanishing like that from their holiday apartment. Scary.'

'What about the parents?'

Harding came closer, shrugging his shoulders. 'I know they were looked at. You know, it's usually the parents or a friend of the family and all that, but they didn't find any evidence.'

'Tom Dyer. He's a chef, isn't he? Like Mario Black?'

'That's right. What's this got to do with him? Is there a connection? Don't tell me he's got something to do...'

Moone shook his head. 'No. Can you look into the working relationship or friendship between Black and Dyer, see how they worked together or if there's anything unusual about their history?'

Harding nodded, still looking curious, and sat at his desk. After he typed away for a while, he did his meerkat impression again as he said,

'Yeah, they definitely worked and socialised together, but it looks to me as if maybe he's closer with Dyer's wife than Tom.'

Moone stood up. 'How's that?'

'Well, there's quite a few photos of them together at charity events. Not quite together, but he's usually in the background. In fact, they seem to belong to a lot of the same organisations.'

Moone felt that flutter of electricity up his back again, the one that was telling him Black was up to his neck in something, but he just didn't know what it might be. Then he thought of what Black had also mentioned, the memory of which made Moone feel sick to his stomach. He swallowed down the urge to vomit. 'What about Loy Grader? Don't suppose he was in Spain at the time of James Dyer's disappearance?'

'Grader?' DC Molly Chambers was stood looking horrified in the doorway, holding her bag and a cup of coffee. 'We're not dealing with him again, are we?'

Moone smiled. 'Don't worry. I'm sure it's nothing.'

Harding looked from Molly to Moone. 'I can look into it, but it's going to be quite a job trying to find out anything from the Spanish police.'

'Spanish police?' Molly sat at her desk.

'It's a long story,' Moone said, sighing, half

wishing he'd kept it all to himself.

'It's to do with James Dyer,' Harding said.

'Oh,' Molly sat up, looking at Moone. 'I've got a friend who works in the Met now. She knows the copper who was last in charge. Do you want me to put you in touch with him?'

Moone went over to her desk, resisting the temptation to hug her. 'That would be great. Thanks, Molly. Give her or him my number or get their number.'

'OK, no problem.'

Moone smiled, then looked round towards the open door again. 'Butler's late.'

'She called me,' Harding said.

Moone looked at him. 'What? What did she say?'

'Her dad's not in a good way, apparently. She was going to stay with him last night.'

'Why didn't you say anything sooner?' Moone grabbed his stuff together as he began to head for the door.

'Sorry, boss,' Harding called after him. 'She said not to say anything.'

Moone grabbed a coffee from Warren's cafe when he arrived at the hospital and sipped it as he travelled up to Butler's father's ward. All the way up, his mind worked overtime while his stomach seemed to stay on the ground floor. He was trying to gather his thoughts, picking out the right words to say to Butler in case the situation had taken the ultimate turn for the worse. He was no good with handling bad news, or comforting those in grief, he had learnt that much on the job, and now it was the person he had grown closest to who he had to console.

Butler.

His stomach sank, recalling what Parry's theory had been. No. It couldn't be. Butler suffered his presence most of the time, even if they had become kind of close through all that they had been through. Underneath her gruffness there was now a kind of respect, and the feeling was mutual. But that was it, he had no other feelings for her, and he couldn't believe she had any romantic ones for him.

He sipped his coffee as he headed out of the lift and along to the ward, his stomach sinking even further as he was let in. He headed for the nurses' desk, walking past the noise coming from the beds in the different bays. A man was shouting at no one, accusing people of stealing his shoes, machines were beeping loudly. Many of the patients sat with masks over their faces, tubes travelling from them to oxygen tanks attached to their beds or chairs.

Moone showed his ID to a dark-skinned, perhaps Indian nurse, as the smell of breakfast wafted past his face, making him feel a little sick.

'DCI Peter Moone,' he said. 'I'm wondering

how Alfred Butler is.'

Moone balled his hands into fists as the dark-eyed nurse examined his ID, then pushed her chair backwards towards a small kitchen area behind her. He prepared for the worst as heard the nurse saying something to one of her colleagues. A red-headed nurse came to the desk, giving Moone a professional smile as she said, 'You were asking after Mr Butler?'

'I was.'

'Are you family?'

Moone's heart started to thump, imagining Butler in tears, wondering how he was going to deal with that. He would, he would say whatever he could to make her feel better, which he knew would be little. But she'd been supportive when Alice was in hospital, and he was determined to be there for her.

'No, I'm a colleague of his daughter.'

The nurse smiled. 'Oh, I see. Mandy's with him now. It was touch and go in the night, but he's hanging in there. He's a tough old boy.'

Moone could have cried with relief as the nurse told him he could go up the end of the corridor to bay A, which was a private room. He walked up there, his heart calming a little as he searched out the room among the many on his way. He slowed down, spotting the sign over the appropriate door that had been crudely fashioned with a pen and paper after the old one had obviously fallen down at some point.

The door was open a little way, but he was still about to knock when he heard voices inside the room.

'I just don't want you feeling...' Alf said, then his voice seemed to give in to a harsh, painful breath.

'Feeling what?' Butler said with her usual shortness.

'Regret. What happened... well, it wasn't your fault.'

'I know. I'm well aware of that.'

'Are you?' More harsh breaths, then a rattling cough.

'Just stop talking. You'll do yourself a mischief.'

'I wanted to talk about the other...' There was a ragged, painful intake of breath.

'Please, don't you dare try and bring all that up...'

'I need to, this might be my last chance...'

'Don't talk stupid. You're not going anywhere.'

A deep, rattling breath. 'You know I am. I haven't got long.'

'Shut up. Anyway, I've got to get to work. I'll try and pop by later.'

Moone started to retreat a little, hearing Butler coming in his direction, panic overtaking his chest.

'Hang on, Mandy,' Alf called out.

'What now?' Butler said with a deep huff.

'Have you been to see him lately?'

There was a long pause, and one that Moone could almost feel thick in the air, filled with years of unspoken words of anger.

'No, not for a while.'

'Could you take some flowers from me?'

'I'll see.'

'Please, Mand.'

'If I have time.'

Then she was coming towards the door again, so Moone backed away, breathing down his curiosity, still hearing their mysterious conversation. He began walking towards the room and met Butler coming out, her face looking as if it had just been slapped. He also thought he saw the start of tears in her eyes, but decided it was best not mentioned.

'Hey,' he said, then pointed towards the room. 'All OK with Alf?'

'He's fine.' Her eyes took him in, seeming to turn him upside down. 'What're you doing here?'

'Came to make sure you're all right.'

She barged past, heading towards the exit, avoiding a couple of porters pushing a bed along the corridor.

'So, are you all right?' he asked as he watched her reach up near the doors and press the release button. She stopped and faced him.

'I'm fine,' she said, not sounding at all fine. 'False alarm.'

'Well, I'm glad he's... he's OK.' He followed her out of the ward and towards the lifts. His phone beeped and he took it out to see he had message from Dr Parry. The autopsy on their second victim, still a Jane Doe, had been performed.

'Looks like we're wanted in the morgue,' he said as they reached the bank of lifts. He looked up at her, noticing her face, the tears still very much in her eyes. 'But I can pop down on my own, if you're not up to it.'

She glared at him. 'Why wouldn't I be up to it?'

'No reason.' He smiled, then looked down as the lift doors pinged open.

It was Dr Lee Parry that let them into the autopsy room, the same old stretched grin across his face. He was decked out in his usual green scrubs, latex gloves on, his shoulder-length hair tied back. Moone thought he looked different today though, definitely altered since the last time he'd laid eyes on him, but he didn't know what it was.

'Good morning,' Parry said, stepping back and allowing them a view of the table where the pale, almost light blue skinned young woman lay on her front. A green sheet was pulled all the way up to her shoulders, obscuring the view of the latest butterfly tattoo.

'How are you, Doctor?' Moone asked, resting his back against the tiled wall behind him, while Butler stood close to the door, arms folded, looking stern. He looked at her, suddenly realising that perhaps this really wasn't the place for her at the moment. But there was no reasoning with her.

Parry looked at Moone with a surprised expression on his face. 'How am I? I'm good, thank you for asking.'

Moone smiled. 'I came by last night, but Dr Jenkins said you were busy. Family issues.'

Parry's smile lost its glow for a moment, his eyes becoming duller. 'Did she? Well, yes, it's my brother...'

'I didn't know you have a brother,' Butler said, sounding even more shocked than Moone was.

'There's lots you don't know about me,' Parry said, turning up his smile a little more, then winking at Moone.

'What's the trouble with your brother?' Moone asked.

Parry smoothed his latex gloves a little, staring down at the DB on the table. 'He's going through a difficult time.'

'Women?' Butler asked.

Parry nodded. 'I'm afraid so. It's never easy letting go.'

'He's staying with you?' Moone asked, then, 'Sorry, I shouldn't be asking so much. It's her we should be asking about.'

Parry nodded, then took the sheet and carefully folded it down until the butterfly tattoo was revealed, glowing orange and red in the lights that beamed down from the ceiling. 'Well, look at this.'

Moone stepped closer, unable to take his eyes off the more complicated design, the extraordinary colour of it. Then he caught himself, admiring the artist who could create something so perfect.

'Beautiful, isn't it?' Parry asked, looking between them.

'I suppose,' Butler said with a huff. 'I guess some really sick minds can create something artistic sometimes.'

'The Yorkshire Ripper painted and did some drawing,' Moone said.

'But they were juvenile, quite bad really.' Parry ran a finger just above the young woman's back. 'This. This is… I don't know. I think the killer is trying to improve her in some way.'

Moone nodded. 'I agree. He thinks he's making her more beautiful.'

Butler huffed again. 'Like all those dopey young girls that get themselves tattooed all over. What're they going to look like when they're picking up their pensions?'

'But that's the point,' Parry said. 'Now she won't get old. She'll stay like this, in this beautiful state for ever. At least, that's what your killer thinks.'

Butler stared at him. 'But she won't, will she? Not for long, not when she's in the ground or cremated.'

Parry looked down at the dead woman, then nodded. 'No, you're right. I'm just saying it's the way the killer might see it.'

'How did she die?' Moone asked.

Parry pointed to her neck. 'Strangulation like the first victim. He was facing her, and there were signs he stopped, then started again.'

'Sick bastard,' Butler said.

Parry looked at her. 'Her hyoid bone was snapped.'

Butler stepped closer to the table, staring down at the body. 'I'm wondering if this is the young woman our friend met in the park. What do you reckon, Moone?'

Moone broke out of his dream, her harsh voice breaking through his thoughts. He'd been thinking about what Dr Jenkins had said to him the night before. 'Maybe,' he said. 'Let's get him in to identify her. Parry, are her nails painted black?'

Parry lifted the sheet, then took out her hand, leaning in to stare at her fingernails. 'Yes, done quite well. I scraped underneath. Just a light pink beneath them, nothing professional.'

Moone was about to say more, then heard

his mobile ringing, made an apologetic face to Parry, then went outside to the take the call. It was DC Molly Chambers calling, and he hoped she had some good news.

'Hi, Molly,' he said. 'Anything?'

'I've got a phone number for you. My friend managed to get hold of ex-DCI David Redwood's number. Apparently, he was the last one in charge of James Dyer's disappearance.'

'Thanks, Molly. Text it, will you and I'll give him a call.'

'No problem.' She sounded as if she was about to end the call, then she said, 'Any news on DS Carthew?'

'No, nothing. I need to get hold of DI Crowne to see what's happening. She's his problem now. Don't worry, Molly, I'm not going to let her be our boss.'

'Good. Thanks, boss.'

The call ended and he looked round when he heard Butler coming out of the autopsy room. She stood, eyebrows raised in expectation, arms folded.

'So?' she asked.

'Molly got a number for the last DCI in charge of Dyer's disappearance.'

Butler shook her head. 'You're really going through with this? You're going to find out what Black wants to know, even though he's probably our killer?'

'We've got nothing on him. Chances

are, he was travelling when that girl was murdered.'

'We don't know that.'

'Then why don't you find out where he was, while I talk to this ex-DCI?'

Butler stared at him, shook her head, then said, 'Fine. I'll try and get hold of his people.'

'Try Barry. He can look on social media. There's bound to be a post from his lot.'

Butler gave an empty laugh. 'Very good. You're not as stupid as people say, are you?'

'Oi!' he called out, but she had hurried on out of the corridor. He sighed, then took out his phone again and found the number Chambers had texted him. He called it, then listened to it ring for quite a while. The next thing he knew, a voice message was telling him that the caller wasn't available and to leave a short message. He hesitated after the tone, then said: 'This is DCI Peter Moone. Please call me back. Please.'

He grimaced after the second 'please' and ended the call. The more he thought about the message, the more stupid he felt, and decided to call the number again.

'Yes, what is it?' a gruff, pissed off sounding voice said in a South London accent.

'This is DCI Peter Moone...'

'Right, OK, well can you hurry the bloody hell up, as I'm in the middle of a golf game.'

Moone sighed. He already knew the detective's type, the sort of copper who rushed through the job so he could get to the green. 'It's about James Dyer.'

'Jesus. I'm nothing to do with that any more. How many more times. Goodbye…'

'Don't hang up. I've got information.'

'Then call someone who gives a stuff.'

Moone rubbed his face, feeling tired all over. 'A name's come up.'

'Really? Probably one that's come up before, but go on, shoot.'

There was a tired and annoyed sigh on the other end of the line and Moone thought he heard some men in the background telling him to get on with the game.

'Loy Grader,' Moone said, and then there was a pause. The impatient voices continued in the background until ex-DCI Redwood told them to 'Shut the fuck up.'

Then Redwood's breathing came back on the line. 'You met Grader?'

'Yes, I certainly have.'

'You talked to him about this?'

'No, not yet.'

'You sound like you're from London.'

'I am. In Plymouth now.'

'Right, Plymouth. Out in the sticks. I could do with a couple of days off.'

'You're coming here?'

'Yeah, why the fuck not. Where are you stationed?'

'Charles Cross. You're actually coming

down here?'

'Didn't I say so? Jesus, pay attention. See you soon, mate. Hang on, what was your name again?'

'DCI Peter Moone.'

There was a dry laugh on the other end. 'Moone? Right. See you soon, Moone. We're going to have a really interesting chat.'

CHAPTER 14

Crowne stared at the computer screen, watching the CCTV image of the only female figure to head towards Armstrong's room. It could have been any woman with a hood up. Whoever they were had deniability. It could either be Carthew or Mrs Armstrong. He replayed it again, getting closer to the screen, trying notice one thing that might tell him who it was. The image was too grainy, so he sat back and turned it off.

'You're not watching that again?' DS Rivers said behind him. 'There's no way to tell who it is. Whoever planned all this was some kind of genius. All they've done so far is have us running round in circles.'

Crowne sighed. 'That's the point, isn't it? That's what we're meant to do.'

'I'm wondering if we're ever going to solve this...'

Crowne turned and stared up at her. 'We will. In fact, I found something out about Wise and Armstrong's so-called grieving widow.'

'You're not going to tell me...'

Crowne nodded. 'They've been at it, which gives them a motive. But I can't prove anything. There's no evidence either of them were there, or that they planned it. Nothing.'

Rivers nodded, frowning. 'Do either of them know Carthew?'

'Maybe. I asked, and I thought I saw this look...'

'So, if they know her and she's a complete psycho, then what's to say they're not in on it together?'

'So, you're suggesting that Carthew wants him out of the way, and somehow she knows about Wise and Mrs Armstrong and convinces them to contrive to murder DSU Armstrong?'

Rivers shrugged. 'I don't know. It sounds crazy, but crazier things have happened.'

'Moone did say she was determined and crazy.' Crowne stood up and stretched. 'But if it's true, then Wise and Mrs Armstrong are the weak links.'

'Then we get them in and grill them separately and see which one sells her down the river.'

Crowne nodded. 'It's all we've got at the moment. Let's go and pick them up, so they can help us with our enquiries.'

It didn't take long for Barry, the musty smelling

IT guy, to locate Mario Black. Butler parked up outside the hotel where his restaurant was based, right where the posh penthouse would usually be. She looked over at DC Molly Chambers who was checking her phone for something, then looked back at the glass doors beyond and the holidaymakers wandering the reception area, not a care in the world. She sighed, thinking of her dad lying in hospital. She told herself off for feeling a tinge of sadness for him, remembering all the bad stuff that happened. Then it came back to her, that one moment on her darkest day. Her father had been there, and she could see him walking in, the tears blurring her vision. Her head had been pounding, throbbing from all the crying.

No, she blocked out the memory, refused to let it in.

'Come on, Chambers,' Butler said, pushing open the car door. 'Before you get lost in a world of your phone.'

Chambers looked up, a little startled, then hurried to follow her. 'Sorry, just checking to see if there's anything about what happened in Bristol.'

Butler looked at her briefly as she pushed through the glass entrance and headed through the plush, tile-floored reception area and headed for the lifts. 'You mean with Carthew?'

Molly joined her at the lifts. 'Yes. Do you

think they'll get her for it?'

'If she did it.'

'Don't you think she did?'

The lift doors opened so they stepped in and Butler pressed the button for the restaurant. 'Of course she did.'

'Then do you think they'll get her for it?'

Butler let out a harsh breath. 'No, I don't.'

'Really?'

Butler turned to her. 'She hadn't just decided to murder our potential boss out of some whim, Molly. She's thought about this, planned it all out for weeks, maybe months or longer.'

'But she's probably made a mistake and they'll find...'

'Nothing. They'll find nothing because there isn't anything to find. She's extremely clever and a complete psycho. She doesn't think like us, doesn't feel guilt and she won't have made a mistake.'

Molly looked down. 'I really don't want her to be my boss.'

'Oh, and I can't wait for the day.' Butler rolled her eyes.

'Sorry.'

Butler sighed. 'I can't think about her at the moment, I've got other things on my mind.'

Molly looked up, a little red in the face. 'Oh, yeah, sorry. Do you want to talk about it?'

'No, I do not.'

'It might help.'

'Don't give me that might help bollocks, Chambers. Let's get on and talk to this piece of work.' When the lift doors opened, Butler stormed down the carpeted corridor, past the enormous monochrome photos of Mario Black and out into the restaurant. Butler was approached by a dark-haired, pretty young woman in a waitress outfit, so she took out her ID. 'DI Mandy Butler. We need to talk to Mario Black.'

Butler had hardly finished her sentence when a deep voice bellowed out from the kitchen. Someone was getting a roasting for something, she thought as she realised the shouting voice sounded a lot like Mario Black's.

'He's busy right now,' the young waitress said, looking awkward.

'Well, tell him to get his arse out here,' she said with a huff. 'The police are here.'

Butler walked away from the waitress, then sat at a table near the bar and one of the huge windows that looked down on the Hoe. She tried to enjoy the view, but she couldn't, not with all the thoughts crashing around her head. She kept seeing him lying in the hospital bed looking all weak and pathetic. She wanted to feel sorry for him, to give him some kind of comfort in his last days, but she couldn't find it inside herself to forgive him. That's what he wanted, all he desired in his last days or weeks.

DC Chambers sat down on the opposite side of the table and stared towards the window. 'What a view.'

Butler nodded, staring out the window for a moment. 'Yeah, lovely. Where is this bastard?'

She had barely finished her words, when she caught sight of a figure heading for their table. When she turned, she laid eyes on the smiling face of Mario Black who was wiping his hands on a piece of cloth, dressed in his chef outfit.

'Here I am,' Black said and threw the cloth on the table. 'I knew you'd show up again after last night's business. Where's Laurel?'

Butler huffed. 'He's busy elsewhere.'

Black nodded. 'Very well. Did he send you with the information I wanted? Are you his lapdog?'

'Believe it or not, we don't run around getting information for you. We've got a murder to solve. Two, actually. In fact, where were you last night between eleven and one in the morning?'

Black smiled, then playfully put a finger to his lips, squinting as he stared towards the window. 'Let me think. No, I can't quite remember.'

Butler stood up, folded her arms. 'You all arrived in Cornwall about eight last night or thereabouts?'

'You were there when we arrived.' He

smiled.

'You didn't arrive any earlier, say a day or more before that?'

Black gave an empty laugh. 'No, I didn't. I was too busy overseeing my restaurants in London. I had several meetings to attend before I could get down.'

'So, what did you do after you attended your friend's restaurant last night?'

'That's personal.'

'Let me remind you that our first victim was found with one of your meals in her stomach.'

Black shook his head and gave another dry laugh. 'A meal that anyone could have recreated. Try again, Detective. If that's all you've got to go on, I feel sorry for you.'

'Why won't you tell us where you were last night?' Chambers asked, finding her voice at last.

Black looked at her, seemed to give her the once-over before he said, 'Tell me, do you have any tattoos?'

'Don't answer that,' Butler said and stepped closer to him. 'What about this young woman who died in your restaurant from anaphylactic shock?'

Black raised his eyebrows. 'Now you're really getting desperate. Jesus. They proved she didn't consume the peanut oil in my restaurant. Next question?'

'Didn't she used to work for you?'

Black lost his smile, his dark eyes starting to dig into Butler's. 'She did. She left when she decided she didn't want to be involved in the restaurant business any more. Not everyone can take it.'

'Did you ever have a relationship with her?'

'No.'

'Didn't draw on her?'

A grin grew across Black's face. 'No, I don't even think I'd started tattooing then. Look, I've got plenty to tell you, and I might have a suspect for you. But only when your friend tells me what I want to know. What's it called? Quid pro quo?'

Butler stared at him, then looked at Chambers. 'Come on, Molly, let's get out of this place.'

As they were leaving, Black said, 'I look forward to seeing you when you have my information. Bye now.'

'Thanks for coming in,' Crowne said as the female constable showed Mrs Armstrong to a seat opposite him in the interview room. She gave an uncomfortable smile, her face a little red, definite signs of fear in her grey eyes. She was a beautiful woman, who had, he noticed from photographs in her house, once looked like a model. Even when he saw her the first time, he thought she'd retained some of her beauty, but now it had been eroded by the waves of guilt and fear.

'It's fine,' she said, her voice quiet and brittle. 'I just don't understand why I'm here.'

'You remember our last conversation?' He sat back.

'Of course, and we told you we had nothing to do with his... my husband's death.'

He nodded. 'I know. I don't think you killed him.'

She stared at him, her eyes flickering for a moment before she nodded. 'Good. I'm glad of that.'

'But you were involved. That I'm certain of.'

Her face and eyes became rigid again. 'So, you're going to arrest me? Do I need to get a solicitor?'

'Not right now.'

She watched him for a moment, then leaned forward. 'You haven't got any proof of anything, have you? You haven't a clue who did this. You're stumped.'

'I can't discuss that.' He saw a flicker of something in her then, a new kind of confidence. But the words didn't seem to be hers, as if they had been fed to her by someone else. Perhaps Jason Wise. No. It was Carthew. They had probably gone running to her for advice that night.

'Can I go, then?' she asked, putting on a look of annoyance.

'Can I ask you something else?'

She shrugged. 'I suppose that's your job.'

'It is. When did she come to you? Did she pretend to bump into you somewhere, in a supermarket or a cafe? Or a pub?'

Mrs Armstrong stared at him. Nothing.

He nodded. 'Maybe she approached Wise first. Got in his head. I'm guessing he's obsessed with you. More in love with you than you are with him. Am I right?'

'He's just a friend.'

'You do stand to gain financially, but it's not a massive amount. Not the sort of money to murder for.'

'I didn't kill anyone. I told you.'

'Then tell me who did. We can work something out.'

She huffed, gave a kind of dry laugh. 'Right. You're trying to trick me into saying I had something to do with his death.'

'Was it Wise, then? He'd do anything for you, wouldn't he?'

Mrs Armstrong shook her head, the anger now in her eyes. 'I'm starting to feel this is an interrogation. Are you going to charge me with something? Arrest me?'

'No, not today. But I probably will be one day. You'll always be looking over your shoulder.'

'Am I free to go now?' She stood up, her face flushed, eyebrows raised.

'Yes, I think so.'

Moone found himself back in the hospital, ready to face the dead again. But this time the DB was in a special room, beyond a window, all well presented on a table with a purple sheet drawn up to her neck, a small pillow under her head. He got close to the glass, staring in at the young woman who had been discovered only recently in Saltram. He sighed at her hollowed-out face, her milky white shoulders. They had done their best to make her look as if she was only sleeping, but Moone knew it never really worked.

There was a knock on the door to his right. Moone turned and opened it to see a blond uniformed officer standing there, and behind him was the lad from Ryland House. Daryl Pawsey. Moone thanked the uniform and told him he'd take over. Daryl stepped in when Moone opened the door, a waft of stale cigarette smoke coming with him. Moone breathed it in like it was a kind of perfume.

'Hello, Daryl,' Moone said, putting on a smile. 'Nice to see you again.'

But Daryl looked at him blankly. 'Have we met?'

'A few days ago.' Moone shook his head. 'Doesn't matter. You said you met a girl, and she stayed in your room?'

He nodded, looked down. 'Yeah, she was lovely. You found her?'

'We might have.' Moone looked towards the window. Daryl hadn't seen it yet, and Moone assumed his brain was a little muddled right then. 'Did the constable explain why you were here?'

Daryl shrugged. 'Said something about identifying someone.'

'That's right. I'm afraid a young woman, matching the description of the one you met has been found murdered.'

Daryl's eyes grew a little, the cogs seeming to turn behind the dullness of his eyes. Then a light switched on somewhere inside his skull. 'She's dead? She's really fuckin' dead?'

'We don't know, Daryl. That's why you're here. If you stand in front of this window then you'll see the body of the victim. She's lying on a table. Look at her and see if you recognise her.'

Daryl looked round the room for a moment before his eyes jumped to the window. Moone gently directed him closer until Daryl was staring through the glass. There was a change to his face, a colour growing through it, his eyes growing wider. Then his hands touched the glass as he bent in closer.

'Poor cow,' he said.

Moone nodded. 'Yes. It's a shame. Awful. We need to stop this person.'

'Who is she?' Daryl looked at him.

'We don't know. It isn't the young woman you met?'

'No, I've never seen her before.'

'Do you remember the name of the woman you met that night?'

'Yeah, course I fuckin' do, I'm not mental. Bobbi.'

Moone let out a sigh and looked towards the window, realising once again that they had another mystery dead girl. He just hoped her prints might show up something. He turned back to the young man. 'I'm sorry, Daryl for dragging you down here.'

'You looking for Bobbi?' he asked, a sadness filling his eyes.

'We don't know anything about her really. Do you remember anything about her? Anything she mentioned about her life?'

He shrugged. 'Sorry, I was out of it. Please look for her.'

'OK, Daryl, we will. We'll let you know if we find her.'

As he watched the addled young lad head off down the corridor, escorted by the police constable, Moone ran everything through his mind, all the events of the last few days. Nothing stuck, nothing really made much sense to him, just like it never seemed to in those early days. At some point, and he hoped it would be true this time, things would start to make sense and he might even see a pattern forming. He hoped, he prayed. Please let me find a way through this mess, he thought to himself.

They had two dead bodies, two young women had had their lives snuffed out after having butterflies tattooed on their backs.

Why?

Change?

Metamorphosis?

He sighed, unable to get his mind to work.

Butler. Her dying father. That was the problem, he was far too distracted to think straight. At least he kidded himself he was, as if normally he would be on his game, tracking down their killer using his keen brain, instead of blindly moving through a maze in the hope of discovering the way out.

He lost his train of thought when his phone rang, which was extremely ironic. It was a number he didn't recognise. 'Hello, DCI Peter Moone.'

'It's Redwood,' the gruff voice said, sounding full of tiredness. 'I'm staying at the Jury's Inn. Come by for a drink later, about seven. I'll meet you in the bar.'

'Right, OK.' Moone noted the time on his phone. 'I can make time now…'

'Later. I need a nap.' The call ended, leaving Moone staring at the wall opposite, his mind whirring a little. The thought of meeting the ex-copper at all was making Moone feel on edge, but when he added the prospect of a drink he felt like he was falling over the cliff.

Crowne was about to head to interview room four when he heard his name being called. He heard the familiar voice and immediately felt a little sick. He knew what was coming, or at least suspected it. He turned and saw DSU Tucker storming towards him. She didn't look best pleased. She stopped and folded her arms, staring at him.

'Tell me it's not true,' she said, raising her eyebrows. 'Please tell me you didn't drag Mrs Armstrong in here. The widow of our murdered colleague.'

Crowne sighed, then ran a hand over his stubble, trying to decide the best way to handle the situation. 'I only had her here for a brief chat to clear up a couple of matters.'

'Then you go and see her. You go to her home, apologise for existing and then ask your questions. Getting her in here makes it look like you suspect her of…'

Crowne looked her in the eyes.

'What?' she asked. 'What's that look, Vincent? You think she had something to do with her husband's murder?'

'Did you know she's seeing DC Wise?'

'Tell me you're joking.' She stared at him.

'Wish I was.'

'How do you know? Have you got them under surveillance? Tell me you haven't…'

'No, I was heading to her home to ask her a couple of questions and then I spotted Wise knocking on her door.'

'And?'

'And I confronted them.'

Tucker closed her eyes for a few painful seconds, then glared at him. 'Bloody hell, Crowne, what do you think you're playing at?'

'They didn't deny it. Well, they tried to, but you should've seen the look on their faces, like two kids been caught out stealing.'

'Right, maybe you're right about the affair, I don't know, and I don't really care. But murder? Really? Wasn't Wise out for a run or something? Wasn't she tucked up at home?'

'She's got no solid alibi. But I don't think it was them who actually killed him.'

She narrowed her eyes. 'Then who?'

Crowne looked round the corridor to make sure no one was listening. 'DS Carthew. Faith Carthew. She's not right.'

'She's not right? That's what you're basing this on? She's not right?'

'DCI Moone knows her. He's worked with her, and he told me she's… she's mentally unstable.'

'Really? Then why is she still working? Has he reported her for something? Is she being investigated?'

Crowne sighed and shook his head. 'No.'

'No. Sounds like Moone had a thing for her and she spurned him or something, and now he's got it in for her.'

'I don't think it's like that.'

She held up a hand. 'Stop. Listen, do you have any evidence against her? Any eye witnesses that saw her go to his room?'

'No, but we've got CCTV footage of a woman wearing a hood going towards his room…'

'A woman who you can't identify?'

'No.'

And do you have any evidence that Wise or Armstrong murdered him? DNA? Witnesses?'

'Nothing.'

She nodded. 'I didn't think so. Leave them alone. You do not bother them again with this.'

'What about Carthew? She hasn't even got a solid alibi apart from she was in her room! Armstrong was going to be the DSU of the station she was heading back to. She's been fast tracked. She wants to be DSU by all accounts. She's up to something. I feel it in my gut.'

She stared at him, her eyes seeming to burn right into him. 'OK, get her in. Make it official. Record it. I want to see what her story is.'

'Good.'

Then she pointed a finger in his face.

'But if you balls this up, Vincent, and we end up looking like morons, you'll be for the high jump. Got it?'

He nodded, but secretly he was praying that Carthew might let something slip. Anything. Or he was fucked.

CHAPTER 15

Moone didn't bother driving over to Jury's Inn, deciding it was better to take a walk in the fresh air. He was desperate for a cigarette though, and the sensation marred his whole walk. Then there was the fact that he was about to meet some ex-copper and poke his nose into an investigation he had no right having anything to do with. It was getting dark and by the time he entered the reception area of the hotel, his shoes tapping loudly against the marble style flooring, the whole sky had sunk to a dark blue hue. The interior of the hotel glowed, especially the bar area. He headed to it, looking out for anyone he thought might have been on the job. His eyes immediately jumped to a man probably in his fifties with dark, thick hair, greying at the temples. He had a gaunt face, hollow eyes that jumped up to Moone. The man raised his glass of what looked like whisky and signalled for Moone to come over.

'You must be Moone,' the ex-detective

said, his voice thick with an East End accent. 'Redwood.'

Moone nodded and was about to pull out a chair when he sensed someone was stood right behind him. He turned and found himself staring at the chest of a huge, mountain of a man in a grey suit. He had a shaved head and stared at Moone without any expression.

'That's former Sergeant Benson,' Redwood said, getting up and necking his whisky. 'He used to be on the armed response team.'

'Thought you were coming alone,' Moone said, giving Benson a polite smile but getting nothing back.

'I never travel alone.' Redwood pointed up to the ceiling. 'Fifth floor. Come on.'

'What's going on?' Moone asked as Benson gripped him under his arm.

'You've got a meeting upstairs,' Redwood said as if Moone was eight years old. 'Chop chop. She's waiting.'

'Who is?' Moone was pushed out of the bar area and towards the bank of lifts. The lift doors opened and a few other hotel guests tried to get in, but Benson glared at them until they backed off.

When the lift was going up to the fifth floor, and Redwood was stood with his hands behind his back, whistling, Moone said, 'Can someone tell me where we're going?'

'Told you.' Redwood sighed. 'Fifth floor.

For a chat. Don't worry, Moone, nothing bad's going to happen to you.'

'That's a relief.' Moone huffed, pissed off that he was in the dark.

'As long as you behave.' Redwood stepped out on the fifth floor and headed down the corridor, then turned left. Moone followed with the huge Benson pushing him onwards every now and again.

'Can you leave that out?' Moone said over his shoulder, then noticed that Redwood had stopped at a door along the corridor and taken out a key card. The door buzzed and he went in. Moone looked into the open doorway, and saw the hallway, then the double bed beyond. Standing by the large window was an attractive, middle-aged woman with platinum-blonde hair, her arms folded. She was smoking a cigarette, her eyes narrowed at Moone.

'Come in,' the woman said, then took another drag of her cigarette. 'Hurry up, you're causing a draft.'

Moone stepped down the hallway and into the small bedroom area, half noticing that Redwood was already there, pouring himself another drink. There was someone else too, a slightly more rotund man in spectacles, dressed in a shirt and tie with a cardigan over the top, who was sitting on a chair in the far corner.

'I'm ex-DSU Jane Thendrick,' the woman

said, then pointed to the bespectacled man. 'Former DCI Colin Smith. You've met Redwood and Benson.'

Moone nodded, a new emotion now washing over him as he realised he'd heard of two of the members of the group. Both Jane Thendrick and Colin Smith had led murder teams to great success and had both bagged infamous serial rapists and murderers. He could feel himself shrinking in size as they all stared at him.

'It's nice to meet you all,' Moone said, his voice drying up. 'I've heard a lot about most of you. But why am I here?'

Thendrick stepped closer. 'I thought you were meant to be pretty clever, Moone.'

'Am I?'

She nodded. 'I heard good things while you were in the Met. God knows why you're here, but there you go. Anyway, we're not here to gossip or catch up, are we?'

'I suppose not.'

'James Dyer,' Colin Smith said, sitting back and folding his arms. 'Disappeared from his parents' holiday apartment five years ago. No one's ever been charged for it.'

'It's not my case,' Moone said.

'No, but you've been digging around.' Thendrick dug her cigarette into the windowsill and left it there. 'You mentioned a name.'

'A name?' Moone looked round the room.

'Loy Grader,' Smith said and stood up. 'Why exactly did you mention him?'

Moone shrugged. 'I'm not sure I should be discussing a…'

'Don't go all soft, Moone,' Thendrick said, lighting another cigarette. 'It's not your case, remember?'

'I don't think you're supposed to be smoking in here,' Moone said, nodding towards the No Smoking sign.

'I'm not meant to do a lot of things in here,' Thendrick said. 'Doesn't stop me. I'll take a dump in the shower if it takes my fancy.'

'Jesus, Jane,' Redwood said, taking a big gulp of whisky.

'Try and stay sober,' Thendrick said, shaking her head. 'At least for another half hour, then you can go back to killing yourself. I apologise, Moone. I should explain, each of us, apart from Benson, headed the Dyer case over the last five years. And it ended all our careers.'

'It's a tough case.' Moone nodded.

'It is when you're not allowed to follow the evidence,' Smith said. 'They told me not to take up the reins on it, but I didn't listen. I thought I could solve it. But they wouldn't let me follow the evidence. Told me in no uncertain terms that I was to go chasing after some mysterious paedophile gang that were meant to operate in the area. Problem was, we could find no such gang.'

'So, who took him?' Moone looked back at Thendrick.

'We have a theory,' she said, taking a puff of her latest cigarette. 'What do you know about Loy Grader?'

Moone's stomach tried to take the lift to the reception area. 'I know he's a monster. My first case here involved him. A lot of people got hurt.'

Thendrick nodded. 'Sounds like him. We all worked the case, and we all heard rumours that Grader was in Spain about that time. But we had no proof, no paper trail, just possible sightings. We also had a woman come forward who saw Grader, or someone who looked very much like him, having a drink with a man who looked very much like Dyer's father. This was a week before Dyer went missing. But again, we weren't allowed to interview Tom Dyer or his wife.'

'Why not? They're possible witnesses.'

'And suspects,' Smith said. 'But Dyer is also in the Masons. Rumour has it in the same lodge as some of the top brass in the Met. They like to protect their own people.'

'Jesus. But this woman you mentioned, she saw Grader? Is she reliable?' Moone asked, 'I mean lots of people come out of the woodwork...'

'She was the head of a child protection

team at the time. She'd seen Grader's photo before and she'd been holidaying in the same complex as the Dyers. I think she's pretty reliable.'

'Then she made a formal statement?' Moone asked.

'But we were told to discount it,' Smith said, a bubble of anger seeming to rise up in his throat.

'What? Why?'

'That's what we could never find out,' Thendrick said. 'As soon as we all started following the trail, then we ended up being forced out.'

'They made up sexual harassment charges against me,' Redwood said, pouring another drink. 'Fucking bastards.'

'Yeah, of course they did.' Thendrick shook her head and looked at Moone. 'We can't get near Grader. We've tried. Anyone involved in the Dyer case is persona non grata.'

Moone looked around the room, noticing that they were all staring at him. He shook his head, holding up his hands. 'No way. I'm not going to see him. Anyway, why would they let me go and see him?'

Thendrick pointed her cigarette at him. 'Because you're neutral. You haven't been involved in the Dyer case. You just need to put in a request to visit him, put down something to do with your first case, whatever, and bang, you're inside, sat across from the evil little bastard.'

Moone shook his head. 'Yes, and that's exactly where I don't want to be. Look, I'm busy trying to solve two murders at the moment, I can't get involved in this.'

Smith stepped closer, poking his glasses tighter to his nose. 'Tell me about the murders you're working on.'

'You know I can't.' Moone looked at Thendrick. 'But while you're here, what do you know about Mario Black?'

Thendrick gave an empty laugh. 'Oh, I see how it is. You don't scratch our backs, but we get to give you a full body massage?'

'He probably expects a happy ending, too,' Redwood said, now slurring a little.

'Shut up.' Thendrick stepped up to Moone and ran a hand down the collar of his suit jacket. 'Black was in Spain at the time, opening a restaurant.'

'I know. He told me he paid someone to look into the case and they also brought up Grader's name. That's why I'm here, because Black wants me to look into the case or at least confirm Grader was involved. If I do, he names a possible suspect in my case.'

Thendrick nodded, then pointed at Moone. 'But you like Black for the murders, and you want to know if Black is capable of murder?'

'Yes.'

She shrugged, toying with his lapel. 'Who knows? He's friends with Tom Dyer, and he's definitely not right in the head. Best person you can talk to about him is Dyer's ex-wife. She's kept a very low profile since her kid went missing. Even changed her name.'

'Where would I find her? I haven't got time to head up to London.'

Thendrick smiled. 'Well, there you're in luck. She lives down here now. In fact, she works for one of Black's chef friends.'

Moone took out his notebook. 'What's she called now?'

'Was Lara Dyer. Now goes by Lisa Brunning. Brunning's her nan's maiden name or something.'

Moone looked up, the realisation flooding him. He pictured the woman with the tattoo of a butterfly, the one who had suggested they go for a drink. He had that strange sensation again, the hairs standing up on the back of his spine. What had been the chances? But then Cornwall was a much smaller place than London. He nodded to Thendrick as he put his notebook away. 'OK, I'll look her up.'

'You do that.' Thendrick stubbed out her cigarette. 'Don't forget to go and see Loy Grader for us.'

Moone sighed. 'I can't get involved in that...'

'You can't face sitting across from him, you mean?' Thendrick looked almost sympathetic for a moment, then it faded, her face hardening as she pointed a finger at him. 'You listen, DCI fucking Moone. We've worked long and hard to solve this case. We're not about to let it go now. We can't get to Grader, but you fucking can. You don't think we can make your life hell? We've got lots of friends in the force, and in the Masons. We can fuck with your life. Don't think we can't.'

Moone looked round the room, seeing that Smith stared at him blankly, while a drunk-looking Redwood nodded and smiled. He looked back at Thendrick, realising that she was ruthless and determined to get to the bottom of Dyer's disappearance any way she could. He had little choice. He felt sick to his stomach at the thought of being in the same building as Grader, let alone the same room. It would only be a short time, he told himself. Grader would clam up, toy with him, try and climb in his head, then he would leave.

'I'll try,' Moone said, and immediately saw a light come on behind Thendrick's steely eyes. She came over and put her arms round him, pulling him tight to her.

'Good boy,' she whispered in his ear. 'We can solve this. You can be the hero. You be good to me, I'll be good to you.'

She let go, and looked into his eyes, her

face softening, a smile on her lips. She was an attractive older woman and he imagined all the younger officers that had probably fallen over themselves trying to impress her.

'I better go,' Moone said, turning towards the door.

'Two dead young women?' Smith asked.

Moone looked at him. 'Maybe. I can't discuss it.'

'I read about two dead women being found in wooded areas recently,' Smith said.

'You'll have to forgive, Colin,' Thendrick said. 'He'll obsess about this now. Let the man go, Colin. It's not your case.'

'You think Black was involved?' Smith said.

Moone shrugged, not wanting to say too much, but knowing Colin Smith had an amazing clearance rate during his career.

Smith nodded. 'He likes young women. I know that. But he uses them, throws them away when he gets bored. I think he's capable of it. Anything else you can tell me. M.O?'

Moone shook his head, then looked at Thendrick. 'I'll be in touch.'

She was brought in the back way, escorted up to the desk and officially booked in. She wasn't under arrest, and she had said she didn't want her union rep present. Crowne shook his head as DS Faith Carthew was taken from the desk and headed past him. She looked at him and smiled, the smile of a cat about to fall into a vat of cream. He sighed, wondering if it was an act she was putting on, a calm appearance, or was she really convinced that she had nothing to fear? Crowne followed her through the station, with Rivers behind him. They had little to go on, but he had to convince her that they had plenty and were about to pounce. There were two weak links. Wise and the widow. If she thought they were going to break, then she might break first. Yeah, right, he thought as she was shown into the interview room and sat down.

She sat back and smiled at him, then Rivers before she said, 'To what do I owe the pleasure this time?'

Crowne stared at her for a moment, then pressed record on the tape machine. 'We're going to record this interview, if that's OK with you?'

She shrugged. 'I don't mind. I've got nothing to hide. Things must be getting official now.'

Rivers read out the details, the date and time, then sat back, arms folded. Crowne couldn't help notice that Carthew's smile grew even brighter, as if she knew something they didn't. It unnerved him, to say the least, but he didn't show it as he sat back, smiling politely.

'You said you were in your room at the

time of Armstrong's murder, is that right?'

She nodded. 'That's correct. I think I've told you several times now. I was alone. No alibi to speak of, because I didn't think I would need one.'

Crowne nodded, looking down at his notes. 'You'd never met Armstrong before the course started?'

She shook her head. 'Never, as far as I know. I sat through his pretty interesting lecture, then I saw him again in the restaurant, we chatted about nothing much, and then I went on my way. Next thing I know I'm being told he's dead.'

Rivers sat forward. 'Would you say you're ambitious?'

Carthew looked at her blankly, then shrugged. 'Quite ambitious, I suppose. Now you're going to ask me if I bumped him off to get his job? Is that right?'

'You tell me.' Rivers raised her eyebrows.

Carthew laughed. 'Do you think I'm crazy or something? I knock off the man who's got the job I want? I'm not stupid.'

'So, it was the job you wanted?' Crowne asked. 'You're not denying that?'

Carthew looked to the ceiling, rolling her eyes. 'No, I'm not. Of course, I would love that job, but not like this. He seemed like a nice... guy. Why would I kill him?'

Crowne nodded, then looked down at his

notes again, pausing for dramatic effect. 'Do you know his wife, sorry, his widow?'

'No, never met her.' Carthew sat back. 'I keep meaning to send my condolences.'

'I'm sure she'd appreciate that. Did you know she was having an affair?'

Carthew put on a look of surprise. 'No, of course not. I don't know her. Was she really having an affair?'

'We think you know that she was.' Crowne folded his arms.

She narrowed her eyes. 'Why would I know? He didn't tell me that night. I chatted to him for ten minutes, if that.'

'No, I'm not talking about that night. Before that night. I'm wondering if you met Mrs Armstrong long before the night her husband was murdered.'

'No, why would I have done?'

'I have this theory, you see? That she wanted to find a way out of her marriage, so she could be with her new lover.'

'That's a very old story. Bit of a cliché really.' She smiled.

He nodded. 'But it's a cliché for a reason, isn't it?'

She smiled. 'Because it keeps happening, time and again?'

He nodded.

Carthew stared at him, then laughed. 'Why wouldn't she just get a divorce?'

Rivers leaned forward. 'If he dies in service, then she stands to gain quite a bit of money, doesn't she? Plus, there's the life insurance.'

Carthew nodded, seeming to mull it all over. 'Then they cooked up a plot between them, she and her fancy man decided to knock him off, and collect the money and live happily ever after. The ultimate cliché.'

Crowne looked at Rivers. 'Did you hear that? Her fancy man. Why did you say her fancy man? Maybe she's got a lesbian lover.'

Carthew shook her head. 'Shoot me. I naturally assumed it was a man, seeing as she's married to a man. It's not rocket science. Who is this person, anyway?'

'We can't divulge that,' Crowne said. 'But I think you know perfectly well who she's having an affair with.'

Carthew narrowed her eyes for a moment, then looked to the seat beside her. 'Should I have representation with me? Are you thinking of arresting me, because the questions you're asking seem to be thinly hiding some accusations.'

'I haven't accused you of anything really.' Crowne smiled.

'It's Moone, isn't it? He's the one with the accusations. I don't know what DCI Moone has said about me, but it's all lies. Did you know I saved his life? And his partner's? But for some reason they hold that against me, and now they're pointing the finger at me, aren't they? Thing is, Moone had a thing for me, but I told him it was over and...'

Crowne laughed. 'Very good. Well done.'

She looked at him strangely. 'You think I'm lying? He's really pulled the wool over your eyes.'

Crowne leaned towards her. 'Like I said before, I have this theory, they planned to knock him off. But I don't really think it was their idea. I think it was someone much smarter than them. Much smarter than the two of them put together.'

Carthew raised her eyebrows. 'There's that tone again. Are you thinking of arresting me? I mean, if you really want to, you can. Perhaps you can talk to my commanding officer, Chief Superintendent Laptew, see what he makes of it all.'

Crowne sat back. 'I hear he's unreachable, lost in the wilds of Cornwall. Anyway, I don't think I need to. I just have to wait.'

'Wait for what?'

'For one of them to crack.' He smiled.

Carthew stared at him, her smile having vanished. She looked almost fearful beyond her cold hard eyes, he thought. Maybe he had her worried for the first time.

There was a knock on the interview room door, so Crowne asked them to come in without taking his eyes off Carthew.

DSU Tucker poked her head round the door. 'Crowne, can I see you outside?'

'What is it? I'm in the middle of...'

'There's been a development. You need to step outside, now.'

Crowne looked up at her and saw she was staring at him with urgency in her eyes. Then he looked at Carthew, who was smiling as if she'd just found out she had won the lottery. They paused the tape, then Crowne stepped outside and found DSU Tucker facing him, her arms folded.

'What's happened?' His stomach knotted.

'Your surveillance team hadn't seen Mrs Armstrong or Wise for a while, and the letters and milk had started piling up.'

'Jesus...'

Tucker sighed. 'They ended up entering the house...'

'They're dead? Both of them?'

She nodded. 'Looks like murder suicide. And they left a note.'

CHAPTER 16

Moone stopped off for a couple of coffees in the morning then went straight to the station. He sipped his, stood outside the incident room, waiting for Butler to appear. Everyone else seemed to turn up first, all greeting him and looking at him suspiciously, probably wondering what he was loitering for. In the meantime, he had time to digest last night's meeting, the way all the ex-coppers looked at him as if he might be the second coming.

Then he thought about the other potential meeting he might have on the agenda and immediately felt sick. Even the vague notion of facing that detestable monster across a table made his skin crawl. Meeting Hannibal Lecter would have been preferable.

Butler came up the stairs slowly, as if she was carrying the whole world on her shoulders. She saw Moone and sighed, then looked at the other coffee in his hand.

'That for me?' she asked, sticking out her hand.

'It is. How're you sleeping?'

She opened the coffee, took a sip and shot him a look. 'Why? Do I look that bad?'

'No. No, not at all.'

'Then why ask?'

He shrugged. 'How's your dad?'

'Same. What's new with the case?'

Moone let out a breath, preparing himself. 'I met with Redwood last night. The ex-copper? Well, not only did I meet him, but I met with a gang of ex-coppers led by the former DCI Jane Thendrick.'

'Thendrick? Jesus. She headed the Dyer case a couple of years ago. She took early retirement after…'

'I know. They all headed the Dyer case. They're obsessed with it. Said they weren't allowed to follow the evidence, just had to go where they were told to look.'

Butler huffed. 'Look, I don't get why we're getting involved in this. Black is just trying to mess with our heads. Misdirection, it's called.'

'I know. I know. But we've got nothing else. No one even seems to know who these girls are.'

'Daryl Pawsey didn't help?'

'No. Not the girl, apparently. But he's pretty messed up. If it wasn't for the fact that other people saw him with a young woman, then I'd think he was imagining it all.'

'We've got nothing round the areas where the bodies were dumped. No CCTV. No suspicious vehicles so far. Only an ambulance parked up briefly around the time of the second body dump.'

Moone straightened up. 'An ambulance? Have you checked it out?'

'The camera only gets half of it, so we can't get any identification from the images.'

'Have you checked to see if there was an ambulance sent out there at that time?'

'I was about to.' She huffed. 'I have had other things on my mind.'

'I know. But we need to be…'

She held up her palm. 'Don't finish that sentence. Fine, boss, I'll get on it. Sorry, boss.'

She stormed past, and Moone called her back, but he knew she wouldn't respond. Her personal life was affecting her work. He laughed at himself, as if he wasn't living in a glass house. Shit. He thought of Grader, and the fact they had no other solid lead.

He sighed, then started towards the doors of the incident room, preparing himself to apologise to Butler and then make the dreaded call to Dartmoor Prison.

'Excuse me,' a voice said behind him. He turned and saw a woman, probably mid-forties, with light brown hair that had started to grey and was tied up in a ponytail. She wore a dark grey trouser suit.

'Can I help you?'

She took out her warrant card and opened it. Moone read DSU Fiona McIntyre. He looked up at her, the realisation hitting him. 'Are you here to take over from DSU Stack?'

'That's right,' she said, then put her hands in her pockets and stood by the doors of the incident room and looked in. 'Only temporarily. They're looking for someone to permanently take over.'

'I see.'

'I'm supposed to be heading to Edinburgh. That's where I was born.'

Then he noticed it, a hint of a Scots accent veiled by a well-educated voice. 'I've heard it's nice. Never been there.'

'It's a beautiful city.' She smiled, then it faded, and she took on a more serious expression. 'Anyway, where are we? I've been told you've been looking into two murders? Something about butterfly tattoos?'

'Yes, ma'am...'

'Boss will do.'

'Yes, boss. You can read the murder book, but basically we followed the leads to Mario Black, the chef...'

'I've heard of him. He's your number one suspect?'

Moone shrugged. 'He's our only suspect. We had another, a porter at the hospital, but he's got an alibi. He was working.'

'Not a lot to go on, then, and I suppose Black isn't being helpful?'

'No. He even says that he knows who might have killed these women, but he won't tell us unless we go and talk to Loy Grader...'

'The child murderer? What's he got to do with this?'

'Remember the missing child, James Dyer? Well, Black's friends with Dyer's family, and he reckons he hired a private detective to look into it all. The name Loy Grader surfaced, along with the allegation that he was seen in the area not long before Dyer went missing.'

DSU McIntyre frowned. 'Surely the Spanish and our detectives would've looked into it already, if there's any substance to it.'

'You'd think, wouldn't you? But I've talked to a few of the officers that were previously in charge, and they say that they weren't allowed to look into the connection between Dyer and Grader.'

'They weren't allowed? That can't be right.'

'Well, I'm just telling you what I was told.'

McIntyre looked towards the corridor, seeming deep in thought. 'So, Black wants us to look into a case that has nothing to do with us? Cheeky sod. Do you think Black might actually know something about our case or not?'

Moone shrugged. 'I really don't know. We

found a meal in our first victim's stomach that matches a recipe created by Black. Not only that, boss, but he likes to tattoo his girlfriends.'

The DSU gave an empty laugh, then shook her head. 'He's trying to divert attention from himself. Right, let's fight back a bit. Tell Black we'll do what he wants, as long as he agrees to come and make an official statement. That'll give us a chance to get under his skin. In the meantime, you go and see Loy Grader and see what he has to say.'

Moone's stomach tied itself up in knots. 'Really? I mean Grader won't just spill his guts, boss...'

'Maybe not, but what if we make him some kind of deal? Let him out on a visit or something?'

'Grader? I'm not sure we should...'

'Just promise him something, get what you can.'

'If I can get in to see him.'

'You will. I've got some sway at Dartmoor. I'll have you in there this afternoon. Go and get ready.'

Moone sighed, nodded, giving in to the rising tide of fate that was now pulling him down.

'Guess what?' Butler said, coming out of the incident room, her eyes jumping to McIntyre with confusion filling them. 'Who're you when you're at home?'

'This is DSU Fiona McIntyre,' Moone said. 'This is DI Mandy Butler. MacIntyre's in charge for a while.'

Butler smiled briefly, then lifted the grainy image of a parked ambulance in her hand. 'Anyway, I just found out that no official ambulance was parked anywhere near the second body dump.'

Their new boss took the image from her hand and started examining it. 'This doesn't look a modern ambulance to me. Looks quite old.'

Butler took it back. 'I know. I emailed the photo to someone at the hospital and they said it's definitely an old model, maybe ten years old.'

'Jesus,' Moone said, then stared at the photo himself. 'So, we've got to find the bastard who owns this ambulance and we could have our killer.'

'Maybe,' Butler said. 'Going to be hard to track it. Thing is, there is this strange old fella that collects old ambulances. He's got a big bit of land near Princetown, where he stashes them.'

McIntyre turned to Moone, her eyebrows raised. 'I've always been a great believer in synchronicity. Something's telling us that you two should go to Dartmoor Prison, talk to Grader, then talk to this ambulance collector.'

Crowne took the takeaway coffee that DS Rivers held out to him as he sat in the mobile command unit that was parked up from Mrs Armstrong's house. The SOCOs had been coming and going all night and into the morning, not allowing him and his team to get a good look at the scene. In a way he was glad, as he wasn't sure if his stomach and heart could take it. By all accounts, it looked like Wise had cut her throat, then hanged himself.

'So,' Rivers said, sitting down beside him and opening her coffee. 'Moone was wrong.'

'How's that?' Crowne sipped his coffee and grimaced. There wasn't any sugar in it. Rivers was always doing that, always leaving it out for the sake of his health.

'They reckon, even at this early stage, that they've both been dead around two hours, give or take. That doesn't give DS Carthew much of a window to stage a murder suicide, does it?'

'I don't know.'

'Plus, there's the printed note they left, signed by Wise.'

Crowne gave an empty laugh as he heard the tone in Rivers' voice, the ease in which she was beginning to believe the story they were being spoon fed. 'A printed note? Not handwritten?'

'It was signed by him.'

Crowne shook his head. 'All a bit neat, isn't

it?'

'Boss, sometimes these things look the way they are. We thought she did it, but it looks like maybe they did. They couldn't take the fact we were onto them, or the guilt got to them...'

'She is very clever...'

'Who? Carthew? Come on, she was in police custody. Even if you really believe she somehow pulled this off, is anyone going to take you seriously?'

Crowne lowered his head, the sickness rising in him, knowing Rivers was right. He could already hear DSU Tucker telling him to neatly tie it all up and pass it on to the coroner. He looked at Rivers. 'She did it. She won, didn't she? She was that bit cleverer. Maybe it was my fault, putting the pressure on them. She probably got worried that one of them might crack...'

Rivers put a hand on his arm, engaged his eyes. 'They planned it, boss. One of them, probably Mrs Armstrong, went to his hotel room...'

He pulled his arm away. 'You met her, right? Mrs Armstrong? Did she seem like the sort of person...'

'People surprise us all the time, you know that.'

Crowne stood up, put down his coffee and faced the door. 'I've got to tell Moone.'

He turned and faced Rivers, shaking his

head. 'I've got to tell that poor bastard that his worst nightmare might actually happen, that she might actually get to be his boss one day.'

Rivers shrugged, making a face that said it all, said that she thought he was losing it.

'What's the point?' Crowne turned and stormed out of the mobile command unit.

He turned on the hose, then started walking across the gated yard, feeling the water expanding the pipe, the pressure building. He pointed the spray gun at the back of the ambulance and started washing it down. He washed the outside first, then fetched a bottle of bleach and mixed it in with a bucket of water. He climbed into the back and started scrubbing down the walls and the floor. As the stench of the bleach started to burn at his nostrils, he stopped and looked round the small space. They came to his vision, the young women, their eyes wide and with terror. The mumbled cries, the pleading to be released muffled by the gag around their ugly faces. He swelled with the beauty of it all, especially the moment when he would deliver them to the perfect spot he had carefully picked out. Then he would release them and watch them flutter away.

He smiled to himself and kept on scrubbing. In half an hour, the old ambulance gleamed at him and he stood, arms folded, looking it over with pride. It was ready for tonight's little outing.

Then his mind turned to the one that had got away; Bobbi-Jane was her name and he wondered about her, a kind of admiration for her rising in him. Of course, there was a great deal of annoyance that she hadn't been delivered to him and he hadn't had the chance to create something beautiful out of her hollow ugliness. Some might call her pretty, beautiful even, but it was an attractiveness born of an age of great ugliness. Life had become polluted by a cultural poison. Only nature could fight back and survive, and long after humans had been wiped off the earth, the plants, trees, and all the tiny creatures would be left to be truly beautiful again. What he was doing was giving them a chance to be beautiful now.

Where was Bobbi-Jane now? High on drugs, he decided, maybe even dead in a gutter or some derelict house that drug users inhabit. He hoped she was dead, prayed for it, even though he doubted the police would believe her story that some man had tried to abduct her and put her in the back of an ambulance. In a way she had given birth to all of this, he told himself. He remembered the butterfly she'd already had tattooed on her back, a perfect creature, a piece of art he knew he had to try and recreate. Now she had escaped, and he hoped she was dead. In death she would be more beautiful.

No, he shook his head, telling himself not to think of her as he carefully reeled in the hose, then swept the remains of the water towards the drain. He lifted his head, sniffing the air, trying to rise above the odour of bleach and to smell all the pretty flowers of his garden. He turned and walked towards his allotment, delicately running his hand over the roses and then the sunflowers that were now starting to die. It was all part of the cycle of life. Autumn was almost here and soon winter would sweep in bringing an icy death. Sadness swept over him, knowing that he would have to forgo his mission until the spring brought its new life.

He didn't have long. He would have to take the ambulance out tonight and catch another. He walked through the yard, round the back of the house and through the back door. He went down the stone steps and arrived in the basement. He pressed the light switch and it flickered above him, making him blink. The light came on, and he could see the cells across the stone floor, beyond the barber's chair. The house was so empty now, so quiet. He missed the exquisite sight of them staring at him through the grey darkness, the lack of understanding in their eyes. He would feed them, keep them warm, right up until it was time for their metamorphosis and then their release. It was in that glorious moment, when they were transformed into a beautiful butterfly, that he witnessed the change in their eyes. The beauty would burst out, rising up from the black of their eyes. In that final moment he knew he would see gratitude, for making their pathetic lives mean something.

He looked up when he heard the sound of a car. He hurried towards the light switch, turned it off, shut and locked the door and went back up into the day.

Butler pulled on the handbrake, then turned to look at Moone, who was staring up at the huge stone archway of the prison entrance. Beyond it were the large doors that would allow him to enter and be delivered to his interview with the devil himself.

'Remember,' she said. 'Do not touch or approach the glass. You don't pass him anything but soft paper.'

Moone turned to her, giving her a sarcastic smile. 'Funny. I didn't know you knew the whole script.'

'I don't.' She huffed and faced the windscreen. 'I just Googled it, and memorised it for this joke.'

'I'm so glad. I really don't want to do this.'

She nodded. 'I know. Just don't let him in your head. He'll want to dig around in there, but thankfully there's not much treasure to find.'

'Thanks a lot.'

Butler sighed, then reached across him and pushed open the passenger door. 'Go on, bugger off and find out what the sick bastard knows. Doubt you'll get much, but best to try, I suppose.'

He took a deep breath, then climbed out. He shut the door, then leaned in the window as she lowered it. 'You're not going off to see this ambulance guy without me, are you?'

She huffed. 'No, I'm not. I don't see why not, but I won't.'

'Because he could be our psycho.'

'Doubtful. I'll make sure your car's here when you get out.'

'Hang on, I thought we were…'

'Right, go on, stop faffing, Moone.'

He saw her roll her eyes, start the engine and put it in reverse and head out of the car park and up the steep road back towards Princetown. When she was out of view, he took out the box of twenty cigarettes he'd bought when she hadn't been looking. He put one shakily between his lips and lit it, then stared up at the forbidding looking building. He could almost hear all the screaming and shouting that would echo inside the walls. The stench of sweat and fear would be thick in the air.

He took a long drag, then prepared himself for facing the evil child killer. He wanted to throw up, but he tucked it away, took a deep breath and threw away his cigarette. He headed towards the prison doors as his hands continued to tremble.

CHAPTER 17

Butler pulled up across the way from the weather-beaten old house that had a massive piece of land round it that backed onto the moors. The prison museum was just up the road, and other small houses were crowded around it. She climbed out and headed towards the gates of the house, wondering if the old man was there. Moone had told her not to go in without him, but she knew the old guy was just a little eccentric, and not dangerous. But of course, she wasn't going to take any chances, and had brought her Casco baton, tucked into her coat.

She thought about ringing the doorbell, but then she heard movement inside the yard, the scraping of boots on the ground. She pounded her fist on the large grey wooden gates, until a gravelly voice said, 'Who's banging on me gates?'

'Police,' Butler said, then took out her ID and held it up so the old man, or whoever was inside, could see.

'Police? Don't need no police, thank you very much.'

'Open up. I need to ask you a few questions.'

There was a pause, then the sound of a bolt being dragged across. The large gates screeched open, revealing a man, probably nearly seventy, with a thick wiry silver beard, dressed in an ill-fitting brown suit that looked moth bitten. His trousers, Butler couldn't help notice, seemed to have had a serious disagreement with his socks. Beyond the old man, she saw the horde of old and ancient ambulances. They filled every inch of the yard and spilled out into the field beyond.

She showed her ID again as she stepped in. 'What's your name?'

'George,' the man said. 'That's the name me old mum gave to me and I've stuck with it ever since. Although I've always preferred Albert.'

Butler gave an empty laugh. 'You've got a lot of ambulances, George.'

'Have I?' the old man laughed, shook his head, and took out a large ornate pipe. 'Could've fooled me.'

'What're you going to do with them?'

'Open an ambulance museum. When I get the money together.'

Butler nodded, looking round the yard.

Most of the vehicles looked to be covered in rust and ready to disintegrate, but she noticed a few newer looking ones. 'Are any of these drivable, George?'

'Daisy, Daisy, give me yer answer do,' the old man sang to himself as he lit his pipe.

'George? Did you hear me? Can you drive any of these?'

'Me? No. Don't have no licence, do I?'

'But are they roadworthy?'

'They may be. But is the road worthy of them, that's the question.' He laughed, sucking on his pipe.

Butler huffed and carried on her inspection, realising the old man was a few pebbles short of a beach. Then she remembered the photo of the ambulance she had in her pocket, so took it out and held it up to his face. 'Do you have an ambulance like this one?'

As he puffed away at his pipe, the old man said, 'Got a couple of that model. Not in very good nick, mind. After buying one, are you?'

'No, George. I'm trying to trace one. Do you know anyone else who might have an ambulance like this one?'

'Only person I know who might have one like that,' he said, then started sucking hungrily on his pipe.

'Yeah? Who?'

'Who what?'

Butler sighed, but tried to put a smile

on her face as she said, 'Who might have an ambulance like this one?'

'The fella I sold one to.'

'You sold one just like this?'

'Didn't I just say that?'

'Who to? Who did you sell it to?'

George puffed at his pipe, then relit it. 'Don't remember his name. Don't remember much about him really. Only that he wanted an ambulance.'

'Don't you have a record of the sale?' Butler lowered her arms in case she gave in to the desire to shake the answers from him.

'No, no need. Just paid cash for it, then drove it off.'

'That's it? When was this?'

'Oh, I don't know, bout two year ago. Give or take.'

Butler let out a giant huff and ran a hand over her face.

Moone was sent through a plain, lime-green corridor as the cries and echoes of the prison found his ears. He couldn't escape them, even in the visitor section that he was travelling through. He was searched and then sent into the empty room that had chairs and tables dotted around the place. He sat down near the door, still hearing the faint noises of the prison. He shuddered a little, watching the secure door opposite where he knew Loy Grader would eventually appear. He had been given fifteen minutes with the sick bastard, which was fifteen minutes too long for Moone. His heart began to hammer in his chest, his stomach threatening to rise up and empty itself on the desk.

Then there was a buzz from the glass door and it clicked open. A guard came out, a thick set, shaven headed guard who looked as if he might have once been in the army. He turned and helped the squat figure behind him come into the room.

Moone looked away for a moment as he saw Grader, the same dead eyes, the receding hair slicked back, and the hooked nose. When he looked back, he saw Grader coming towards him slowly, a smile on his lips.

'Behave yourself, Grader,' the guard said, nodded to Moone, then retreated to a table near the door.

Grader looked down at Moone for a moment, smiling, then used his cuffed hands to pull out a chair and sit down.

'Well, well, DI Peter Moone,' he said, his voice rising, the sound of it hitting Moone in his stomach. 'I didn't ever see you here. Miss me, did you?'

'It's not a social visit.' Moone sat forward. 'I need to ask you some questions.'

Grader shook his head. 'That's not the way it works. You know that. I want a little chat first. I want us to catch up, like old times.'

'Old times? Like when you murdered your guard, John? Remember him?'

Grader sighed. 'I do indeed. I'm still being punished for that one. I nearly got away, too, but you and your bitch of a partner suckered me. I'd like to see her again sometime. Is she not with you?'

'No. Let's get on.'

'How's the family?'

Moone didn't look up, didn't dare. 'Have you heard of James Dyer?'

'Have you had any more children since last I saw you?'

Moone sighed. 'James Dyer.'

'Answer my question first. Time's running out, Peter Moone.'

Moone sat back. 'No. No, I haven't. I'm not married any more.'

'I know. I just thought maybe you'd squirted your seed into some other poor sad bitch. Like your partner. Or some other dirty slag.'

Moone laughed, despite the sickness and the anger welling in him. 'Try again. Let's talk about Spain.'

'Spain. Oh, for the sunny beaches of Spain. It's been so long since I've been there. Happy days.'

'How long exactly?'

'You ever been to Spain, Peter? With the

family, I mean?'

'When were you last there?'

'Did your wife ever go topless? Her pale breasts displayed for the men on the beach. I think they like to titillate, don't they? Especially the young, prepubescent males.'

Moone stared at him, trying to think of pleasant things, like the cigarette he was going to enjoy after he left the prison.

'What about your daughter?' Grader leaned in closer. 'Alice, isn't it?'

'How the fuck do you know that?' Moone's hands trembled, the sickness poisoning every inch of him.

'It's easy really. You ask around. Does she like to go topless? Does she like to show off her small…'

'Shut the fuck up, Grader. Just answer my question.'

'Spain? Oh, years maybe. Ten years. I can't remember.'

'James Dyer went missing nearly five years ago.'

Grader smiled. 'I know. Such a shame. Just like Danny Sawyer. But you gave him some peace, didn't you? Now his family can get some well-deserved rest from all the mental torment. Well done.'

'Were you in Spain when he went missing?'

'Was I?' Grader put a finger to his lip, then

looked up at the ceiling. 'I might've been. It's possible. Have you checked to see if there's any record of me?'

'I have. There isn't.'

'Then I can't have, can I?' He smiled, showing his yellow teeth.

'There's quite a few eyewitnesses that say they saw you in the area.'

'Perhaps I was, then. In fact, yes, I definitely was there when he was taken. I remember reading it in the Spanish news at the time.'

Moone felt invisible hands tying his gut in knots. 'You're admitting you were there? When Dyer was abducted?'

Grader smiled, folded his arms. 'I am. What I'm not admitting to was taking him.'

'No, I didn't expect you would. Next question is, have you ever met Tom Dyer? Ever had a drink with him?'

Grader raised his eyebrows. 'Well, oh well, look who's going for the jugular. I'll have to say no to that and that's all I'll say about Tom Dyer.'

But Grader gave a wink.

Moone nodded. 'OK. So, tell me, if you were there, how did you get into Spain? There's no record of you leaving the UK or entering Spain.'

Grader smiled even more, a smile that made Moone want to vomit. The child killer leaned forward. 'Tell me about Alice.'

'Fuck off.'

'I bet she's pretty. I expect your ex-wife is very pretty. Do you still think about her, Peter? Do you think about her and knock one out? Yes, I bet you do.'

Moone clenched his fists under the desk. 'How did you get into Spain?'

'Has she got small breasts? Your daughter, I mean, not your wife. I imagine after all those kids sucking away at them, your wife's are probably quite saggy.'

Moone shook his head, forcing a smile to his lips, imagining the cigarette he was going to enjoy in a few minutes. 'You can't get to me like that.'

Another sickening smile. 'That's no fun. OK, so, how did I get into Spain without anyone knowing I was there officially?'

Moone shrugged.

'Oh, Peter. You are thick. Because I was allowed to enter the country… unofficially.'

'Bollocks.'

Grader opened his hands. 'Very well, choose not to believe me. It doesn't matter to me. We've got a few minutes to go. What shall we talk about, your other kids?'

'Who arranged it, then? Let's pretend I believe you.'

'People high up, who wanted me there.'

'Yeah, right.'

Grader leaned in, lowering his voice.

'Aren't you the police officer who smashed a paedophile ring not so long ago? Didn't you find an MP and a councillor involved in that?'

Moone stared at him, the sickness returning, now forming a wave that threatened to drown him. 'Who then?'

Grader shrugged. 'That I don't know.'

'What happened to Dyer? Where is he?'

Grader laughed. 'Oh, come on, that's the thought that keeps me cozy at night. We've got to have some secrets. Anyway, the fact that you're here must mean you've talked to someone involved in the case. Am I right?'

Moone didn't say anything.

Grader nodded. 'Yes, maybe one of those crazy ex-coppers or even Tom Dyer? Now, Tom Dyer. He's a one.'

'What do you mean?'

Grader winked. 'He's just, special. Look into him.'

'I will.'

Grader nodded. 'But this isn't your case, is it? It's the Spanish police's case. Or maybe even the Met's, but not someone like you, Peter.'

'I'm doing someone a favour.'

'A favour? Interesting. Or maybe Dyer's mother? I heard she's in this neck of the woods. Oh, Peter, you're not dipping your wick in her, are you?'

'No.'

Grader laughed. 'Come on, then, tell me

who you're doing this favour for.'

'I can't.'

'Then I'm definitely thinking it's Mrs Dyer. She is a beauty, I'll give you that. A bit of a dark horse, that one.'

'Far too old for you, I would've thought.'

Grader smiled. 'Oh, you're getting cheeky now. I like it. But, yes, you're right. By the way, she's the one you need to go and see.'

'Why?'

'Because she's a woman. Women know things, deep inside.'

'You think she might know something about her son's disappearance?'

'I think she might have suspects, don't you?'

'Like you? What if she points the finger right at you?'

'She wouldn't do that.'

'Why not? Maybe she saw you that night. She might not have known who you were.'

'Everyone knows who I am.' Grader smiled. 'But Mrs Dyer hasn't had the pleasure.'

'The pleasure? You mean the pleasure of meeting a man who probably destroyed her life?'

The child killer laughed. 'You're trying to put words in my mouth. Just go and see her, Moone. I think you might learn a lot.'

'Just tell me how you really got into Spain.'

Grader stood up. 'I believe time is nearly

up.'

'Come on, Grader. Tell me and I'll see if I can find a way to make things a bit more cushy for you in here.'

Grader shook his head. 'Please don't beg, Moone. Come on, don't do yourself down, Peter. You're clever, you just don't realise how clever. You think you stumble through life, but it's more than that. You can do it. I'm rooting for you. Anyway, keep me posted. Maybe send me some nice photos of your daughter?'

Moone stuck up his middle finger.

'Worth a try. Bye, bye.' Grader turned and headed towards his prison guard. The security door was opened for him, then he went on through, disappearing back towards his safe wing in the prison. If he was allowed into the main section of the prison, with the ordinary criminals, then Moone knew he'd be ripped to pieces in seconds. He wondered if that might be justice for a moment, then ignored the anger that rose in him as he turned to the door behind him and went through it.

He would have to visit the ex-Mrs Dyer. Chances were Grader was yanking his chain, but he had planned to ask her about the butterfly on her shoulder anyway, so there would be no harm in asking her a few questions. No harm at all, he told himself, even though his gut bit down on itself.

He carried on out of the prison once he

had been back through security and had signed out. He shakily took out a cigarette and put it between his lips, then lit it. He took a deep drag and almost coughed. It didn't taste the way he had hoped it would. It was as if everything had been tainted by Grader and his layer of scum that got on everything. Moone took out his phone, thinking about getting in touch with Mrs Dyer, or Lisa Brunning as she was now known.

He almost dropped his phone as it started ringing. It was Crowne calling, a fact that made him want to run for the hills.

'Moone,' he said, taking another drag.

'Are you smoking, Moone?' Crowne asked.

'No, of course not.'

'Are you sitting down?'

Moone looked around for somewhere to sit, then opted for his car when he spotted it now parked close by and leaned on it. 'Go on.'

'They're dead.'

'Who?'

'Wise and Mrs Armstrong. Murder suicide. There's even a note admitting guilt.'

Moone let out a laugh that was echoed back to him on the phone line, allowing him to hear how absurd and crazy it sounded. 'Yep. Of course there is.'

'It looks like Wise cut her throat then he hanged himself.'

'*Looks like.*' Moone nodded, his heart

hammering, knowing Carthew would be back soon, racing up the ranks again. 'She's done it. She's tidied up after herself.'

'How?'

'What do you mean?'

'I mean, how did she do it? She was in police custody for most of the timeline, give or take.'

'She's clever, I told you.'

'She's more than a genius. She must've had help. She can't be in two places at the same time. How would she manage to hang someone who didn't want to be hanged?'

Moone nodded, realising the futility of the situation, and hearing the despondency in Crowne's voice. 'She always finds a way. So, what's our next move?'

Crowne gave a tired, empty laugh. 'There isn't one Moone. I've been told to drop it on pain of death. They prefer the notion of the wife and her lover killing the husband and then doing themselves in. They can live with that...'

'She's going to be in charge one day...'

'I know that. I really appreciate that, but what can I do? Please, tell me what I can do to prove she did it?'

Moone let out a sigh, a deep tired sigh. 'There isn't anything. She won't have left us a scrap. If someone else was involved, then they are probably dead. Maybe one of the lovers did help, I don't know. Now we'll never know.'

'What I don't understand, is why was she even there?'

'What do you mean?'

'Well, if she's so clever, then why put herself in the middle of the action? She didn't have a proper alibi.'

'Because she wanted to prove how clever she is to me or anyone paying attention.'

'I guess. Misdirection, I suppose.'

'Yep. Well, thanks for your help, Crowne.'

'Vince.'

'Vince. Thanks, anyway. I've got to go.'

Moone ended the call, then stood for a moment, looking around, feeling a little lost, his eyes seeing the surrounding prison and the moors beyond. Then he saw her, the smug expression she wore the last time he'd faced her, and he realised that not too long from now Carthew would be back, with the very same look on her face. He rubbed his jaw, trying to rise above it all as he unlocked his car, climbed in and started the engine. He drove towards the main road, then stopped, checking the traffic was clear, which it was. He started back towards Princetown, trying to absorb all that Grader had said, pushing Carthew out of his thoughts. He would have to visit Lisa Brunning, find some kind of excuse to talk to her again. He saw the tattoo on her shoulder, thinking of the two dead girls yet to be identified with a similar piece of art on their bodies. The two cases somehow connected.

Moone looked in the rear-view mirror, having caught the sight of a car a few hundred yards behind. It was getting closer all the time, speeding towards him. If they wanted to overtake, that was fine by him, there was plenty of room. But then the car was even closer, gaining on him, their engine groaning as they got right behind Moone. He waved them on, but the car didn't overtake and just moved closer, practically nudging him onwards.

What the hell was going on? He was staring at the driver, noticing they looked pretty familiar as the car's lights started to flash. Moone sighed, the anger rippling across his chest as he flipped his indicator and started to slow down and pull over.

The car pulled in behind him, then the driver got out and stood by the car for a moment. Moone watched the spectacle wearing, slightly overweight, man in the rear-view mirror. Then the man was walking towards his car and that's when he realised who he was; former DCI Colin Smith was heading to the passenger side of Moone's vehicle, then pulled open the door and climbed in.

'Afternoon,' Smith said, nodding, then looking straight forward.

'What do you want?' Moone asked. 'I take

it you've been sent by your gang?'

Smith looked at him, seeming a little confused. 'My gang?'

'Redwood and that lot?'

Smith nodded. 'I see. No, they didn't send me. But I suspect that Grader admitted to being in Spain at the time of the abduction. Am I right?'

Moone turned to him. 'How did you know?'

'It's Grader. He loves to be in the thick of it. He'd admit to almost anything, as long as he got some attention.'

'So you think he's lying?'

'Oh, no, I'm certain he was there. Did you ask him about Tom Dyer?'

'Yes.'

'And he was a little cryptic but didn't quite deny he'd met him.'

'Were you listening?'

'No. But I'm not here about that.'

'What are you here about?'

Smith folded his arms and faced Moone. 'The dead girls in the woods.'

Moone shook his head. 'I can't discuss that.'

'Two dead young women. How did they die? Strangulation?'

'It's not your case. You're not even on the force any more, Colin.'

Smith nodded, still staring at Moone.

'Black. I don't think it'll be him. No, he's a sexual predator, but not a killer. Strangulation wouldn't be his MO if he was the killer.'

'And what would it be?'

'Black grew up on a farm. Then he worked in a slaughterhouse for a while. More than likely he'd use one of those stun guns, then slit their throats.'

Moone rolled his eyes. 'Are you sure he's not our killer? He worked in a slaughter house?'

'Yes, but he couldn't stomach it. Ended up being sent to Cambridge and the rest is history. Why did you suspect Black? No, don't tell me. Stomach contents?'

'I can't answer that, Colin.'

'Yes, food in her stomach. Something expensive, I'm guessing. One of Black's recipes? Interesting.'

'Why did you leave the force?'

'Health issues. Blood pressure, stress. My wife at the time bugged me until I took early retirement. Thing is, when she got to spend a lot more time with me, she found me disagreeable.'

Moone nodded. 'Sorry.'

'It's OK. Now I get time to write books and spend time putting my website together.'

'Well, I appreciate you trying to help.'

'But you want to solve this yourself? Prove to yourself that you've got what it takes?'

Moone shrugged. 'I don't know. I just want

to do the right thing.'

Smith looked out across the moors. 'I understand. But I can help, if you need me.'

'I appreciate that, Colin. I really do. I'll be in touch.'

'Do you promise?'

Moone thought he saw a look of desperation in the former copper's eyes, so he said, 'Scout's honour.'

Colin smiled, then climbed out and went back to his car and drove off, leaving Moone alone again. The sky was getting darker, the heavy clouds drawing in. He wanted to get off the moors before it started raining. He was about to start the engine, when his phone rang.

It was Pinder.

'DCI Moone, what is it?' Moone said.

'Thought you'd want to know, we've got two distraught parents here at the station. They say their daughter went missing a couple of weeks ago. By the looks of the photograph, she looks a lot like our victims.'

'I'm coming,' Moone said, and started the engine.

CHAPTER 18

Moone mentally prepared himself as he reached the family room, where Mr and Mrs Todd were waiting for him, probably hoping that he had good news, that their daughter wasn't one of their victims. He looked down at the photograph of the young woman looking at the camera, a drink in her hand, a female friend next to her, taken in some dark nightclub. She looked like their victims, had the right colour hair, right build, same age.

Then he thought about her name. Bobbi-Jane Todd, he'd been told their daughter was called. Daryl's mysterious friend. It would all be a glimmer of hope for their daughter, but not for Moone.

The door opened and a redheaded woman poked her face out, looking around the corridor. She was mid-thirties, dressed in a trouser suit. DC Casey Yates, he presumed, the family liaison officer hurriedly assigned to the case.

'DCI Moone?' she asked, her eyes jumping to him as she stepped out and closed the door behind her.

He nodded. 'Yes, that's me. How are they?'

Yates looked towards the room. 'As you'd expect. Shaken up. They've heard about the two dead girls, and their minds, well...'

Moone lifted the photograph. 'I don't think she's one of the victims.'

'No?'

'No. We've got a guy called Daryl, a troubled young man, who said he met a girl called Bobbi-Jane a few nights ago.'

Yates took the photograph, examining it. 'That's good, then. For them.'

'Yes, in a way. But our killer, he likes to tattoo his victims. That means, he takes them, keeps them alive, tattoos them, then...'

Yates nodded. 'So, he could still have her.'

Moone nodded towards the door. 'Let's go and see what they say.'

Moone knocked then went in, his eyes jumping to the slender, tired-looking woman on the blue sofa, next to the thickset, balding man. They were sat close, but weren't touching. Mrs Todd had tears in her eyes, a tissue balled in her hand.

'I'm DCI Peter Moone,' he said, sitting down on the sofa opposite them as Yates joined him. 'Thank you for coming in.'

Moone put the photograph on the coffee

table positioned between the sofas. 'And thanks for this.'

The mum looked at the photo for a moment, then picked it up, and stared at it for a while before looking up at Moone with obvious questions in her eyes.

'I'm pretty sure she's not one of our victims,' he said, and saw a physical change in them, their bodies loosening a little, the colour reappearing in their faces.

'That's great,' the dad said, but the mum turned and stared at him, annoyance in her eyes.

'She's still missing, John!' she hissed.

'I know!' The dad looked at Moone. 'Are you looking for Bobbi?'

'Yes, yes we are.' Moone sat forward. 'Thing is, we have a couple of witnesses that saw her on Milehouse Road a few nights ago. At least they met a young woman going by the name Bobbi-Jane...'

'Milehouse Road?' the mum said, looking at the photo. 'Why would she be there?'

'She was in a building there, a place set up for troubled young people.'

'What?' the dad said. 'What do you mean? What would she be doing there?'

'She went there with one of the residents,' Moone said.

'One of the residents? Who the fuck...'

'John, shut up for once,' the mum

snapped. Then she looked at Moone, her eyes widening. 'So, she was staying there with someone? Do they know where she went?'

'No.' Moone sighed as the worry returned to the mum's face.

'Has Bobbi-Jane ever left home before?' DC Yates asked, and Moone noticed the mum shoot an accusing look at the dad.

'No, not until this time,' the mum said, looking down at her hands.

'Was there trouble at home?' Yates asked.

'We had a falling out,' the dad said, his voice quiet.

The mum huffed, shook her head. 'He had a row with her, wouldn't let her go out the way she was dressed...'

'Well, you saw what she was bleeding wearing, Stace. Jesus, I've never seen a bleeding skirt so short.'

'Oh, come on, John. It wasn't that short. Anyway you didn't need to shout at her!'

'Please,' Moone said, raising his palms. 'I just need you to answer some questions so we might be able to find Bobbi-Jane. I know you both must be going out of your minds.'

Both parents looked awkward. Moone sat back, feeling their collective pain, imagining it was Alice who had been taken. His stomach lurched, remembering how he felt when *it had* been her.

'We've been in touch with her friends,'

the mum said, wiping a tear from her eye as she looked up at Moone. 'None of them know anything.'

'I wouldn't trust 'em,' the dad said. 'If you lot go and talk to them, they might sing a different tune.'

Moone nodded. 'We will, don't worry. Chances are, seeing as Bobbi-Jane hasn't done this before, then she'll just turn up soon. She will be a priority. If you can tell everything you know to Detective Constable Yates, as she's your family liaison officer.' Moone stood up, shook the parents' hands and went to leave the room. Then a thought occurred to him, all the aspects of the investigation pouring through his brain. He recalled the girl who Daryl described, tattoos and all. He looked at the parents again as he said, 'Does Bobbi-Jane have any tattoos?'

It was the dad who huffed, then shook his head as he said, 'Does she ever? Two of the bloody things. A bloody tattoo right on her back, and this awful one right over her backside. Bloody thing, makes her look like a tart or something...'

'John!' the mum snapped again, then stared up at Moone. 'Is that important? What does it mean?'

'Maybe nothing. Can you tell me what the tattoo is on her back?' Moone kept the sudden overwhelming feeling of enthusiasm from his face; he was getting somewhere, close to a breakthrough, he sensed it.

'It's a butterfly,' the mum said, looking worried while the dad stood up, staring at Moone.

'Come on, why're you asking that?' the father demanded to know.

'Just eliminating her from another inquiry,' he said, the lie filling up his throat. 'But it might help if you can find out where she had it done.'

'Her friend, Jenny, would know,' the mum said.

'Good, give her details to DC Yates. Try not to worry. I'm sure she'll turn up soon.'

Moone got out of the room as quick as he could and backed up against the wall, his mind spiralling. A missing girl with a butterfly tattoo on her back. His head spun, trying to work it all out. He pulled himself together and headed to the incident room, only to find Butler stood at the centre of it, arms folded, staring at the door with a face like a slapped arse, as the locals liked to say.

'Oh, shit,' he said, remembering about the collection of ambulances. 'Sorry, I got this phone call…'

She huffed. 'So, after all that don't go in there without me bollocks, you still left me to go in alone. Lovely.'

'But you had my car delivered to the

prison, so you must...'

'Just forget it, Moone.'

He watched her storm past and head to her desk where she started searching through her paperwork, slapping everything down that she moved. He stared at her, wondering how long it would be before she could be approached without him getting bitten.

'What?' She stood up, looking at him, her face red, eyebrows raised. 'Are you going to stare at me all day?'

'Sorry. Just thought you'd want to know that the two suspects in Crowne's case are dead.'

Her expression changed, softening a little. 'Dead? How?'

'Murder suicide, it looks like...'

Butler looked down, shaking her head. 'Don't tell me. Wise kills the ex-wife, then himself? She's a sly one.'

Moone nodded. 'Yep. That's the way it's going to look on the paperwork too, the way she wants it to look. All neat and tidy.'

'Which means she's heading back here.' Butler slumped into her chair. 'To one day be in charge of us. Bloody lovely. Well, I'm not going to stick around for that.'

Moone stepped closer. 'You're joking, aren't you? You can't leave us to deal with her all alone.'

Butler looked up, her face straight. 'Can't

I? I can't stick around and have that... woman in charge of us, can I?'

The door of the incident room opened and DSU McIntyre came in. She stopped, and looked questionably between Butler and Moone as she said, 'Everything OK?'

'Yes, boss,' Moone said.

'How did it go with Loy Grader?' McIntyre asked, coming closer.

'He was his usual creepy self,' Moone said, still half watching Butler as she started typing on her keyboard. 'But he admitted he was in Spain when James Dyer went missing.'

'He admitted it?' McIntyre said, her eyes widening. 'So, he took Dyer?'

'He wouldn't admit that, obviously. But I suspect he did. Thing is, there's no record of him being in Spain, only a couple of witnesses who say they saw him. Question is, how did he get into Spain without it being registered?'

'Fake passport,' Butler said, not even looking up from her screen.

'That's not what Grader says,' Moone said. 'He's saying someone official arranged for him to be there. But he's probably yanking my chain.'

'He has to be,' McIntyre said. 'Is there anything else?'

'He pointed the finger at Dyer's dad, Tom Dyer. Said he's up to no good, and I should check him out.'

McIntyre nodded. 'OK, sounds interesting.'

'And that I should talk to the former Mrs Dyer, Lisa Brunning. She lives near here.'

'Thing is,' Butler said, turning round in her chair. 'This isn't our case. This is just Mario Black trying to keep us busy while he goes off and grabs another poor girl. We can't waste time on this.'

McIntyre nodded, looking at Butler. 'She's got a point. We are letting ourselves get distracted. Maybe that's what Black wants. Have we got anything else to go on with our tattooed girls?'

'Only the ambulance,' Butler said. 'I talked the old guy who's got the collection in Princetown. He's harmless enough. He said though, that he sold one a couple of years ago. No evidence of the sale, cash in hand. He hasn't even got CCTV either.'

'So it's a dead end?' Moone asked. 'Well, I've just talked to the parents of a missing girl who looks very similar to the two dead girls we found. Her name is Bobbi-Jane and she has a tattoo of a butterfly on her back, or so the parents tell me.'

'Just like our dead girls?' McIntyre said, her face brightening. 'Where did she get it done?'

'I'm waiting to find out, they're trying to get hold of the missing girl's friend who was there when she got it done.'

'That's got to be the breakthrough,' McIntyre said, sounding excited. 'Perhaps whoever designed the tattoo became obsessed with her, or the whole idea of it all and now they're trying to recreate that moment...'

'It might be,' Moone said, then had a thought, his mind rewinding to the beginning of the case. 'There's a woman who lives opposite Ryland House. She told us she heard a lot of noise the night Bobbi-Jane went missing. What if what she heard was Bobbi being abducted? I think we should send a uniform to check if she saw an ambulance that night.'

'Good, do that,' McIntyre said, looking excited, but Moone glanced at Butler and was disappointed to see that she was still looking pretty pissed off as she typed something on her computer.

'We'll go and visit the tattooist as soon as we find out where it is,' Moone added.

'Good.' McIntyre headed to the door with a smile. 'Let me know as soon as you find out anything.'

As soon as Bobbi-Jane's eyes opened, her head swimming a little, she saw the same stained ceiling, the same dark patch of mould in the far corner. There was a deep musky smell too, the hideous smell of damp that greeted her every time she woke up. It was a house that had seen better days. She could hear the sound of traffic not far away and guessed she was close to town or Mutley. She moved her right hand and heard the chink of the handcuffs and the chain that kept her captive, secured to the radiator. She had tried to pull her hand free several times, but all she had to show for it was cuts and bruising on her wrists. It was cold in the room, a breeze always coming from the old, battered window behind her. Covering most of the wooden frame, that had paint peeling off it, was a blackout blind. Behind the blind was a sheet of wood, nailed to the frame. She didn't know what time of day it was. The only light in the room was from the three light bulbs in the cobweb covered chandelier high above her head.

    She looked down over the edge of the bed, where she had left the empty plate and the bottle of water. They were gone. He had put something in the food or the water to make her sleep, as he always did.

    She heard a creak somewhere in the house. The front door had closed, then footsteps travelled through the house. He was back. She followed the sound of his steps, hearing them going upstairs, across the landing. Doors opened and closed, then more creaking steps. Then they were getting louder, coming down towards her. She sat up, staring at the door, waiting. There was a pause after his footsteps stopped outside the door, as there always was and she wondered once more what he did in those moments. Then the locks started coming undone, the bolts drawn across noisily. The door creaked open painfully slowly, then his masked face appeared through the gap. All she could see was his dark eyes through the plain white mask. He wore a beanie hat too, pulled down over his ears. She took comfort in the mask; if he was planning to kill her, why would he wear a mask?

He stepped into the room and headed to the radiator, checking the chain. He nodded, then looked at her as he lifted a Burger King takeaway bag. The smell came with him then, flooding her face, making her feel instantly sick. It was a strange smell, something she couldn't identify, except she feared it was something to do with death. Yes, she shivered, it was a deathly smell. She didn't say anything, and kept her face free of emotion as he took out a cheeseburger, fries and a milkshake, and put them all before her on the bed. She wasn't scared of him; she had stopped being scared of him days before. There never seemed to be any malice in him, no hint of a depraved mind waiting to burst out. But he was troubled in some way, she could tell that, a constant battle going on behind his eyes; he was trying to decide what to do with her, which meant he had n io real plan. That was the element that scared her the most about it all, the fact that he didn't have a plan. What decision was he having to face?

Why was she even there if he didn't have a plan for her?

'Eat up,' he said, then pulled over the old battered wooden chair from the corner and sat down. He crossed his legs, watching her, a smile in his eyes.

'You're going to watch me eat?' she asked, looking down at the food. She was hungry, there was no denying that, but she wondered what he had slipped into the food this time.

'No, I just want to make sure you eat something.'

She poked the top of the slightly warm burger. 'What's in it?'

'You want me to list every ingredient? Do you know there used to be a song about what was in one of these burgers? They used it in the advert...'

'I mean, what did you put in it?'

'Actually, it wasn't Burger King. It was the other company. Maccy D's, they call them, don't they?'

'I asked what's in it. What have you put in it to drug me?'

He uncrossed his legs, then sat forward. 'Nothing, I promise.'

She huffed. 'Yeah, like I'm going to believe you.'

'I mean it.'

'You put something in my dinner! Don't lie and say you didn't.'

He nodded. 'It's true. I did. I'm sorry, but I wanted to make sure you slept.'

'Why?' She took out one of the fries and started to chew it.ea

'Sleep matters. People really don't appreciate the importance of it. People say, "I'll sleep when I'm dead", don't they? But how can you appreciate it then? You can't. Why spend your living days so tired?'

'What do you do when I'm asleep? Take photos or video for your own fucked up amusement?' She put another chip in her mouth, staring at him.

'No, I don't. I honestly don't. You're safe here. I don't want you under the impression I'm some kind of pervert. You really are safe here. I promise.'

She gave a laugh, shaking her head, a burst of anger and spite racing up into her chest. 'Then fucking let me go. I'll be safer if you just let me go. Please. My family will be looking for me!'

He seemed to stare back at her for a moment, watching, maybe wondering if he could trust her or not. 'I'm sorry, but I can't do that. I wish I could.'

She almost let out the tears, but managed to hold them in, to swallow down the sob.

She pushed the food aside, then stared at him again, thinking it all through. 'Why did you kidnap me? Just to bring me to this shithole? To keep me locked up? I don't fucking get it.'

He sighed, then looked down at his gloved hands. 'I know. I know there's so much you don't understand. I saved you. If you want to understand something and take comfort in it, then understand that. I saved you. I risked so much to save you.'

She listened to his words that made no sense, thinking that maybe he was some kind of God botherer, a nutcase who'd seen her on a night out, maybe kissing a lad. He didn't like the way she acted, and so he *saved* her. *What did it mean? How would it end?*

'Can I see it?' he asked suddenly, his voice low, almost a whisper.

'See what?!' she moved back, her stomach knotting, the repulsion making her tremble.

'No, it's nothing sexual.' He pointed towards her shoulder. 'On your back.'

She turned her head, looking down at her shoulder, trying to see what he meant. 'What?'

'Your tattoo.'

She moved away again, pushing herself up the bed, getting closer to the cold wall. 'Why? What the fuck do you want to see my tattoo for?'

'I just want to see it. Please.'

'Will you let me go?'

His eyes lifted from her shoulder and looked deep into her. There was a pause, then he nodded slowly. 'Yes, I'll let you go.'

'Now? Right now?'

'I can't right now. You won't be safe. But I will let you go. One day, not long from now, I'll let you go.'

'You swear?' She moved closer to him, her voice trembling, her heart beginning to thud in her chest. 'Do you swear on your life, on all the people you care about?'

He nodded. 'I swear. On every person I care about. On my mother's life. I will let you go.'

She stared at him, a flicker of hope appearing somewhere on a very dark horizon. He could be lying, she thought. Could be. But somehow she believed him, something in his words made him sound genuine. It was a ridiculous notion, but she took what comfort she could in his promise.

'Can I see it now?' he asked, his voice so soft.

She felt a little sick, but she turned round as she took hold of her top and lifted it. She flinched as she felt his gloved hands helping lift her top further up until it was all bunched up around her neck. She shivered from the cold and from his touch. His hands stayed on her, and when she turned her head, she could see the blurry shape of his face as he stared at her back.

'It's beautiful,' he said, lifting his hands and stepping backwards. 'It's a work of art.'

She turned and lowered her top. 'I'm cold. It's freezing in here.'

He nodded. 'I'm sorry. I've got an electric heater. I'll bring it in.'

He kept staring towards her back, transfixed, so she asked, 'What is it about my tattoo? It's just a tattoo of a butterfly. No big deal.'

He nodded. 'I know. It may seem a minor thing to you, something you decided to have done in a moment of weakness or on a whim… but it's much more than that.'

'Is it?' She shook her head, getting a little freaked out by his obsession. 'So, when do I get to go?'

He looked away as he headed to the door. 'I'll get that heater now.'

'I asked when you're going to let me go.'

He stopped, his hand on the door handle. 'Soon. Not long from now. I will you take you from this house, out somewhere far from here. Then, when the time is right… I'll release you.'

CHAPTER 19

It took only two hours for the parents of Bobbi-Jane to get hold of her friend and find out where she got her tattoo done. They also emailed a photo the friend had taken of Bobbi's back not long after she had the tattoo done. A uniform had also visited the nosey neighbour who lived opposite Ryland House. The uniform reported back that the neighbour had indeed looked out of her window late that night when she heard a woman cry out, and had seen an ambulance drive away. As soon as they received all the information, Moone and Butler raced over towards Union Street, a long road in the city centre lined with clubs, pubs, tattoo parlours and a few supermarkets. It was a part of Plymouth that had been in a state of disrepair for many years, Butler told Moone as she drove them over there. Many times there had been plans to redevelop and build plush new flats, and even at one time add a canal, but nothing ever came of it. They parked opposite a rundown building covered in bill posters that Moone could imagine standing bright and impressive a long time ago.

'That's an old theatre,' Butler said as they climbed out. 'Was a club when I was in my twenties. In fact, this whole strip used to be clubs. JFK's, Jesters, Boulevards, Millennium. I could tell you a few horror stories.'

Moone laughed, happy to hear her sounding a bit cheerier as they headed up the street, farther away from the city centre. 'I can't imagine you going to clubs.'

She stared at him, narrowing her steely eyes. 'That's because you didn't see me all dolled up, wearing a belt for a skirt. I did have a social life once.'

'I'm sure you did.'

Butler pointed across the street. 'Copped off with Gareth Meadow over there. I used to think he was so fit. Saw him a while ago and he's bald and he had this massive beer belly. I pretended I didn't see him.'

'You pretended you didn't see him?' Moone stared at her.

She shrugged. 'I know, but I didn't know what to do. It was a bit awkward. I just hid. I'm not proud of myself, Moone. Look, the shop's just up there.'

Moone followed her as they headed past a large weather-beaten shop front that advertised used and cheap furniture, a small kebab house, then a gentlemen's club. He stopped outside the club, hearing music somewhere among the seedy darkness, beyond the blacked-out windows. He tried to imagine what weird stuff could be going on within, and found himself a little creeped out.

'Don't get any ideas,' Butler said and pulled him away. 'You don't know where they've been.'

'I wasn't thinking anything.' He followed Butler into the next, much narrower and darker shop. The outside had been painted black, with ornate and obviously hand painted designs covering the whole exterior. As they went into the grungy and dark entrance, Moone looked over the framed photos of various customers, most of who were absolutely covered in intricate tattoos.

'Come on,' Butler said, gesturing towards the back of the building where the sound of buzzing was coming. Moone found himself going through an archway into a brighter room that was narrow but stretched quite far back. Tattooist chairs lined the walls either side, but there seemed to be only two customers being worked on. Butler pointed to the middle-aged rocker-type tattooist, who wore thick round rimmed glasses as he concentrated on a young woman's leg that was being languished before him.

The rocker looked up from the leg, the

tattoo gun still buzzing in his hand. He gave a slight smile and nod as he said, 'Alright, Mand? Ain't seen you in a fair while.'

'Been busy, Doug,' she said. 'This is my partner, DCI Peter Moone.'

Doug sat up and turned off the machine. He smiled up at Moone, showing a set of crooked and discoloured teeth. 'Glad you added the rank, Mand, otherwise I'd think you meant sex partner.'

Butler huffed and brought out her phone and the photo of Bobbi-Jane's butterfly tattoo. 'Is this you? It looks like you.'

Doug readjusted his glasses, took the phone and seemed to examine it. 'Yeah, Mand, that's mine. I remember that. I was on a roll that day. You won't find another tattoo like that in Plymouth, in fact the whole world probably.'

'There is another,' Butler said. 'In fact, two others.'

'Fuck off,' Doug said. 'Not of that quality. Not like that design. That's a one off.'

'Didn't some uniforms come by here a few days ago?' Butler asked.

'Am I ever going to get this leg finished?' the young woman asked, stifling a yawn as she laid there.

'In a min.' Doug looked up at Butler as he folded his arms. 'Yeah, we had uniforms come here. Least that's what Rick said.'

'Did they ask about these tattoos?' Moone

asked and brought up the crime scene photos of the dead girls' backs.

Doug leaned forward and Moone watched his eyes widening at the sight of them. 'Fuck me. Who did these? They're fucking good. I mean, not in my class, but they are fucking intricate designs.'

'You mean, this is the first time you've seen these?' Butler asked and huffed. 'Bloody uniforms.'

'Yeah, first time I've seen them.' Doug looked closer. 'I've never seen anything like these.'

'So, you or your people didn't design these?' Moone said, feeling the hope dwindle away as he watched Doug shake his head. Then the tattooist was narrowing his eyes, tapping the image on Moone's phone.

'You know what,' Doug said as he looked up at them both. 'The more I look at them, the more there's something familiar about them.'

'So you have seen them before?' Butler said, folding her arms tightly over chest.

Doug sat back with a shrug. 'I feel like I have, but I just can't place 'em. It'll come to me sooner or later.'

'We'd prefer it if it was sooner, Doug.' Butler glared down at the old tattooist.

'Sorry, Mand, the old memory ain't what it was. I'll let you know if anything comes to me.'

Moone showed the missing girl's tattoo

again. 'So, you definitely did this tattoo?'

'Yeah, like I said.'

Moone nodded. 'Anything special about the design?'

Doug shrugged. 'Just something I came up with on the spot. The girl wanted a butterfly tattoo, said she wanted it to be unique. So I sat down and drew that and she loved it.'

Butler sighed, shook her head and looked at Moone. 'That's it. We're on to a loser. Let's go.'

Moone lifted his phone towards her face. 'This has to be something to do with it all. We've got two dead girls, both with butterfly tattoos and now this.'

Butler glared at him. 'I know. I know all that. But Doug did Bobbi's tattoo, he's not some deranged killer. Are you, Doug?'

Doug stared up at them both. 'No, not the last time I looked.'

'You don't own an ambulance, do you?' Butler asked him.

'An ambulance? No, why the hell would I own an ambulance? It's bad enough trying to park round my way as it is. Where would I park it to?'

'Forget it, Doug,' Butler said. 'But we will need you to confirm where you were on certain dates. Come to the station tomorrow.'

'Tomorrow?' Doug called out as Butler started pushing Moone towards the dark corridor and out towards the street. 'I have to bloody work, you know!'

Moone faced her as she came out after him, tutting to herself, and asked her, 'What do you make of it all?'

She looked up the street, seeming to stare off as she said, 'What do I make of it all? You know what I think.'

'Do I? I'm not sure I ever know what you're thinking.'

She looked at him, her face pinched. 'What's that supposed to mean?'

He shrugged. 'Nothing.'

'No, go on, spit it out.'

'I mean, this, the job, and with your dad.'

She took a deep huff, shaking her head as she looked away again. 'That's my business, isn't it? My dad being ill and everything, I mean. It's my business, no one else's.'

His mind rewound to what Parry's colleague had suggested that ill-fated day, the suggestion that had started to run noisily round his brain like a single marble since she had said it. The words, the many questions hovered on his tongue, partly wanting to ask the truth of the matter, but mostly terrified that if he did she might confirm it. He liked Butler, admired her for her brain, her stubbornness and even the way she punctuated every sentence with a huff, but he didn't feel anything more than that for her.

'You lost your tongue now, Moone?' She

raised her stern eyebrows.

He started to retreat into his mind again, dragging the words back to their dark cave. 'You definitely don't think your friend, Doug, had anything to do with this?'

She narrowed her eyes at him for a moment, a look on her face that suggested she wasn't happy about his change of tact, but then the storm seemed to pass over. 'No, not Doug. Look at him. When he's not in that chair working, he can hardly move. Got arthritis in his legs and back or something. No, it's not Doug, and it's not any of his employees. We've checked them out.'

'So, we're back to square one?' Moone sighed, wondering which way to go now.

'It's got to be Black.'

Moone looked at her. 'We've had a team keeping an eye on him. He's either been at his restaurant or this big grand design house he owns out in the sticks near Padstow.'

'See, that's what our killer needs, a nice big house in the middle of nowhere to do his dirty little deeds.'

Moone nodded. 'Yes, he does, but we can't search the place. We haven't got reasonable grounds.'

Butler huffed again and started walking towards their car, so Moone followed, hurrying to keep up. 'What's our next move, then?'

As Butler unlocked the car, she stared at

him. 'Why're you asking me? You're the boss, you come up with something. Didn't your mate, Grader give you any clues, or just the runaround?'

They both climbed in the car and sat there motionless, watching the passers-by and the traffic groaning past. Moone looked at her. 'He just gave me the creeps and tried to point the finger at Tom Dyer. I can't see him being involved in his own kid's abduction, can you?'

Butler looked at him like he had loudly passed wind. 'Oh, come on, how many times has a mum or dad or some other relative murdered their kid? Everyone's capable of it. This is a cruel world, or hadn't you noticed?'

'No, I've noticed all right.'

'But that case isn't our business, as I keep saying. It's a distraction. We need to find out where he picked up the girls. He drives an ambulance, probably even has a paramedic outfit. He probably seems harmless to the poor girls he approaches.'

Moone nodded. 'I agree. But we don't even know who the two dead girls are, do we? We've got two Jane Does.'

'That must be why he picks them up. He knows no one's going to miss them.'

Moone shook his head. 'Neither of them showed signs of drug abuse or malnutrition. So it doesn't seem likely they were living on the streets, does it?'

'No. But they were living somewhere.'

'So why hasn't anyone reported them missing?'

Butler looked at him suddenly. 'Have we been focusing on this locally? I mean, missing persons wise?'

'Yes, we have. What, you think he goes up the line or somewhere to abduct them?'

'Yeah, I do. We need to reach out nationally. We've been idiots. He's been fishing out of our waters, I reckon. What about London? A few missing girls in a place like that wouldn't stand out.'

'But we reached out as far as London and had no one matching their description going missing.'

Butler started the engine, then gave a strange sound in her throat and turned it off again. She faced Moone, a fire seeming to burn behind her eyes. 'That's because we've been looking at this all wrong.'

'Have we? How?'

'We've been looking for two slender missing girls with light brown or blonde hair, haven't we?'

'Yes, we have. That's because our victims match that description...'

'Maybe we should be looking for two missing dark-haired young ladies who used to be quite heavy.'

Moone stared at her, seeing her wide

eyes, her raised eyebrows, as she stared at him. The penny dropped and his mind tried to imagine the two dead girls a little bigger, more flesh on their bones, their hair darker. 'Jesus. He's transforming them, making them more beautiful in his eyes. He decides they're ugly somehow, so he takes them, starves them, changes their hair colour... bloody hell, you've got it. You're right, we've had this all wrong.'

It wasn't long before the sun started to go down, the shadows stretching out, elongating the buildings and the silhouettes of the late shoppers. He kept driving around the city centre, heading along Royal Parade, knowing that no one would pay him much attention. No one really took much notice of an ambulance, not unless it had the sirens and lights going. He turned the wheel, half watching the few cars behind him, and the bodies on the streets. He saw pretty young things hobbling along on high heels, all done up for a night out, in the hope of being groped by some young hungry lad. He shook his head, noticing that most of them were young enough to be someone's child and should have probably been tucked up in bed. It was disgusting. Even though they looked attractive on the outside, he knew that there was ugliness within. He knew the type very well, had approached similar creatures in bars and clubs, had offered to buy them drinks, only to find their eyes turn to him with a look of absolute disgust. They'd laugh, make fun as they hurried off.

No, it wasn't their type he was after; he kept his eyes trained on the streets for a very different kind of animal. As the sky grew even darker, and a little rain started to be blown along the grey streets, he knew he would have to be patient. The young people started heading towards the pubs, throwing caution to the wind, not seeming bothered by the fact that coronavirus had only taken a short break before re-emerging stronger in the winter in all probability. He paid it no mind though, and he was glad to see them scantily dressed, showing off their outer beauty and inner ugliness.

He caught sight of something as he was about to turn away from Union Street. He turned the wheel back again, annoying a car that was far too close to his rear end. He received a shout and toot for his trouble, but he still turned the ambulance towards the strip of clubs and rundown pubs. There was a steady stream of young people and some older, all addled by drink. Normally he would have taken the ambulance further afield, picked up one of the ugly ones from up the line. He preferred a larger hunting ground. There was so much ugliness to be found in the big cities.

He saw them, two of them, staggering and giggling past a club that thumped with the beat of dance music. He shivered at the sound, the tortuous thought of entering its dank, sweaty walls and having the noise assault his ears.

It was two females he had spotted, hardly wearing much at all, dolled up, lips bright red, faces brown with thick make up that was designed to make them look just like all the other sluts on the streets. These two were ugly on the outside, their flesh bulging in their tight and short dresses. He licked his lips as he crawled along, watching them heading for the nearest club, approaching the tall bouncer on the door. He slowed down, staring at the girls as they had banter with the man on the door, flirting with him. Yes, they were perfect, he decided, smiling to himself as he put his foot down.

CHAPTER 20

Moone and Butler stood in the dark of the autopsy room as the lights flickered on above them. Moone held his hand over his eyes, blinking and frowning as the room lit up, every metal surface glinting under the cold, harsh light.

Dr Parry stepped towards them, decked out in his scrubs and apron, pulling on a pair of surgical gloves. His usual bright smile was absent, and Moone wondered if family life was getting him down. He made a mental note to ask the doctor to go for a drink, to get him to open up a bit, if indeed he did drink. Moone realised he knew little about the man who he spent most weeks visiting.

'This is a late call,' Parry said, smiling a little. 'You said it was urgent.'

'We need to see the dead girls,' Butler said, all hint of friendliness evaporated. Moone looked at her and saw her blood was up and she had at last found the scent. In his head he heard her voice telling him off for even comparing her to a dog.

'Yes, you said on the phone,' Parry said, then opened the large doors that revealed the morgue fridges. 'Got a breakthrough?'

'We might have,' Moone said, as he heard the rattle of a trolley out in the morgue. One of the orderlies was pushing the trolley towards the autopsy room, where Parry helped him direct it inside. Moone stared at the human shape under the green covers, thinking how slender the young woman had looked when they found her lifeless, hollowed out. Somehow their killer saw them as beautiful after he had starved them, marked their skin and then strangled the life out of them. Had he starved them? He thought of their last meal, a delicious and expensive consumption just before the killer "released" them. His stomach knotted.

'This is your first Jane Doe,' Parry said, neatly folding down the sheet, revealing the cold, grey skin, the almost peaceful, but hollow face. Moone shivered a little as he stepped closer.

'Can you uncover them down to their waists?' Butler asked, standing over the dead girl.

Moone noticed Parry looking at her quizzically before he did as he was requested. The doctor stood back, watching them both as they examined the girl's torso.

'What are you looking for?' Parry asked, joining them.

'Stretch marks,' Butler said, then pointed a finger at the girl's hips, and then her stomach. 'Look, stretch marks. Aren't these the sort you'd find on a girl who used to be overweight?'

Parry stepped closer, coming round the table, looking where she was pointing. He nodded. 'Yes, oh my God. I never noticed that...'

'You weren't looking for it,' Moone said, noticing the look of surprise and sadness on the doctor's face. 'We think he targets big women. Starves them, tattoos them, changes their hair colour. All before he strangles them.'

'Look,' Butler said, pointing to the dead girl's scalp. Moone bent in, spotting the dark roots below the blonde hair.

Moone nodded, looking up at Butler. 'You've done it. You've sussed our killer out. Well done.'

Butler straightened up and huffed. 'Hardly. We've still got to find the sick bastard.'

'Anyway, we're a step closer.'

Butler had a strange, quizzical look come over her face as she stared at the body on the table.

'What is it?' Moone asked.

'Bobbi-Jane.' Butler looked at him. 'She wasn't overweight, was she? She looked slender to me. Just like our victims when we found them.'

Moone nodded. 'And she already had two tattoos. And one of them is a butterfly.'

'So, chances are the bastard we're after knows her or is obsessed with her. She's from down this way too.'

'We need to look into her past and we might find the psycho. We're getting closer.'

'I thought you had a suspect,' Parry said, looking between them. 'The chef?'

Moone nodded, then sighed. 'We did. But I'm not sure he's our man.'

'Wasn't it his food in her stomach?' Parry asked.

'His recipe, but nothing substantial tying him to any of this. Apart from his tattoo obsession. He did say he might know who's doing all this. What if he really does somehow?'

Butler stared at him. 'What about this ex-wife of Tom Dyer? She's got that tattoo. And she probably knows a lot bleeding more about Black than anyone. Apparently, they used to go on holiday together, so I've heard.'

'You think we should go and talk to her, then?' Moone asked, listening to the very different tune she was starting to play.

She shrugged. 'What else have we got to go on? We'll start looking for missing person reports from further afield. Larger young women. That might get us closer to identification. In the meantime, you should go and talk to the ex-wife. Use that cockney charm on her.'

'I'm not a cockney. I was born in...'

Butler sighed. 'Whatever, London boy. Just arrange a date.'

Moone watched her turn and storm out of the room, while he was left wondering what her motivation was. Yes, she was desperate to find their killer, but he noticed another look in her eyes, one he had never seen before, something very alien. Whatever was going on in her head, he wasn't sure he was going to like it when he discovered what it was.

He drove the ambulance back along Union Street, then parked in a road opposite the club that the ugly creatures had entered after they'd had their sickening flirtations. He pulled on the handbrake and listened as the engine cooled, making clicking noises, and knowing that the ambulance wouldn't be roadworthy much longer. He would have to find another way to lure them in. He didn't want to though, as the official uniform of a paramedic seemed to put them at ease. Along with the alcohol in their system, it was the perfect way to get them close enough to the vehicle. But that had been a different place, another city, and this was only the second time he had tried to lure one in closer to home. It was a big risk, but he had started to worry that the authorities might be getting wise to his operation. If they knew about the ambulance, they might have figured out more.

He sat up, seeing the door of the club opening, the red and blue of flashing and spinning lights hitting the puddles on the pavement. A tall and wide meaty doorman with a shaved head stepped out and allowed a young man and woman onto the street. He relaxed again, noting it was an overly made-up, pretty skinny thing that the young man had latched on to like a parasite. Even as they staggered past the kebab shop, they stopped awkwardly and backed into a wall as their hands and mouths hungrily groped at each other. Sickened, he turned away from the view, and just in time to see more silhouettes emerging through the door that the bouncer had opened.

His eyes widened when he saw the young woman who had stepped onto the pavement, her phone in her hand as she typed at a million miles an hour. It wasn't one of the big young women he had seen earlier, but she was almost interchangeable with them. She was squeezed into a short, dark pink dress, her large bosom almost spilling out of the low-cut top. Her face was covered in dark make up that didn't match the paler tone of the rest of her. She was truly ugly, he thought to himself and started the engine as he couldn't help stare at her. He was about to pull out and get closer, when he saw a young lad appear behind her, his arm wrapping round her back. She turned to him with a drunken smile as her thick lips devoured his face.

He swore under his breath, watching them head off towards the city centre. She was too perfect to let her get away, he decided, and started the engine again. He crawled along behind them, watching them stop and kiss every now and again pressed up against a shop doorway or wall. Then they moved away from the busier part of the city centre and headed into the quieter, darker back streets. He nodded, feeling his heart beat harder. This was it, he decided and checked his equipment was on the passenger seat. He nodded, put his foot down and overtook them, then swung the ambulance towards the pavement and parked up. They took their time travelling the street, staggering sideways, stopping for more groping. He watched them in the wing mirror as he opened his bag of tricks. He took out a taser and the syringe he had ready, then climbed out of the ambulance.

It was only the young man that looked at him briefly, before he went back to chatting up the girl.

'Excuse me,' he said, smiling. 'You haven't seen an injured young woman round here, have you?'

But the two of them paid him no attention and carried on laughing and trying to pass him. He took out the taser and fired it straight at the young man's chest. The lad jerked, gave a gurgled cry then collapsed to the pavement. The young woman stood there, her hands to her face, her eyes wide as she stared in confusion and horror at her convulsing boyfriend on the pavement.

Then the girl was staring at him, accusing, angry eyes digging into him.

'What've you done to him?' she demanded to know. 'You sick bastard. He didn't do nothing to you!'

He lurched towards her, expertly, grasping her round the neck, dragging her towards him. The needle went in, and he plunged the drugs into her. He let her go then, and watched her try and run away, her terrified eyes even wider, so scared and confused. He almost laughed when her chubby legs started to give way. He was waiting to put his arm round her, when she almost collapsed. No longer could she communicate properly, and only a mumbling sound came from her mouth as he guided her weak legs towards the back of the ambulance. By the time he opened the back doors, she had passed out. He rested her on the edge of the ambulance, then lifted her legs and dragged her inside.

After he closed the doors, his eyes lifted

towards the young lad who was groaning as he seemed to be coming round. He let out a breath, shook his head, then fetched his baton and went over to him.

'Are you all right?' he asked, crouching beside him.

'No, someone... someone did something...'

'Don't worry, I'll help. What's your name?'

'Rory...'

'It'll be OK, Rory.' He lifted the baton, then brought it down, striking Rory hard on the side of his head.

Moone hadn't had much sleep when he finally did get back to his mobile home that night. The caravan seemed emptier than ever, and he rattled around the place, trying to clear his mind of everything that had been building up, but it was no good. He'd left word for the team to stretch the search for missing young women wider, to keep an eye out for larger, more overweight young women. Molly had been tasked with looking into Bobbi-Jane's past more closely. He'd also contacted the former Mrs Dyer by sending a friendly text, reminding her of where they had first met. As soon as he had sent the text, he'd wished he hadn't. It felt odd, and more than a little weird to contact her out of the blue, especially when he was only after picking her brains.

In the morning there were no messages from anyone, so he headed to the station, his mind suddenly rushing back to his Bristol colleague, Crowne, and wondering what he must be feeling. Carthew had got away with it, had managed to actually kill three people and there wasn't a thing they could do. He almost felt desperate enough to reach out to Laptew, but he didn't want to disturb the Chief Super, or his wife. It would wait until he was back. Maybe it was time to lay everything on the line, and tell him everything that had been going on, even at the risk of looking like a jilted ex-lover.

When Moone entered the incident room, he found Butler already at her desk, her eyes searching some paperwork in front of her, seeming almost mesmerised.

'What've you got?' he asked, looking over her shoulder.

She sat back, letting him see the two Misper reports she had printed up. 'The intelligence team sent these over, after I asked them to stretch our search a little wider.'

Moone looked at the first report, which had a photo of a young and plump woman smiling brightly, a sunny sky behind her. She had thick dark make up on, eyes heavy with mascara and fake lashes. He read the name aloud: 'Chloe Gillard. From Cardiff.'

Butler nodded. 'Last seen two months ago. Went out in Cardiff, hasn't been seen since. Her phone was tracked to Westgate Street. That's the last place she made a call from. Phone hasn't been on since.'

'We need to get on to Cardiff police, get them to check CCTV and ANPR for that night.'

Butler sighed. 'Already contacted them. Didn't seem very excited about the prospect, but they're going to get round to it.'

'Nice. Who's the other girl?'

Butler tapped the other photo of a blonde young woman, also smiling, also heavily made-up. She too was quite chubby. 'Angelina McLean. Lived and worked in Oxford. Went missing three months ago. Three months, Moone. He's basically locked them up, starved them, drawn a fucked up tattoo on them, and then strangled them.'

Moone straightened up. 'Are they definitely our victims? They look pretty different.'

'I ran their photos through a slimming app. They match. We need to contact their families.'

'I can do that,' a voice said from across the room.

Moone looked up to see DC Molly Chambers giving him a polite smile. 'Thanks, Molly, that would be really helpful. Have you been looking into Bobbi-Jane's past?'

'Yes, nothing much of interest so far. No stalkers.'

'OK. We also need CCTV footage from the times the girls went missing. Has the McLean girl's phone been tracked?'

Butler nodded. 'Went off just outside Oxford city centre.'

Moone sighed. 'Right. So, he takes his ambulance up to Cardiff and Oxford and stalks the nightclubs until he sees an overweight, overly made-up young woman...'

'How does he get them in the ambulance?' Molly asked.

Moone shrugged. 'Drugs them? Approaches them, talks to them? No one's going to think twice about a paramedic, are they?'

'Sick bastard,' Butler said. 'Are we looking at a medical professional, then?'

'Could be. Or anyone with an ambulance.'

Butler sat back, staring at Moone thoughtfully.

'What?' Moone asked, seeing something was going on behind her eyes.

'Nothing. Just that... well, did you know Black trained as a nurse before he ended up as a chef?'

Moone enclosed his face in his hands, taking in and absorbing the news. 'Jesus. OK, then we need to find out if he was anywhere near Oxford or Cardiff at the times of the abductions.'

'He's got restaurants in Cardiff and

Oxford.' Butler raised her eyebrows.

'Of course he has.' Moone was about to say more when he heard his mobile ringing. He took it out and saw an unknown number calling. He held up a finger to an unimpressed Butler and headed to the stairwell. 'DCI Peter Moone.'

'Hi, it's Lisa,' the woman said on the other end of the phone. 'Lisa Brunning. You sent me a text. Is everything OK?'

Moone's stomach tightened and his heart started to race a little, even though he didn't really understand why. She was an attractive woman, and she had shown some interest in him. That was it, he thought, remembering the attractive, popular girls at school that only ever teased him and only ever went out with older boys with cars. He shook it all away, remembering he was a police detective with a job to do.

'Hi, yes, I did call you. I needed to talk to you.'

He took in the hesitation on the other end, so added, 'It's nothing bad. Just some follow up questions.'

'Oh, right. Do I need to come to your station?'

'No, it's OK, I'll come to you.'

'OK, why don't you meet me for lunch?'

'Yes, all right. Where?'

'Meet me at the restaurant. Where we

were the other night, is that OK?'

'That's great. I'll see you then.'

Before Moone knew it, the call had ended and he was left with a strange sense of something uncomfortable that he couldn't communicate, not even to himself. Then there was a glimmer of understanding, or almost, as an idea or hunch almost came to him.

'Want the latest?'

Moone looked round, his idea dispersing and crumbling before it had time to take form. Butler was stood before him looking tired, her eyebrows raised. 'What now?'

'We've got a young lad bludgeoned almost to death,' she said, sighing. 'They've rushed him to Derriford.'

'Haven't we got enough to deal with?'

Butler nodded. 'Yes, but you're SIO on duty, so we have to look into it. Come on, his mates are at the hospital. Let's go see what they have to say.'

There were two lads sat nursing machine coffees in a corridor just off the main entrance. One had his head back, resting it against the wall, his eyes closed. The other was yawning and rubbing his tired eyes. Even from a couple of yards away, Moone could smell the stale alcohol emanating from their pores.

Butler lurched forward and grabbed the sleeping lad's coffee cup before it dropped to the floor, then straightened herself. The sleeping lad hadn't even stirred, so she looked at the other one.

'Any news on your mate?' she asked as she fished out her ID and showed it.

He shook his head. 'Na, they've taken him to get scanned or something. Can't believe this has fucking happened to Ryan.'

'Did something happen in the club?' Moone asked. 'Any trouble?'

'Na, nothing like that. He's not like that.'

'What is he like?' Butler asked with a huff. 'Because someone was pissed off with him enough to knock the sense out of him.'

The lad shrugged. 'You know. Just a normal geezer. Into football and girls.'

'Did he meet a girl tonight?' Moone asked, taking out his notebook.

'Yeah, copped off with this bird he met at the bar,' the lad said, taking a sip of his coffee. 'She was alright, bit on the large size, pretty though, if you get what I mean?'

'Yeah, we get you.' Butler rolled her eyes at Moone. 'Where's this girl now?'

The lad shrugged again. 'Fucked if I know. He was taking her home last time I knew.'

'Hang on,' Moone said, holding up his palm. 'He was walking a girl home, then at some point he's attacked?'

'Yeah, I suppose.' The lad sighed and sat back. 'Maybe she had an ex or something. You should check that out.'

Moone smiled sarcastically. 'We will, thanks. Do you know this girl's name?'

'Na, didn't catch her name.'

Moone nodded, thinking it all through, then looked at Butler. 'We need CCTV checked around the place he was found, and along the route from the club.'

'Do we really?' Butler shook her head. 'I hadn't thought of that. Maybe we should let one of the other DIs take charge of this.'

Moone looked at her, seeing the complete disinterest in her eyes, then signalled for her to follow him down the corridor. When they found a quiet little treatment room, they went inside.

'You OK?' he asked.

She stared at him, narrowing her eyes. 'Yes, why? Because I'm not chomping at the bit to take on another case? Are you?'

'No, of course not, but we're on call. Let's take all this down, then hand it over to a DS or DI. Thing is, I'm worried about the girl. Where did she go to?'

'Probably ran off, or maybe she did it to him. He tried it on and she didn't like it...'

Moone caught sight of a uniform heading past the room they were in. 'Hang on.'

Moone went out and saw the same male uniform looking lost. 'You looking for us?' Moone asked.

The uniform came over, taking out his notebook as his radio mumbled away in the background. 'Are you DCI Moone?'

'That's right.'

'Glad I found you, sir.' The uniform looked at his notes. 'I was making enquiries round where the boy was found. I talked to the owner of a restaurant just up the way. He says he saw a lad and girl kissing and groping as they passed his place...'

'OK, and did he see the attack or see anyone following them?'

'No. But he did see an ambulance going by, crawling along just after they went past. He thought it was odd. I only mention it because I hear you've been looking into an ambulance...'

Moone turned to raise his eyebrows at Butler, then stormed along and found the two tired-looking lads.

'Tell me about this girl your friend met.'

CHAPTER 21

The whimpering had gone on all night, the constant whine of it finding his ears even when he lay in his bed and tried to find some rest. But he lay there for what seemed hours, listening to the distant sound of the creature. Eventually, he couldn't stand it any longer, and got up and dressed himself and went downstairs after grabbing a coffee. He stopped at the small window on the way down and stared out at the barren land, the distant cloud shape of the sheep all crowded around a single tor. Nothing for miles, maybe only the occasional rambler or dog walker. He donned his mask and took his coffee to the basement where he unlocked the door and entered the bare room. Only the barber style chair and the cells at the far end of the room greeted his eyes. In the corner was his small office space, the desk with the drawing board and his previous designs taped to the wall.

'Please!' her voice came wearily from the

dark. 'Please let me go!'

He ignored it and sat at the desk, looking at his latest design. It was more magnificent than the last, something he had felt was impossible, but there it was. So many colours and the hidden words crafted into the illustrious wings. Before his eyes, they beat, and he saw the creature lift off the page and fly across the room. His vision dropped from the imagined insect and found her eyes glistening in the darkness, wide and full of terror.

'Please...'

He stared at her, remembering the large shape of her. It would take many weeks to get her anywhere close to perfect.

'You've got a long way to go,' he said quietly. 'A long way to go before I can release you.'

He saw the glimmer of hope in her eyes as she came closer to the bars. 'You're going to release me?'

'Of course I am.' He smiled, stepping closer. 'But like I said, you've got a long way to go. I mean, look at the state of you.'

'I don't know...'

'Yes, you do. All the stuff on your face. Those clothes I had to peel off you. What did you think you looked like? And that boy, all over you. What a disgusting display.'

She started crying again, the whine reaching a new height of annoyance, so he turned and headed for the door, thinking of all the other tasks he had to complete before he had to return to his actual job.

'Please, don't leave me down here...'

He let out a laugh, then faced her. 'Why? Are you afraid of the dark?'

'Please...'

'Frightened of monsters?' He smiled. 'You've got nothing to worry about. There are no monsters here.'

She whimpered, snot starting to run from her nose, the remainder of her eyeliner and mascara running onto her cheeks.

'You think I'm a monster,' he said. 'I know you do. But you don't understand. I'm an artist. A great... creature. A little like, dare I say... God?'

She began to cry uncontrollably, so as he laughed, he took himself out of the basement and up the stone steps until he was stood on the landing above, ready to think about what he had to do next.

He had it all straight in his mind when he heard it, the sound of a car engine grumbling in the distance. He hurried to the window at the end of the landing, which allowed him to see along the muddy lane and the woods beyond. There was the main road that ran round the woods and led towards the house. *His* house.

The car kept coming. He stared at it, his heart beginning to thud a little, trying to make out who was at the wheel.

The car came closer, slowing as it reached the lane and turned into it. He sighed, shaking his head as he recognised the car. But the sight of it filled him with concern. Why was he here now?

He went back down the stairs, hurrying towards the front door. He unbolted it, and stood watching as his half-brother climbed out of the car. As usual, he had the hood of his coat pulled tightly over his head and a mask covering the lower part of his face. He was still so paranoid about catching the virus.

'There's no one to see you here,' he said, laughing a little as his half-brother hurried towards him and pushed past and entered the old house.

'I don't care,' he said, standing in the hallway, his skin paler than usual. 'I can't risk it. You've taken another one, haven't you?'

'What are you talking about?'

'Don't give me that rubbish. Don't lie. You have, haven't you?'

He stared back at him, looking deep into his worried eyes, thinking it all through. 'What if I have?'

His half-brother looked down, let out a pained breath, his head shaking. When he looked up, his eyes were wet with tears. 'I told you, this had to stop! Didn't I tell you that?'

He stepped closer. 'I know. And I really

tried to stop...'

'Did you? I doubt that.' He wiped his eyes, sniffed.

'Listen...'

'No. You listen. This has to be the last...'

He smiled, nodding. 'Absolutely the last.'

His half-brother gave a choked laugh, then looked up at him. 'You'll want me to... you know, mark her.'

'Not yet. She has quite a bit of weight to lose yet.'

'We haven't got time for this. You took her from here. It's too close. The police will be onto you soon.'

'No, don't panic. They don't know anything yet.' He put a calming hand on his shoulder, squeezed a little. 'This one will be perfect. I know it.'

His half-brother nodded. 'I hope so. This has to be the last. You have to promise me that.'

'I swear. On our mother's grave. But, you have to remember, that I wouldn't have to keep doing this if you hadn't fucked up.'

His half-brother shrugged his hand away, then looked down. 'I know. I'm sorry, but she got away. She was fast.'

'I know. You keep saying. She was the one. *The one*. Do you understand?'

'I know.' His half-brother reached into his pocket and pulled out a piece of paper and unfolded it. On the paper was a design. A butterfly.

He took the piece of paper and stared at it. He let out a breath, then looked up. 'This is it. How? How did you do this?'

His half-brother didn't look at him. 'It came to me. Like, you know, in a dream.'

He nodded, and looked at the design, ecstatic that he was looking at the one element that had been missing all this time. But there was another feeling poisoning his happiness, a strange sensation that had been born weeks ago. It had started as a suspicion, and slowly grown until it was a substantial fear. He looked up at his half-brother and smiled, while in his head and heart he knew he had been betrayed.

They now had a great deal of information about the missing young woman, along with a recent photo from her Instagram account. Her name was Cody Barton and her distressed parents had now been informed. Like a lot of young women, Moone realised with a sense of distaste and fear, it seemed that she liked to take snaps of herself and post them online, as if as reaching out desperately for some kind of approval. He thought of Alice and knew she wasn't like that. He hoped she wasn't like that. He made a mental note to ask her about her online presence as he headed towards Padstow. His stomach had tightened as he'd set off, thinking about the attractive woman waiting for him and the difficult questions he would have to ask. It was his job, he told himself, as his mind absorbed what the poor woman had been through. He couldn't imagine losing a child. He had almost lost Alice, a memory that always came with a thudding heart and a stomach full of black moths.

He parked up close to the harbour and hurried from the car as light rain started falling. He headed into the town, which was already quite busy with tourists. He found the restaurant and was about to go in, when he heard someone call out his name. He turned to see Lisa Brunning waving at him from a doorway a hundred yards away, so hurried over and followed her into a narrow cafe.

'I thought this place might be better,' she said, directing him to a booth opposite the counter. 'The restaurant will be really busy.'

'Fine by me,' he said and sat opposite her.

She sat back and smiled. 'I wasn't sure I'd hear from you again.'

He nodded and smiled, then looked at the paper menu on the table. 'Sorry, I've been busy.'

'I can't imagine doing your job. My job's pretty easy. Smile, greet people.'

'Trust me, it's better than what I have to do.'

She smiled again, then lost it as her eyes dug into him. 'Last time I saw you, you were asking about Mario. Are you still looking into him?'

'I can't really discuss that.'

She nodded, her cheeks reddening. 'No, sorry, of course not.'

'What's good to eat here?'

'All of it. Close your eyes and point at the menu.'

He laughed but when he looked up at her, he saw she had lost some colour and was staring at him strangely. 'You OK?'

She nodded. 'I think so. But...'

'But?'

'I'm wondering... well, I'm wondering if there's something you've found out about me.'

He put the menu to the side, his stomach clenching. 'There is.'

She looked down. 'That's why you're here, isn't it? Officially.'

'I'm sorry for what you went through... I can't...'

'I'm glad you can't. No one should...'

Then she looked up at him, eyebrows raised. 'So, you wanted to ask me some questions and this isn't a date?'

'Well, I do have to ask you some questions, it's my job, but I wish I didn't have to.'

She smiled a little. 'Then let's get it out of the way. Go ahead and ask.'

He sat back, preparing himself, watching her preparing herself. 'Your tattoo. The one on your shoulder...'

She looked towards her arm. 'My tattoo?'

'It's a butterfly, isn't it?'

She looked at him strangely. 'Yes, it is. What's this got to do with my tattoo?'

'Bear with me. Who designed that tattoo?'

She narrowed her eyes. 'I think you already know.'

'Mario Black?'

She didn't say anything for a few seconds, just stared at Moone, while she absent-mindedly touched her shoulder. Then she nodded. 'So, you're still investigating him?'

'He's a person of interest.'

'He is that.'

'Why do you say that?'

She shrugged. 'I don't know. I suppose because he's successful, a bit weird, short tempered. All the things that make people strange. I'm none of those things. I've always been ordinary, boring even.'

'I doubt that.'

She leaned towards him. 'It's true. It's always been fine with me. Then... then everything changed when...'

'I have to ask you something.'

'That sounds ominous.'

'Have you heard of a man called Loy Grader?'

'I have.' Her face tightened. 'He's a monster. That's what the papers said... is this to do with what happened? You think...'

'I think he might have been in Spain at that time. Close to where you were staying. But I can't prove that. If you know anyone looking into it, or if anyone involved talks to you again, you should ask about him...'

'I will.' She looked down.

'Thing is... it was Loy Grader who suggested I talk to you.'

She looked up, staring at him. 'What do you mean? Talk to me about what?'

'I don't know. That's all he said. He mentioned your ex-husband too.'

Her face changed he noticed. She became almost unrecognisable as her face became rigid. 'Tom? What about him?'

Moone shrugged, trying to keep his face clear, even though his stomach was ready to scramble out of the restaurant. 'I think he was trying to suggest something.'

She kept staring. 'That he had something to do with...? He would never...'

'I know, but that's Grader for you. Likes to mess with people's heads. It's his voice too.'

'Creepy.'

The hairs stood up on the back of Moone's neck as he saw the look in her eyes. The look of someone caught in a lie.

'You've met him?' Moone asked.

She looked down. Nodded. 'Briefly.'

'Where?'

'Spain.'

'Spain? So you knew he was there?'

She looked up, her eyes wet with tears. 'Yes. I knew.'

Moone sat back, trying to understand what the hell was going on, and what the hell *had* gone on. 'I don't get it.'

She sighed. 'Mario Black opened a restaurant in Spain. He sold it later. He invited us there one evening. Before that awful night. Tom seemed distracted that night. There was this man in the restaurant who kept staring at us. Then he came over, said hello. He gave me the creeps…'

'It was Loy Grader?'

She nodded.

'Tom knew him?'

'He seemed to know Tom. He took him back to his own table, chatted to him, then the man left. I only recognised the man as Grader later.'

'How did Tom know him?'

'Said he was someone who'd worked for him. But I didn't believe him. I didn't believe much of what he said after I found out who he was.'

'Did you tell the police this?'

'Of course.'

'What did they say?'

'They'd look into it. But then later they said they'd ruled him out. But Mario was obsessed with him, convinced he'd…'

'That's why he's put us on to him.'

'I think he used it all, the fact that Tom knew Grader, to get into my head and split us up.'

'Why?'

'Because Mario had a thing for me. But I think I was just something he couldn't have. Then he finally did have me and afterwards, well, he wasn't interested.'

'I see.' Moone wanted to leave suddenly. He'd had enough of the conversation, unable to look at the woman opposite and not see Grader or Mario Black. 'That's when he did the tattoo on you?'

'No, he didn't give me tattoo.'

'But I thought you said he did?'

'He designed it.'

Moone sat back, the bewilderment clogging up his brain for the moment. 'OK, then who actually performed the tattoo?'

She looked up towards the ceiling as a memory tried to form, her fingers tapping at the tabletop. 'I can't remember the guy's name. He was a friend of Mario's. He'd worked for him. Yes, that's it. He worked for him.'

'He worked for him?' Moone took out his notebook. 'You're sure?'

'Definitely, I remember him saying he was one of his promising chefs.'

Moone nodded, noting it all down. 'Anything else you can remember about him, a description, maybe?'

She leaned forward. 'Well, he was quite tall. Well, taller than Mario. Light brown hair. He was big…'

'Big?'

'Overweight, you know.'

Moone looked up. 'Overweight? That's interesting.'

'Is it? Why?'

Moone smiled apologetically. 'Sorry, I can't really say. Is there anything else you remember about him?'

'He was pretty… well, he was creepy to be honest.'

'In what way?'

She shrugged. 'Just, the way he looked at me. Having him touch me was pretty sickening. I know that sounds awful. And I remember he was upset and a bit angry when I said I wanted the tattoo on my shoulder…'

Moone felt the invisible, icy hand brush its fingers up his spine. 'Where did he want to put it?'

'On my back. Right between my shoulder blades.'

Moone stared at her for a moment, his stomach circling itself and squeezing. He was so close now, he could feel it deep inside, swimming about in his blood. 'Lisa, try and think, try and remember more about him.'

Her face changed, a little shock

brightening her eyes. 'Do you think he's who you're after?'

'I can't say. I just need to find him.'

'Then you need to talk to Mario. He'll remember him. He has to.'

Moone nodded, smiled, but he couldn't see the self-obsessed chef, who had already given them the run around, just opening up and dropping his friend in it. 'Yep, don't worry, I will talk to him.'

She nodded, looking down.

'I'm really sorry for what you've been through.'

She looked up briefly, nodding.

'What's he like? James, I mean.'

Her eyes closed for a moment, a ripple of pain crossing her body, making him feel awful.

'I'm sorry,' he said.

She shook her head. 'No, it's OK. I should talk about it all. James. James was... he was full of energy. He was a chatterbox. Never wanted to sleep. Never, not even as a baby...'

'Tell me about it.'

'How many children have you got?'

'Three. My eldest is Alice. I don't think any of them are very impressed with their old man.'

'I'm sure they are.'

Moone stood up. 'Maybe one day they will be.'

'Are you going?' she asked, standing up too. 'We haven't eaten.'

'I'm really sorry, but I need to find this man. Maybe we can do this another time?'

She smiled, but he saw a flicker of something cross her face, perhaps the realisation that he had only been there to feed on what she knew.

'OK, I'll call you,' she said, and he smiled, then turned and hurried away.

He slowed down a little when he got past the harbour and reached the car park, the squawk of ravenous seagulls filling his ears. He got to his car, climbed in and took out his phone. He dialled Butler and waited.

'That was quick,' she said, a strange note in her voice. 'Can't have had much time for a smooch.'

'Very bloody funny. Listen, we need to talk to Mario Black.'

'Right, OK. Why?'

'Mario Black didn't perform the tattoo. A friend of his did, and it was someone he worked with.'

'Right. Well, I better let you know that someone's here asking to talk to you.'

'Who?'

'Your favourite person in all the world.'

'You're joking? You don't mean who I think you mean?'

'I do. Carthew is sat in one of the interview rooms waiting for you. And she's looking particularly pleased with herself.'

Moone ended the call, then started the engine, his mind running in every direction. What the hell did she want now?

CHAPTER 22

Moone held out one of the coffees he'd grabbed on the way and Butler took it as she rested her back on the whiteboard. She raised her eyebrows as she opened the cup and blew on it.

'You going in?'

Moone looked towards the corridor, envisioning her waiting for him, undoubtedly hungry for the attention. 'Let's keep her waiting a bit longer. Did she say anything?'

'No, not much apart from she needed to talk to you. She had a particularly smug look on her face. One that said *aren't I clever for getting away with murder*?'

Moone let out a harsh breath and sipped his coffee. 'She is, though. Three murders and we can't touch her.'

'We have to take this higher.'

Moone gave an empty laugh. 'Take what? There's nothing to take. The widow and her boyfriend did it, then the boyfriend killed her and himself. It's all neatly tied up for us. A nice little early Christmas present from her.'

'She could've got me some new bras, my old ones are looking a bit minging.'

'Funny. Any news on the whereabouts of our favourite chef?'

Butler huffed. 'No. His people are being vague on the subject. So, you think this friend of his is our killer?'

'Well, it's a bit of a coincidence that he's got a creepy friend tattooist who wanted to put a large butterfly tattoo on her back, isn't it?'

'I suppose.' She sipped her coffee. 'Don't suppose she said he turned up driving an ambulance?'

'No such luck. Any CCTV showing our ambulance in town or where it went?'

'Harding's your man.' Butler looked over Moone's head. 'Harding?'

The DC's confused face appeared over his monitor, his jaw moving as he chewed something. 'What?'

'CCTV?' Moone said. 'ANPR?'

'SFA,' Harding said, grinned and then lost it as he seemed to catch sight of Butler's glare.

'Sweet fuck all?' Moone asked. 'It isn't caught on CCTV at all? That can't be right.'

'Oh, no, CCTV caught it all right. Just no number plate visible. Don't get a good look at the driver either. Sorry.'

'Where does it head to?'

'Last camera picks it up heading out to towards Dartmoor.'

Moone nodded. 'Makes sense. He takes these girls and holds them somewhere while he starves them and changes their hair. He'd need somewhere out of the way. We need to start looking for anywhere out there where he could hide.'

Butler huffed out a laugh. 'Good luck with that. It's three hundred and sixty odd square miles. Do you know how many old farms and pubs and God knows what else is out there?'

Moone sighed, knowing she was right and he was grasping at straws. Then he remembered the ambulance. 'They'd need somewhere to stash an ambulance.'

'Again, there must be hundreds of places out there. And we don't even know if he's in Dartmoor.'

Moone rubbed his face, then remembered Carthew was waiting. 'Keep looking for Black, I better talk to her majesty in there.'

Butler pushed herself away from the whiteboard and sat at her desk. 'Yeah, go and run along. Can't keep her waiting.'

Moone headed out of the incident room and along to the interview rooms. Before he went in, he took a few deep breaths and put on his poker face. He went in and found Carthew sat waiting, already staring at him, her arms folded. She smiled, then gestured to the chair opposite.

He sat down, raised his eyebrows. 'What did you want, Faith? I'm very busy.'

'I'm sure you are. Trying to catch a killer who likes to tattoo his victims, I heard.'

'Who from?'

'Does it matter?' She leaned forward. 'I've missed you. Have you missed me?'

'You've killed three people. Murdered three people. Doesn't that have any effect on you?'

She put on a look of mock surprise. 'I've murdered three people? When? I happened to be in the same hotel when a police officer was murdered, I'll give you that. But they know who did it. The widow and her lover. That sounds like the title of some cheap romance, porn novel, doesn't it?'

'How did you do it? How did you manage to kill them both and make it look so perfect?'

She smiled. 'It probably looks so perfect because that's what happened. Murder, suicide. You just have to accept it.'

He didn't say anything for a moment, just stared into her eyes, trying to detect a glimmer of anything human. He saw nothing, just a predator out for whatever she could get. 'I don't have to accept it. You're wrong, Faith. Sooner or later, you'll make a mistake.'

'Sooner or later, I'll be your boss.' She leaned forward, smiling. 'How will that play out? You'd better start being nice to me now.'

'That isn't going to happen.'

She sat back. 'Are you going to tell on me? Go running to Chief Super Laptew? He won't listen to a thing you've got to say.'

'Why won't he? Because you've charmed him?'

Another smile. 'Sometimes you've got to use the gifts God has given you. What are your gifts, Peter? What are you going to use to catch this killer you're after?'

He stood up. 'I think we're done here.'

'Sit down. I can help. Come on, remember, I'm part of the team.'

'Not my team.'

'So, he takes these girls, or young women, and he transforms them. Tattoos them. Why, do you think?'

Moone huffed out a laugh, then shook his head. 'OK, Lecter, let's wrap this up. I've got work to do.'

'How's the ex-Mrs Dyer?'

Moone was about to leave the desk, but stopped when he heard her words. 'How did you know I'd been to see her?'

Carthew smiled. 'I hear things.'

He sat down, staring at her, a strange, uncomfortable feeling spreading over him, a dark cloud settling over his head. 'You've been following me, haven't you?'

She shrugged. 'Maybe. What do you think

of her? Do you think Mario Black and she used to fuck?'

'I don't care.' He stood up again, determined to ignore her mind games.

'Do you fancy her?'

'That's none of your business.'

'What do you make of her?'

He shrugged. 'She's a woman in pain. Not knowing where your child is, it must mess you up. But there's…'

'What? Something doesn't sit right?'

'I don't know what it is. Anyway, I'm not discussing it with you.' Moone headed to the door. 'Don't come back to Plymouth, Faith. Please, do us both a favour.'

She turned in her seat to face him. 'But I like Plymouth. I love being close to the sea.'

He rubbed his eyes. 'This is an island, there are plenty of places by the sea. Please, just find somewhere else. Be the boss up country or somewhere. Just not here.'

'Why? Because you're afraid?'

'Yes. If you like. I'm afraid of how this is going to end.'

She smiled brightly. 'I'm not. I'm looking forward to it.'

He shook his head, then opened the door.

'Your killer is medically trained.'

He stopped and faced her. 'You know about the ambulance?'

'It's not that. I looked at the victims. He

put in cannulas. Did you notice?'

Moone nodded. 'Yes, we did.'

'They were put in very well, expertly. Most nurses and doctors don't put them in that well. They've had plenty of experience.'

Moone didn't say anything, just digested the information, nodded and left the room. Butler was waiting for him, arms folded, eyebrows raised. 'Interesting conversation?'

'Sort of. Everything OK?' he asked, walking round her and towards the incident room.

'I've found Mario Black. Thought you'd be interested.'

Moone stopped. 'I am. Where… what's it you locals say? Where's he to?'

Butler huffed out an unimpressed laugh, then overtook him. 'Nearly. You won't be getting your Janner passport yet. Come on, I'll drive you out to wildest Cornwall.'

Moone recalled a programme Mario Black had presented that he'd watched one day on BBC Two. It had been about the self-important chef touring the country, reinventing traditional British foods. In the Cornish edition, he had taken the cameras to his home which was near Padstow. He remembered a bird's eye view of the white, glass and stone house that seemed to have been bolted onto the side of the cliff itself, designed by another self-important architect.

It took them a while to find the narrow road that ran parallel with the coastline, where Butler said they would find another narrow, gated road that would lead down to Black's house.

Moone spotted the large metal gate which had "private land" written upon it in massive letters. Butler pulled in close to the gate, then they climbed out. There was an intercom system attached to a post next to the gate, so Moone pressed it while he stared towards the sea and the white stone outline of Black's art deco style home.

'Do you think we're really looking for someone medically trained?' Moone asked, still looking out to sea.

'Our murderer?' Butler asked. 'Well, I told you Black studied medicine, so yeah, I do. Why?'

He shrugged, then pressed the buzzer again. 'Something Carthew said.'

Butler turned towards the narrow road with a huff. 'What's that crackpot been saying now?'

'She heard about the cannulas.'

'So? The killer administers drugs. So what?'

'It's difficult to get cannulas in. They were fitted expertly.'

'Well, we've had people checking for medically trained people with a history of similar crimes, and so far nothing. Like I said, Black's had some medical training.'

'Then we'll ask him about it.'

Butler gestured to the road. 'Someone's coming.'

Moone turned to see a silhouette moving towards them, coming up the road gradually.

'Is that Black?' Butler asked, sounding astounded.

Moone gave a surprised laugh when he focused in on the chef who seemed to wearing a silk robe over his naked body and carrying a Champagne glass in his hand.

'Welcome, welcome,' he said brightly and pressed a button on the gate, which opened it. 'It's so nice to see you two lovely detectives again.'

'You're drunk,' Butler said, and headed along the road.

Moone nodded to Black, who held the gate open for him. 'Thanks. We need to ask you a couple of questions.'

'Of course you do. It's your job. Come and see my lovely house. I designed it myself. Well, mostly.'

Moone followed the chef, watching him striding back towards the house, sipping his drink, where Butler was already waiting, arms folded, face frozen in a look of annoyance.

'Come in, officers,' he said and slid open one of the glass French doors that made up the entire exterior of the ground floor. Music was playing inside, echoing round the grey stone walls. Dark wood flooring covered the wide expanse of the open plan area. A hard, black, sixties style sofa sat opposite a large wall-mounted TV. Huge painted portraits of Black himself hung on the walls. The chef took his Champagne to the kitchen area at the far end of the room and refilled his glass.

'Can I get you both a drink?' he asked, lifting his glass.

'No, thanks,' Moone said. 'Like I said, we've got some questions.'

'Fire away.' The chef smiled, then sipped his Champagne.

'Is it true you nearly became a doctor before you took up cooking?' Butler asked.

Black narrowed his eyes at her, while pointing a finger. 'You've been reading up on me. Yes, that's right. My father, bless his soul, was a doctor. You know how it goes. Same old story. But I can't stand the sight of blood.'

'Really?' Moone asked.

'Unless it's pouring out of a steak. Actually, do you know that's not blood pouring out of your steak? The blood's been drained away already. No, it's actually muscle tissue protein, called myoglobin, mixed with the meat's water content.'

'Delicious,' Butler said, not hiding her annoyance. 'Where were you last night?'

Black looked up at the ceiling, tapping his chin. 'Last night? I think, yes, I was here. All night.'

'Alone?' Moone asked.

Black looked at him, giving a big grin. 'I was. All alone. I take it some horrendous murder took place? Of course it did. And I have no alibi.'

'Tell us about the tattoo you designed for the ex-Mrs Dyer,' Moone said, carefully watching the expression change on the chef's face. Some of the mirth left his eyes, and was replaced by a look of almost surprise.

'You know about that?'

'We know everything,' Butler said.

Black smirked. 'Apart from who murdered those young women, it would seem. Anyway, yes, I designed a tattoo for her. Big deal.'

'It's not your design we're interested in,' Butler said, folding her arms and squaring up to the chef. 'It's who actually drew it on her skin.'

Black stared at her for a moment, then turned away, sipping his Champagne as he said, 'That was me, so what? Have I broken some tattooing law?'

'Mrs Dyer told me that you didn't perform the tattoo at all,' Moone said, staring at Black's back. He had stopped moving, then slowly turned round, his face a little drawn and tight.

'Did she?' Black said with a shrug. 'I don't

seem to recall.'

'You remember all right,' Butler said. 'Who're you trying to protect?'

Black's angry eyes flared a little at her. 'No one. No one at all. Lisa must be remembering it wrong.'

'Funny thing to remember wrong.' Butler huffed. 'First tattoo? I think I'd remember who performed it. Say if it was a big fella. Someone who used to work for you.'

Moone noticed a flicker of some kind of emotion, perhaps slight panic, cross the chef's face before he regained his composure.

'Big fella?' Black repeated. 'Someone who used to work for me? How am I supposed to remember everyone who worked for me? Do you know how many people I've had…'

'Not everyone,' Butler said, squaring up to him again. 'Just one person. A big fella, someone able to perform tattoos. The same person who put that butterfly on the ex-Mrs Dyer. Now do you recall?'

The chef simmered away, staring back at her. For a moment, Moone feared a fight was about to break out. He feared for the chef, if it did. He decided to step up, so moved closer and said, 'It's just a name, Mr Black. An ex-employee, and someone who might know who killed two young women. Don't you want to help us find out who did that?'

Black dragged his angry eyes from Butler

and looked at Moone. 'Of course I do. I'm not a monster, despite what other chefs have said about me in the papers. It's all just a show, the shouting and all that business. It's what people expect.'

'The name?' Butler asked.

Black kept his eyes on Moone. 'Are you any closer to finding out what happened to my friend's missing boy?'

'We're not involved in that,' Moone said. 'It's not our case.'

'Loy Grader was in Spain at that time, wasn't he?'

'I can't comment on that,' Moone said. 'It's not my case. Go and see the Met officers who are looking into it.'

Black shook his head, then sipped his Champagne. 'You know what? I don't seem to be able to recall the name of the man who performed that tattoo. Funny, isn't it?'

'What do you expect me to do?' Moone said, now feeling his level of annoyance growing, a little tempted to leave the chef alone with Butler. 'It's not our case.'

'Have the Met looked into Tom Dyer?' Black asked. 'Do they know that one of the people he went on holiday with the time before his son went missing reported him to the child protection people?'

'No, we hadn't heard that,' Moone said. 'Why did they do that?'

'Because they overheard him and one of his friends talking very inappropriately about the kids they were with. I'm telling you, Tom Dyer is a sick individual.'

'Did he know Loy Grader?' Moone asked. 'Mrs Dyer told me that a man made a bit of a scene at your restaurant opening. She said she recognised him later as Loy Grader.'

Black nodded. 'Yes. I didn't see him, but I was told he seemed to know Tom. I didn't find this out until much later.'

'OK, I'm going to pass all this information to the Met. But you need to go and tell them what you know. Everything.'

'I can't.'

'Why not?'

The chef looked down, shrugged a little. 'It's complicated. You wouldn't understand.'

'Just bloody tell them,' Butler groaned. 'It's simple.'

'I don't want the bad publicity,' Black said. 'It could kill my career. It doesn't take much these days, not with social media.'

'You selfish bastard,' Butler said through her teeth.

Black ignored her and looked up at Moone. 'Patrick McGrady,' Black said. 'The guy who performed the tattoo. By the way, I did design the tattoo, but it was McGrady who insisted it was a butterfly. He was adamant, in fact. I think Lisa agreed in the end, just to get some peace.'

'Where did this all happen?' Butler asked.

'Here.' The chef refilled his glass, took a sip and walked to the windows.

Butler stood behind him. 'So you, Mrs Dyer and some weird, butterfly obsessed chef come here and convince her to get a tattoo? Was this some kind of sex party thing?'

Black turned round, the anger back in his eyes. 'No, it wasn't. Is your mind completely in the gutter? McGrady would come here and cook for me. Why have a dog and bark yourself? Anyway, Lisa came over to let her hair down. We had a few drinks, got a bit... merry... and the next thing I know, McGrady has joined us and we're planning a tattoo. It was all a bit wild.'

'I bet. I take it drugs were involved in this little party?' Butler raised her eyebrows.

Black looked at her, seething a little. 'No comment.'

'Do you know if this Patrick McGrady is medically trained or used to work at the hospital?' Moone asked.

Black nodded. 'I believe so. I can't recall what department, but I'm pretty sure he had some kind of medical training.'

'Like you?' Butler stared at him. 'Ever put a cannula in someone?'

Black laughed, shaking his head. 'No, I trained for a while as a junior doctor, but I dropped out quite soon into it. Wasn't the life for me. So, no, I wouldn't have a clue how to put a cannula in.'

'Convenient.' Butler turned away with another huff.

'No, it's not convenient,' Black said, his face reddening as his eyes burnt out to Moone. 'None of this is convenient. Being suspected of murder is not convenient, especially if the papers get hold of this and the customers stop coming to my restaurants. You know the restaurant business is very fragile, you understand that? One bad review or a piece of bad press...'

Moone held up his hand. 'Yes, you said before, you don't want the bad publicity. We understand. We won't be talking to the papers.'

'How do I know that?'

'You have my word.' Moone smiled. 'Scout's honour.'

'Scout's honour?' Black downed the rest of his Champagne. 'I hope you catch this nut job, detectives. Go and talk to Patrick McGrady. He's your man. Obsessed with butterfly tattoos. Always thought he was crazy.'

'We will.' Moone started to follow Butler to the open door.

'But be careful,' Black called. 'He's violent. He's sick. He may seem calm on the outside, but inside he's raging with anger. I know, I've worked with him.'

CHAPTER 23

'This guy sounds like a right psycho,' Butler said, reading the file from her tablet device as Moone drove them to the hospital, an incident response car not far behind them.

'Why, what's he done?' Moone looked over at her, then back to the Tavistock Road, the traffic slowing up, the mass of brake lights flashing on.

'He was in the British Army, serving in Northern Ireland. It says he was dishonourably discharged for torturing IRA suspects. Jesus. And he used to be a chef.'

'Is he medically trained?' Moone asked and took the Derriford roundabout and headed towards the main entrance of the hospital.

'Doesn't say, but he's bound to have picked up a few tips in the army.'

Moone nodded and took them to the smaller car park opposite the parade of restaurants that sat under the new multi-storey car park. He turned off the engine, thinking it all through, and remembering that Butler's father was still staying at the hospital. Chances were that he would never leave. He looked at Butler who was still engrossed in the file she was reading, wondering if he should broach the subject again.

'How's your dad doing?' he asked, bracing himself, ready to jump and roll out the car if needs be.

She huffed, then looked up through the windscreen. 'He's struggling to breathe. On oxygen most of the time now. It's not looking good.'

'I'm sorry.'

She looked at him. 'Why do people say that? When other people have relatives who are dying or dead, they say I'm sorry. Why?'

'Sympathy?'

'It's ridiculous. They're not sorry, they're glad it's not them in that situation.'

'Well, I can't speak for them, whoever they are, but I am genuinely sorry that you're both going through this. Are you going to see him?'

She shrugged. 'I don't know. Why should I?'

Moone braced himself and put one hand on the car door handle. 'What happened between you two?'

She glared at him, almost making him flinch. He held up a hand. 'It's fine. I won't ask.'

Then her face seemed to soften as she

looked forwards again. 'I suppose you'll keep asking. So, I'll tell you...'

'You don't have to.'

She huffed and stared at him. 'Just shut your cakehole, Moone and listen.'

'OK, cakehole closed.'

'This might surprise you but, well, a long time ago I was pregnant...'

Moone held his face together, held back the raging torrent of questions, and managed a nod.

'Everything seemed OK,' she said. 'Had all the scans. No problem. Then with a couple of weeks to go. Well, I started bleeding. Heavily.'

Moone's stomach turned over.

Butler looked down. 'I tried to get hold of my dad, who had been taking me to appointments and stuff like that. Couldn't get hold of him. So, I end up going round to my neighbour. They took me to the hospital. Mr Jarvis from Number sixty-seven. Lovely Mr Jarvis. Retired Policeman. Funny. Anyway, he took me to the hospital and he held my hand when they scanned me and they told me they couldn't find a heartbeat.'

'Oh...' Moone almost reached out to touch her hand.

'He even cried when I cried.'

'Where was your dad?'

Butler huffed, a deep cavernous huff. 'He was off with his fancy woman. Mavis Wright.

The same woman he cheated on my mum with. Bastard. Why should I care that he's dying?'

Butler was staring at him, the question thick in the air between them, almost solidifying and filling Moone's mouth and throat.

'He's your dad. I know that's unforgivable, but he's still your dad and if you don't go and see him and he... you know, then you'll never forgive yourself.'

Butler nodded. 'You're a wally, Moone, you know that?'

'I know.' He climbed out and Butler followed, so he headed out of the car park and towards the main entrance of the hospital.

'So, we don't even know if this psycho still works here,' Butler said as they headed into the hospital and towards the reception desk, the two uniforms they'd brought along not far behind them. There was a bulky, shaven headed, middle-aged man sat reading a paper at the desk. Moone showed his ID, which barely raised a response.

'DCI Peter Moone,' he said, causing the man to put away his paper and stand up. 'We're looking for a Patrick McGrady.'

'Is he a patient?' the man asked, stifling a yawn.

'Either works here or used to,' Butler said. 'Big fella by all accounts.'

The man ran a hand over his shaved head,

sighing deeply. 'Do you know how many people work here?'

'No, but just tap at the keyboard and it shouldn't take long,' Butler said.

The man shook his head but did as he was told. 'One Patrick McGrady. Works as a porter. Go down the corridor, turn left, then go right down to end. You can't miss it.'

Moone nodded. 'Thanks, I know where it is.'

As they headed towards the porters' office, Butler said, 'Isn't this the second porter we've had dealings with?'

'Bit of a strange coincidence, isn't it?' Moone asked, looking over his shoulder at her.

'Unless all the porters happen to be weirdos.'

Moone shrugged. 'Not entirely implausible, but doubtful.'

'Patrick McGrady?' Moone said, and showed his ID to the middle-aged lady who was sat in the small office.

The woman put on her glasses and stared at Moone's ID. 'Patrick? Not in trouble, is he?'

'We just need a word,' Butler said, folding her arms.

'He should be on his break,' the woman said. 'Try the staffroom round the corner, through those double doors. I'll let you through.'

There was a beeping sound, so Moone

pushed open the doors, then quickly pushed himself against the wall as a hospital bed came speeding towards him. At one end was a young woman with pink and purple hair, and at the other was a large, bearded man, probably in his mid-forties.

'Patrick McGrady?' Moone asked the young woman and noticed she flashed her eyes towards her colleague before she shrugged and said, 'I don't know...'

But by then the big man swung round and was hammering his boots back down the way he had come, moving at a surprisingly fast speed. Moone spun round, trying to spot the uniforms.

'He's doing a runner!' Moone shouted at Butler, but the uniforms had appeared, running past him and heading down the corridor.

Moone started to jog in pursuit, seeing the big man sprinting far ahead with the uniforms struggling to keep up. He was pushing beds and patients out of the way as he pumped his arms madly. Then he stopped dead, panting, and slowly turned to face the uniforms. He straightened up, a big grin appearing on his face as the male uniform reached him and slowed down.

'Fancy your chances, young man?' Moone heard Patrick say, just before he lunged at the uniform, stuck his massive foot behind the constable's leg and pushed him backwards.

The big man bellowed out a laugh as he turned back round and started running along the corridor.

'Stop! Police!' Moone yelled and started running after him. He didn't know quite what he was going to do if the big bruiser stopped and faced him. He glanced behind and looked for Butler but she was nowhere to be seen. Typical, he thought and turned back to see the huge shape of Patrick McGrady hammering his way out of the corridor. Moone had got to know the hospital pretty well over the last couple of years and knew there was a corridor that spliced McGrady's escape route in two. He sprinted back down the main corridor, then through the stairwell that joined the two corridors and rushed back out into the hallway, just in time to cut McGrady off.

McGrady slowed up, his face red and covered in sweat. He seemed to think for a moment, then smiled as he clenched his giant fists and stepped towards Moone.

'Think you can take me on, do you, you pig bastard?' McGrady said, unaware of the two uniforms about to pounce on his back.

Moone stepped backwards as the uniforms went to work, wrestling the giant man, trying desperately to pull him to the ground. But with one swipe of his thick arms, McGrady threw the male uniform against the wall, then swung round on the female uniform and sent her flying with a sickening punch to the face. With both uniforms lying comatose on the floor, McGrady turned his breathless attention back to Moone with a smile.

'Now, where were we, my man?' McGrady said and balled his fists, blood smearing his right one.

Butler seemed to appear out of nowhere, throwing out her arm that held a taser. The big man jerked, letting out a deafening roar as his body convulsed. Then he seemed to shake himself out of it and looked at Butler as if she'd merely slapped him on the cheek.

'Sneaky fucking bitch,' he said, and gripped her entire face in his hand and pushed her back against the wall, pinning her.

Moone saw her lift her knee and flinched with imagined pain as it made contact between the big porter's legs. McGrady howled, gripping his crotch as he crumpled to the floor, a big thick tree being felled.

Butler recovered quickly and secured his hands behind his back then looked at Moone. 'Do you want to do the honours?'

Moone took a breath and approached the sweating, grunting lump on the floor. 'Patrick McGrady, I'm arresting you on the suspicion of murder...'

McGrady yanked his head up, staring up at Moone. 'Murder, is it? Fuck me...'

'You do not have to say anything…'

'Murder? I haven't fucking murdered anyone… well, not since the fucking eighties. It was a different time back then, so it was.'

Moone ignored him, and helped Butler get the big man to his feet. 'But it may harm your defence if you do not mention when questioned something which you later rely on in court. Understand?'

McGrady straightened himself, half laughing. 'You think I committed some murder?'

'Why did you run?' Butler asked.

'Because I thought you thought I was stealing from the hospital.'

'And are you?' Butler pushed him towards the exit.

'No, darling. I'm innocent as the day is fucking long.'

It was nearly an hour later that Moone and Butler had Patrick McGrady delivered to the custody suite, then escorted to interview room one after a medical examination. His duty solicitor arrived half an hour later, a small man with balding red hair, wearing square glasses.

Moone stepped in, a mug of black coffee in his hand, a file in the other. Butler followed and they both sat down, facing the giant Northern Irishman who smiled at them, trying to appear calm and friendly. But Moone could sense it, the underlying tremor of violence the man carried around in his frame, in his past.

'Patrick McGrady,' Moone said. 'Just to remind you that you're under caution. We will be recording this interview.'

'You shouldn't be wasting your time with me, fella,' McGrady laughed. 'You should be out there, finding your man.'

But Moone didn't reply. Butler started the recorder and read out the relevant information.

'You are Patrick McGrady, aren't you?' Moone asked, sitting back.

'That's what my ma named me,' he said and sat back. 'I hope I didn't hurt no one.'

'Just their pride,' Butler said. 'And a broken nose, I might add.'

'Sorry,' the big man said, looking convincingly ashamed.

The duty solicitor leaned in towards McGrady and mumbled something, which caused the Irishman to stare at him as if he was naked. 'Too fucking late now, fella. Anyway, about a dozen people saw what I did. Don't suppose I'll have me a job after this little affair.'

'Probably not.' Butler sat back. 'There are certain dates we need you to confirm where you were.'

'Because of a murder?' McGrady laughed. 'No, I didn't commit a murder. Who is it I'm supposed to have knocked off? A few patients?

Jesus, Mary... the ones I spend my days pushing around are ready to drop anyway.'

'You used to work for Mario Black, that's right, isn't it?' Moone asked, folding his arms across his chest.

'Aye, so I did. Quite a while back. What of it? Your man made a complaint against me?'

Moone shook his head. 'Just making sure of a few details. Do you have any tattoos?'

'Any tattoos?' McGrady raised his bushy eyebrows, then rolled up his sleeve, revealing an army tattoo that covered most of his thick forearm. 'How's that? That do yer?'

'Ever performed any tattoos?' Butler asked.

'Performed?'

'Yes,' Moone said, 'performed, as in applying the tattoo to the skin.'

McGrady stared at them both in turn before the solicitor whispered in his ear again.

'Oh, shut the fuck up,' McGrady growled at the small man, then looked at Moone. 'No, I've never performed any tattoos. Why the fuck would I? I spent twenty years in the fucking British Army, getting spat on by my own people. Then I'm stuck in the fucking desert... What do I do now? Push people about all fucking day long. It's killing me back, so it is. I don't hardly sleep now.'

'We don't want your life history.' Butler huffed.

'Oh, don't you?' McGrady glared at her. 'Well, boo fucking hoo, cause you're fucking getting it.'

Butler pushed a piece of paper with the dates and the estimated times of the murders printed on. 'Where were you on these dates at those times?'

McGrady shook his head, then looked down. He tapped the paper with his huge forefinger. 'Working. Plenty of fucking witnesses. Got drunk with Brendan Taylor. Working. You can check with the fucking head porters if you don't believe me.'

Moone nodded. 'We will. Do you know a young woman called Bobbi-Jane Todd?'

McGrady narrowed his deeply buried, wrinkled eyes. 'Bobbi who? No, never heard of her. The only young girls I meet are patients.'

'Are you sure you've never met her?' Moone pushed a photo of Bobbi across the table, and watched McGrady look at it blankly.

'Never seen her before. What the hell're you pulling here? I wouldn't hurt a wee girl.'

'You know your way around a kitchen, don't you?' Moone asked.

McGrady's brow creased. 'A kitchen? Aye, just about.'

'Just about?' Butler laughed. 'You worked for Mario Black, didn't you?'

McGrady laughed and sat back. 'Oh right, oh yes, I worked for Mr Black. But he didn't let me anywhere near his fucking kitchen.'

'Why not?' Moone asked.

'Cause I can't boil a fucking egg.' McGrady laughed some more. 'I drove his car and generally looked out for him. You thought I was one of his chefs? Why did you think that?'

Moone looked at Butler and found she was looking back at him with a tired, pissed-off expression on her face, much the same as he felt.

He was careful not to park too close to the road that led to Black's costal home. He knew there were cameras pointed at the road, but none before that. No one would see him coming or going. The next house along was a couple of hundred yards away, and the whole reason Black had bought the house was for privacy.

He walked the rest of the way, avoiding the eyes of the occasional dog walker or insane swimmer. He climbed the metal gate and jumped down into the lane, then walked towards the house, watching the dark water smashing against the rocks below and spitting up into the air. Seagulls hovered high above, screeching, then dive-bombed downwards.

He knocked on the glass and saw movement inside, then heard the distant sound of shoes tapping against hard wood flooring. He caught sight of his own reflection, the hood covering his head. He looked down as the door slid open, the beat of music coming from deep within the huge house and its clean, uncluttered interior. He immediately liked the place.

'You're early,' Black said, adjusting his tie. The chef was decked out in a dark suit, a waft of heavy aftershave clouding the air between them. The chef's eyes widened. 'Oh God, what happened to you? You look so different.'

'Do I?' He stepped inside, admiring the interior, keeping his hands in his pockets and fighting the urge to touch anything. 'You've done well for yourself.'

Black overtook him and picked up a glass of what was probably Champagne. 'Lots of hard work, I can tell you. Let's make this quick, as I have to go to a meeting.'

'OK, what did you want?'

Black huffed. 'You know. You've been using one of my recipes.'

'Have I?'

'They found it in the stomach of a dead young woman.' Black stared at him for a moment, then held up his hands. 'It's fine. I don't want to know what this is all about, but you need to stop feeding them my food. They think it's me.'

'You don't seem flustered.'

Black sipped his drink. 'Want one?'

'No.'

Black nodded. 'No, I'm not flustered. I've

seen my fair share of horrific things. I've met a lot of interesting people. Loy Grader, for one. He's a very bad man.'

'A child killer. The worst.' He looked round, wondering why the chef was bringing up that particularly sick individual.

'You must be wondering why I mentioned him.'

He shrugged. 'I don't care. I have my own agenda.'

'The bastard snatched the son of a friend.'

He looked at him, then stepped closer, examining Black's face, trying to perceive any sign of real emotion. 'You're talking about that woman. The one I tattooed?'

'Yes.'

'You're in love with her.' He laughed.

'I wouldn't say love...'

'Grader took her son?'

'I'm pretty sure.'

'And if you can tell her that you've arranged retribution, then you'll be the hero. I suppose she would let you do anything you want to her, wouldn't she?'

Black shrugged. 'Perhaps. Will you do it?'

'And if I say no, you'll expose me?'

Black nodded.

He thought for a moment, wondering what it would be like to be an avenging angel for once. It would not produce the same high, the same ecstasy as staring into his painted ladies as the life drained out of them. But it would be an experience. 'How would I get to him?'

'He comes to the hospital every month for a health check-up. Two guards keep him in line. They clear out the ward before he arrives. If you can get close...'

'That wouldn't be a problem.' He looked round the kitchen area of the house, admiring the cleanliness of it all. His eyes stopped on an object. He looked at Black. 'You're scared of me.'

Black laughed. 'What? As if I'd be scared.'

He pointed to the knife block that had all the blades removed and hidden somewhere. 'Then where are all the knives?'

Black lost any of his mirth. 'Being cleaned. Anyway, can I count on you to help me?'

He smiled, then stepped closer, keeping his hands dug into his pockets. 'Of course you can. But, it's not always going to be the kind of help you need.'

Black stared at him, the first glimmer of perhaps a little realisation behind his dark eyes. 'What is that supposed to mean?'

He smiled at the chef, then turned his attention to the bottle on the kitchen counter. He picked it up, turned it upside down and let the contents pour out onto the floor.

'What the fuck do you think you're doing?' Black snapped. 'Do you know how much a bottle of that stuff costs?'

'Oh, yes, I do.' He held the stem of the bottle in his gloved right hand and stepped closer to Mario Black, making the chef retreat, the fear beginning to mix with anger on his formerly smug face. This he would enjoy, even though there would be no real beauty created within the act. No, there would be a kind of beauty, he realised when he turned such an ugly soul into something so still and peaceful.

The chef raised his open hands, forming some kind of martial arts pose as he stepped backwards.

'I'm a black belt in four different martial arts,' Black said, gritting his teeth, putting an edge into his voice.

He couldn't help laugh as he threw the bottle across the room where it smashed. He put his gloved hand into his jacket and brought out the knife he had brought along, just in case. 'Did they teach you how not to get stabbed?'

The chef's eyes jumped to the blade, widening, while his hands lowered. 'There's no need for all this. I'm on your side, remember? We have a deal, don't we?'

He stepped closer, swapping the knife hand to hand, unable to keep the grin from burning across this face. 'Not really. Well, I might actually kill Grader. I mean, why not rid the world of a child murderer?'

'Then we have a deal?' Black tried to smile, but his skin had lost any colour as he backed up, his eyes now jumping about the kitchen. He was looking for a weapon and cursing himself for removing all the knives. He laughed as Black made a sudden lurch for one of his kitchen drawers, trying to pull it open in time.

He struck out, digging the knife into the chef's back, making him howl and try and reach round to defend himself. He screamed when the blade went in again, and again.

He stepped back, watching the chef stagger about the kitchen, groaning, swearing, trying to reach the wounds on his back. His skin was white, and he was trembling all over. The smugness was gone, sapped away from him and pure fear shone in his eyes.

'Help me,' Black said, begging, falling to his knees. 'Call an ambulance.'

He shook his head, then put a finger to his lips as he grabbed the chef by his hair and brought the knife hard into his chest.

He didn't know how many times he stabbed him, but he had blood all over his clothing by the time he came to his senses, breathing hard. He stripped off his first layer of clothes and took them to the chef's garden. He loaded the barbecue with coals and fire lighters and bundled the clothes on top. He grabbed the lighter from the shelf under the barbecue and carefully lit just one fire lighter brick, adding more fire lighter bricks to fuel the flames.

He looked about at the view, breathing it

all in, feeling the beat of victory and ecstasy in his chest until it slowly ebbed away, leaving him a little empty. Not for long, he thought, and remembered the young woman locked in his house. Her time to be beautiful was coming.

CHAPTER 24

There was a wind coming up from the sea, bringing with it the scent of everything dark and rotting left on the beach. The sun had sunk down beneath the waters, colouring the sky with a deep burgundy glow. Moone watched the horizon as he walked, then turned to see that the cordon had been set up and the blue and white tape was being toyed with by the same stale breeze. Seagulls rode the thermals, squawking at him as they dived towards the cliffs. The silhouettes of uniforms danced along the side of Black's home, made eerily long by the lights that had been set up.

Moone showed his ID, then ducked under the tape that a uniform held up for him. He signed the crime scene log, then looked round to see if any onlookers or press had caught wind of the situation. That would be all they needed.

He went down the path, moving out of the way of the SOCOs travelling back and forth.

He stepped onto the duckboards and headed along to the side of the house where the French window was open. The curtain was sucked in and blown out.

There was a flash of blue light as a SOCO photographed Black's lifeless body by the doorway. Moone blinked, trying to remove the swirling glowing blue blob from his eyes so he could focus on the body again.

'Twenty-six stab wounds,' Butler's voice said and Moone looked up, focusing in on her tired, drawn face.

'I didn't think you'd be here,' Moone said. 'I thought you'd gone to the hospital.'

She shrugged, and looked down towards the SOCO photographer. 'He sleeps most of the time.'

Moone walked over to her. 'You haven't talked to him yet? Made your peace?'

'I haven't had a chance.' She pointed to the body. 'I bet our killer did this.'

'What happened?' Moone looked round the room for someone in charge of the crime scene.

'No sign of breaking and entering,' a man's voice said across the room, where one of the SOCOs was getting to their feet. The SOCO faced Moone, revealing a ginger bearded man. 'The French window was open. Looks like our victim and his killer had words. Victim was drinking. One glass. The bottle's lying smashed in the corner. Possibly thrown by the killer, which might suggest anger. Then there was a struggle, and the victim was stabbed repeatedly. Castoff suggests the killer was above average height.'

'Fingerprints?' Butler asked.

'Only the victim's so far,' the SOCO said. 'His killer came prepared. Probably wore gloves.'

'Thanks,' Moone said and turned towards the door, listening to the seagulls squawking and the sea lapping at the shore, thinking it all through.

'He knew who killed our young girls,' Butler said, joining him as she stood by his side, looking out of the window.

Moone nodded. 'Looks like it. Maybe he decided to contact our killer.'

'Or our killer could've decided to pay him a visit to tidy up.'

'Perhaps.'

'Or what's more likely is that Black and our killer are friends and he wanted to give him the heads up. Or Black was involved, like I said earlier.'

Moone looked at her, saw the look of sad triumph in her eyes. 'It's possible. Hence the food in their stomachs... but why do that? Why use ingredients that would have us knocking on his door in seconds?'

'That's obvious.' Butler huffed.

'Is it? Enlighten me.'

'He was arrogant. Self-obsessed. People like that can't wait to wave it in our faces, show us how clever they've been.'

Moone looked back out of the window, thinking it through, then headed out into the night, feeling the chill grip him. Butler had a point, he knew that, and so much of the evidence pointed at the chef being involved. But he also had that whispering doubt at his ear.

'You still don't agree, do you?' Butler said behind him.

He faced her. 'I don't know. Everything's pointing to him being involved…'

'He even pointed us in Patrick McGrady's direction so he could have a good laugh at us.'

Moone nodded. 'Yes, he did. So, he contacts his cohort and they have words, fall out or whatever, then he gets killed?'

Butler shrugged. 'That's what it looks like to me.'

'So who's the other killer? Who killed Black?'

'I don't know. But we're getting closer.'

'Are we? Doesn't feel like it. Does Black have any CCTV cameras?'

'Yes, further up the road, but the killer must have snuck past them. One of the houses along here might have picked something up.'

Moone nodded. 'Get uniforms to check,

then go and be with your dad.'

She stared at him, a strange look coming over her face, a look he had hardly ever seen before. For a moment he thought there might be tears, but there was a soft huff as she came closer. 'I don't know what to say to him.'

'You'll know what to say. Just go and be there. If you don't, you'll regret it.'

Butler gave a fleeting, awkward smile. 'I'll tell the uniforms to check on CCTV, then I'll be off.'

'Good. See you later.' Moone headed to his car, his mind dragging itself away from Butler's problems and towards the dark and obscure mystery that still lay in front of him. He thought of the killer, who drove an ambulance, perhaps had some medical training and had an obsession with tattoos. Then his mind travelled to the young woman that their killer had taken, who was probably locked up somewhere, scared, and waiting to die. He thought of the extra weight she carried, and wondered how long it would take the killer to get her down to the weight he desired her to be. They perhaps had two months, maybe weeks to find her before their killer marked her with his design and released her.

DI Crowne hadn't been to bed yet. He was sat in his living room, staring out at the night through the bay windows, avoiding looking back down at the crime scene photos scattered over the carpet. By rights, he shouldn't be looking them over at all, for he had his orders to file it all away, to pass it all onto the coroner, to be used in the short inquest that would follow.

He looked down at the battered body of Armstrong lying in the hotel room.

He rubbed his tired eyes, then stood up and stretched. He looked at the time and groaned. If he went to bed now, then he'd get a couple of hours sleep, maybe three. But it would take him ages to get to sleep now as his mind buzzed with it all.

Carthew came to mind, and he wondered if she had indeed been so clever and managed to get away with the perfect murder. No such thing, he told himself. Yes, there was. They had two dead people who seemed guilty of murder, who had motive, the most powerful motives of all. Love and greed.

He jumped when he heard a knock on his window. He went down the hallway, peering at the glass panel by the front door. There was a shape and he stopped, realising it was a female shape. He took a deep breath, wondering if Carthew would have the gall to come to his house.

He opened the door slowly and let out a breath when he saw DS Rivers stood there holding a sheet of paper in her hand.

'You all right?' she asked as she stepped inside. 'You looked a bit scared then.'

'Me? Scared?' He laughed, and followed her to the lounge to see her raise her eyebrows at the sight of the crime scene photos lying about the floor.

'We're not supposed to be looking into this,' she said.

'No,' he said and started picking up the photos. 'You didn't see this.'

'Then you didn't see this.' Rivers held up the photograph. It was a large printout of a grainy image of a front view of a car. It was clear enough to make out Jason Wise in the passenger seat and Armstrong's merry widow behind the wheel.

'OMG, as the kids say.' Crowne took the photo and examined it.

'Please don't ever say that again,' Rivers said. 'By the way, that was taken the night Armstrong died, about the time he was killed.'

Crowne stared up at her. 'What? So, they couldn't have murdered Armstrong?'

'Doesn't look like it. Unless they paid someone to do it. Someone who knew how to get away with it.'

Crowne sat back down on the sofa with a pain-filled sigh. 'So, basically we're back to square one? We've got to prove Carthew went to Armstrong's room and murdered him? Jesus.'

Rivers sat down next to him, taking the photo from his hands. 'I know, but she did it somehow. She's not God or the devil. She's a woman. A clever as fuck woman, but nonetheless a woman. Maybe she took money from them and paid some dodgy offender she's met on her way up.'

Crowne sighed and shook his head. 'I don't think so. And even if she did, then that offender would be dead by now. No, she did it somehow. But we're not allowed to bring her in.'

'But now we can prove it wasn't the wife or Wise. That's got to count for something. And she's got no alibi.'

He nodded. 'Because she thought she wouldn't need one. We need to go over everyone's story. Drag everyone in, all the people on Armstrong's course. We need to verify their alibis, and everything.'

'Including Carthew?'

Crowne felt his heart rate ramp up a beat, imagining the bollocking he'd get from above for dragging in Carthew again. He took a breath and looked at Rivers. 'Yep. Bring them all in. Leave her until last.'

DC Cara Banerjee was the second to be interviewed after the probationary Detective Constable Danielle Halligan, whose account of the evening had been very hazy after admitting she had quite a few shots bought for her by

DC Banerjee. The caramel-skinned DC Banerjee came into the interview room where Crowne and Rivers waited. She was dressed smartly in a grey trouser suit and black shirt, her dark shiny hair pulled back in a tight ponytail. She smiled politely as she was escorted to the desk and then sat down with her arms folded.

'Thanks for coming in, Detective Constable Banerjee,' Crowne said, smiling brightly, while watching her body movements, the way her eyes moved a little nervously.

'I heard that you'd ended your investigation,' she said, her dark eyes taking them both in.

Crowne nodded. 'That's what we thought, but there's a few unanswered questions we'd like to go over. Don't worry, you're not the only person we're talking to.'

'I wasn't worried,' Banerjee said, her voice tense. 'I've done nothing wrong.'

'Good,' Crowne said. 'I'm glad to hear it. Now, the night DSU Charlie Armstrong was murdered...'

'I was out in town,' Banerjee said. 'I've said it all before. I made a statement. DC Halligan should verify my whereabouts.'

'That's the thing,' Rivers said, smiling. 'She can for some of the evening. I mean, in her original statement, she said you were together the whole evening. But today, she seems a little unsure as you apparently bought her quite a few shots.'

'I don't know about that.'

'Well, she seems pretty sure about that,' Crowne said.

Banerjee let out a breath and raised her eyebrows. 'That detail she's sure about, but my whereabouts, she isn't?'

Crowne sat back. 'No, she doesn't seem sure about when you left. Nor are the others you met out that night, because you bought them a lot of drinks. You can see where we're having trouble. Thing is we decided to check CCTV around the club, just to check your comings and goings as it were.'

Banerjee looked awkward he noticed for a moment before she regained her composure and said, 'I didn't see many cameras outside the club.'

'You noticed the security cameras?' Rivers asked, with a laugh of surprise. 'Do you usually notice such things on a girls' night out?'

The DC stared at her, a tight smirk appearing. 'I'm a police officer. I'm always a police officer. I notice things like that. Sue me.'

Crowne laughed. 'Good. But there is a shop opposite the club you went to. It has a cashpoint outside. The camera catches the doors of the club. So we saw what time you left. You said in your original statement it was after one a.m.'

'It might have been a little earlier.'

Banerjee tightened her folded arms.

'A little?' Rivers asked.

'Yes.' The DC kept her face blank, but her eyes said it all, told of the panic within.

Crowne smiled. 'Maybe a lot? Before the murder, maybe?'

'I didn't murder anyone.'

'I didn't say you did. I don't think you did. But you left the club earlier than you first said. A lot earlier, didn't you?'

Banerjee was breathing harder, her eyes making calculations before she nodded. 'Yes, before the murder. I didn't say because obviously I didn't want you thinking I had anything to do with DSU Armstrong's murder.'

'Obviously,' Rivers said, eyeing the DC suspiciously. 'Which is what we are now, understandably, suspecting.'

Banerjee's eyes blazed. 'I didn't do it. Why would I? I didn't even know the man before a few weeks ago.'

Crowne leaned forward. 'Well, then tell us exactly why you got your colleagues drunk, so drunk that they didn't notice you sneak off halfway through the evening from a club within walking distance from the hotel where Armstrong was killed.'

The DC took a breath then looked down, her hands starting to fidget. 'I left the... I left the club early so I could meet someone.'

Crowne nodded. 'And this someone... did

you meet them at the hotel?'

She nodded, then she looked up, the look of realisation spreading like wildfire across her face. 'It wasn't DSU Armstrong, if that's what you're thinking.'

'We are,' Rivers said. 'But back to this mysterious meeting at the hotel. If you did return to the hotel, then why is there no CCTV of you walking through the lobby?'

'That's because I didn't walk through the lobby,' she said, looking down again.

'Interesting,' Crowne said, sitting back. 'Then how did you enter the hotel?'

'There's a back way in, through the kitchen.' Banerjee shrugged. 'No CCTV.'

'Convenient,' Rivers said. 'The perfect way to get into the hotel without being seen, so you could murder someone.'

'Why would I?' The DC's face flooded with panic and desperation. 'I didn't know him. I didn't have any reason to kill the man.'

Crowne nodded. 'OK, let's forget that for the moment, and why don't you tell us who you were meeting.'

Banerjee's face changed, the desperation sinking away and a strange fearfulness rising. 'I can't.'

'You can't?' Crowne exchanged disbelieving looks with Rivers. 'You're talking about your alibi. So far, we have you entering a hotel earlier than you said you did, basically lying to us. You're already risking your career. Just tell us who you were meeting.'

She shook her head. 'I'm sorry, but I can't. You have to understand, if my family ever found out.'

'You're afraid your family might find out?' Rivers asked. 'They would disapprove?'

'Very much. They have plans for my future.'

'I see.' Crowne shook his head. 'We're not here to get involved in your private life, Detective Constable Banerjee. We're here to investigate the murder of a fellow police officer. And at the moment, you're interfering with that investigation. We could by rights charge you. You do understand that?'

Banerjee looked down, then a strangled sob escaped her. 'I know. I know. I just…'

Crowne folded his arms, watching her cry. 'Then all we've got is you sneaking back into a hotel where a man, a police officer, was murdered. That makes you our chief suspect.'

Banerjee sat back, sniffing, wiping her eyes, seeming to bring herself back to a state of almost being calm. 'Then I guess you'd better arrest me.'

Crowne looked at Rivers. 'DS Rivers, I think I'm beginning to understand what happened.'

'Are you?' Rivers said, a little confusion showing in her eyes.

He nodded. 'It's obvious. DC Banerjee headed back to the hotel for her late-night date with this person she's too afraid to expose. So ashamed of, apparently, that she would rather lose her job and go to prison than reveal who they are. Well, what if DSU Armstrong saw Banerjee and this mysterious person together...'

'He didn't.' Banerjee's eyes widened again.

'It's the only thing that makes sense,' Rivers said, nodding. 'It's the only motive that makes sense.'

'Oh my God.' The DC hung her head for a second then looked at them both, tears in her eyes. 'I didn't murder him. You've got to understand.'

'Help us understand,' Crowne said, putting a sympathetic tone in his voice. 'This person you met with, were they on the course?'

Banerjee nodded, then started crying again.

'So, we know where Wise went,' Crowne continued. 'Your friends were drunk, thanks to you. So, that leaves... DS Carthew?'

Banerjee didn't look up, just let out another sob.

'You were meeting Carthew?' Crowne looked at Rivers and exchanged another shocked glance.

She nodded, swallowing down another choked sob.

'Was this...' Rivers began, 'A romantic thing?'

Banerjee looked between them. 'Please, I don't want anyone finding out about this. Please, if my family ever found out.'

Crowne sat back, his head beginning to spin with it all. Then a question rose up in it, a feeling of unease rising with it. 'Banerjee? Was Carthew with you all evening?'

The DC nodded. 'Yes, we were together all night.'

Crowne looked at Rivers and saw they shared the same look of disappointment. He rubbed his eyes, the realisation invading his body. If Banerjee was telling the truth, then Carthew couldn't have killed anyone that night.

CHAPTER 25

There came a sound, somewhere above her. Her eyes shot open, her cry muffled by the gag over her mouth. It took a moment for Bobbi's eyes to adjust to the thick, inky darkness of the room. Her left arm was stuck under her body, and was numb. She tried to move and the cuff rattled, along with the chain keeping her attached to the radiator. She lay still and listened, waiting for the sound of his footsteps. It had been a day or so since he had come to see her. As much as she was scared when he came in to see her, she was more fearful of the dark, and the dreadful loneliness it brought. She had only her memories to keep her company, and they came with terrible imaginings, images of her family in despair not knowing if she was alive or dead. Would they ever stop looking for her? She couldn't be sure.

There were the footsteps, coming down, slowly. It was always a painful journey, a slow and deliberate torture he inflicted on her, or so it seemed.

Her heart started to race as the footsteps sped up, almost turning into a run. The lock was fiddled with, her captor dropping the keys in the process and cursing. The door was flung open and he stood there in the doorway, breathing hard, his eyes beyond the mask staring at her. When he took a sudden step towards her, she retreated, flinching, ready to fight for her life.

'It's time for you to go,' his muffled, breathless voice said.

She looked at him, her mind spinning, wondering what hidden message the words carried.

He stepped closer, holding up his gloved hands. 'I'm not going to hurt you. I know you don't understand, but I saved you. If I hadn't taken you, then he would have, and you'd be in a cell in a dark basement right now. You might even be dead.'

She looked away, her heart pounding, tears filling her eyes. She wanted to believe him. Really needed to believe he meant her no harm, but he had taken her, drugged her and dragged her into the back of an ambulance. How long ago did that happen?

'You have to trust me.'

She let out a harsh breath, then more tears.

'I'm going to undo your cuff, then take

you out the back way.' He stepped closer. 'Please don't try anything. In an hour, you'll be gone from here.'

She stared at him, looking into his dark eyes, trying to tell if he was being genuine.

'I need...'

There was a strange look in his eyes, and suddenly she knew what he wanted. She shivered, turned her back on him, and closed her eyes.

'I need to see it. One last time.'

She flinched when his gloved hands touched her back. He was always gentle, never grabbed her, but still she hated feeling his hands on her. There was something about the way he handled her, touched her, as if she was... as if she was just an object, a dead thing. And there was the smell he carried, the awful smell he always brought with him. A deathly smell. She pushed the terrible thoughts from her mind, tried to ignore the scent, ridding herself of the sickness it brought.

He pulled her top up, then let out a harsh sigh. She heard him step back, the creak of the floorboards.

'Do you know how beautiful you are?' he said, his voice barely a whisper. 'I see so many young women. So many pass my eyes, but none of them are truly beautiful like you. They are all grey and empty. Lifeless.'

He pulled her top down, then placed his

gloved hand on her shoulder and squeezed. She shuddered again, feeling the vomit almost rise up to her mouth.

'Are you ready to go?'

She turned and looked up at him. She nodded, sniffing, feeling the hope rise in her.

'Don't worry, I'll get you to the van and I'll take you somewhere far from here.' He nodded and she could tell that beneath the mask he was smiling brightly. 'When we're far from here... then I can release you.'

Moone rubbed his tired eyes as he stood outside the incident room, taking the lid off his double espresso. Butler was at the hospital, and the sun was barely up. Sleep kept edging into the corners of his eyes, but so were the questions the case kept throwing up. Black, their prime suspect, was dead. Now would the murders cease, or would his partner in crime continue his horrific work? Moone was about to push open the door to the incident room, when his phone started ringing in his pocket. He answered when he saw it was Crowne calling him, trying hard to balance his coffee in the crook of his arm.

'Crowne?' Moone said, leaning against the wall. 'Didn't think I'd hear from you.'

'No, I didn't think I'd be calling,' Crowne said, a heavy sigh in his voice.

'What's happened?'

'You're never going to believe this.'

'If this is to do with DS Carthew, then I'll believe anything.'

Crowne gave an empty laugh. 'Me too. She's got an alibi.'

'What? Apart from being in her room alone?'

'I'm afraid so. Seems she's been romantically involved with one of the students on her course.'

'Who?'

'A DC Cara Banerjee. She says they were together in her room all night.'

'What? Then she must've got Banerjee to lie for her.'

'I don't think so. This young lady is so terrified of her family finding out about all this, she was prepared to lose her job...'

'Then that's it, Carthew's blackmailed her. Threatened to expose her to her family...'

Crowne sighed. 'I don't think so. I believe her. Someone else must have killed him. I'm sorry.'

Moone lowered his head, his heart diving once more, knowing Carthew had managed to pull off the impossible. No, he thought, no one could be that clever. She would have made some error. 'There must be something. She did this, I know she did. Even if she didn't commit the murder herself, there must be something tying her to this. I'd talk to this DS Banerjee again. I mean, where did they meet? How did this so-called romance start? Carthew's stringing her along, using her, I know she is.'

Crowne sighed again. 'OK, fair point. It would be interesting to know how this love affair started. I'll let you know.'

The call ended and Moone breathed out, trying to relieve some of the tension in his back and shoulders. He rubbed his neck as he took his coffee into the incident room and headed for his small office.

'Oh, morning, sir,' DC Chambers said, jumping up from her desk.

Moone held up his hand. 'Molly, it's boss, or hey, you there, but never sir.'

'Sorry, boss.' She blushed, then pointed at her desk. 'I got here early and I was here late last night...'

'Don't you have a home to go to, Molly?' Moone sipped his coffee.

She shrugged, her mouth turning down. 'Not really. I mean, I've got a house my mum left to me. My dad's in a home. Early onset Alzheimer's. My boyfriend buggered off about a month ago now...'

'I'm sorry,' Moone said, half feeling guilty that he knew little about his team, apart from Butler and half feeling too tired to entertain her woes. He smiled. 'It can't be easy.'

'I prefer to work.' She raised a smile, then picked up a printout from her desk.

'I was looking into our victims' pasts. The background checks came back from Cardiff police. Chloe Gillard worked at a hospital in Wales as a domestic assistant about a year before she went missing...'

Moone carried on towards his desk with his coffee. 'Another hospital connection, that's interesting. Good work.'

'Well, she started off as a domestic assistant, then she became a porter for a while.'

Moone stopped mid sip and stared up at her, the hair seeming to catch fire along the back of his neck. He stood up and took the printout from her. 'A porter? That's really interesting. This will be the third hospital porter connection. Right, get on to University Hospital Wales, and find out who was working with her when she was a porter...'

'OK, then I'll run the list against our people of interest.'

Moone smiled. 'Yep, and we might just get a new suspect. Well done, Molly.'

He never looked out of place anywhere really, especially not in the hospital. Yes, sometimes people, the patients and other staff, looked at him in a way that said how weird and ugly they thought he looked. But they were prejudiced, filled to the brim with the hate and ignorance the media had presented them with. They didn't understand true beauty. He smiled as he walked through the hospital, ignoring the bustle of patients, the chatter and noise coming from the restaurant. He stopped to take some gloves from the dispenser on the wall, then pulled them on, watching everything around him. Most people came and went without making eye contact. He was just another body in a uniform. He looked at his watch and saw that he had another half hour before the police van would deliver Loy Grader to the hospital for his monthly check-up.

Black was dead, and therefore he had no obligation to hold up his end of the bargain, but there was something about his request that sparked his interest. It was the thought of the former Mrs Dyer, the memory of designing the tattoo and drawing it on her skin. The images of that day flashed in his mind, how he had tried to recreate the tattoo on her flesh. It had been a beautiful thing, but yet it wasn't right. She had been beautiful already and a desire for her had made his heart beat so much faster than usual. She had not noticed him, or he suspected had found him unattractive, ugly even. It would feel good somehow to visit her and see the old tattoo. He smiled, nodding to himself, imagining how good and proud he would feel seeing her again and informing her that her enemy had been vanquished forever.

He moved on, unseen as always, nodding

to his fellow workers, smiled at by some of the nurses he knew. Most of them paid him no mind and today he was glad of it. He turned left, heading towards the porters' office, but he had arranged to start later that day and only swung by to say hello to his colleagues and to hear them discussing Patrick's arrest. He made himself a cup of tea in the staffroom, listening to everyone gossiping, half watching the clock on the wall.

It was nearly time. He slipped out again, his heart beginning to pound in his pigeon chest and he wondered if anyone noticed the harsh rise and fall of it. But no one took much notice of him as he headed for the back lifts, the ones they used for patients that preferred not to exhibit their injuries to the world. He swiped his pass on the lift's sensor, then typed the passcode. No one stepped out when it arrived and so he had time to think all alone as the lift rose and groaned all the way to the cardiology department. When he left the lift, he took a turning on his right, and hid in the small cupboard area where the domestic assistants stored their equipment. He rested his back on a vacuum and waited, absorbing the sensations, imagining how it would feel to release another young woman.

Bobbi's hands were tied behind her back, her ankles bound together, her face pressed down on a mat he had laid on the floor of the van. He had gagged her and apologised all the time, and she wondered for a moment whether he was truly sorry or if it was some game. She had thought she had seen genuine regret in his eyes, and a hint of sadness. Then he would smile, a big grin that lit up his eyes and it would make her unsure again, as if it was all a joke. Now she was in a van, the engine rumbling, her body shaking as it made its way out of the city. The sound of traffic and people had faded away half an hour ago, and all hope that he would release her somewhere public had faded with it. Then she had started shaking, trembling all over, feeling an iciness crossing her back. Her heart was racing at the realisation he was taking her into the countryside, maybe even the moors. Tears came, fear filling her heart, flashes of him marching her out into the woods. She hated the woods. Even as a child it would fill her with a terrible sense of terror if they even passed by one.

She started to sob when the van began to slow down, then turned and shook as it made its way along an uneven road.

Then it stopped and the engine rumbled to silence.

Silence.

Nothing but the blood pounding in her ears. He was still sat in the driver's seat, not moving. She tried to lift her head to see if she could see him through the glass partition. It was no good, she couldn't get a good look.

The van door creaked open and he stepped out. She began to sob with all her heart, her eyes blind with tears, her head pounding and aching. The side door slid open and the silhouette of him stood there, silent for a moment, black against the bright day. There was a little rain in the air. She smelt damp earth. She started crying again.

She saw a grave in her mind. A shallow grave in the woods.

'What's all the crying about?' he asked.

'Please... please don't do this...'

'You don't want to be released?' He gave a laugh and shook his head as if she had told him she didn't want to go to school. It was almost the way her dad had spoken.

She sobbed again.

'Come on, it's time to go. It'll soon be over.'

'We heard anything yet?' Butler asked, stepping into the incident room, and sighing when Moone looked at her blankly. 'About what you texted me? The hospital connection? Come on, Moone, wake your ideas up.'

Harding laughed behind him, but stopped when Moone stared at him. His mind was on other things at that moment, namely the woman in Cornwall who had lost a child.

'No, nothing yet,' he said. 'Cardiff police

are dragging their feet.'

'Probably too busy...' Harding started to say.

'Don't finish that sentence.' Butler glared at him, raising a finger, then looked at Moone. 'So, we're pretty definite that our killer works in the hospital?'

Moone nodded. 'All points to it. It's where we keep ending up, isn't it?'

'Good point. Let's hope they come up with a familiar name, then.'

He nodded and was about to say something when a uniform appeared in the incident room. It was a red-haired female constable and for a moment Moone was taken back to his first days when he had met Faith Carthew. He shook it all away and smiled up at the uniform.

'Can I help you?' he asked.

'Sorry, sir, there's a man downstairs who wants to talk to you,' the uniform said. 'Says he used to be a DCI. Colin Smith.'

Moone nodded, then sighed, wondering why the former detective was poking his nose in again. 'Thanks. I'll come down.'

Moone had Smith directed to the small waiting room next to the custody suite, and found the spectacled man sat upright at the table, staring blankly ahead.

'Colin?' Moone said, stood in the doorway.

'Why're you here?'

Smith flickered out of his dream and smiled at Moone as he stood up, almost to attention.

'My apologies,' he said. 'I didn't want to drag you away from your duties.'

'It's fine. What did you want? Did the others send you?' Moone took a seat at the table and Smith sat back down.

Colin shook his head. 'Oh no, it's my brain again. Thoughts just get trapped in there. It's all this business with Loy Grader, it's got me thinking.'

'Well, the only link to Grader in this was our chief suspect, Mario Black, but he's now dead.'

'The chef? He's dead?'

'Yep. So, I'm not really pursuing…'

'I see. I take it you're not going to interview Grader again?'

'No, thank God. I mean, there's a part of me that would like to know what happened to the boy, but better people than me have tried and failed…'

'That's because they were never given the chance. Every police officer who tried to start a fresh review of the case, were told they couldn't look into certain areas.'

'What areas?'

'The parents. I mean, when investigating a case involving a dead or missing child, you look at the parents first...'

Moone sighed, feeling the hankering for a coffee taking him over. 'I know, we've been through this. But there wasn't anything substantial to tie the boy's father to it. Plus, he had several witnesses that said he was at the restaurant over the road...'

'Doesn't mean he didn't help dispose of the boy's body.'

'You're convinced he's dead?'

Smith nodded, looking a little regretful. 'I'm afraid so. The cadaver dogs found the scent of death in the child's pushchair. I believe the father walked the kid out like that in the middle of the night.'

'Risky.'

'One witness gave a description of a man fitting Tom Dyer pushing a pram in the early hours of the morning.'

'It's not my case. Sorry.'

'You've talked to Mrs Dyer?'

'I have.'

'What do you make of her?' Smith stared at him intently.

'I don't know really. She's a woman with a lot of sorrow in her past.'

'True. She's also a bit of a wild one, by all accounts, or she used to be.'

'So? Is this to do with the fact they left the child alone for an hour?'

'Tom Dyer left him alone for an hour, if

the rumours are true, she went out partying until late.'

'Rumours?'

He nodded. 'I know. But there are a few people who came forward to say she was out in a local club that night. But, yes, nothing substantial. The same witnesses said she was seen talking to a man that night.'

Moone stood up, feeling a little annoyed at where the conversation was heading.

'You're leaving?' Smith said, sounding disappointed.

'I've got to get back to work. And all you've given me is rumours.'

'No one else knows about these witnesses. Because I found them. I found the people who were in that club on that night.'

'And what does it all mean? She went to a club, maybe met a man, and lied about it? I'm not surprised she did, seeing that she comes home to find her boy missing.'

Smith stood up, stepped around the table, and looked Moone in the eye. 'I gave those witnesses a few photos to look at. Most of those photos were of random people, some ex-cons, and one was a very well-known child murderer.'

'Loy Grader?' Moone shook his head, his stomach turning over, going into a spin. 'I suppose they picked him out as the man they saw her with?'

Smith nodded. 'They did. So why would she be meeting with Grader? That's what keeps going round in my head.'

'Eyewitnesses often get it wrong,' Moone said, his words not quite convincing himself of that fact.

'They do. But I think they've got it right this time. As I said before, every time an officer gets assigned to review the case, they are given certain parameters. Don't look into the parents. Particularly, the mother. Why?'

Moone shrugged. 'Why don't you tell me?'

'I looked into her past. I couldn't find much before she met and married Tom Dyer. No social media certainly. And what I did find, was clean, not so much as a parking ticket.'

'So?'

'Well, when someone's personal history is that boring, that pristine, it usually means they're a government agent of some kind.'

Moone laughed at the absurdity of it all, feeling a little sorry for the man who had little better to do than follow up conspiracy theories. 'I very much doubt that.'

'What about the extremely expensive lawyers and media companies representing them right out of the starting gate? The same lawyers who work for the royal family? How did they afford them?'

'Dyer is a celebrity chef.'

'Yes, but at that time he was struggling to

make ends meet. He hadn't quite made it and he was up to his eyeballs in debt.'

'What are you getting at?'

'I'm not sure. But it would be interesting to ask Grader about his meeting with her, wouldn't it?'

'You've had all this information and you've been sitting on it, haven't you? You've even kept all this from your former colleagues. Why?'

'I was waiting for fresh eyes to take a look. Someone with a good brain and a good sense of people.'

'Me?' Moone laughed. 'I don't think so.'

'I do. Go and talk to Grader. Ask him about the mother.'

Moone stared at him, feeling the dark cloud filling his head again, Grader's whispering voice. He shuddered. 'I'll think about it.'

'He has his monthly check-up today at Derriford Hospital.'

Moone headed out of the room. 'I'll think about it.'

CHAPTER 26

She blinked out into the daylight, only a beam of bright yellow burning her eyes. Then the trees formed, the birds singing overhead, traffic roaring past. She huddled her arms around herself, then looked round and saw the van still parked in the lane. He was sat at the wheel, his face half covered by a mask, a baseball cap on his head. He nodded, telling her to move on. She looked around again, her heart pounding. Then she jumped when the van's engine rumbled, and he started to reverse it. She walked backwards, watching him make his manoeuvre, then putting the vehicle in gear and driving slowly in her direction. Perhaps it was a game, she thought, a sick game. Was he there to hunt her?

He braked close to her and wound down the window, the engine rumbling away. 'Go. Go on, you're free.'

She looked around, then back at him as she stepped backwards. She stumbled on a fallen branch, her eyes jumping back to him, making sure he hadn't left the van.

'It's not a trick,' he said. 'You're free. You're safe. Someone will see you and pick you up. Go on, carry on through the woods. You'll reach the A38. Someone will stop.'

The engine roared and he drove the van away, leaving her in the opening, staring round at the woods, listening to the crows squawking, the traffic rumbling along. She turned and slowly headed into the woods, trembling all over. Was it a game? She started walking faster, looking around for him, her heart thumping. She reached a muddy path and started hurrying along, tears forming in her eyes.

There was movement again and she froze. From the trees and bushes around her came the sound of someone. A twig snapped and she got ready to run.

A dog burst out of the undergrowth and raced towards her with a stick in its mouth. She let out her harsh breath and started crying as she crouched down and stroked its grey fur.

'He's pretty friendly,' a voice said, and Bobbi looked up to see a woman in a raincoat and wellies. The woman smiled kindly and Bobbi found she couldn't hold in her tears.

'Are you OK, love?' the woman asked.

Bobbi tried to communicate between the tears, but nothing made sense. Then she managed to say, 'Police.'

The woman had her mobile out and up to her ear in seconds.

An uneasy feeling had filled every part of Moone by the time he had reached the incident room. The former detective's words were haunting him and he kept getting flashes of Lisa Brunning, the ex-Mrs Dyer talking cozily with Loy Grader. Every aspect of the case filled his brain with flashes, imagined scenarios. He shut his eyes, pushed the case away from him. *It was not his case.*

But he was getting a sense of something, something bad and it had grown since his meeting with the ex-Mrs Dyer. He thought of the incident involving Grader, coming into the restaurant to talk to Tom Dyer. Maybe it was something he should talk to Grader about.

'What did Smith have to say?'

Moone looked up to see Butler stood by his desk, arms folded. 'I don't know. He's got a bee in his bonnet about the whole Dyer case.'

'That's not our case, I hope you put him…'

'I did, I did. That's what I told him. He wanted me to go and talk to Grader again.'

Butler let out a laugh filled with disgust. 'Jesus. Don't they think we've got better things to do than to go gallivanting around chatting to paedophiles?'

Moone shrugged. 'He's been investigating the boy's disappearance since that night. I think he's become obsessed with it. Sounds like he's been pouring his own money into it.'

'Well, he's a bleeding fool then.'

Moone nodded. 'Perhaps he's trying to do the right thing.'

'Perhaps he's got nothing else in his life.'

Moone sat back, finding himself feeling a little sorry for the ex-copper, a man so lost in his own empty life that he has to build an imaginary world made of conspiracy theories. 'You're probably right. He seems to think Mrs Dyer might have known Grader, or at least met with him...'

'Come off it.' Butler huffed and headed to her own desk and sat down. 'There are so many theories about this case. You go and look it up and you'll read a million different theories. The parents did it, a ring of paedophiles took him... aliens abducted him.'

Moone smiled despite himself. 'I know. I've read a few. But there is something odd about it all. Things that don't quite add up. I can't help feel like there's something right in front of me... something obvious that I'm missing and everyone else is too.'

'Well, no offence, Moone, but better brains than yours have come up empty.'

Moone laughed, but the uneasiness was sitting heavy in his stomach. 'We could pay a visit to the hospital.'

'Could we? Why?'

Moone shrugged, scratching round for an excuse. 'We need to find out if any of the hospital staff, mainly the porters, worked for a while in Cardiff.'

Butler narrowed her eyes. 'Aren't we waiting for Cardiff Police to let us know?'

'Yes, but...'

Butler sighed and got up with a powerful huff. 'All right. You're not going to be satisfied until we talk to that sick bastard, are you?'

'Believe me, I don't really want to talk to him.'

Butler grabbed her jacket. 'Come on then, and you'd better bring us a couple of sick bags, too.'

He heard the calls coming from the other end of the ward. It was the prison guards making sure no one was around that might be in danger from the infamous child killer, Loy Grader. He put on his face mask, then opened the cleaning cupboard and stepped out in time to see two guards stomping their way towards him.

'We've got a prisoner coming in,' the first, muscular, bald-headed guard said, laying his deep set eyes on him. 'You might want to leave this area. He's an interesting character.'

'Any need for a porter?' he asked, smiling at the guard, and looking at the nurses behind him who were at the main desk, preparing themselves for the arrival.

'I'm not sure,' the guard said and turned to look at the nurses. 'Are you going to need a porter?'

One of the nurses flickered to life, looking at the guard and registering what he had said after a moment. Then her eyes sprang to the porter as he waited, smiling. She gave a smile, then said, 'Oh, hello, didn't know you were working today. Yes, we might need a hand. But you know who's coming in, don't you?'

The porter nodded, rolling his eyes. 'I know, some prisoner from Dartmoor.'

She huffed. 'Not just any prisoner. It's that Loy Grader. Makes my skin crawl. If I'd known, I would've tried to get today off.'

'Well, doesn't bother me,' the porter said. 'I've met all sorts in this job.'

'Is that sorted, then?' the guard asked, looking between the nurse and him. 'Good. Let's clear the rest of the area and we can get him in.'

He went and stood in the doorway that led to one of the bays. There was only a couple of elderly patients sleeping there, no one that Grader could get any joy from teasing. He watched the nurses getting the equipment together, smiling occasionally as they looked his way. They were used to him by now, had long since got used to the way he looked.

'Actually, could you get a wheelchair?'

He fluttered out of his thoughts and realised the guard was stood at the end of the corridor, staring at him.

'Sorry?' he asked.

'Could you get a wheelchair and bring it to the maternity entrance? That's where we're bringing him in. I know, not ideal, but there's not many kids about. Well, not born yet anyway.'

He ignored the guard's laugh, nodded and headed off out of the doors of the cardiology ward and started looking for a chair. He knew that there was a line of locked up wheelchairs close by. He managed to find one and pulled it all the way back to the cardiology ward and found the prison guard waiting.

'Which way to maternity?' the guard asked, looking round at the signs.

The porter nodded to the far end of the corridor. 'There's a lift down there. Hardly anyone uses it. Follow me.'

He pulled the wheelchair along behind him as he walked to the bank of lifts tucked away round the corner. The guard followed and joined him in the narrow interior. He pressed the button for the ground floor and felt a shudder as the lift went down. There was silence for a moment.

'Been a porter long?' the guard asked.

'A few years. I was in Cardiff before here. I've moved around a bit.'

The guard nodded. 'Better than being a screw, I bet. Scum we have to look after. People like Grader. You have to watch him. Last time there was... an incident. People got hurt.'

The lift doors opened, so the porter guided the wheelchair out. 'That's terrible.'

'Yeah, it is.' The guard followed him as they went round the corner, then past the maternity reception. No patients were around, he noticed, only the staff. They must have cleared the way already, he decided and looked towards the white prison van parked outside the entrance. Another broad, thickset guard stood leaning against the van, a cigarette between his fingers. He saw them coming and dropped the cigarette and stamped it out.

'Are you ready for him?' the smoking guard asked, turning to the van's side door.

'Yeah, let's get his Majesty out.'

The porter brought the wheelchair close to the van while he watched the guards opening the secure doors. He could see the narrow corridor inside the van, the doors of the three secure cubicles where the prisoners would sit. There was only one today.

The sound of keys jangling came from within, then voices. Chains rattled, then their collective shadows fell on the porter. The squat figure of the prisoner came first, taking tiny awkward steps because of the chain between his ankles. His chubby wrists were also locked together. The porter looked up into the pallid face, saw the dark eyes, the receding dyed hair. The evil eyes took him in, giving him the once-over.

'Couldn't they have found an uglier porter?' the prisoner said, then gave a deep rattle of a laugh.

'Keep quiet,' the prison guard said behind him. 'Be nice for once, Grader.'

As he was helped down from the van, Grader said, 'Where's the fun in being nice? It's not often I get to chat.'

The porter ignored it all, going about his business, making sure the patient was safe and comfortable in the chair before he started to direct it towards the entrance of the maternity ward, the two prison guards following close behind.

There came a throaty, rattling laugh from the prisoner as he was pushed into the maternity reception area.

'This is a new one,' he said and laughed harder. 'Have they got them lined up for me, ready to squeeze out the delicious little kiddies?'

'Shut up, Grader,' the guard said, the porter hearing the tight anger in his voice. 'Or do you want to wear the mask? It's up to you.'

'Just having some fun.' Grader turned his head, so one of his dark eyes peered back at the porter. 'You don't look like the type who has kids.'

The porter decided not to answer, even though the desperate need to was rising in him, beating in time with the pulse that thudded in his neck.

'Too ugly for kids.'

He found himself wanting to laugh as he stopped the wheelchair by the lift doors, then pressed the code into the keypad. He stood by the doors, arms folded, half listening to the guards' idle football chatter, half feeling Grader's eyes on him.

'There's something about you,' Grader said, hesitation and great thought in his words. 'I can't quite put my finger on it... not that I'd want to put my finger on it. Too old for me, you are. You need to eat. You're too fucking skinny.'

The porter felt the burn of rage in his chest and saw it as a deeply red moth trapped in his rib cage.

'There it is,' Grader said, nodding. 'I thought so. I can smell it on you.'

'Shut up, Grader.'

'I can't believe we're doing this,' Butler said for about the tenth time since they had left the station. Now they crossed the road outside Derriford hospital and headed into the entrance.

'You don't have to come along,' Moone said, smelling the aroma of freshly cooked food from the cafe. Normally his stomach would have yearned for a bacon turnover, but the thought of talking to Grader again had poisoned his gut.

Moone stopped by the entrance to Smiths, then faced her. 'Go see your dad.'

Her face tightened as if an invisible hand had pinched her cheeks. 'I told you, he sleeps most of the time.'

Moone sighed and shook his head. 'Well then, why don't you go and talk to the porters and see if any of them worked in Cardiff?'

She looked up at the sign that directed visitors to the X-Ray department and let out a huff. 'Can you handle the sicko by yourself?'

'Of course, Mum.' He smiled even though he felt like throwing up. 'I'm a big boy now.'

'Big boy?' She huffed out a laugh. 'In your dreams. Right, I'll see you in a mo. Call me if there's any trouble.'

He nodded, then watched her turn away and head to the X-Ray department. Moone looked round, his stomach starting to roll over. He spotted the men's toilets and hurried towards them, unsure whether he was just going to splash water in his face or actually throw up.

He was a couple of feet from the men's loo when he saw the door of the ladies' toilet open and a woman stepped out. His eyes jumped to the figure, taking her in and then recognising her, but not at the same time. It was like that sometimes, seeing a familiar face in the last place you would expect to see them.

Her eyes jumped to his before he could duck into the men's loo, so he smiled, tried to look pleased to see her.

'Oh, I didn't think I'd bump into you here,' Lisa Brunning said, her cheeks reddening a little. He thought for a moment she had the look of a teenager caught smoking.

'Didn't expect to see you either,' he said, folding his arms. 'I hope everything's OK.'

She nodded. 'Oh, yes, just a... you know, check-up. Are you here officially?'

'I'm afraid so. Have to grill a suspect.' He laughed and heard the awkwardness in his own voice.

'Well, I bet you get your man,' she said. 'Or woman, of course.'

'Hello, hello,' a voice said from along the corridor, and it was a sound that made a knot twist in Moone's stomach. He sighed, then looked round to see DS Faith Carthew slowly walking towards them, a big grin on her face as she looked from Lisa to him.

'DS Carthew,' he said, nodding to her, then watching Brunning's confused face.

'My name is Faith,' Carthew said, looking at the ex-Mrs Dyer. 'He used to call me Faith all the time when we were sleeping together.'

'Alright, let's not,' Moone began and saw

Carthew's burning eyes staring at him.

'Let's not?' Carthew looked at her. 'Are you the replacement? He's quite the mover when he gets going, isn't he?'

'This is a witness I've been talking to,' Moone said, feeling the burn of awkwardness covering his back.

'I'd better go,' Lisa Brunning said, but Carthew cut off her exit, her eyes narrowing.

'I know you, don't I?' Carthew said, pointing a finger at her.

'Please, Faith,' Moone said, but she held up her palm to his face.

'Yes, I know you now.' Carthew nodded, but Lisa looked away, sighing inwardly.

'I'm sorry,' Moone said, wanting to run off and hide.

'You're the ex-Mrs Dyer,' Carthew said, nodding. Then a look of almost genuine sadness and sympathy masked her usual blankness. 'I'm so sorry about your little boy. He must be a little angel.'

Brunning nodded, smiled a little. 'He was. Such a little… angel.'

'Bet he never wants to go to bed.'

Brunning smiled sadly. 'Never. He would always have an excuse. And when he would go to bed, he'd always wake up. I'm sorry, but I've got to go…'

Carthew stepped back, smiling at her, then watching the distressed woman heading at speed along the corridor.

Carthew then turned and faced Moone, the usual look of emptiness filling her eyes again. 'Isn't she... interesting? I can see why you fancy her.'

'I don't.' He sighed.

'Oh come off it.' Carthew folded her arms, her eyes travelling up the corridor in the direction Lisa Brunning had vanished in. 'But it was a very interesting conversation, wasn't it?'

'Was it? You hardly said two words to each other.'

Carthew stepped closer to him. 'That's all you need sometimes. It's all there.'

Moone stared at her, watching the way her eyebrows rose and her eyes glistened a little with triumph. 'What is?'

'The truth. What happened to her boy.'

Moone turned to look where the boy's mother had gone, running back through everything they had talked about. His mind was empty. He looked at Carthew. 'What happened?'

Carthew laughed, then shook her head. 'Oh no, this isn't my case. You've got to figure it out for yourself.'

Moone smirked. 'Well, actually, it's not my case either. Now, I have to be somewhere else.'

I've got another psycho to talk to, he said in his head and hurried off.

The porter directed the wheelchair and the ugly load inside it, down the corridor of the cardiology unit and into the examination room. The guards followed, still chatting, one of them playing a gambling game on his phone the whole time.

'You used to be fat and ugly, didn't you?' Grader said, his black eyes digging into the porter's skin.

'One more word out of you,' one of the prison guards said.

Grader looked at the guard. 'Just remember what happened to my last guards. Dear old John. Was he a friend of yours?'

The guard's face twitched, his jaw grinding as his eyes narrowed. 'You want the fucking mask on? Do you want to watch the TV tonight?'

Grader lost his look of pure hatred and smiled, and mouthed, 'Sorry.' Then his black eyes fixed on the porter again as he said, 'Must be boring pushing people places.'

The porter shrugged and put on the wheelchair's brake. He looked at the guards as he headed to the open door, noticing one was still staring at his phone and the other was staring intently at Grader. They didn't see him.

He went to the door to shut it, but one of the nurses appeared, about to come into the room.

'Right, Mr Grader,' she said, smiling, trying to sound cheerful, but the porter heard the quiver of disgust just beneath the surface.

'Have you got a blanket for Mr Grader?' the porter asked, smiling.

The nurse looked beyond him, towards the creature in the wheelchair that obviously offended her eyes. 'A blanket?'

The porter looked back at Grader and winked. 'You'd like a blanket, wouldn't you?'

Grader grinned. 'Oh, yes, would you be an absolute sweetheart and fetch a blanket? I'm a little chilly.'

The nurse looked a little sickened, but nodded and left the room. The porter moved swiftly and shut the doors to the room, then locked them. He turned and saw the guards hadn't seen what he had done. But Grader eyed him with great interest, his beady black eyes staring hungrily towards him.

The porter reached down into his trousers, digging around until he ripped away the small metal bar that was taped to his leg. He raised it high above his head as he crept towards the first guard who stood, arms folded, staring at Grader.

He smashed it down, whacking the guard on the side of his head, knocking him to the ground. He managed a second blow to the first guard before the gambling guard had realised what was happening and reached for his taser.

He wasn't quick enough. The porter smashed the bar across his jaw, the echo of the cracking sound pounding over the ceiling. He smashed it again into his face and stood back, watching the guard's legs wobble then crumple away beneath him.

He stood back, staring down at both guards as they lay silently on the floor.

There was a knock at the door, then the nurse's panicked voice.

'Is this a rescue?' Grader smiled, his high voice coated in excitement. 'Who sent you? Was it Graham?'

The porter had been staring at the door, listening to the nervous nurse's voice calling out, but then turned to look at the ugly creature in the chair who was now shining bright with hope.

'No, this isn't a rescue,' he said, stepping towards him. 'This is an execution.'

CHAPTER 27

All the way up to the cardiology department, Moone was bothered by the same feeling of growing unease. He couldn't quite grasp exactly what was making him feel out of sorts, as he had plenty of situations to choose from. He pictured the crazy eyes of Carthew, the way those eyes burned through him. She had got away with murder, three times in all probability and he felt responsible somehow. Then there was Lisa Brunning, the beautiful woman who had suffered such tragedy in her life. He had found her attractive, but since his chat with her in Padstow, there had been some other much more disturbing feeling. Carthew's words kept coming back to him, her taunt that all he needed to know about that case was in that short conversation with Brunning. His mind ached as the lift reached the floor the cardiology department was on. He stepped out, feeling a little sick knowing he was about to talk to another deeply disturbed individual.

As he headed through the doors, Moone heard panicked voices. A woman somewhere along the corridor was shouting at someone. Moone hurried, following the shouts and found a few members of staff, mostly nurses, gathered at a set of doors.

He showed his ID. 'Is there some trouble?'

All their eyes fell on him with relief, but it was a blonde nurse who said, 'We don't know what's going on. One of our porters has locked himself in there with a patient.'

'With a patient?' Moone came closer, an iciness drifting up his spine. 'Who's the porter? What's his name?'

The nurses looked at each other blankly.

'Can't remember his name,' the blonde nurse said with a shrug. 'Does anyone know? He's the skinny one, the one who looks ill.'

'Oh him,' an Indian-looking nurse said. 'I know who you mean, but don't know his name.'

'Is it Paul?' Moone asked, the same rush of unease now racing through him as he stepped towards the locked doors.

'I think so,' the blonde nurse said. 'Yes, I think it's Paul, come to think of it. What should we do? I was about to call hospital security.'

'Call them,' Moone said. 'And call Charles Cross station and tell them DCI Peter Moone needs assistance.'

As one of the nurses headed back to the

nurses' station, Moone got closer to the door. 'Paul? Can you hear me, Paul? It's DCI Peter Moone.'

'I think he plans to kill me, Peter!' Grader's voice called through the door.

'Shut up,' another muffled voice said.

'There's nowhere to go, Paul.' Moone's chest started to thump, the blood echoing his heartbeat in his ears. 'Come out and we'll talk about this.'

There was a short, strange kind of laugh inside. 'You should see it in here, Detective whatever your name is… trip hazards everywhere. I keep telling them. But no one listens.'

'I'm listening. Why don't you tell me about the girls?'

There was silence in the room for a moment before Grader said, 'Yes, Paul… tell us all about the girls. You're sounding very interesting to me all of a sudden.'

'Shut your sick little mouth,' the porter shouted. 'I'm not like you. I'm nothing like you.'

But Grader was laughing his throaty laugh.

'What's your plan for Grader?' Moone asked, pressing his ear to the door and hearing footsteps behind him.

'I thought that was obvious,' the porter called through the door. 'He needs to die.'

'What's he done to you?' Moone turned his

head and caught sight of two tall and meaty-looking security men.

'Nothing. It's just his time. Don't tell me you'll shed a tear for this sick bastard.'

Moone sighed, lowering his head, a large part of him wanting to walk away and let him get on with it. Then his mind thought of the prison guards. 'Who else is in there?'

'His useless guards. Don't worry, they'll live. They're tied up right now.'

At least that was something. But he had to find a way into the room that wouldn't result in more violence.

'Let us get through,' one of the security staff said.

Moone turned and faced a bearded man who was at least a foot taller than him. 'This is a delicate situation. I'm a police officer...'

'We can open the door, steam in there. Job done.'

'There are two guards in there that might get hurt, and believe it or not I have to make sure Grader stays alive too.'

The security man folded his arms. 'What're you going to do then?'

Moone turned back to the door again, knowing there was only one course of action he could take, even though it terrified him and made him want to throw up. 'Paul. Let me in.'

There was laughter from the porter before he said, 'Do you think I'm stupid? Give me some credit.'

'I know you're not stupid. You're the opposite, I know that. You've had us running in circles. Let me in and we can talk.'

'What's to talk about? I kill Grader and you have one less sick bastard to deal with. Don't pretend you don't want me to kill him.'

'Peter,' Grader said, 'Tell him you wouldn't want to see your old friend die. I've always enjoyed our chats.'

Moone tapped his head on the door, thinking. Lisa Brunning came to mind. 'I've just seen the ex-Mrs Dyer, Loy.'

'Really?' Grader called out. 'I hope you sent my love.'

'Shut up,' the porter said. 'Stop this talking. It's getting on my nerves.'

'You know her too, don't you, Paul?' Moone asked. 'You gave her a tattoo at the request of Mario Black. The chef you murdered.'

'Lisa? Yeah, I remember that tattoo. That was a very singular, beautiful tattoo.'

'But not the one you've been trying to recreate?' Moone asked.

'What did Mrs Dyer tell you?' Grader asked. 'Anything interesting?'

'Shut up!' the porter shouted, then there was a thud, and a high-pitched scream.

'Paul!' Moone shouted, his heart pounding, realising that he may never get his answers from Grader. He didn't give a stuff about the weird little man and his sick and evil ways, but he knew that he still had so many secrets in his brain. 'What have you done, Paul?'

'Grader's having a little nap. Don't worry, your friend is still breathing. But not for long.'

'We need to get an armed response team,' the first security guard said.

Moone sighed and shook his head, not even bothering to look at the man. 'No. Grader would be dead by then.'

The security guard stepped closer, lowered his voice. 'Seriously, mate. Are we that bothered what happens to him? You know what he's done, don't you?'

'I know. But he's got information. Important information.' Moone stepped back, straightening up, a decision being made in his head, and one that filled his head full of bile. It was a stupid decision, and Butler would call him crazy, but he knew he had no choice if he had any chance of finding out the truth of what happened to Lisa Brunning's little boy.

'Paul,' Moone said, his voice crumbling a little. He cleared his throat. 'I need to come in there...'

'No way.'

'You've got no way out.'

'I don't care. As long as I do this one thing. This will be something beautiful, something perfect.'

Moone looked down at his hands, half wishing Butler was there to talk some sense into him.

'I have to come in there. If I don't, then the armed response will come in all guns blazing. I don't think you want that.'

There was quiet for a while.

'Paul?'

'You can come in. It won't do you any good. You won't save Grader, but you can come in.'

'OK, Good.'

'But you get someone to tie your hands behind your back first. Or you aren't coming in. End of story.'

Moone let out a sharp breath, then nodded. 'OK, fine.'

'You're not really going to do that, are you?' the bearded security guy said, while the nurses started chatting nervously.

'Get everyone back,' Moone said. 'Get them all back to the nurses' station.'

The security man folded his arms, staring at Moone as if he'd just streaked naked down the corridor. 'You can't do that. That's crazy.'

'I know. But what else can I do?'

'Let us steam in there or wait for the armed response team.'

Moone turned and looked beyond the big security guys and saw all the worried and expectant faces of the staff. 'Please, can you all get back? Please, just get out of this area.'

The security guard shook his head, then turned and started clearing the area, moving the nurses back along the corridor. Then quietness descended, giving Moone the chance to think clearly and realise it was a completely stupid thing to do. *So what if Grader died? It was one less evil bastard.*

He thought of the little boy, wondering where he was, if he was still alive. He shut his eyes, tapped his head on the door again.

'Are you coming in, then?' the porter asked. 'I haven't got all day.'

'I am. Hang on.'

'Get your arms tied behind your back or you're not coming in.'

Moone turned away and found the bearded security man coming towards him. 'Your lot won't take long to get here. Just keep him talking.'

'He wants me in there. Have you got some restraints?'

'Cable ties.' The big man brought them out, so Moone put his hands behind his back. Then he felt the ties being put around his wrists, and pulled tight.

'There is a way out of these ties, you know?'

Moone nodded. 'I know. Right. Here I go. Wish me luck.'

DC Cara Banerjee looked nervous as she took a seat in the interview room again opposite DS Rivers and DI Crowne. She smiled awkwardly, her hands fidgeting a little.

'You look nervous, Cara,' Crowne said with a slight smile, trying to fool her into feeling somewhat calmer. 'We just need to ask you some more questions.'

'OK, I will if I can,' she said, looking between them. 'I've told you all I know, really.'

Crowne sat forward. 'I know. But there's a few details that need clarifying...'

'Like what?' Banerjee looked worried again.

'Like... this relationship you were having with DS Faith Carthew. When did it begin?'

DC Banerjee shrugged, let out a sigh and looked down. 'We met at another training session. It was down here.'

'So you met in Bristol?' Rivers asked.

'Yeah, we got talking... went for a few drinks.'

Crowne nodded. 'Who initiated things?'

'I don't know.' Banerjee shrugged again. 'I can't remember. I'd had a few drinks. We ended up in her room. Next thing I know... I was shocked really. I mean, she'd been giving me signs, but I didn't really think anything would happen...'

'She initiated it though?' Rivers asked.

'Would you say that?'

Banerjee nodded. 'Yes, I think so. Yes, I'm pretty sure she did. Why?'

'No reason,' Crowne said and sat back, watching the DC. 'Did anything ever seem out of the ordinary about it all?'

'What do you mean?'

'Well, did anything seem... strange? Did she seem...'

'You think she was using me?' Banerjee asked, looking a little annoyed.

Crowne sighed. 'I'm not saying that. It's just that the picture we have of Carthew is one that's very different than yours. We're just trying to understand all this.'

'I see. Well, there's nothing I can think of. Can I go now?'

'Not right at this moment, no,' Crowne said. 'Try to think back to the times you spent together. For instance, were you ever aware of any meetings she had in Bristol? Anyone she met up with while she was here?'

Cara sat back, the frustration and annoyance in her eyes. But she was thinking anyway, Crowne noted. Then he saw it, a flicker and a shrug.

'What is it?' Crowne asked, sitting forward.

'Nothing. It's nothing,' Banerjee said.

'No, go on. You thought of something.'

The DC shrugged again. 'The second time

we met up, she left me sitting in the pub for a while. Seemed like ages, and it pissed me off...'

'What pub?' Rivers asked.

Banerjee looked over at her. 'The Crown Bar. We were there for like five minutes then she said she had to talk someone and that she'd be right back.'

'Who did she talk to?' Crowne asked.

'I don't know. I asked her, but she just said it was for work, and she'd be right back.'

Crowne nodded. 'That was that? You didn't see who she talked to?'

Banerjee shook her head, but looked away.

Crowne looked at Rivers and saw she had a suspicious look on her face that mirrored what he was feeling. He sat back, folded his arms. 'I think, if it was me, I would've had a look at who she was meeting with.'

The DC shrugged, but didn't say anything.

'Thing is,' Rivers said, nodding, 'It comes with the job, doesn't it, boss? Being nosey. Especially if someone tells you it's to do with work.'

'Come on, Cara, don't tell us you didn't have a cheeky look.' Crowne raised his eyebrows.

Banerjee sighed, gave an empty laugh then looked Crowne in the eyes. 'Fine. Yes, I went to find her... satisfied?'

'Who was she with?' Crowne asked.

'I didn't see.'

'You didn't see?' Crowne huffed.

'No. I'm telling the truth.' Anger flickered in the DC's eyes. 'I found where she'd gone, but it was round a corner. Whoever she was talking to, she was sat by a pillar...'

'She?' Crowne exchanged looks with Rivers. 'It was a woman?'

Banerjee nodded. 'Yes. All I could see was strawberry blonde hair. It was covering her face. That's it. I didn't want Faith to see me, so I hurried back to our table. She came back and that was that. That's all I know. I swear.'

Crowne watched her, seeing that she looked as if she was telling the truth. 'And she was with you all night in the hotel? Never left the room?'

'No, I told you.'

'So, all we need to do is get the CCTV footage from the pub that night...'

Banerjee shook her head and sighed. 'No, you can't...'

'Why?' Crowne asked, a sickening feeling invading his stomach. 'What did you do?'

Banerjee lowered her head as she looked ready to weep. 'She convinced me to go to the pub a couple of days later and retrieve the footage...'

'She convinced you?' Rivers asked, disbelief thick in her voice.

The DC nodded, sniffing as a few tears came. 'I know how all this looks. I get it, but she told me that it was important that the person she met wasn't seen with her and that if the CCTV footage of them together fell into the wrong hands...'

'What did she tell you it was, what was going on?' Crowne asked.

'That it was to do with corruption on the force. In Bristol. She said the person she was meeting was an informant. I didn't know what to do... then she said that if the pub footage ever came to light they'd see me there, then it might come out... that she and I... I couldn't have my family finding out.'

Crowne huffed, then looked at Rivers and saw she was looking just as astounded as he felt. 'Banerjee, you're going to have to write this up in an official statement. Then sign it.'

'And if this goes to court? What then?' Tears were in the girl's eyes again, ready to stream out.

'I'm going to do my best to keep this in house.' Crowne looked her in the eyes, did his best to convince her that he had the power to make it happen. He didn't like manipulating her, but she was all they had.

'I don't know.' The DC wiped her eyes, shook her head.

'You're in a lot of trouble. You've lied to us. You haven't got a lot of choice. You've got to trust us. Look, I think Carthew is dangerous. I think you might be in danger, so you need to find somewhere to go in the meantime. At least for a couple of weeks. Is there somewhere you can go?'

She thought for a moment, then nodded. 'I've got a cousin in Birmingham. I can stay with him.'

'Good.' Crowne sat back. 'Stay here and write up everything and then we'll get you there.'

The door of the bay opened slightly, enough for Moone to squeeze through. He had trouble, unable to use his hands to propel himself into the room. A gloved hand grasped him by his shirt and dragged him inside. The door was locked behind him. Moone's eyes fell on the figure lying on the floor. He took in Grader, his squat, ugly body lying on the ground, blood caked over the side of his head. There was groaning coming from him and Moone let out a sigh of relief. Then his eyes jumped to the two battered and unconscious guards. He could see faint signs of breathing. 'Why don't you let these men go? They need medical help.'

'Kneel down,' the porter's voice commanded behind him. He turned and saw the gaunt, pale and withered form of the killer.

'You really want me to kneel and get my suit dirty on this floor?' Moone said, stalling, trying to think of a way out of all this with

Grader still alive. But there was so much more at stake than just Grader, like the young woman, Cody Barton who the porter had locked up somewhere. He had to concentrate on her.

'Quit stalling and fucking kneel,' the porter said.

Moone did as he was told. 'You're a very talented tattooist.'

'Me?' The porter laughed. 'Shows what you know.'

'Meaning?'

'I'm a terrible tattooist. I can do it, but I'm not great.'

'But I've seen your work on those girls.'

The porter stared at him for a moment, then nodded. 'Beautiful, weren't they? How unremarkable they were in their lives, and how distinguished they were in death.'

Moone swallowed down his revulsion and nodded. 'Beautiful. Truly artistic.'

The porter glared at him. 'Don't try and flatter me. I know your game. I'm not stupid.'

'No, you're not. You fooled us. So, if you didn't tattoo them, who did?'

The porter raised a long bony finger and tapped the side of his nose. 'That's for me to know.'

'It's over now,' Moone said, hearing Grader groan next to him. 'Tell me where Cody Barton is.'

'Who?' The porter nodded, a look of realisation coming over his gaunt face. 'Oh, right, the chubby pretty girl.'

'Where is she? If you're here, no one's there to feed her, give her water...'

'She'll be fine.'

'How?'

'Jesus... my head,' Grader groaned, grasping his skull as he clambered to his knees. 'That skinny bastard hit me.'

'I'll do more than that in a minute,' the porter said, lifting a metal bar in his hand. 'You only have minutes to live. Enjoy them while you can, you freak.'

'I'm the freak?' Grader laughed and coughed. 'Have you looked in a mirror lately?'

'Why do you want to kill him?' Moone asked.

'Why not?'

Moone shrugged. 'Won't exactly be in line with your other art, would it?'

'Art is... well, it's art, isn't it?' The porter smiled.

'Is this to do with Black, the chef, your old mate?'

The porter laughed. 'My mate? That narcissist? Don't make me laugh. If you must know, yes, he mentioned this child molester... and I thought why not kill him?'

'He asked you to kill him? As some kind of revenge or what?'

Grader laughed.

'What are you laughing at?' The porter lifted the bar, staring at the little man on the floor.

'Nothing,' Grader said. 'Revenge. Yes, he probably thought he was getting revenge. He sent you after me, didn't he? To avenge his friend's little boy? Oh, what delicious fun.'

'You're a sick little bastard.' The bar came whipping through the air.

'No!' Moone shouted, but the thud of the bar hitting the child killer's head echoed round the room, bellowing into Moone's ears.

The porter went to strike again, but Moone shouted for him to stop. The killer turned to him, his gaunt face tight, pale, his lanky body pounding visibly. 'Why? Why save this despicable creature?'

'I need answers. He's the only one who can give them to me.'

The porter looked down at the still man, the blood pouring from the wound to the side of his head. 'Too late now, I think. Shame, but it looks like you'll never know. But at least all those grieving parents can rest.'

'Can they?' Moone looked down, his stomach strangling itself. 'I doubt it.'

'It's me you should be talking to.'

Moone looked up, nodding, clearing his mind, deciding he should be getting something from the mess. 'Why? Why do all this?'

'Why?' Fabre looked thoughtful. 'I don't know. I remember as a kid being taken to a gallery... I think it was in London... anyway, I remember staring at the art, the paintings, the sculptures and thinking how their beauty would live on. Then I saw this thing walk in, this great big fat lump. Hideous she was, but I could see beneath it all she had the makings of a beautiful work of art. I was only young, and I didn't understand the meaning of it all, but later... well, I had a mission...'

'From God?'

The porter laughed. 'God? Fuck no. God? God is dead. His days of making art are long over. But he did make art. Butterflies. From something ugly to something so beautiful. It's perfect, isn't it? The metamorphosis, I mean.'

'Well, it's over now.'

The porter's eyes widened. 'Over? Remember there's the young girl to think of. Chubby Cody. No, my dear detective friend, it's only just beginning. Let's get out of here and I'll explain further.'

'Out there?' Moone nodded to the door.

The porter nodded, then lifted the metal bar in his hand and placed it on a nearby table. He then turned to the door and unlocked it before raising his hands to shoulder height. He smiled and stared at Moone as he said, 'Security men, you can come in now.'

CHAPTER 28

Bobbi-Jane pulled the blanket round her body, listening to the voices outside the small room they had put her in. She could also hear the sounds of the emergency department, the echoes of chatter, of machines beeping, and kids crying. She couldn't quite make out what was being said about her by the nurses and the doctor that had left her moments earlier, but she felt like they didn't believe her. She shivered and pulled the blanket tighter around her. They had given her some scrubs to wear, but they rubbed against her skin and made her feel queasy.

The door opened slightly, the voices and the din becoming louder. There was a beeping sound every few seconds, while a garbled voice said something as if they were on the end of a badly tuned radio. Then she understood when the figure of a female policewoman came in. She smiled at Bobbi, then looked back at her taller male colleague who settled by the door, arms folded.

The female officer had light brown hair tied back, a ruddy complexion and a friendly, almost bright smile. She approached Bobbi slowly, one hand quietening her radio.

'Hello, I'm PC Jessica Bennett,' she said, smiling again, then looking at her colleague briefly. 'You can call me Jess. This is my partner, PC Daniel Irwin. Just ignore him.'

'That's work partner,' Irwin said, smiling. 'Not anything else. My wife would be annoyed if she heard that.'

PC Bennett pulled up a chair. 'Can I sit?'

Bobbi nodded.

'Thanks.' Bennett took out a notebook and pen and found a page. 'I know you've been through quite an ordeal, but to help you we need some details. Are you OK to do that?'

Bobbi nodded. She managed to say yes, but her voice was hardly there.

'Good. Let's start with your name.'

Bobbi cleared her throat. 'Bobbi. Bobbi-Jane Todd.'

She saw the way PC Bennett reacted, the surprise in her eyes as she looked up from her notebook. Then Bobbi saw that the male uniform stepped forward, his eyebrows raised.

'You're Bobbi?' he asked, smiling. 'I'm glad to meet you. Everyone's been looking for you.'

'Bobbi,' Bennett said, her face losing any signs of her former smile. 'Do you know where you've been?'

'Can I see my mum and dad?' she asked, the tears starting to arrive.

Bennett nodded. 'You will. Soon, I promise. I'll call them. But we really need to know where you've been.'

Bobbi fought away the tears, clearing her throat. 'A house.'

'A house? Do you know whereabouts this house was...'

'Jess?' Her colleague stepped closer. 'We should probably notify the detectives in charge of the search for her.'

Bennett looked back at him, then at Bobbi and nodded. 'OK. Bobbi, I'm going to get in touch with some detectives. They'll want to ask you some questions. OK?'

'Can I see my mum and dad?'

Bennett stood up. 'Soon, I promise.'

Moone rubbed his wrists again as he started walking along the corridor, his heart still thudding. The two prison guards both had severe injuries, but they would live. Then he watched as the medical team put the unconscious Grader on a bed and wheeled him out, taking him to intensive care. He had a severe head wound, they said. It would be touch and go. He swore and turned to see DC Molly Chambers and two uniforms escorting the cuffed Paul Fabre out of the room.

'Sir, boss,' Molly called out. 'Shouldn't you let someone take a look at you?'

He kept on walking, just raised a hand and hurried along the corridor and headed for the ward where Butler's dad was being treated. He wanted to share the good news with her that they had their man and the bad news that Grader might not recover. How could that be bad news, he thought, laughing to himself.

Then he heard his phone ringing in his pocket and took it out as he reached the main lifts. It was DI Crowne calling, but he didn't have the head or stomach to take the call. He cancelled the call and put his phone back in his pocket and headed into the lift, squeezing himself to the back wall as a patient in a bed was wheeled in towards him. He watched the porters stand by the bed, listened to them chatting and felt a little sick.

He arrived at the ward where Butler's dad was staying and slipped in through the doors as a visitor came out. The same old beeping sounds, chatter and patients crying met his ears as he went in. He pulled out his ID ready in case he was stopped, but the nurses seemed in a hurry to get somewhere. The crying he had heard was now louder, coming from the corridor on his right, on the way to where Butler's dad...

His stomach dropped. He started hurrying towards all the noise, following the nurses that hurried along the corridor. Then he saw her. Butler stumbled out of the small room, tears flooding her face, a strange noise escaping her mouth. She was directed by a nurse who helped her to a chair in the corridor.

'Butler?' he said, stood by her. Butler looked up at him through red, wet eyes.

'Can you look after her?' the nurse asked, so Moone nodded, and crouched down by her chair, watching his partner sob her heart out.

'He's... he's,' she managed to say between breaths. 'They're trying...'

Moone nodded, then put his hand on hers and squeezed. He looked into the room but could only see bodies moving, and heard commands and questions being asked. Then there was beeping and a robotic voice warning that a shock was about to be administered. Then he understood what was happening.

'His heart...' Butler cried, pointing behind her. Then she turned and looked towards the room. 'He wouldn't want...'

'What? What wouldn't he want?'

'That... all that going on.' She looked down, shaking her head.

'You want them to stop?' Moone stood up.

'But I didn't... I didn't get to say...' She looked up at Moone, tears pouring over her cheeks. 'I never said anything...'

'He knows. He knows.' Moone squeezed her hand again. 'What do you want to do?'

Butler looked towards the room again, then wiped her eyes and stood up. She took a shaky breath then headed in. He listened outside, hearing Butler's muffled voice telling them to stop trying to resuscitate him.

Then a few seconds later she came out and stood staring into space. He stepped up to her and held her hand, but she kept staring for a few minutes, saying nothing.

Then she looked at him blankly and said, 'You're a soppy wally, Moone. You know that?'

He nodded. 'So they tell me.'

'Grader?' she asked.

'Unconscious. Might not wake up.'

She nodded. 'Not that bad, then?'

He smiled sadly. 'It was the porter. Paul Fabre.'

'What was? Our butterfly obsessed killer? The skinny porter? Oh, right, now I get it.'

'Do you? Because I don't.'

She shook her head. 'No, nor me. Let's go and talk to him and find out where he's got this girl.'

'DCI Moone?'

He turned see DC Chambers coming towards him. 'Sorry, but I've just found out that a young girl's in A and E, says her name is Bobbi-Jane Todd.'

They rushed down to the emergency department and headed through the corridors that were lined with patients of all ages lying on beds and gurneys, the nurses and doctors running about as if they were on speed. Moone showed his ID to a young-looking doctor and asked for Bobbi-Jane, and got only a distracted answer and a slight point of his finger towards a room close by. Moone found the room where the thin, pale young woman lay on a bed, a blanket wrapped round her. There was a cup of something warm in her hands as she was being interviewed by a female uniform. The constable turned to Moone, nodded and followed them both outside.

'She's in a bad way,' the PC said, shaking her head and looking forlorn.

'I'm sorry, what's your name?' Moone asked.

'PC Jessica Bennett, sir.'

'Good work,' Moone said, and looked at the scared girl in the cubicle who stared back at them.

'I haven't done much.' The PC shrugged.

'You've done all you can,' Butler said. 'Has she said anything?'

The PC looked at her notes. 'Only that she's been held in some rundown house somewhere. Somewhere built up. She could hear traffic.'

'Built up?' Moone rubbed his stubble. 'That's not what we were thinking.'

'Let's just hurry up and see what she knows.' Butler moved into the room, putting on a smile as she headed over to the bed, where the girl looked up at her warily.

'DI Mandy Butler,' she said, showing her ID. 'This gormless sod is DCI Peter Moone.'

'Thanks,' Moone said, then smiled at Bobbi. 'We've been looking everywhere for you.'

She nodded. 'I didn't think anyone would be.'

'Of course they were,' Butler said. 'Your parents are worried sick.'

'Are they?' She looked down, shrugged.

'They really are,' Moone said, then pulled over a chair and sat down, watching the tears begin to pour from her eyes.

'Here, love.' Butler took out some tissues and passed Bobbi a couple. 'Can you tell us where you've been?'

Bobbi sniffed and wiped her eyes. 'Not really. Just a house somewhere.'

'And you could hear traffic?' Moone asked.

'Yeah. I felt like I wasn't far from the city centre.'

Moone jotted it down in his notebook. 'Where were you when he took you?'

'The end of Stoke Village. There's this building I was staying at. I met this bloke…'

'Daryl,' Moone said and nodded.

Bobbi looked surprised. 'Yes. How did you know?'

'We've talked to him. He got worried when

you disappeared. He had the feeling you were scared of something that night.'

She nodded, sniffing. 'Yeah, I was. Someone was following me. I kept seeing them. I left my friends and walked through the park. It was getting dark and I heard someone behind me. There was someone following me. It must've been him, the one who took me to that house. He must've followed me to Daryl's. I left there cause I thought I'd better leave and get home. I thought he'd be gone and I'd be safe...'

'But he wasn't?' Moone said.

She shook her head. 'He must've been waiting for me. He grabbed me, and I felt something sharp in my neck. Then I woke up in that house.'

'Did you notice an ambulance nearby?' Butler asked.

She shook her head. 'No, I don't remember seeing one. Will I be able to go home soon?'

'We'll get you home soon.' Moone smiled. 'We just need to ask you a few more questions. I'm sorry. Did you get a look at the man who took you?'

'He always wore a mask when he'd come into the room.'

Moone nodded. 'OK. Was he tall, skinny?'

'No. He wasn't very tall. Average height, I think.'

'Not very skinny?'

'No. Sort of normal looking. I remember he had this smell about him...'

Moone looked at Butler, exchanging raised eyebrows. 'What sort of smell?'

She shrugged. 'A horrible smell. Sort of chemical, but I don't know. Like death or something. Please can I go home now?'

'Soon. Was there anything else that stood out? Anything he did or said?'

She shrugged, then she looked at her shoulder. 'The only thing I can think of is... it was weird...'

'What is it?' Moone asked, his gut tightening.

'He kept asking to see my tattoo. Then he'd stare at it for ages. I think he was... you know...'

'What, a weirdo?' Butler said and smiled at the girl.

'But I never really felt like he was going to do anything. Hurt me, or anything, do you know what I mean? He was never angry or anything.'

'That's interesting.'

'Will you call my parents? I'd like to see them.'

Moone nodded. 'We're going to call your parents right now. But I'm going to get PC Bennett to write down everything you saw. And we're going to get you to look at some photos. OK?'

She nodded, sniffing.

Moone stood up and signalled for Butler to follow him into the corridor. He was about to talk shop with her, put his theories to Butler, but then he saw her red and swollen eyes.

'Should you really be doing this right now?' he asked instead.

She huffed, glaring at him. 'Do you really have to ask that? Get on with it, what're you thinking?'

'Well, what are you thinking?' He nodded towards the room where Bobbi lay.

Butler looked over. 'Well, doesn't seem quite right, does it?'

Moone nodded. 'No, I didn't think so. Why don't you think so?'

'If it's the porter who took her, then she'd be describing someone very different…'

'Exactly. And he takes her to a house in a built-up area? Doesn't seem right, does it? I mean, they've probably had more than one girl locked up at a time. I can't see them using a run of the mill house, can you?'

Butler shook her head. 'No. So, we think there's two of them out there, do we?'

Moone ran a hand down his face and sighed. 'Well, Fabre told me Cody would be OK without him and said that things were only just beginning.'

'Great. So we've got two nutters on our hands.'

Moone sighed. 'But only one of them

locked up, so let's go and talk to him.'

Paul Fabre had been delivered to the station, booked in and read his rights again, then placed in one of the cells in the custody suite. Moone and Butler waited while a doctor examined him to make sure he was in a state of health that would allow him to be interviewed. He was, the doctor told them, but he was concerned about his weight. Moone smiled, nodded and listened, as did DSU Fiona McIntyre, whose care he was now under.

'So, you think there's more than one of them?' McIntyre asked as they stood just outside the secure door of the custody suite. They had been ordered to leave the area while paperwork was filled out and the prisoner was checked over. In the custody suite, the custody officers were solely in charge and answered only to themselves. What they said, Moone knew, might as well be the word of God.

'Looks that way.' Moone looked past her, trying to see into the next room. 'But we're thinking we have the killer. For some reason, Bobbi was being held in a house somewhere near the city centre. But whoever kept her there, treated her well, and was kind to her. And the description of her captor doesn't fit with the porter.'

She nodded. 'He's all skin and bone, isn't he? Is he well?'

Moone shrugged. 'Maybe I'll find out in a few minutes. I might even find out where Cody is too.'

'Let's hope so. Listen.' McIntyre stepped closer. 'How's Butler? I can't believe she's come back to work after...'

'That's Butler. Best not to try and understand her too much. I've been trying to and I haven't got anywhere.'

Fiona smiled. 'Another thing, I'm going to be leaving soon.'

'Off up to Edinburgh?'

She nodded. 'My fiancé is getting restless.'

'Understandable.' He smiled. 'Well, hopefully we'll get this all tied up before you go.'

She smiled. 'Good. Maybe we can get a coffee or go for a drink before I head off.'

He nodded, a little confused. 'Yes, that would be good.'

'Right, then, best you get talking to your suspect.'

Moone sat down opposite Paul Fabre who was dressed in a thin blue forensic outfit, his hollow white skin seeming to glow eerily under the strip lights above. A duty solicitor, a slight podgy man with curly greying hair, was sitting by his side taking notes. Butler read out all the relevant information for the recording, then sat back.

'Where do you live?' Moone asked, smiling politely.

The solicitor leaned in and whispered something to the porter.

'None of your business,' Fabre said, smiling slyly.

'I'm thinking out in the sticks somewhere.'

The porter laughed. 'This is Devon. Everywhere's out in the sticks.'

'Where is Cody Barton?' Moone asked.

'Never heard of her.' The porter grinned as the solicitor whispered something again.

Moone sat back, wondering if there was another way to get under his skin, and asking himself if it was a place he really wanted to visit. There was only one way he could see, even though he was loathe to do it.

'I couldn't help notice your appearance,' Moone said, and saw a flicker around Fabre's eyes as his smile seemed to flatten out a little.

'What about it?' Fabre said.

'You don't look like a well man,' Butler said with a huff.

Moone looked at her, seeing her usual pissed off exterior and wondered what was going on in her head.

'You're not afraid to speak your mind,' the porter said, nodding. 'That's refreshing.'

'So, is it cancer?' Butler asked, folding her arms.

'Is this relevant at all?' the solicitor asked, robotically, not even looking up.

'It may be,' Moone said.

'It's OK, I don't mind talking about it,' Fabre said, staring at Butler. 'No, it's not cancer. Have you ever heard of Whipple's disease?'

'No,' Moone said. 'What is it?'

Fabre looked at him. 'A very rare illness. Only one in a million people get it. Mostly men. I'm one in a million. How about that? How lucky I am. You see, it's a bacteria that you ingest, and when it gets inside of you, it buries itself deep into your cells. It's almost impossible to give rid of, even though they put you on a smorgasbord of drugs. If you get it in your gut like me, then it disallows your body any nourishment from the food you eat. So you end up looking... well, like me.'

'There's no cure?' Butler asked.

'Only treatment.' He looked at her blankly.

'So you take a lot of drugs?' Moone asked.

'No. I used to. Every day. Pill after pill, until I rattled. But then I had an epiphany and I stopped taking them.'

'Presumably you'll die then without the pills?' Moone asked.

The porter nodded. 'Yes, I will, but I've made my peace with it. I realised one day that this was how I was meant to be, that I was in some kind of metamorphosis stage. I was becoming something else...'

'A monster?' Butler asked.

Fabre smiled. 'If you feel comfortable calling me a monster.'

'I do. Very. You transformed into this monster and you started kidnapping and killing young women. Overweight young women.'

The solicitor leaned in, but the porter shook his head at him. 'It's all right. I want to talk. I don't expect you two to understand, you're just mindless drones. No offence.'

Butler huffed out a laugh. 'Plenty taken.'

'They had so much potential. So much beauty ready to burst out of them. I could see it in their eyes, that desperate need for beauty and approval. The way they snap those selfies, posting them online for every pervert to comment on. And you should read the comments...'

'So you started targeting overweight girls?' Moone asked. 'In Cardiff?'

Fabre nodded. 'That's where it started, yes.'

'But you saw the tattoo first, didn't you?' Moone asked, leaning forward. 'The butterfly?'

Fabre looked up towards the ceiling. 'Oh, yes, that perfect butterfly. The painted lady.'

'On Bobbi-Jane?' Moone asked.

Fabre nodded. 'That's right.'

'We've got her now.'

'You've got her? Now?' Fabre looked away,

his eyes full of confusion for a moment. Then he let out a laugh. 'I see.'

'You see what?' Moone sat forward. 'You didn't take her, did you? Someone else had her.'

'I'll talk about that in a minute. All this... it was fate that laid it all out for me.'

'Really?' Butler shook her head.

'Yes.' Fabre's eyes ignited as he leaned closer. 'I'd started to grow butterflies. You can send off for baby caterpillars and feed them, nurture them, and then release them once they transform... I was talking about it in the staffroom one day, and someone laughed. It was this dopey idiot who worked there... anyway, he said for a minute he thought I was talking about real ladies. Capturing them and then releasing them. Then I knew. It was a sign.'

'That you'd gone mad?' Butler raised her eyebrows.

'Where's Cody Barton?' Moone asked.

The porter looked at Moone. 'She's fine. Soon she'll be looking slim and beautiful, ready to be released.'

Moone sat back, seeing the sickness in his eyes. 'But that's the thing, isn't it? You're not there to release her.'

'She'll be released.' Fabre smiled. 'Don't worry yourself.'

'How?'

'By the person who has been looking after

Bobbi all this time.'

'But they let Bobbi go,' Butler said and laughed.

The porter looked at her. 'So?'

'So, he couldn't kill her. How do you expect him to release, I mean, kill Cody Barton?' Butler huffed out another laugh.

The porter stared at her blankly, then smiled. 'Oh dear. You are clueless. I'm not the artist. He is. He's the one who paints them, makes them beautiful.'

'And you kill them?' Moone asked.

'A couple.' The porter stared at him. 'But the rest... was he. And although he tries to fool himself into believing he's a good man... he enjoys it, he enjoys seeing them transformed before his very eyes. I'd say Cody hasn't got long now until she is a much more beautiful creature.'

CHAPTER 29

When Moone stepped back into the incident room, he got a bit of a shock to see DI Vincent Crowne stood talking to his boss, Fiona McIntyre. Moone went over, his heart still pounding, his stomach rolling over and over, knowing they had been mistaken all along.

'He's winding us up, isn't he?' Butler said behind him.

Moone faced her. 'Is he? I don't know.'

'He has to be. He's the killer.'

'She's out there, somewhere and we have no idea where and no idea who this other person is.'

'Moone?'

He turned round to see Crowne smiling, coming towards him with his hand ready to shake. 'It's good to see you. I've got good news.'

'That's nice. I could do with some.'

'We've got her.' Crowne smiled even brighter.

'Who?'

'Carthew. She's made a mistake. We talked to her partner in crime, the detective constable she was seeing, and she told us they met up at a pub one night, and Carthew went to talk to some woman in the pub. I think that woman was Armstrong's dead wife. I think that's when they were planning it all.'

'Did your PC witness hear them planning it?' Moone asked, praying the answer was yes.

'No, but she said that Carthew convinced her to go to the pub and take the CCTV footage. Gave her some bullshit about it being part of a secret police operation.'

'Where's the footage now?'

Crowne sighed. 'I don't know. She gave it to Carthew, but now we can use this knowledge to break her.'

Butler laughed aloud as she sat at her desk.

'What?' Crowne stared at her.

'You'll never break her.' Butler folded her arms. 'You've got no CCTV footage, no evidence of the meeting...'

'We've got an eyewitness.'

'To what?' Butler shook her head. 'She'll deny it. It's this eyewitness's word against hers. She's far too clever to get caught up in this.'

Moone looked back at Crowne and saw the moment that the realisation hit him.

'We've got to try,' Crowne said. 'Put it to her, see her reaction.'

'It depends how you word it,' DSU McIntyre said, stepping closer. 'If you say you've got an eyewitness in the pub who says they saw Carthew meeting with Armstrong's ex-wife...'

Crowne nodded. 'That's exactly what I thought. I've already contacted her to come in for a chat. Here, if that's OK?'

Crowne seemed to look at them all with almost a child's need for confirmation.

'Of course,' McIntyre said. 'Use one of our interview rooms. DCI Moone can sit in on the interview with you.'

Crowne raised his eyebrows at Moone. 'What do you think? Together we can crack her?'

Moone looked at Butler and saw her shake her head and sigh before returning to her desk as if nothing had happened. 'OK, I'll sit in, but I don't think it'll do much good.'

'Thanks,' Crowne said, the glint of relief in his eyes. 'How's your case going?'

Moone leaned on the desk, noting McIntyre was now paying even more attention. 'Well, we've got one of our killers. Paul Fabre, a porter working at Derriford. He's obsessed with butterflies and transformation, and I don't know what else. Thing is, there's someone else out there helping him. They've got Cody Barton.'

'How are we going to find her?' McIntyre

asked.

Moone shrugged. 'I don't know. Fabre won't tell us. And he's got a disease that's going to kill him pretty soon.'

'There must be a way,' Crowne said.

'We've had uniforms going to farms and smallholdings near here, but there's so many,' Moone said, and rubbed his tired eyes.

'What about an appeal?'

'Appeal to his sympathy?' Butler asked. 'According to our crazy porter, he's also a killer and he enjoys it. If that's true, there'll be no point appealing to him.'

Moone agreed with her, but he couldn't see what else they could do. 'It's worth a shot. We can sit there and just talk about Cody, maybe get her parents in...'

'What about Bobbi?' Butler said. 'She's met him. He let her live, maybe having her appeal to him...'

McIntyre pointed to her. 'That's great. I think that might work. Talk to her, Pete, convince her to come in and we'll record an appeal. I'll call the local news channels, and Plymouth Live.'

Moone watched the DSU head off in a hurry, still not convinced it would work. But then he had let Bobbi go. Why had he let Bobbi go? There was only one person who might be able to answer that question. Fabre was still in the interview room, waiting for them to return, sweating it out, in conference with his solicitor. Moone hurried back out of the incident room and along to the interview room. He knocked, then went in and stood facing an amused looking Paul Fabre and his bored solicitor.

'Why did he let Bobbi-Jane go?' Moone asked, folding his arms. 'If he's this hardened killer that you say he is, then why just let her go?'

Fabre shook his head. 'You just don't get it, do you?'

'No, I don't. Explain it to me.' Moone sat down.

'You shouldn't say…' the solicitor began, but the porter waved away his words.

'She started it all. She's the mother to all this. That perfect tattoo. She's perfect. Beautiful. Everything was almost in her image. We could never destroy that.'

'Then why take her?'

Fabre leaned in, flames behind his eyes. 'We needed inspiration…'

'But she never turned up. He hid her from you.'

Fabre nodded, sat back. 'That's brothers for you.'

'You're brothers?'

'Well, half-brothers to be exact. But don't bother looking it up, because you won't find any record of it. We only found out ourselves about two years ago.'

Moone sat back. 'I take it you're close?'

'Of course. He'd do anything for me, and vice versa. Don't even think about trying to get me to turn on him. I'll never do that.'

Moone nodded. 'I know. But it must upset you a little that he's out there having all the fun.'

The porter laughed. 'I've had my day in the sun. I knew it was going to end sooner or later.'

'I don't believe that,' Butler said with a laugh. 'It must ache inside of you that he's with her and you're not. Imagine the things he'll get to do.'

Fabre turned to her slowly, blank at first, then a thin smile spread across his face. 'You've been visiting the hospital a lot, Detective. I've seen you…'

'Don't, Paul,' Moone said, watching Butler's face change, a redness coming to her cheeks.

'Someone poorly?' the porter asked. 'I'm thinking they're on their way out…'

Butler jumped forward suddenly, putting her face a foot from Fabre's, making him jolt backwards. She stared at him, then laughed a laugh full of anger and ridicule.

'Look at you, shitting your pants,' Butler said. 'For the recording, I, DI Mandy Butler went to get up and the suspect got scared.'

'What is this?' the solicitor said, his eyes

wide with worry. 'Do I need to report you?'

Moone held up a hand as Butler got up and stormed out. 'For the tape, DI Mandy Butler just left the interview. Let's finish it there for the moment.' Moone stopped the interview and hurried out of the interview room to catch up with Butler. He found her in the incident room putting on her coat.

'Are you going home?' he asked, seeing the tears in her eyes.

'I don't know. I'm not sure where I'm going.'

'Well, let me come with you…'

She stopped and stared at him. 'No, Pete. I appreciate it, but no, I need to be alone. I thought I could come back and carry on as if nothing had happened, but obviously I can't.'

'You need time.' He smiled.

She huffed. 'Time. That's what they say, but there's never enough time, is there? Never enough time to say the things you should say. Never enough time to tell the people you care about that you… that you love them.'

Moone stared at her as she looked into his eyes, holding his gaze. He wasn't sure what he was meant to say, so he just nodded.

She huffed again. 'I'll be in touch. Tell McIntyre that I'm sorry.'

'I will.'

She grabbed her bag, then opened the door and looked at him again. 'I'm hoping they can get Carthew, trick her into giving herself away, but… I know they won't. She's too clever, that one.'

'We'll get her in the end.' He nodded, heard her huff again, then watched her walk out.

Moone felt something drain out of him, the remains of whatever it was lying in the pit of his stomach, infecting the rest of him with unease. Her words kept coming back to him, the way she looked at him.

He shook his head, pushed it all away, and sat at his desk as he reminded himself that she was a woman who had just lost her father, who was confused. It meant nothing. Slowly he lowered his head to his arms and enveloped himself in darkness. He needed some peace, time to think.

'She's here and waiting for us.'

Moone groaned and looked up, blinking and seeing Crowne stood in the doorway. The detective's face looked concerned as he said, 'You all right, Moone?'

Moone sat up, nodding. 'Yes, I'm fine. A-OK.'

'Are you sure?'

Moone stood up. 'Scout's honour. Let's get this over with.'

'You don't have to do this, I can get…'

Moone raised a hand. 'I'm fine. I need to do this.'

DS Faith Carthew was sat smiling, sipping a coffee and chatting with her Union representative when Moone and Crowne entered the interview room. She looked at them both as they took their seats, raising her eyebrows, a smirk on her face.

'It's Batman and Robin,' she said and laughed. 'Not sure who is who though. I'd have to see you both in tights.'

Moone took a breath and sat back. 'DS Carthew...'

'Faith,' she said, still smiling. 'You know my name. You've used it often enough. I remember you saying it just after I saved your life.'

Moone let out a sigh.

'I don't think you ever thanked me,' she said.

'Thank you.' Moone looked down at the notes he had in front of him. 'June 18th, last year.'

Carthew raised her shoulders. 'What of it?'

'You went for a drink in a pub in Bristol,' he said. 'You went to the Crown Bar in the city centre with DC Cara Banerjee. Is that right?'

Carthew's smile faded a little. 'If you say so.'

'We do say so,' Crowne said. 'We even managed to find you and Banerjee together in the city centre.'

'OK, good,' Carthew said. 'So?'

'Do you remember that particular evening?' Moone asked.

'I think so. Why?'

'We tried to find the CCTV footage from the pub that evening, but guess what?' Moone sat back, keeping his face blank.

'They've deleted it? They only keep it if there's an incident.'

'Someone came in and took the footage away with them. A police detective.'

'Really? Why?' Carthew sat up, pretending to look confused, but Moone saw the glint in her eyes.

'Because another detective of a more senior rank asked them to,' Crowne said.

'Who?' Carthew looked between them, and Moone thought he saw a faint glimmer of a smile, a smile of victory wanting to shine through.

'You know who,' Moone said.

'Isn't that the way elderly ladies call each other?' Carthew smiled, a little laugh coming with it. 'You know who! Yoohoo, over here, darling.'

'You're not taking this very seriously, DS Carthew,' Crowne said, the anger cracking in his voice. She was getting to him, getting to him like she did everyone she met. Moone knew she had the power to make people either love her deeply or hate her with everything in their soul.

'I'm sorry,' she said, shaking it off, and sitting up straight as if she was a schoolgirl being told off. 'OK, I'm listening. Tell me what you think has happened or what you think I've done.'

Moone let out a breath, tired of it all already, feeling them sliding towards defeat. 'We believe you met up with Mrs Armstrong that evening, in the pub. DC Banerjee has claimed that she...'

Carthew let out a sigh and hung her head.

'What is it?' Crowne asked. 'Ready to come clean?'

She looked up, a sad expression on her face. 'No, I haven't done anything. You were about to say Cara, bless her heart, claims I met with Mrs Armstrong that evening... I take it this is all to support your ridiculous theory that for some unknown reason I met up with DSU Armstrong's widow to help plan his murder? Is that right?'

Crowne sat back, not saying anything, just raising his eyebrows.

Carthew sat forward in a conspiratorial fashion. 'Look, I don't want to start name calling or anything like that, but Cara Banerjee had issues. Very serious mental health issues.'

Crowne swapped incredulous looks with Moone before he said, 'Go on.'

'That evening, for instance, in the pub, well, I went off to the bar to get us some drinks. I ended up chatting to this young woman at the bar, passing the time of day... in fact, I even helped her take her drinks to the table she was sitting at... maybe she misconstrued that? Anyway, I'm digressing... anyway, when we leave the pub, she starts accusing me of having an affair with this woman I talked to at the bar. She was going crazy...'

Crowne laughed, sat back and stared at the ceiling.

'You obviously don't believe me.' Carthew sat forward.

'No, quite frankly, I don't.'

'There must be CCTV footage. We walked out of the pub and headed along the passage towards the market. There must be some footage of us arguing.'

'There might be,' Crowne said. 'But why did she go and get the CCTV footage?'

Carthew shrugged. 'I don't know. Maybe because I said nothing happened and she was obsessed that it did. She probably went and got the footage to catch me out, but obviously she would have seen that nothing did happen.'

'Nice little story,' Crowne said with a sigh and Moone could hear the defeat in his voice. 'So, you're painting a picture of a crazy and obsessed girlfriend?'

'I don't want to,' Carthew said, putting on

a look of anger. 'You're not giving me much choice. But, seeing as the truth's coming out, and she's accusing me of all this, whatever it is, then let me tell the truth.'

'I wish you would.'

'DS Carthew is doing her best to help,' Carthew's Union rep said, then folded his arms.

'Thanks,' Carthew said. 'That night, the night Armstrong was murdered, Cara came to my room, she started to accuse me of crazy stuff she'd made up in her head.'

'Like what?' Moone asked.

Carthew looked at him. 'She'd seen me chat to DSU Charlie Armstrong. I only wanted to ask him a question about the course, but she started accusing me of doing all sorts…'

'But you went to his room, didn't you?' Crowne asked.

'Yes, because he wanted to show me something course related. As I've stated before, I left a few minutes later.' She sat back. 'Now, that night, she came to my room and started accusing me of stuff. We argued for a while, then we went to bed. Thing is, I fell asleep pretty quickly, a lot quicker than I normally would. I hadn't even had that much to drink…'

'What are you saying?' Crowne leant forward. 'Are you suggesting DS Banerjee drugged you?'

Carthew shrugged. 'I don't know. I'm just saying what happened. It's possible that she thought I was seeing Armstrong behind her back and went to have it out with him...'

'So she murdered Armstrong?'

'I don't know.'

'DSU Armstrong, the man who had the job you wanted. Desperately.'

Carthew looked surprised. 'That I wanted? In Plymouth? I have no plans to come back to Plymouth. In fact I've put in a transfer request to Scotland.'

'When did you put in for this transfer?'

'A while before the course started. You can check.' Carthew smiled.

'Oh, I will.' Crowne looked at Moone, but he just shrugged. 'That's an interesting story,' Crowne said.

'It's her word against mine, I guess. But you can check it all out.' Carthew folded her arms. 'Am I free to go yet? Am I under arrest?'

After Carthew and her Union rep had left the interview room and exited the building, Moone sat with Crowne in the interview room in silence for a moment.

'What?' Crowne said.

'We've got nothing,' Moone said. 'Nothing to hold her with. Just a lot of circumstantial stuff.'

'That won't hold up,' Crowne said, then looked at him. 'She's clever, isn't she?'

Moone nodded.

'You told me so.' Crowne dragged a hand down his face. 'What is it all for? I don't get it. We thought she had motive, but she says she's relocating to Scotland...'

'You'll find what she said is true.'

'I don't doubt it. Then why did she do it?'

Moone couldn't truly fathom it, and could only think of one reason. 'To show off. To prove that she could get away with this. To get the attention.'

Crowne laughed, but it was an empty, hollow sound. 'And now she's off to Scotland. At least she'll be out of your hair.'

Moone sighed. 'She won't go to Scotland. She'll come back to our station. I guarantee it. She's not done with us.'

'I'm tired all over.' Crowne stood up. 'I'm going to check out what she said, and if it all adds up, then I'm afraid I'm going to have to draw a line under all this.'

Moone nodded, feeling a little sorry for Crowne, but mostly sorry for his team and for the storm that was on its way. He couldn't let her be their boss, but he just didn't know how to stop her. He stood up, and put out his hand for Crowne to shake.

'I understand,' Moone said. 'Thanks for trying. Now I have to go and try and find a missing girl.'

Cody Barton was shivering all over, sat in the

darkness of the cell, clutching her arms around her naked body. There was only a blanket in the cell and she had wrapped it around her, but still she was shaking. Cold and fear was making her tremble. She thought of the lad she had been with and wondered if he was alive or not. The tears came for him and for what might happen to her. She thought of her family. Flashes of them all filled her mind as she started to weep.

Her head shot up when a sound echoed down through the building. It sounded like a door slamming shut, then footsteps. She trembled even more, her heart thudding.

Another door squeaked open, then more slow steps. Nothing after the steps stopped. She watched the doorway, but no one appeared.

Her heart pounded.

'Please,' she called out. 'Please let me go.'

Then a shape appeared. The person stood in the doorway, staring in her direction, or they seemed to be.

He came into the room, taking his time, his eyes on her. As he got closer, she could see the mask under the hood he wore.

'What am I going to do with you?' he asked, his voice strained, breaking up.

'Please, just let me go.'

'I wish I could,' he said as he stepped closer. 'I really wish I could.'

'You can.' She came closer to the bars. 'Just take me far from here and leave me. I haven't seen your face. I don't know you. Please... please...'

He seemed to stare at her for ages, before he said, 'But you're not ready to be released yet. Look at you. You've got a few weeks to go before you can flap your wings and fly off.'

'Please...'

'You're so close to being truly beautiful.' He stepped closer.

'I don't know who you are, I haven't seen your face... you could let me go.'

Then his hand grasped at his mask and ripped it from his head.

She looked away, clenching her eyes shut, the tears still bursting out.

'Look at me,' he said, quietly.

'Please...'

'Look at me or I'll end you now.'

Her heart pounding, she looked up and opened her eyes. He was staring down at her, a big smile stretching his face as he said, 'I haven't even painted you yet.'

CHAPTER 30

Although he hated being there, and felt a little sick about it, Moone was sitting in a chair close to the hospital bed that Loy Grader was lying in. He hadn't been able to sleep, so he had decided to visit Bobbi-Jane again and make sure she was OK. Then he had found himself staring at the child murderer with so much revulsion filling his stomach. He had been informed that Grader had a bleed on his brain which they had operated on. It was touch and go and now he was in a medically induced coma. Moone leaned forward and buried his face in his hands, moaning to himself.

'Do you think he'll ever be able to tell us the truth?'

Moone sat up and stared round at the man stood in the doorway. It was Colin Smith, the ex-detective obsessed with finding out what happened to the little boy. Moone huffed to himself, knowing he had caught the same contagious obsession.

'I don't know.' Moone stood up. 'He's in a coma. It doesn't look good. What're you doing here?'

'Assessing the devastation.' Smith looked at him with a blank expression and pushed his glasses back up his nose. 'Well done for catching your killer.'

'One of them. There's another out there. But I don't know how to find him.'

'Anything to go on?'

Moone saw a flicker of life in the ex-copper's eyes. 'Not much. We think he holds them out in the sticks somewhere. Thing is, this accomplice had one of the girls somewhere else, a house somewhere. Near the city centre, we think. They use an ambulance. An old ambulance, but so far nothing on ANPR. Once they get out into the wilds of Devon, they disappear.'

Smith nodded. 'It's not easy. It's never easy. You'll get a break sooner or later.'

'I hope so.' Moone looked at their sleeping patient, almost looking calm and peaceful, not at all like the monster he knew he was. 'And I hope this... creature makes a recovery. I didn't think I'd ever hear myself say that. Anyway, I better go.'

Smith only smiled, so Moone headed out, past the uniform guarding the patient and out into the corridor. All the time he walked, myriad thoughts swept through his mind.

They slowly morphed into rats, running this way and that, escaping him at every turn. He tried to concentrate on the man they were hunting, who had Cody Barton. Was she in danger? The porter had promised him that his partner was equally as ruthless as him, he just kidded himself that he wasn't.

Bobbi-Jane had been released from the hospital and was at that moment being taken to the family room at the station to be interviewed. Perhaps more information about her kidnapper would be revealed, he hoped.

Butler came to mind, and the fact that she had lost her father. He knew how it felt to lose a parent, but he didn't know how it felt to lose one that you hadn't had the chance to make up with. Then his mind drifted back to what Dr Jenkins had said to him about Butler and her feelings for him. He had put them out of his head, tried to blot it all out, but as he walked through the hospital, they only rose. He took a left turn, deciding to head down to the morgue to talk to Dr Parry about it, as he knew the rumour had started with him.

After leaving the lift, he went along to the plain white door of the morgue and knocked. The door was opened by one of the technicians, so Moone asked for Dr Parry.

'He's not here,' Jenkins called out from the inner office, then poked her smiling face out. 'I'm here, if you need help.'

He smiled, then walked past the morgue fridges and into the autopsy room where Dr Jenkins went back to writing something up on a tablet device.

Not wanting to discuss the Butler situation, Moone said, 'We made an arrest.'

She looked up and smiled. 'You arrested someone for your butterfly murders?'

He nodded. 'Yep. But there's another one out there and he's got Cody Barton. I just don't know where and the man we've arrested won't talk.'

'You'll figure it out.' She smiled.

'That's what people keep telling me. I'm not convinced.'

'I've hear you've been doing pretty well. What about the missing boy? Did you solve that?'

'James Dyer?' Moone shook his head and sighed. 'No, and the only person who might tell me, is now in a medically induced coma.'

Jenkins made a sympathetic face. 'Oh dear, you're not getting a break are you? I feel sorry for his parents. Not knowing if he's alive or... you know.'

Moone had a flutter of thought in the back of his mind, trying to break through. He stared at the pathologist, pointing at her, knowing there was something there in what she said.

'Are you OK?' she asked. 'Did I say something?'

'If it was your boy or girl missing... what would you say about them?'

Jenkins shrugged. 'I guess I'd say all nice things about them, the way they played... what sort of...'

'You'd talk about them in the present, wouldn't you? Not in past tense, I mean?'

Jenkins frowned. 'Well, you wouldn't know if they were alive or dead, so... you wouldn't talk about them as if they were dead. Why?'

Moone held up a hand and took out his phone, and brought up Mrs Dyer's, or rather Lisa Brunning's phone number. 'Sorry, I need to make a call. Oh, can you get Dr Parry to come and see me or I'll come and find him.'

'OK.'

Moone hurried out of the morgue, hurrying down the corridor as he rang Lisa Brunning's phone number. It rang for a while then went to her voicemail, so he left a message asking her to come to the station.

DI Crowne and DS Rivers headed down the narrow thoroughfare where the Crown Bar was situated, wedged in between a few more touristy shops. The clouds were drawing in, promising rain, reflecting Crowne's grisly mood as he stormed into the pub. It had low ceilings, but stretched quite far back, with tables in alcoves and booths. There was a stage and a long bar that ran along the far back wall.

'Cheer up,' Rivers said as they reached the bar. 'I might even buy you a pint.'

He let out a tired laugh. 'Cheers. What are we even doing here, Rivers? She's running rings round us.'

'You're giving her too much credit.' Rivers signalled to a young man behind the bar, who had floppy emo style blond hair, a piercing in his lip. 'We will trip her up. Or she'll trip herself up. I talked to the manager of this place on the phone and he told me about the footage being taken away. I thought it wouldn't hurt to find out some more from the barman who actually dealt with her.'

Crowne turned his back on the bar, shaking his head. 'Whatever. Make mine a Coke.'

'Full fat?'

He stared at her. 'Look at me. What do you think?'

She laughed as the floppy haired barman came over.

'What can I get you?' he asked, looking between them.

Rivers showed her ID. 'DS Rivers, this is DI Crowne. I talked to someone on the phone about CCTV footage…'

'Oh, right, yeah, that was me,' the barman said, resting his hands on the bar.

'You said a police detective came and took

the footage,' Rivers said.

'Yeah, like I said, she showed her badge. What could I do?' He looked nervously between them.

'It's fine.' Rivers brought up a photo of DC Banerjee on her phone and held it up. 'Is this the detective?'

He nodded. 'Yeah, I'm pretty sure that's her. I remember cause she was acting a bit... weird.'

'Weird?' Crowne asked.

The barman looked at him. 'Yeah, she was like... upset or angry. I thought she was going to cry at one point. I asked her if everything was all right and she bit my head off. Anyway, she took the footage and left.'

'She didn't say anything else?' Rivers asked.

'Na, that was it. It was all a bit weird. I'm not in any trouble, am I?'

'No, you're not,' Crowne said, then turned round and headed out of the pub. He stood outside, watching people go past, heading into the other restaurants, waiting for DS Rivers. She came out and stood next to him, writing in her notebook. 'That was productive.'

She looked up. 'Sarcasm, boss? Doesn't become you. So, she's upset and takes the footage. Why is she upset?'

'Because she thinks Carthew is doing the dirty on her. She's jealous.'

Rivers nodded. 'That night, the night Armstrong was murdered... she went into the bar and saw Carthew and him having a chat and a drink.'

'Yes, so?'

'Well, what if she got jealous that night?' Rivers raised her eyebrows.

Crowne looked at her and let out a dry laugh. 'What are you thinking? That she gets up in the middle of the night and goes to see Armstrong and murders him? You're joking, aren't you? DC Banerjee?'

Rivers looked at her notes again. 'Why not? Murders are committed by jealous people all the time.'

'DC Banerjee? Really?'

'What room was she staying in that night?'

He sighed. 'I'll have to check. But what of it? What do you expect to find? It's been cleaned since then.'

Rivers nodded. 'I know. I just want to look at it, see how far it was from Armstrong's room. I don't know really.'

'It's a waste of time.'

'Come on, what have we got to lose?'

He stared at her for a moment, noting her subtle smile. Then he threw his hands into the air. 'Fine. We look, and if we don't find anything, we bugger off back to the station and draw a line under this. I'm tired all over.'

Rivers patted his back, then headed for the hotel.

Moone headed down to the main desk of the station when he was told Lisa Brunning had turned up. He smiled as he opened the secure door and let her through. He noted that she looked slimmer than before, and her skin had lost its tan. She was still attractive but there was a haunted quality to it. Then he wondered if it was all in his mind. He directed her up the stairs towards the floor where there was a more comfortable family room.

'Thanks for coming in,' he said, opening the door for her.

'It's fine,' she said, quietly, then looked round the small room, at the green sofa and the red armchair facing it.

'Take a seat,' he said, then closed the door behind him. He watched her sit on the sofa, fidgeting a little.

He stood for a moment. 'Would you like a tea or coffee? Or water?'

'Water would be good. Thanks.'

He nodded, left the room and found WPC Carly Tomlin who was waiting in the small kitchen area.

'She'd like some water,' he said.

'OK, sir,' Tomlin said and took a bottle from a small fridge and poured a glass. 'So, what are we doing?'

'Chatting to her. I'm worried she might get upset, so I'd like you to be there in case.'

'Right, sir.'

'Let's go in.' Moone let Tomlin go in, rehearsing what he was going to say in his head. He smiled at Brunning as he came back in, then watched PC Tomlin sitting close to her.

Moone sat down and nodded, sliding the glass of water closer to her. 'We really appreciate you coming in like this.'

'It's fine.' She touched the glass, moved it round with her fingertips.

'I know it must be hard going over it all again and again.' He sat back, his whole body tensing, his words forming in his throat, threatening to choke him.

She nodded, looked up briefly, and slightly shook her head as she said, 'It's OK, it's fine. What did you want to ask me?'

He leaned forward, looking at her, trying to see beyond her beauty at what lay beneath it. 'Tell me about James.'

She looked up, blinking. 'You want to know about James?'

'Yes. Please. Unless it's too hard.'

She shook her head. 'It's OK. James was… he was a loving child. He loved playing football…'

Moone felt his gut tighten at her words and his eyes found PC Tomlin. The uniform was nodding, looking sympathetic. His words rose to his lips as he took a breath.

'You say *was*,' Moone said. 'Forgive me, but I've noticed that you always talk about James in the past tense.'

Brunning looked at him, blinking, her face reddening. 'Do I? I don't mean to. He's...'

'Why do you think you do that?' Moone asked, and saw Tomlin staring at him, concern in her eyes.

She shrugged. 'I don't know. I suppose it's so long since...'

'When was the last time you saw him? I mean, the absolute last moment you saw him.'

He saw the flutter across her face, the flinch in her jaw. A memory. A painful memory.

'When did you last see James?' Moone said again.

'I can't remember.' She looked down.

'You must remember the last time you saw him...'

Brunning looked at Tomlin, a tear in her eye. 'I don't think I can do this. I'm sorry...'

'It's OK,' Tomlin said. 'Sir...'

'Was he alive when you last saw him?' Moone asked, clenching his fists, digging his nails into his palms.

Brunning looked down. 'Of course he was.'

'What's his favourite toy?'

Brunning shook her head. 'It was... it is, I mean...'

Moone leaned forward. 'He's dead, isn't he,

Lisa?'

She didn't look up. He could see she was trembling as she started sniffing.

'I need Tom here,' she said.

'Where is James, Lisa?' he asked.

'I don't know,' she said. 'I don't know. Please...'

'Do you not know because you got someone else to take him somewhere?'

She looked up, the tears now streaming down her face. 'I want to go home.'

Moone looked at PC Tomlin and saw the horror in her eyes. 'Loy Grader.'

Brunning let out a strange sound, grasping her hands together.

'Did he help you?' Moone asked, lowering his head, trying to make eye contact. 'I think he did, but I just don't understand why. Why would he help you?'

She lowered her head, sobbing.

'Can you explain?'

Tomlin produced a packet of tissues and held one out to Lisa Brunning. She took it in her trembling hands and wiped her eyes and nose. Then she looked up, blinking, staring at Moone. He could feel it, the need to talk welling inside her.

'It's OK,' he said. 'It's OK.'

She nodded. 'I don't know what happened.'

'Just tell us about that night. You went out

to the restaurant near the hotel...'

She nodded, sniffing. 'James used to wake up a lot after we'd put him to bed. He'd have these bad dreams, night terrors...'

'One of my kids used to have them...'

'We used to give him these...' He saw the memory dig into her and twist.

'Pills?'

She nodded. 'Only a little bit. Just a little bit. I don't know what happened. I came back to check on him... I could see he wasn't...'

She started sobbing again, so Moone sat back and watched PC Tomlin try and comfort her. She regained her composure, and wiped her eyes and looked up at Moone.

'I'm not a monster,' she said. 'People say all this stuff online, like I... like I did things to him. I loved him so much...'

'But there was nothing you could do to help him.'

She nodded.

'Where does Grader come into it?'

'He was there. I came out of the apartment... I think I was in shock... and there he was, just stood over the other side of the street, like he'd been waiting all that time. I recognised him from the restaurant... from when he tried to talk to Tom. Tom told me that Grader had worked for him for a bit, but then he'd found out what he was. Then Grader started saying he could ruin Tom's business, tell people all kinds of stuff... said he needed money...'

'Tom was paying him off?'

Brunning nodded.

'So, he was outside the apartment...'

'He... he just walked over and he knew... he knew something bad had happened. He stormed past me and went in. I found him staring at James and I started hitting him, pushing him away... but then he said he could help. That he could make it all go away. He said our lives would be over, we'd go to prison and we'd lose everything we had worked for.' She looked up at Moone, a kind of pleading in her eyes. He smiled kindly even though he wanted to walk out and be sick in the corridor.

'So you let him take James away?' Moone said, his words crumbling, feeling his own hands start to tremble.

She nodded. 'Yes, I did. Oh God. Oh God. Why did I? I don't know where he is. I don't know where my poor boy is...'

Moone sat back, staring at her as she broke down, sobbing uncontrollably, his own body shaking almost violently. He looked at Tomlin, nodded, and stood up, desperate to get out of the room that seemed to be getting smaller by the second.

He walked out calmly, then closed the door behind him and stood in the corridor. He almost didn't know what had happened at first, but he found himself slipping down the wall, his eyes blinded by tears. He was shaking, sobbing and gasping for breath.

CHAPTER 31

'What the hell're you doing down there?' Butler asked, appearing in the corridor. 'Moone, you alright?'

He wiped his eyes and fought to get to his feet, and tried to put a smile on his face. 'I'm fine. It's all good.'

Butler gave him a look that told him she didn't believe a word of it, then nodded towards the interview room. 'How did it go?'

He coughed away the dryness of his voice, his mind flickering back to what Lisa Brunning had said, his stomach sinking again, the wave of emotion threatening to rise over him. 'She... she gave him a tablet. Sleeping pill or something. It was an accident, or so she says.'

Butler widened her eyes. 'She admitted to it? Just like that?'

He nodded. 'Just like that. If it's worth anything, I believe it was accident, but it's the other thing I can't get my head round.'

'What other thing?'

Moone looked over Butler's shoulder and saw Dr Parry approaching, his usual bright smile having deserted him. He nodded to the doctor, then returned his eyes to Butler. 'Loy Grader. She said he was outside their apartment that night. Like he was waiting. He helped her... dispose of her boy's body...'

'He did what? What sort of person lets... Jesus Christ, I don't care what you say, she's not right in the head.'

Moone nodded. 'You may be right. Hello, Doctor.'

Butler turned and saw Parry looking at them. 'Oh, if it isn't the illusive Dr Parry. Where have you been?'

He shrugged. 'Busy I guess.'

'You guess?' Butler huffed, then looked at Moone. 'By the way, Bobbi-Jane is here, ready to be interviewed.'

He nodded, then looked at Parry, realising that the reason he was here was of a delicate nature and not for the ears of Butler.

'You wanted to see me?' Parry asked, looking between them.

'Yes,' Moone said, putting his hands into his pockets. 'I'm just trying to remember why.'

Butler looked at him, her eyes narrowing as a low huff escaped her lips. 'All right, I can see when I'm not wanted. I'll go and talk to Bobbi, ease her in.'

When Butler had left, Moone stepped

towards Dr Parry, noticing he seemed a lot less happy than he used to, and that he looked skinnier too. 'You OK?'

'Of course. I take it you didn't want to talk in front of DS Butler?'

'No.' He took a breath. 'I heard a rumour that you think... well, that you think that Butler...'

'Spit it out.' Parry put on a smile, but it didn't stretch his face like it normally would.

'Does she like me? Like, really like me?'

Parry stared at him for a moment, then laughed. 'Butler? That's funny. I think she's fond of you. Probably fonder than she is of anyone. But no, I don't think you've got anything to worry about.'

Moone let out a sigh of relief. 'That's good. I was worried for a moment.'

'Was that all? I was told you wanted to see me urgently.'

Moone shook his head. 'Not urgently. Sorry, that was it. I didn't expect you to rush down here. In fact, I don't think I've seen you here before.'

Dr Parry looked round at the walls, then shrugged. 'It's not often I'm here. Only occasionally.'

'Sorry, I better go and talk to Bobbi-Jane, our witness.'

Parry straightened up and nodded. 'Yes, you better had. Is she all right?'

'Bobbi-Jane?' Moone sighed. 'She's as well as can be expected. Thing is, she was held somewhere different than the rest of the girls. We think he had an accomplice, but whoever they were kept Bobbi to himself.'

Dr Parry nodded. 'To save her?'

Moone frowned. 'I don't know about that. It seemed to start with her tattoo, seemed to start off their obsession. I really don't know.'

'Maybe it was because her tattoo was bigger, more intricate?'

'Maybe. Right, I can't chat here all day. I'll come by and see you later.'

'Anytime,' Parry said, then headed off down the corridor, leaving Moone alone to absorb all that had happened. He felt sick, could have easily bent over and puked his guts up. But he had a job to do. First, he found some officers to go in and take Lisa Brunning's full statement, then headed along to the family room, where he suspected Butler would have taken Bobbi-Jane. By the time he got there, Butler was opening the door and escorting the poor young girl out. He was about to approach, trying to find some kind words to say that wouldn't sound trite, but nothing came to his lips.

Bobbi-Jane had stopped in the corridor, her face losing all colour as she held on to the wall. Moone started moving quickly towards her, as he saw her slump to her knees, her body beginning to heave. He got down beside her, holding back her hair as she vomited on the floor.

Crowne opened the bottle of water he had bought as soon as he arrived at the hotel. It cost him a pound more than it would have in a newsagents, and he was half tempted to call for backup to arrest them for daylight robbery. He had told the person running the shop the same thing, but DS Rivers had dragged him away. Now she was putting on a pair of latex gloves, getting ready to swipe the electronic key card and enter the room.

'This is a waste of police time and resources,' Crowne said, leaning against the wall and watching her.

'You sound like our boss,' Rivers said, then put the keycard in the reader. It took her a couple of goes before the light went green and the door clicked open.

'That's because I know what the stuck-up cow will say.'

'Come on,' Rivers said and stepped in gingerly, as if she thought there might be landmines under the carpet.

He sighed, shook his head and pulled out a pair of gloves and put them on. He followed her in, watching her as she examined the empty, neatly prepared room. It was much the same as all the others he had seen in the hotel. The duvet was white with grey and red stripes, there was the coffee and tea making facilities by the tiny TV that was mounted on the wall. White tiled bathroom. He sighed again and folded his arms.

'What are you hoping to find?'

She shrugged. 'I don't know. Something. I'm thinking that maybe Carthew fell asleep, then DC Banerjee got up and headed to Armstrong's room...'

'You really think Banerjee did this?' He gave a shake of his head. 'Banerjee? Really?'

'Why not? She's jealous, obsessive. I got off the phone to her ex a little while ago. She said the same thing, she was possessive, jealous...'

'Did she murder someone?' Crowne raised his eyebrows. 'Oh, and by the way, how did she manage to murder the widow and her lover and make it look like murder suicide?'

Rivers closed her eyes, then looked up at him again. 'How did Carthew?'

'What's your point?'

'Well, we seem to be treating her like some master criminal genius, because DCI Moone said she is. Maybe he's wrong about this. Perhaps Jason Wise did kill her, then take his own life. I mean, if it looks like and smells like shit...'

Crowne nodded. 'I get it. So, what are we looking for?'

Rivers looked round the room and

shrugged. 'I don't know. But this is the only place we haven't examined, because stupidly we didn't even consider her as a suspect because we were blindsided by your mate.'

Rivers got on her knees by the bed, and started examining the mattress itself.

'You're not going to find anything.'

She stared at him. 'I won't if I don't look.'

Crowne turned away and looked towards the window as he started to question everything he believed about the case. Perhaps Rivers was right, Moone was a jilted ex-lover with an unhealthy obsession. He just didn't know any more.

'Jesus,' Rivers said. She had her hand under the bed, feeling around for something.

'What is it?'

'There's something stuffed into the bed slats. Help me. Lift the bed up.'

'With my back?'

'Hurry up.'

Crowne took off his jacket, then rolled up his sleeves. He was careful to bend his knees as he got hold of the end of the bed and lifted and let out a grunt.

Rivers got under, tugging at something. 'That's it. Let it go.'

Crowne let the bed back down and Rivers was holding a squashed-up carrier bag which had something in it. She looked inside, then up at him with her eyebrows raised. 'You're not going to believe this.'

'What?'

She put her hand in and brought out a long blonde wig and held it up. 'Look at this. There's a hoodie in here too, and it matches the one the woman was wearing on the CCTV footage. What's the betting we get DNA from this that matches DC Banerjee?'

Crowne couldn't find the words. He was staring at the wig, trying to compute it all, realising for the first time in a long while that he might have read the whole case wrong. He looked at Rivers. 'We better find her and bring her in.'

Moone passed Bobbi-Jane a cup of water as he sat down in the family room. Butler was sat beside her, looking at the poor girl with something close to sympathy. The young woman had some of her colour back, her cheeks flushing a little as she picked up the water and took a couple of sips.

'I'm sorry,' she said, shrugging. 'I don't know what happened.'

'It's OK,' Moone said. 'You've been through quite an ordeal. It's probably the shock.'

Bobbi-Jane nodded. 'I suppose so. It was the smell too.'

'The smell?' Butler asked.

She made a face as she sipped more of the water. 'Yeah, even the thought of it makes me want to chuck up.'

Moone leaned forward, feeling a little lost. 'The smell? Sorry, Bobbi, what smell do you mean?'

She shrugged. 'I don't know… I thought I could smell him again. Just for a moment.'

'Smell him?' Butler asked. 'The evil bastard who took you?'

The girl nodded, looking down. 'Yeah, it was an awful smell. I can't even describe it.'

'Like death you said before.' Moone sat back, his mind running through everything, trying desperately to make sense of it all.

She looked up, nodding. 'Yeah, but it was kind of, I don't know… like chemicals or something.'

Moone's whole body became rigid for a moment, while his stomach wrapped round itself tightly. 'Chemicals? And death?'

'I suppose. It was horrible.'

Moone thought of the area where she had caught the scent, of where she had been sick. He looked at Butler, his heart beginning to pound in his ears and chest. 'Did anyone come through there before I did? Just before?'

'No, I don't think so. I was stood outside waiting to go in to see Bobbi.'

'No one at all? You're sure?' Moone stood up.

He saw Butler's eyes going up to her left, signifying the retrieval of memory. 'Well, I saw

Dr Parry go by. But that's all.'

Moone grasped his face, enclosing it in pink darkness. When he looked from his hands, he saw Butler staring at him strangely.

'He knew about her tattoo,' Moone said.

'Who?'

'No, it can't be.' Moone turned to the door, then stopped. 'But how did he know about Bobbi's tattoo? I never showed him it, did you?'

Butler got up in a hurry, then pushed Moone outside into the corridor and stared at him. 'What the hell're you getting at? Are you trying to say Parry's involved in this? Don't be ridiculous...'

Moone put his fingers to his temples, racing back over the last few weeks. 'He's not been himself. Then there was the trouble with his family. He said he had a brother... He knew about the tattoo, and he passed by shortly before Bobbi smelled the smell... have you smelt him when he's at work?'

Butler nodded, stepping back, shaking her head slightly. 'I can't believe...'

'Where does he live?'

'I don't know.'

Moone was about to head to the incident room to look up his address, but Butler's hand grasped his arm and yanked him back. 'What?'

She sighed and shook her head. 'We can't arrest him.'

'Why?'

'Think about it. He's the pathologist, he's been the pathologist on a lot of our cases, other cases. If we arrest him, then a lot of those cases could be reviewed, or thrown out. Lots of criminals back on the street.'

Moone stared at her, his stomach sinking even further as he realised she was right. 'What do we do?'

'Go and see him. Have it out with him.'

'Then what?'

'Fucked if I know. But let's make sure we're right first.'

The incident response cars were leading the way, their blue lights flashing as they cleared the way along the M5. Crowne was driving, with DS Rivers in the passenger seat reading through some files. They had been in touch with Birmingham's major investigation unit and passed on their intelligence to them in the hopes they would assist in the arrest of Banerjee. They would send officers to help, they said, but it was Crowne's operation, his arrest.

'How far now to Birmingham?' Crowne asked, putting his foot down, and racing round a line of traffic.

'Not too far.' Rivers didn't look up. 'Her mind must've snapped. She saw Armstrong and Carthew together or she saw her go into his room…'

'I just don't buy it,' Crowne said.

'Why not? People have murdered for less.'

'Oh, come on. This is Carthew. You've seen the smug look on her face every time we talk to her.'

'Maybe she's just a smug person.'

He laughed. 'Where's she staying?'

'A flat where her cousin lives. The uniforms have got the address. Just don't lose them.'

He sighed. 'I'll try not to.'

The incident response cars took them through Birmingham city centre. Soon they were heading to towards the suburbs and turning off towards a housing estate. As Crowne pulled in behind one of the response cars, just across the road from a row of shops, he shook his head. He still couldn't buy it, still couldn't see DC Banerjee as a psychopathic killer who got into a jealous rage. Then he started to wonder as he climbed out of the car and followed Rivers and the uniforms towards the archway entrance to the estate; could he have got it all wrong because of what Moone had been telling him? He sighed and walked into the courtyard that sat below two grey tower blocks.

'It's the fifth floor,' Rivers said to the uniforms before they started hammering their boots up the stone, urine-stinking stairs until they stopped at a red, scratched door.

'You want to do the honours?' Rivers

asked, turning to Crowne.

'Be my guest,' he said, and stood to the side, resting his back on the low wall behind him.

Rivers rang the bell, then thumped her fist on the door as she called out, 'DC Banerjee? It's DS Rivers and DI Crowne. We need a word with you.'

There was no answer, so Rivers banged again.

'Maybe she's not home,' Crowne said and shrugged. 'Maybe she's done a bunk.'

Rivers made an unimpressed sound and knocked again. But there was still no answer.

'I ain't seen her for a couple of days,' a woman's voice said, and they all turned to see a black woman, perhaps in her fifties, staring at them from a doorway a few feet away.

Crowne walked over and smiled. 'Do you know her well?'

'I know the young lady who lives there and I saw her cousin turn up. But haven't seen either of them for a while.'

Crowne nodded, looking towards the flat, wondering, getting a slight discomfort in the base of his gut. 'Thanks. Have you seen anyone else turn up?'

'I can't remember. Oh, there was an Indian lad, yesterday I think it was. He knocked on the door, then went in. I didn't hear him leave though. Is everything all right?'

'Yes, all good,' he said, lying through his teeth as he smiled. 'Nothing to worry about.'

The woman looked past him and towards Rivers and the two uniforms. 'Doesn't look like there's nothing to worry about.'

'It's fine. Just go back inside.' Crowne sighed and walked back to Rivers. 'I don't like this. We should go in. We've got reasonable suspicion. What do you think?'

Rivers nodded. 'We've got an arrest warrant for her, so...' She turned to the uniforms. 'Let's get in there.'

One of them produced a small red battering ram Enforcer and swung it at the door a couple of times before it flung open and hit the wall inside. Rivers went in first, pulling on some latex gloves, with Crowne following hot on her heels. He nearly slammed into her back, when she stopped dead towards the end of the corridor where daylight streamed in from the windows of the living area.

'Can you smell that?' Rivers asked, turning to him, her face tightening as her eyes widened.

Crowne sniffed the air and caught the deep pungent and macabre smell. He'd smelt it before on two other occasions, only one of them being part of a murder enquiry.

'We need to get forensics here,' he said, turning to face the uniforms coming down the hall. 'Seal this off. Let's keep traffic to a minimum.'

'Where's it coming from?' Rivers asked, stepping toward the living room. Then she paused, turning her head. 'Is that a bedroom?'

Crowne shrugged as he pulled on a pair of gloves and watched his partner grip the door handle and slowly open it.

The smell rushed towards them, burning into Crowne's nostrils. He gripped a gloved hand over his face as he fought against the odour and stood by the double bed.

'Banerjee,' Rivers said as she stood on the other side of the bed, looking down at the almost grey naked woman lying across the white duvet. Her body was dark around her chest, her forearms, where blood had dried and caked itself to her skin. Crowne bent over and saw her eyes were open, but glassy. He turned away, the smell too much for him and hurried back out and then through the front door.

He leaned over the balcony, taking shaky breaths, seeing life going on, a market bustling, women pushing prams.

'Are you all right, boss?' Rivers asked, standing next to him.

'I can never get used to that smell.'

'No. But my guess is that she's been dead about forty-eight hours. I think that's when the body starts to decompose and, well, smell. It's quite warm at the moment too.'

'OK, Quincy.'

'Who?'

'Never mind. When did we last interview her?'

'Just over two days ago, give or take. She must have left London, headed up here, and...'

'Where was Carthew?'

Rivers let out a sigh. 'We interviewed her during that time. The timeline doesn't add up.'

He nodded. 'She's smart. Very clever.'

Rivers stared at him. 'You're kidding, right? How did she do it? We interviewed her, then she drives up here at high speed, and kills her ex-lover?'

'What if she could have sped up the decomposition process somehow?'

'How?'

'Heat? All you'd have to do is close the windows, put some heaters on.'

Rivers shook her head, then put her fingers on her temples. 'Listen, boss, but I just don't think she did this. And I found a knife under the bed. Blood all over it. Maybe that will tell us something. Plus, we need to find out who visited her the other day. I've just noticed the shops across the way, they might have a camera that captured something.'

'Good, let's get the footage. Let's just process all this and see what we come up with. Sorry, you're right. I think Moone's warped my mind.'

She smiled and patted his arm. But as soon

as she started to walk off, his mind started to race again, scrambling in every direction to work out how she could have done it. In his mind's eye he could see her, sitting across an interview room desk, smiling with a big smug look on her face.

'We need to contact her boss, Moone's boss,' Crowne called out to Rivers. 'Tell him what's been going on. If she is involved, he needs to know.'

CHAPTER 32

Butler pulled on the handbrake and turned off the engine, leaving them both in silence, the engine making a clicking noise as it cooled. Moone was staring across the lane where an old farmhouse and barn stood, looking pretty foreboding. They were on the outskirts of Bodmin, outside the property they had learned belonged to Dr Lee Parry. His father, a farmer, had left it to him nearly fifteen years ago when he had died of cancer. They had gleaned this information from some of the people he worked with and a couple of people he had studied alongside.

'Does that look like the kind of place where you could keep young girls and then tattoo and murder them?' Butler looked at him, her eyebrows raised.

'We've got to call this in,' Moone said and took out his mobile.

Butler gripped his wrist, staring at him. 'We can't, I already explained.'

'What the bloody hell do we do? We can't let him just wander off and snatch some more young women… cause we know he's not going to stop. I mean, if this is what he is… then he's not just going to agree to stop, is he?'

Butler huffed. 'No. So we have to come up with an answer. Oh, shit. Moone, look…'

Moone turned and flinched when he saw Parry stood in the open doorway of the house, staring out at them, his face devoid of any signs of his usual smile or anything that seemed human. Then he turned and disappeared inside, leaving the door open.

'Right, looks like we're being asked to go in.' Butler opened her door and climbed out.

Moone watched her, his heart pounding, a strange kind of panic engulfing him that he tried to breathe down. He jumped out and caught up with her.

'But what do we do?' he asked.

'Let's just see what the wanker says and take it from there.'

She went in, and Moone followed, his heart now thumping in his chest, ears, and just about every part of him. He followed her down a grotty hallway, the walls decorated in a flowery patterned wallpaper. There was a huge kitchen that stank of burnt wood, and was covered in dust. Butler kept turning into rooms until she stopped. Moone saw she had entered a living area. There was an old TV, a battered ugly sofa, and a much lived in armchair. Old black and white photos decorated the mantelpiece, cobwebs and dust covering them all.

Parry was sat on another chair, a hard back kitchen type chair. He was looking at them, staring, looking pale, dark stubble covering his jaw.

'You're here to arrest me?' he asked, looking at Butler.

'I don't know what we're going to do,' Butler said. 'Number one, where is she?'

He nodded. 'The basement. Paul liked to keep them locked up down there. I didn't like it, but what could I do?'

'What could you do?' Butler glared at him, stepping closer. 'You could've called us! That's what any normal person would've done.'

Parry looked at his hands. 'But that's the problem, isn't it? I'm not normal. I've never been normal. I mean, I've tried to convince myself that I am normal. But then, look at what I do. I enjoy my job. I enjoy taking them apart, putting them back together. It's so... moving, so beautiful.'

Butler looked at Moone, her eyes wide. He nodded, and came further into the room. 'You need to let her go.'

'I know. I wasn't going to hurt her.' He looked down.

'You weren't?' Butler asked. 'Your mate, whatever he is, told us that you murdered some of them. Was he lying?'

Parry lowered his head further. There was a pause, then Moone's stomach rolled over and over as he saw the Doctor's head shake side to side.

'No, he wasn't lying.' Parry looked up at them. 'By the way, he's my brother. We found out that my mother... his father. We don't know what happened really. But he found me. And he showed me so much stuff, so many dark and horrible, horrific...' Parry looked up, tears welling in his eyes. 'And such beautiful things.'

'Jesus...' Butler hung her head.

'There's a bit in a Sherlock Holmes story,' Parry said, a sad smile appearing on his face. 'He says, Sherlock, I mean, that when a doctor goes wrong, commits a crime... well, he says it's the worst.'

Moone looked down and saw his hands trembling. 'Parry... we've got a problem.'

The Doctor nodded. 'If you arrest me, and they charge me, which of course they will, because I will tell them everything, then every case I've helped with... well, it'll destroy everything.'

Moone nodded, fighting the urge to throw up. 'I'm going to be honest with you. I don't know what to do.'

Parry laughed. 'That's the thing with you, DCI Peter Moone. You always say that you don't know what to do, and you have that look in your eye, that constant fear that you're going to get caught out, and discovered as a pretender. But you know what you're doing. You're clever, you just don't realise how clever.'

'I don't feel clever.'

Parry nodded. 'Probably because of DS Carthew. She's running rings round us all. She's incredibly clever. But you'll get her in the end.'

'How?'

'I don't think the law is going to help. Justice, yes, but not the law.'

'Where's the bloody girl?' Butler asked, looking pale.

'I told you. She's in the basement.' Parry stood up.

'Stay there.' Butler pointed at him.

'But if you go and let her free, then she'll see you. You'll have to take her in and... well, the house of cards collapses, doesn't it? So, if I go and let her out, tell her to run, then at least she's free. Isn't she?'

Butler looked at Moone. He shrugged, the taste of vomit thick in his mouth.

'It might be the only way,' Butler said.

Moone nodded, looked at Parry. 'Let her go. Tell her to head for the main road. Someone will stop for her.'

Parry nodded and started walking.

'We still have the problem of you, Doctor,' Butler said, as Parry reached the door and faced them.

'There's a simple solution,' Parry said, 'I let her go, then drive off and… you know.'

'You can't be serious.' Moone stared at him. 'What about all this? This house?'

'I burn it to the ground. I know how to make it look like an accident. There's a wood burning oven. Wouldn't take much. Maybe the house burning down took me over the edge?'

Parry turned away again and disappeared. They could hear doors opening and closing, footsteps fading away.

'What the hell are we doing?' Moone stared at Butler.

'I don't know. But I can't see any other way, can you? I mean, we've got one killer, and so the other… well, the other gets another kind of justice.'

'It's Dr Parry. Our friend.'

Her eyes blazed at him, her arm shooting out, pointing towards the doorway. 'I don't know who the fuck that is! Do you? He's a murderer. He's not our friend. Do we want murderers to walk free? No. If he goes down for this, that's what will happen. So something has to be done.'

Moone turned away, listening to the distant sounds of doors opening. He walked through the house blindly, and found himself looking through a window towards the field by the side of the house. After a while he saw a figure emerge onto the field, coming from somewhere along the side of the house. It was a young woman, a little overweight, and now clothed, being directed by Dr Parry, who was wearing a forensic outfit, a mask over his face. He ushered her onwards, pointing the way. From where Moone was stood, he could see the girl was shaking, looking around wildly, unsure of what was happening to her.

'He's let her go,' Moone said, and heard Butler's hurried steps behind him, arriving next to him at the window.

'Oh God, the poor cow,' Butler said, and he heard the genuine sadness and remorse in her voice.

'We can't just let her wander off,' Moone said. 'This is insane.'

Butler dipped her head and let out a pained breath. 'I know. I know, but what else can we do?'

'The right thing!'

Butler spun round to him, her eyes wider, a strange look on her face. 'That's the bloody thing, Moone. Doing the right thing doesn't get you anywhere. It's all well and good, but if we did the right thing, everything would go to shit. Take Carthew for instance. We've been doing the right thing with her, haven't we? Where's that got us? Bloody nowhere...'

'What are you saying?'

She looked him in the eyes. 'She's too clever for us. Well, at least she is for a couple of detectives who're trying to do the right thing.'

'So?'

'So, we have to do the wrong thing. We have to do whatever it takes to make sure that evil cow does not get the chance to hurt any more people, and doesn't end up as our boss. Which, by the way, is the right thing to do.'

He stared at her for a moment, then some movement caught his eye, so he turned to the window and saw Parry was stood staring at them. Then his arm was rising, pointing towards the house. Moone turned his head, trying to see what he was gesturing to. A cloud of deeply black smoke came billowing across the window.

'He's set the bloody house on fire!' Butler growled. 'With us still in it!'

'Let's go.' Moone hurried through the rooms with Butler right on his heels. Then he saw the open doorway and burst out into the overgrown garden. He stood there for a moment, half expecting to find Parry waiting for him.

'Where's he gone?' Butler said, coming out and looking round. 'Don't tell me the bastard's done a bunk.'

Then Moone swung round as he heard the sound of an engine rumbling, coming from somewhere close by. He looked past the now thick black cloud of smoke that made its way skyward, his eyes stinging and watering a little.

The car raced around the house, the engine roaring as it headed towards the lane that would lead to the main road and on to Bodmin Moor. Parry's pale face flashed past them, a look of sadness on it, and then he was gone, his brake lights flashing on as he slowed then roared on again.

'Shit,' Butler said. 'Now what do we do?'

'Come on.' Moone pulled her with him as he jogged to the car and got behind the wheel and started the engine. As Butler jumped in, Moone sped them off down the same lane, the chippings and dirt flying everywhere, hitting the paintwork. Moone put his foot down, hearing the engine groaning, wanting to go into a higher gear. He spun the wheel, scraping the car along the bushes and then onto the main road.

'There he is!' Butler called out, and Moone could see him far ahead, driving full pelt towards God only knows what.

'Where does he think he's going?' Butler asked, but Moone's eyes had jumped to the sight of Cody Barton stood by a car full of people and young children. In that split second, he saw one of the adults calling someone, and Cody telling her story, her eyes wet with tears. He turned back, glad to know she would be safe while they followed Parry through Bodmin.

'Do you think he'll try and leave the

country?' Butler asked.

'I don't think so.'

Then his car slowed a little, turned sharply right, taking a narrow and bush-lined turning, and then sped up again.

'Where the hell's he going?' Moone asked and looked out towards the open field before them that only led to row of impressive high tors about four hundred yards away.

'He's heading for those tors,' Butler said, her voice shaky.

Moone put his foot down, but Parry's car was way ahead of them, getting closer and closer to the jagged outline of the tors. Then his car had stopped, and he was running from it, the driver side door still open.

'Jesus... is he going to climb up there?' Moone stared at Butler, but she said nothing, just kept looking straight ahead, with a look in her eye like a lost child.

Moone turned off the engine and sat back, staring as Parry reached the bottom of the tor and started scrambling over it, gripping the rocks, and awkwardly pulling himself up it.

'We've got to stop him,' Moone said and went to climb out. Butler grabbed his elbow and shook her head when he looked at her.

'We can't. He knows we can't. It's over.'

Moone shook his head and jumped out, walking, then running across the grass, his vision bouncing around, the tor swinging side to side as he sprinted towards Parry as he climbed up further and further. He called out, told him to stop, but the Doctor didn't even look back.

Moone reached the tor and put his hands on the rocks, ready to push himself up and start climbing.

'Don't!' Butler called out, so he turned to face her.

'We can't just let him jump.'

'If you go up there you could get hurt.' She stared at him, a strange look in her eyes he hadn't seen before. It was as if he had never really noticed her before, had not really seen the real her.

'We have to stop him,' Moone said.

'I can't lose you too,' Butler said, and she looked down, her head shaking. 'I lost my dad, I've lost everyone. I can't. I can't lose you.'

He stared at her, then broke out of his dream state when he heard someone calling him. It was Parry's voice, distant, strained, echoing down to him. He looked up and saw the silhouette of him staring down.

'The ambulance!' Parry called out.

'Come down!' Moone shouted. 'Please! We can sort this out!'

'You need to burn it! It's out the back. In the yard.'

'Parry!' Moone cupped his mouth, shouting.

'I'm sorry!' Parry's echoing voice shouted.

Butler grasped Moone's collar and pulled him back, dragging him back towards the car as he looked up and saw the shape of the doctor, his arms spreading out from his sides, his whole-body tipping backwards.

Moone's breath was sucked out.

Parry fell, hitting a few edges as he rolled and plummeted to the ground.

Moone went to run to his body.

'You can't touch him,' Butler said. 'We were never here.'

'We can't leave him on his own,' Moone said, his eyes getting wet.

'We have to move the ambulance and burn it.'

He faced Butler. 'Are you serious?'

'We have to. Otherwise all those cases, all the money spent on them, all go up in flames. Murderers and rapists and child molesters walk the streets. Do you want that?'

He shook his head, then looked over at Parry's still body. 'He's all on his own.'

'That's the way he's always been,' Butler said, and held Moone's hand and started pulling him back to the car. 'Then he learnt he had family and that must be when the bad things started. Family, eh? Nothing but trouble.'

At some point, Moone found himself being driven through Bodmin, as if he had blacked out. He felt cold, shivering a little. It was the shock. He looked at Butler, not recognising her, and seeing someone else entirely. His heart pounded in his chest, words trying to form in his throat.

'What?' she asked, catching him staring at her.

'Nothing.' He looked away, knowing everything had changed.

Moone felt the heat reaching him as the flames licked away at the body of the ambulance, the black smoke drifting up into the sky. He had watched Butler pour over the petrol, then stuff an oily rag into the petrol tank. He had flinched when she lit it and ran towards him. They watched as the flames rushed all over the body of the vehicle, destroying any evidence.

This wasn't happening, he told himself, they weren't tampering with evidence, definitely were not risking their careers.

Then he felt it. He looked down and saw Butler was holding his hand, squeezing it tight. He squeezed her hand and looked at her.

What the hell was happening?

'We can never talk about this again.' She stared at him, the same old Butler glare on her face.

'I know. I never want to talk about it again. But what if anyone starts snooping round after his house burns down?'

'You take charge and make sure they don't. We'll have to remove any evidence that hasn't been destroyed when we get the chance.'

Moone nodded, his stomach wanting to rise up to his mouth. 'What about Fabre? What if he starts to talk?'

'By the look of him, he hasn't got long left. Months at the most, I'd say. He'll die in prison and he's not likely to dob his brother in, is he?'

'I suppose not.'

She squeezed his hand again. 'It's going to be all right, Pete. Now, let's get back to work.'

She let go of his hand and climbed back into the car and started the engine. He joined her, his mind turning over, a realisation coming to him.

'We have to tell Laptew about Carthew,' Moone said. 'Everything.'

'He won't believe you.'

'Maybe not. But I have to talk to him.'

'He's in deepest darkest Cornwall, so good luck with that.'

'Someone must have a number for him.'

CHAPTER 33

'I can't get hold of him,' Moone said, a couple of hours later as he put his trembling hands round his espresso. He didn't feel like drinking it all, or ever drinking or eating again. How could he when he had been party to something so terrible? He looked up and saw Butler was staring his way. He nodded and tried to smile, but she looked away. He looked at his watch and saw so much time had passed since the girl had been released from the house. Where was she?

'Congratulations.'

Moone looked up and saw DSU Fiona McIntyre smiling down at him. 'You cracked the Dyer case.'

'I just talked to her, that's all.'

'That's all?' McIntyre looked round the room, catching the eye of the rest of the team. 'Did you hear that? He manages to get a confession from our suspect and he says he just talked to her. Come on, people, he deserves a round of applause.'

Moone tried to protest and held up his hands, but the team were already on their feet, slapping their hands together. Much to his horror they also started a chorus of "he's a jolly good fellow". Inside, he felt like dying, his stomach churning, his heart pounding. Had they covered their tracks efficiently? As soon as the call came in, they would have to rush to the scene, to put their explainable DNA there, just in case. The applause died down as he grimaced, remembering Parry lying on the ground close by the tor.

'Boss,' he said to Fiona, wanting to change the subject, 'I haven't been able to get hold of Chief Superintendent Laptew.'

'Really? Where is he?'

'In Cornwall,' he said. 'Staying at some cottage.'

'Maybe there's no signal.'

'It's ringing. No answer.'

She nodded, making a face. 'OK, I'll send a couple of uniforms to check up on him. I'm sure it's fine. Anyway, well done, Moone. You've done us proud. Now I can move on, knowing we've solved one case at least.'

Then Moone's phone was ringing in his pocket. He looked down, his heart thudding again. He looked at Butler and saw her staring at him.

'You'd better answer that,' DSU McIntyre

said.

He nodded and took out his phone, his hand trembling, his stomach ready to exit through his mouth. 'DCI Peter Moone.'

He listened, nodding, wanting to scream, doing all he could to not put down the phone and blurt out the truth of what had happened to the entire incident room. He kept nodding, hearing that Cody Barton had been found wandering in Bodmin and taken to hospital. She was in shock but she would be fine, he was told. At least she had made it.

'Cody Barton has been found,' he announced to the room and looked at Butler. She gave a sad little smile, and nodded before looking back at her computer screen.

'Where was she found?'

Moone looked over to the door of the incident room and saw DS Carthew stood there, smiling.

'Wandering on Bodmin Moor,' he said, and looked over at Butler and saw her glaring.

'What are you doing here, DS Carthew?' Fiona asked her.

Carthew looked round the room, then at Moone. 'I thought I'd see how your cases are going. I'm glad you found the girl. And I hear you got someone for the abductions and murders.'

'We did.' Moone nodded and looked down at his desk, trying not to see Parry lying dead.

'I heard you thought there were two people involved,' Carthew said.

'I'm not sure you should be here,' DSU McIntyre said, approaching her. 'Isn't there an ongoing investigation?'

'There was. But they haven't charged me with anything, obviously because I didn't do anything. I'm sure I'll soon be properly exonerated.'

'Well, maybe so, but for now, maybe it's better if you leave.'

Carthew smiled at her, then made eye contact with Moone. 'Perhaps DCI Moone would like to see me out.'

'I'm sure he's very busy...'

Moone stood up before he had a chance to think, just wanting to be anywhere else at that moment. 'It's fine. I'll see her out.'

When they reached the corridor, Carthew turned to him and smiled as she said, 'How are you, Peter?'

He let out a sickened laugh. 'Do you really care?'

'Of course I do. I worry about you.'

'Worry about yourself.'

'Meaning?'

'Meaning you're facing a murder charge.'

'No, I'm really not.'

'How can you be so sure?'

She sighed and shook her head. 'Because I didn't murder anyone. It was DC Banerjee.'

'DC Banerjee? Have you told Crowne?'

'He knows. He must have found her by now. She's the crazy jealous type.'

He stared at her, not knowing what to say, the urge to run and hide swelling in his chest. 'I better get back to work.'

'Have you heard from Laptew?' she asked, raising her eyebrows. 'Is he enjoying his little holiday?'

'I haven't been able to get hold of him.'

She nodded, a smile stretching her face. 'Perhaps you should go and see him.'

He stared at her, seeing the glint in her eye. 'Why?'

'No reason.'

A cold feeling moved over his back. 'Faith, what have you done?'

'Nothing. Nothing at all. At least, nothing you'll ever be able to prove.'

He moved away from her, feeling for the door behind him. He turned and hurried into the incident room. 'Where's Laptew staying?'

Butler stared at him. 'He's staying at some cottage in Cornwall. I've got the address, why?'

'We need to go there now.'

Crowne and DS Rivers stood in the interview room next door to the room where two Birmingham detectives were interviewing Anil Banerjee, watching it all on a monitor. The young man was DC Banerjee's cousin, and he looked increasingly nervous as he was being asked the same questions over and over. Crowne was shaking his head, a sickness filling his gut. It couldn't be right, not the way it seemed to be playing out.

'So, tell us again, Anil, when was the last time you saw Cara?' the Brummie DI asked, a friendliness to his voice.

'I told you, I don't remember.' Anil tapped the desk, avoiding eye contact.

'But that's the thing. We've got you on CCTV walking towards the flat where your cousin was staying. We've also got a neighbour who says you paid Cara a visit a couple of days ago, just after she arrived.'

'She's wrong.' He kept looking down.

'I didn't say it was a woman,' the Di said.

Anil shrugged, looked away.

'Then where were you between the hours of ten a.m. and two in the afternoon on Wednesday?'

Anil shrugged again. 'Working. In the market.'

'But that's not true,' the female DS cut in. 'We've been in contact with your boss, and they said you took half the day off that day.'

'If he says so.'

'Your cousin was murdered two days ago, Anil.' The DI leant forward. 'Stabbed several times and had her throat cut. We found a knife at the scene. Your prints were on the knife...'

'I didn't kill her!' Anil's head shot up, the terror clear in his eyes, even from their view on the monitor.

'That's not what the evidence is saying,' the DI said. 'Just run us through that, so we can clarify things.'

Crowne looked at Rivers. 'He didn't do this.'

Rivers looked at him like he'd dropped his trousers. 'His prints are on the knife. It's his knife.'

'He kills her with his own knife and leaves it there for us to find? It's insane.'

Rivers sighed. 'He found out about her affairs with women. He has a history of this kind of thing, bullying members of his family who go against their religious…'

'I know. But there's no way. DS Carthew…'

Rivers let out a deep groan.

'What?'

She looked at him again. 'There you go, singing that song again. Listen, with all due respect, but you've got it all wrong. DS Banerjee was jealous of Carthew and Armstrong. She dressed up to look like his widow and murdered him. She had the means and motive. We found the wig and everything in her room. Her DNA will be all over it…'

'What about his dead wife and her lover?'

Rivers shrugged. 'I don't know. Maybe they couldn't take the fact that we found out about them. Or he snapped, and killed her and hanged himself. I mean, there's no way Carthew could have done all that on her own. Could she?'

'Maybe Banerjee helped…'

Rivers laughed. 'Banerjee? No way. Sorry, boss, but you're reading too much into this. We've tied up the loose ends. We've got a good result. Be happy with that.'

Crowne stared at her, then looked at the monitor and saw Anil Banerjee with his head in his hands, weeping like a child.

It was a good result, he told himself, and perhaps it was actually the way it looked for once. In a way, he was glad it was coming to an end and that he wouldn't have to deal with or even think about DS Carthew any more.

Yes, it was a good result.

Butler stopped the car as they reached the gate that cut them off from the winding road that would lead them to the cottage. The old building was sat back from the edge of the cliffs. Moone got out and opened the gate, his heart thumping, speeding up as they got closer and closer to the house. Something bad was coming. He climbed back in, then Butler drove them down the narrow lane, the bushes scraping the sides of the car, the canopy of trees overhead making it so much darker.

The road led to the side of the

whitewashed old cottage that sat scarily close to the drop of the cliffs. As they hurried from their car, the beat of panic probably sounding in both their hearts, Moone could hear the sea below, crashing on the rocks. Seagulls glided effortlessly on the wind, hovering over the house.

The cottage door was open. They looked at each other, then went in and called out for Laptew.

No answer.

There was one bedroom. The door was shut, so Moone pulled on a glove and opened the door and looked in.

He trembled, the taste of vomit rising to his throat. The buzz of flies bit into his ears. The blackness was moving over her body. Deeply dried blood. Her throat slashed open.

Moone pushed past Butler, raced outside and fell to his knees, retching. Nothing came up but spittle. He wiped his chin as he heard Butler behind him.

'Are you all right?' she asked.

'No, I'm not all right. Jesus Christ. What happened here? Where's Laptew?'

Butler walked past him, heading for a path that led to the cliffs and the big drop below. She pointed to the ground.

'Is that blood?' she asked.

Moone clambered to his feet and looked at what she had seen. Yes, there was droplets of blood. They carried on to the edge. He stepped closer to the drop.

'Careful.' Butler grabbed his elbow as he looked down, seeing over edge. He moved a little closer, seeing the wild sea smashing against the rocks. In a little cove, closer to the cliff, there were more rocks. Something lay there, twisted and dark against the wet stone. A body.

'Oh God.' Moone turned away. 'What the hell has she done?'

'She's done what she set out to do. She's had us looking one way, while she's been doing this.'

'We need to arrest her.'

'There won't be anything linking her to this. She's too clever. Of course, we'll look, but...'

He nodded. 'So what do we do?'

She looked into his eyes. 'We have to play her at her own game. We have to fight dirty.'

'I don't know if I can do any more bad things.'

She gripped his arm. 'We have to. We don't have any choice. This has to end.'

CHAPTER 34

DI Crowne took a seat in DSU Tucker's office, his stomach still turning over and over, his heart beating in what felt like a strange rhythm. He looked at DS Rivers, who seemed calm, at ease. He shook his head, knowing that none of it was right. Carthew had fooled them all.

'Well, Crowne, Rivers,' Tucker said, smiling. 'You've got a good result. Well done. Both of you.'

'Thank you, ma'am,' Rivers said.

'I mean it. We've almost got everything ready to send to the CPS. We've got DC Banerjee for the murder of DSU Charlie Armstrong, and her cousin for her own murder. A strange kind of justice, but there you go.'

Rivers sat forward. 'We figure her cousin found out about her affair with Carthew and the fact she was gay, and he really didn't like it. He's been pretty vocal on the whole gay scene before.'

'An honour killing,' Tucker said and shook her head. 'It's a terrible end to this case.'

Crowne huffed out a laugh before he had a chance to hold it in.

Tucker stared at him. 'Have you got something to contribute, DI Crowne?'

He let out a tired breath. 'No, ma'am.'

'Are you not convinced by the evidence and facts?'

'It's all just a bit... convenient, isn't it?'

Tucker shook her head. 'Convenient? I don't think murder's ever convenient.'

'Crowne has had his doubts,' Rivers said, 'but we've both worked hard on what has been a tough case.'

Tucker smiled at her. 'It hasn't gone unnoticed how hard you've worked on this, DS Rivers. In fact, I think a promotion is long overdue. You've proved yourself very capable, hasn't she, Crowne?'

Crowne nodded. 'She has.'

'Then I'll be suggesting you go up to the rank of DI.' Tucker smiled. 'You'll have to sit the inspectors' exam, but I'm sure it won't be a problem for you.'

'Really, ma'am?' Rivers glanced at Crowne, her eyes beaming. 'Thank you, ma'am.'

'What about DS Carthew?' Crowne asked.

Tucker let out an unimpressed huff. 'Well, seeing as she has committed no crimes that we know of, she gets to go back to work. Unless you have some evidence I don't know about?'

Crowne shook his head.

Tucker sat forward. 'I know that this case has been tough on you, Crowne. You look exhausted. Perhaps you should take some time off.'

'No, ma'am, I'm fine.'

'That's an order. Take a couple of weeks. I mean it. Rivers can take it from here.'

Crowne nodded, his gut tightening, the tiredness indeed hitting him. It would be good to relax for a while and forget about Carthew and Moone, and everything else. 'Thank you, ma'am.'

Another meeting was happening at almost that exact moment, but back in Plymouth. Moone was sitting in the conference room, next to DI Butler, and opposite DSU Fiona McIntyre.

'So, the Birmingham Major Crime Unit will be charging Anil Banerjee with murder.'

Moone nodded. 'OK. I guess there's not much else to say about that.'

'She's gotten away with it again.' Butler huffed. 'She killed them, even our boss, and we can't touch her.'

McIntyre looked at her with sympathy. 'I know it's not what you wanted to hear, but she has an alibi for Laptew's and his wife's murder. When they died, she was here. In this station.'

Moone gave a sickened laugh. 'Of course she was. She planned the whole thing out. The murder of Armstrong was just to throw us off. Misdirection. We look there, she kills over there.'

'But she was here, so how did she kill them?' McIntyre asked. 'Unless she had an accomplice?'

'Probably,' Butler said. 'Must've found another sick bastard to do her dirty work.'

'But who?' Moone asked.

'We'll never know.' Butler looked down at her hands.

'At least you got a good result on the butterfly murders,' McIntyre said. 'And Cody Barton's safe.'

'Bobbi-Jane too.' Moone nodded, trying not to see Parry lying at the bottom of the tor. 'Someone's coming to pick her up.'

'Good.' McIntyre sat back. 'I'm so sorry to hear about Dr Parry. It's all so shocking. Burning down the house his father left him and then... well, doing that to himself.'

Moone nodded. 'He had some issues of late. I guess you never know the troubles other people go through.'

She nodded. 'So sad. Did he have any other relations? Brothers or sisters?'

'No one,' Butler said.

'Shame,' McIntyre said and looked at Moone. 'Are you OK leading the investigation into Dr Parry's death? I can always find someone else...'

'No, I'm fine. I'll do it.' Moone looked at Butler, but she turned away.

'What about Loy Grader?' McIntyre asked.

'He's going to pull through, unfortunately,' Moone said, a bad taste tainting his mouth. 'More time added to his sentence. He'll never get out.'

'Good.' McIntyre smiled. 'How about a drink after work?'

Butler stood up. 'I've got to be somewhere. But you two have fun.'

Moone watched her leave, then looked at McIntyre, saw the smile on her face, her eyebrows raised.

'Just you and me then?' she asked.

He nodded, unsure what she was after, and confused by the fact she was getting married soon. He mentally shrugged, telling himself that life was too short. He had come face to face with death, and had worked alongside it. Why not take the chance to enjoy a nice, pleasurable moment?

A little while later, Moone walked Bobbi-Jane down to the car park where a taxi was waiting, the engine running. There was a figure in the passenger seat that climbed out and faced her. Daryl Pawsey smiled at her and Moone watched, wondering what her reaction would be, his chest tight, feeling nervous for the young man.

Bobbi-Jane was suddenly running at him, flinging her arms round him, squeezing him tight. There were tears in Daryl's eyes as he looked over her shoulder and stared at Moone. He mouthed, 'thank you', so Moone turned away, fighting back the tears that welled in his own eyes. Then he shakily took out a box of cigarettes from his suit jacket and lit one. He sucked it and immediately some of the anxiousness lifted. He would go and see Alice, spend some time with her, spoil her and things would seem better for a while.

DS Rivers parked up, still smiling to herself, delighted with her new promotion. Crowne had seemed unhappy, but at least he would have some time off. She knew he wasn't happy with the result, but it was what it was. She climbed out, locked her car, then headed across the estate, to her building.

She stopped dead when she reached her floor and saw the door to her flat was ajar. She took out her Casco baton and flicked it to full length as she quietly entered the flat. Nothing seemed out of place, so she headed to the front room.

She froze when she saw the woman on the sofa. DS Faith Carthew was staring at her, a smile on her lips.

'What are you doing in my flat?' Rivers asked, her heart thumping.

Carthew stood up. 'We need to talk.'

'About what?'

Carthew came closer. 'About everything.'

'You shouldn't be here.'

Carthew stood barely an inch from her, then took hold of the Casco baton and pulled it gently from her grip. 'You won't need this.'

'You're crazy.'

Carthew nodded. 'Yes. So are you.'

Rivers put her arms round her and pulled her close. They kissed for a while, then stopped and stared at each other.

'I made DI,' Rivers said, smiling.

'What did I say?'

'You were right. Everything you said and planned. You were right.'

Carthew touched her face. 'I'm always right. They can't touch us. Soon, we'll be in charge. Then we can do anything we want.'

About a week later it was raining quite hard over Weston Mill cemetery. Moone was stood outside the chapel of rest, smoking, and watching the dark car approaching. When it parked up, he dropped his cigarette and stubbed it out with the toe of his shoe.

Butler climbed out, along with one of her female cousins. There were only a few family members coming to her dad's funeral.

He watched her walk towards the few people gathered under umbrellas. She chatted to them, but her eyes kept finding Moone. She had lost weight, seemed different to him, almost as if she had blossomed in her grief. He couldn't quite put his finger on it, but it was almost as if he was seeing her for the first time.

And then, as she approached him with a sad smile, his heart thumped harder, butterflies released in his belly. What was this strange feeling?

'What now?' she asked, taking his hand in hers.

'We say goodbye.'

'I meant about Carthew, you wally.'

He nodded. 'I know. We fight dirty, like a wise friend of mine once said. We do whatever it takes to win.'

Butler stared at him, then nodded and pulled him towards the main chapel. He followed, unsure of anything any more, except that something had changed within him.

Bad things were coming, but he would be ready for them.

GET TWO FREE AND EXCLUSIVE CRIME THRILLERS

I think building a relationship with the readers of my books is something very important, and makes the writing process even more fulfilling. Sign up to my mailing list and you'll receive two exclusive crime thrillers for FREE! Get SOMETHING DEAD- an Edmonton Police Station novella, and BITER- a standalone serial killer thriller.

Just visit markyarwood.co.uk

or you can find me here:

https://www.bookbub.com/authors/mark-yarwood

facebook.com/MarkYarwoodcrimewriter/

DID YOU ENJOY THIS BOOK? YOU COULD MAKE A DIFFERENCE.

Because reviews are critical to the success of an author's career, if you have enjoyed reading this novel, please do me a massive favour by leaving one on Amazon.

Yes, I am happy to leave a review- click here

Reviews increase visibility. Your help in leaving one would make a massive difference to this author. Thank you for taking the time to read my work.

THE DCI PETER MOONE THRILLERS

BAD TIMES

TAKE YOUR LIFE

PREPARED TO DIE

Get your FREE eBooks- visit
www.markyarwood.co.uk

MARK YARWOOD

THE EDMONTON POLICE STATION THRILLERS SERIES

SPIDER MOUTH

MURDERSON

LAST ALIVE

THE AMOUNT OF EVIL

WHEN THE DEVIL CALLS

THE FIRSTCOMER

HOLMWOOD

THEY CALL EVIL GOOD

THE EDMONTON POLICE STATION THRILLERS BOX SETS

THE EDMONTON POLICE STATION THRILLER SERIES: BOOKS 1-3

THE EDMONTON POLICE STATION THRILLER SERIES: BOOKS 4-6

THE DCI JAIRUS NOVELS

JAIRUS' SACRIFICE

JAIRUS' SLAUGHTER

JAIRUS' TORMENT

———————————

THE DCI JAIRUS NOVELS BOX SETS

THE DCI JAIRUS NOVELS: BOOKS 1-3

THE SEAN FAINT SERIES

FIRELAND

THE FAINT OUTLINE

THE FAINT SUSPICION

THE FAINT CHANCE

Printed in Great Britain
by Amazon